Holly Bourne is a journalist and best-selling author of several YA novels, including the Spinster Club trilogy. Her critically acclaimed *Am I Normal Yet?* was inspired by her work at an advice charity for young people and her own experiences of blatant everyday sexism, and was chosen as a World Book Night title for 2016 and shortlisted for the YA Book Prize. In 2017, Holly was chosen as a judge of the BBC Young Writers' Award with Radio 1 DJ Alice Levine and author Nikesh Shukla.

Holly enjoys getting lost on long countryside walks, getting lost in very good books, and finding any excuse to go to Pizza Express.

Also by Holly Bourne

HOLLY BOURNE

IT ONLY HAPPENS IN THE MOVIES

USBORNE

To Eryn and Willow

First published in the UK in 2017 by Usborne Publishing Ltd., Usborne House,
83-85 Saffron Hill, London EC1N 8RT, England. www.usborne.com

Text © Holly Bourne, 2017

Author photo © L. Bourne, 2017

Cover images: popcorn © Juj Winn/Getty; popcorn box © Jiri Hera/Shutterstock;
film strip © Alexander III/Shutterstock

A CIP catalogue record for this book is available from the British Library.

JFMAM JASOND/19

ISBN 9781474921329 04085/11

Printed in India

"Romance films are money-spinning cathedrals of love, wobbling on the foundations of unbelievable and damaging stereotypes."

Audrey Winters's Media Studies project

Prologue

I wasn't expecting candles.

They lit the whole cinema – tea lights, the stout white candles you get in churches, thin ones stuffed into candlesticks. My skin itched in their heat.

I blinked and shook my head. "What the hell?"

Then I saw Harry.

He looked so damn proud of himself. His hair sticking up at every angle, his hands sheepishly in his pockets, head cocked, his teeth bared in his trademark smile. The flickering light made him look like a hologram.

Harry...

My body declared instant war on itself. My heart thudded against my ribcage, like it was using the force to try and pull me closer. But everything else fought against it. My intestines cramped, my stomach curdled, bile rose up in my throat.

"Audrey." He stepped through the candlelight, and I took

a step back. His face sagged, teeth disappeared. "Audrey, please. Hear me out. I did all this for you."

That much was obvious but it didn't change anything.

"Harry, you can't just light a few candles and…"

He stepped forward again, reaching me this time. He touched my face, smoothed away a tear with his thumb. A tear I hadn't even known was there.

And I'm thinking… *If this was in a movie, what would you be doing, Audrey?*

Would you be yelling at the girl on the screen? Chucking popcorn or cushions and screaming "DON'T DO IT, YOU MORON"?

…Or would you be sighing – willing her to hear him out?

1

THE GREAT CLASS DIVIDE

A rich girl meets a poor boy.

They come from different worlds.

She's heading towards amazing things but feels suffocated by them.

He's from the wrong side of the tracks. He was in a gang once. He's not any more.

But he looks rough enough around the edges for her parents to disapprove once the two of them fall madly in love, despite having literally no life experiences in common.

"Here's where we keep the pulled pork."

Marianna – *"everyone just calls me Ma"* – pulled up a metal hatch, blasting my face with the stench of dead pig.

"The what?"

"The pulled pork," she repeated. "For the pulled pork hot dogs."

"Cinemas serve pulled pork hot dogs?"

I jumped as Ma slammed the hatch closed. "Flicker is not just any cinema. We're not like CineUniverse. At Flicker, we pride ourselves on a unique, artisan cinema experience." She smoothed down her black silk shirt. "Now, if you just follow me into the kitchen, I'll train you on how to make the fresh guacamole."

Two hours later and I hadn't learned any of the skills I'd thought I would at my first day working in a small independent cinema. Ma had not once mentioned films, or shown me where a projector was. Instead, I learned how to work the till, smush guacamole, shred pulled pork, pour the exact amount of balsamic vinegar into virgin olive oil to make a dipping pot for the "sourdough fingers", oh, and mix "cinnamon dust" for the popcorn. It took an hour for Ma to admit that, yes, they did still have popcorn.

"When do you train me in taking ticket stubs and showing people to their seats?" I asked Ma, midway through washing the avocado out from under my fingernails. The cinema opened in less than thirty minutes, and I hadn't even seen inside the screening rooms.

Ma smiled. "Oh, we don't want you to run before you can walk."

The smile made parts of my tummy hurt, like someone was about to jump out in a horror film. She didn't look older than thirty but she behaved like an android. Her hair was pulled back into a stiff bun and she clopped around in ridiculous heels. "You can just be in charge of food tonight. That's all I've put you down for on the rota."

I'd seen the colour-coded rota in the tiny staffroom upstairs. It had every hour split into ten-minute intervals.

"Great," I tried to chirp.

"Harry will be here in a second to do tickets. The new Dick Curtisfield is out, so it's going to be busy."

Dick Curtisfield. I used to adore his fuzzy, love-y films...

"Is that okay?" Ma gave me a look like I'd be murdered if I dared say anything other than yes. But busy was good. Busy was why I'd taken the job. I didn't care what lies people were happy to watch as long as I was busy enough to not think about the message that had landed on my phone on my walk in.

Mum: Your father wants to sell the house.

He wants us to sell the house. Our house. Our home.

I smiled back at Ma because smiling is sometimes the only way to stop yourself crying. "Sounds good to me. Now, can you explain cinnamon dust one more time?"

Busy was an understatement. The cinema only had two

screens, separated by a purple velvet carpeted area with a ticket booth and a teeny bar. By high tide, it was so packed you couldn't see all the intricate black and white paintings of Hollywood stars on the wall.

Harry turned up two minutes before we opened, stinking of cigarettes and bringing the cold autumn air in on his clothes.

"I know, I know," he said, as Ma tapped her watch. Then, before she could tell him off, he pulled her into a hug and lifted her up.

"Oi, Harry, put me down!"

When he did, she was bright red and smiling.

"There's a queue outside," he told her.

"That's why it's unacceptable for you to be late. Again. The rota says you should've been here thirty minutes ago."

"I'm always late, Ma. Can't you just accept that and schedule it into the rota?"

And she giggled. She actually *giggled*.

I stood behind the bar, nervously polishing the counter over and over. Harry noticed me, waved and walked over.

"Hello, new person."

"This is Audrey." Ma spoke for me, clopping behind him on her heels. "She's a sixth-form student, so she's only doing one school night a week and weekends."

Harry scooched behind the bar and came up right in my face, like personal space wasn't an issue. "I know you." He had dark hair that all stood on end and every part of him was a bit too long and thin, liked he'd been wrung out too harshly when wet.

I shook my head. "I don't think you do."

"No, I do…" He was about to say something else when Ma hissed, "Harry? The queue?" and he leaped back over the counter and opened the door to let the stampede in. Well, stampede is something Bridgely-upon-Thames doesn't do, thank you kindly. It does Chanel No. 5 and Radley purses and detached houses and the *Daily Mail* and oboe lessons until you reach Grade Eight with distinction. The line descended on the bar like a really posh zombie apocalypse, and I dropped my washcloth, stuttering as I asked the first couple what they wanted.

"Can we get two Chilean Merlots, two popcorns with cinnamon dust, the garlic olives…oh…shall we just get a bottle? A bottle of Merlot…"

And I was too busy to think again. Which was fine by me.

2

The films began and there was a slight break in the madness. I nervously asked Ma if I could use the bathroom, and she looked at her watch before mumbling, "Yes, I suppose you need a quick break. Take ten minutes."

I spent the whole break just sitting on the staff loo with my head between my legs. My phone kept vibrating in my pocket. I ignored it.

When I emerged, Harry was in the foyer, collecting the empty glasses people had left strewn on the counter.

"You were in there a while," he stated. His instant familiarity felt strange and warm at the same time. "Are you okay?"

I flicked my eyes upstairs in the direction of Ma's office. "Is she always like that?"

"Who, Ma?" He grinned, revealing a big set of teeth. There was essentially no room for gum. "Oh yeah. She is most certainly always like that. You'll get used to her...

I mean, people got used to Stalin."

I scratched my arm. "Why does she ask to be called Ma? She only looks about thirty."

Harry picked up four glasses with his fingers and shoved them into the dishwasher.

"Oh, Audrey – you've only seen the tip of the *Ma-is-nuts* iceberg."

As if on cue… "Audrey?" Ma's voice echoed down from her office, sharper than a sharpened sharpie. "Your break was up two minutes ago. I hope you're replenishing the black-cherry cordial."

"Audrey, heel," Harry whispered, and I giggled in a short, guilty burst.

…Just like Ma, I realized.

We ran out of guacamole during the second big rush and Ma acted like it was my fault.

"Why didn't you tell me we were out of avocados?" she asked me through thin lips.

"I didn't know I had to."

Ma pushed a stray strand of hair off her high forehead, and I saw her roll her eyes at the disappointed customer. "Sorry, she's new. How about some lemongrass hummus on the house? Hmm?"

It got so nuts that Harry came over to help out, arming himself with popcorn boxes and scooping it out of the machine.

It was immediately obvious that Harry had hints of fuckboy about him. Ma giggled whenever he spoke, as did all the female customers. He dazzled them with compliments on their coats, noticed their haircuts, said "*Good choice*" whenever anyone ordered any combination of food and wine.

"You keeping up, Audrey?" He winked as he handed over some sourdough fingers and I smiled back knowingly.

Trouble trouble trouble.

I'd been there with trouble. Been there, done that, bought the *I-lost-my-virginity-to-an-attractive-but-morally-bankrupt-arsehole* T-shirt.

Eventually, everyone trickled into the screens, the doors slamming shut behind them. With both films playing, we were left in an unnerving quiet in the foyer.

I leaned back on the counter with exhaustion. "Now what?"

Ma shook her head. "Did you not even look at my rota, Audrey? Now we clean up again."

So I anti-bacced all the surfaces, put all the new empties in the dishwasher, and I was just about to sit and rest my aching feet, when a burly man emerged from Screen One. I looked around but Ma and Harry had both vanished.

"Hey, you," the customer called.

I straightened as he walked towards the counter. "Can I help you?"

"I want a gourmet hot dog, with extra farmhouse relish."

No please.

"Okay."

I took his money and turned to the till, trying to remember how the hell to work it. He coughed.

"Is there a problem?" I called over my shoulder.

"I'm missing the film."

"They take a few minutes to make…" I stumbled over my words, flustered by his aggression, just as Ma swooped back downstairs.

"What seems to be the problem here?"

"I've ordered a hot dog," he said.

"Of course, of course." Ma clapped her hands once. "What seat are you in? We'll bring it straight in when it's ready. Sorry" – she rolled her eyes for the second time – "she's new."

The man strode back into the film and I turned to the pulled pork warmer so Ma couldn't see my face.

"I didn't know we took food into the cinema for them," I said, on the defensive. "Won't that disrupt the film for everyone else?"

"We do what the customer wants." She was watching over my shoulder to check I was adding the right amount of meat. "He's sitting in B12, that's on the aisle, on the left. Can I trust you to take it into him when it's ready?"

I just nodded. Feeling about eight years old.

"Good, right. Now I need to check on Harry."

She tip-tapped off and I got to work assembling the hot dog, scooping up organic relish and smearing it onto the artisan bun.

I mimicked her voice under my breath. *"Oooh, don't forget, Audrey, the customer is always right, even if he's a rude bell-end who can't wait the whole half-hour until the film is finished for his overpriced ludicrous hot dog, we do what he wants…"*

"It sounds like Ma has broken you already."

I jumped at Harry's voice and dropped the tongs. They clattered to the floor along with the bun.

"Dammit," I said, staring in dismay at the hot dog.

"Whoops, five-second rule." Harry bent down to pick it up. The air on his clothes was cold again. He blew on the bread and dusted it off before holding it out to me, smiling. "The floor gives it a more delicate texture," he explained.

I found myself giggling stupidly again and took the bun, our hands grazing.

"Ma's looking for you."

"Ah, bollocks." Though his huge toothy grin suggested he was unbothered. "I thought she'd be too entrenched in her rota to notice me sneaking out for a smoke." He ran up the stairs to her office two at a time.

I dusted off a bit of grit he'd missed. "Thanks for saving the artisan bread," I called after him.

But Harry had already reached the top, leaving just a hint of freezing air behind him.

It took a second for my eyes to adjust to the gloom of the cinema when I pushed through the doors. A few heads turned in annoyance as I tiptoed down the aisle.

I glanced up at the screen, using its light to guide my way to B12.

Dick Curtisfield's gorgeous heroine was running through the snow towards some guy, dragging a tiny sausage dog behind her.

"Stop," she called after him. "Wait."

The guy in the snow stopped and I felt the audience take a collective breath. I spotted the outline of the man and crouched down beside him.

"Here's your hot dog," I whispered.

He reached out and took it roughly, his eyes on the screen. He didn't even say thank you.

I crept back up the aisle and, just as I was about to leave, the actor on screen said, "I've tried to stop loving you, Katie, but I can't."

I found myself turning around. I'd always admired this actress. I'd watched her best scenes over and over to try and pick up extra tips. Last year, I would've been desperate to watch this film. The leading male had her face cradled in his hands, pushing her beautiful cheeks together. The sausage dog barked at her feet.

"You have?" she whispered. One tear delicately dripped onto her cheek without ruining her make-up.

He nodded. "I've tried to hate you. I've tried to feel numb about you. I've tried to not even think about you at all. But I'm exhausted, Katie. I can't not love you, even after everything. I can't not feel anything for you. Every feeling I have, every inch of my heart – it's yours. It always has been…"

I blinked hard, my hand on the door, a lump jumping into my throat. I pushed my way out just as the orchestral music signalled the big kiss. I strode past the bar, ignoring Ma as she barked instructions at me and let myself into the staff toilet. And then, with my knickers around my ankles, I put my head between my legs and sobbed – stuffing my fist into my mouth in case Ma came in and heard me cry.

3

The hard work didn't finish once the screens emptied of people, dabbing their eyes and saying it was Dick's best yet. It was almost midnight when Ma handed me a bin bag and sent me in to clean the screens up.

I instantly felt guilty for every time I'd dropped popcorn on a cinema floor. The place was a mess – like feral pigs on acid had just held a house party. I checked my phone.

Two missed calls and three messages.

Mum: What time will you be back?
Mum: Did you see my message?
Mum: I can't believe he's doing this to us.

I put it back into my jeans pocket and dropped to my knees to scrape popcorn from under the seats.

Harry burst through the double doors wielding a giant

roaring Hoover. "You're doing it wrong, Audrey," he yelled over the noise. "You need this."

I stood up, brushing eight trillion kernels off my shirt. "No one told me there was a Hoover."

"We call him Magic Mike. You collect up all the empties, I'll do the carpet."

"Thanks."

I started plucking stray wine glasses out from the nooks and crannies, trying not to yawn. I'd been on my feet for hours and I was still nowhere near my bed. Harry, however, fizzed with energy, like his aura was made of popping candy. He hummed as he sucked up the debris, smiling the whole time. When he shut off the Hoover, the silence engulfed us. I grinned goofily, hating that he was the sort of guy that made you instantly goofy.

He gathered up the lead as I picked up all the boxes previously containing seventy-per-cent-cocoa chocolate buttons.

"This is the most middle class cinema in the world," I found myself saying.

Harry burst out laughing. "And that offends you?"

I shoved another box into the plastic liner. "I just think this place is taking it a bit far. I feel like I'm in a parody."

He perched on the arm of one of the purple seats, his arms crossed, his mouth twitching. "And it's not like *you're* middle class or anything."

"What's that supposed to mean?"

He looked me up and down. "Well, no offence, but I

don't exactly think you're Eliza fucking Doolittle."

I liked the way he casually swore. "Yeah, but I'm not middle class—"

"Please!" he interrupted, gesturing at me. "You're so middle class I'm surprised you didn't buy your disdain for this job in Waitrose."

I narrowed my eyes at him – taking in his artfully-crafted messy hair, his ripped jeans that you know he bought like that.

"Yeah, well, you can talk," I replied. "I bet your hair putty is organic."

"You're so middle class, I bet you had the Sylvanian treehouse as a child."

I opened my mouth. "How did you know that?"

And we both pissed ourselves laughing, which was kind of cool considering we'd only just met each other. I collapsed on a chair next to Harry and I figured it would be okay working here if he was. Yeah he had *player* carved into his dimples, but he was funny and I'd already learned my lesson about boys like him.

"I know where I know you from now." He turned to me. "You're Dougie's sister."

"How do you know Dougie?"

"Your mum knows my mum. Dougie and I went to baby massage together apparently."

I giggled. "Now that really IS middle class."

Harry stood and picked up my bin bag. "Guilty as charged. But I'd much rather work here than CineUniverse – the pay's better, the customers are nicer…."

I opened my mouth to protest.

"I said nicer, not nice. And Ma will calm down once she knows you're not totally incompetent. How's Dougie finding uni? He's at Sussex, right?"

"Yeah, he's enjoying it, I think. We don't hear from him much."

In fact, he'd not come home once yet, leaving me with Mum and her newest drama. I was about to ask him why he wasn't at uni when Ma pushed through the double doors, saw me relaxing, and totally activated.

It was well gone midnight when Ma finally let us out.

"You should go too, it's late," Harry said, but she waved him away with a hefty martyr sigh.

Harry and I emerged onto the empty frozen street together. Our breath crystallized instantly and mingled before floating off into the air. The town was dead and silent. The cinema overlooked a normally crammed crossroads but now the traffic lights flickered from red, to amber, to green, conducting invisible cars.

"So, how was your first shift?"

I heard the unmistakable click and hiss of a lighter. Harry took a breath of his cigarette, plucked it from his mouth, then exhaled, careful not to get his smoke on me.

"It was fine. I need the job."

"Saving up for travelling or something?" He took another drag.

"Something like that."

The roar of a car engine interrupted the quiet. A beat-up Peugeot skidded around the corner and slammed to a stop before us. Harry grinned as the door opened to reveal a very crowded car – like that circus trick when all the clowns cram into a Mini. Obscenely loud rock music hit me through the open door.

"HE'S A FREE MAN," the driver shouted, and the rest of the car cheered. It was all boys rammed in there, bar one girl. The sort of girl who, even through the dirty window, I could see would always be effortlessly cool. I stood there awkwardly, watching as she smiled at Harry from under her faux-fur coat. I wondered briefly if she was his girlfriend.

Harry dropped his still-lit cigarette and punched the air. "FOR TWELVE WHOLE HOURS I'M A FREE MAN."

"LET'S GET WASTED," yelled the driver.

Harry went to climb in, and I wondered how he'd get his long body into such a cramped space. Just as he did though, he stopped, and turned.

"You got a lift home?"

I shook my head. "I'm walking. I'm good."

"You want a lift? Where do you live?"

I shook my head again. "I'm happy walking."

"Harry, come on," the girl shouted from inside the car.

Harry hesitated. "You sure? It's late and it's dark."

I raised both my eyebrows. "It's Bridgely-upon-Thames."

Also, if I walk it will take longer to get home…

"Fair point. See you around."

"See you around," I said, but the car door was already closed, Harry's body folded inside. It took off around the corner, running the red light.

And the town fell quiet again.

The lights were on when I got home, even though it was late. I'd assumed she'd still be up but I tried to sneak in without her hearing. I turned the front door handle slowly to stop it squeaking. Our family home was Victorian – all high ceilings and bay windows and things that made noises. Sneaking in was practically impossible.

I took my shoes off on the doormat and tiptoed into the hallway in my socks.

I heard voices, the clattering of glasses.

Sandra must be round.

I rolled my eyes up to the ceiling, wanting bed, craving bed. I needed a glass of water but the clattering came from the kitchen. I'd just have to drink out of the bathroom tap.

I crept upstairs, brushing my teeth and rubbing my make-up off, before I tiptoed to bed. I chucked my new uniform on the floor and climbed into one of Milo's old T-shirts. He'd asked for it back and I kept claiming it was lost. Then, without reading or anything, I turned off my light and lay back in bed.

I could hear the rumble of their voices through the thin floorboards. The shrieking of laughter, the pop and clink and glug of another bottle of Prosecco being opened. It was

Thursday, she had work tomorrow. I was stupid for getting my hopes up that she was doing better. As my eyelids fluttered downwards, I thought back to that line from the film.

"Every feeling I have, every inch of my heart – it's yours. It always has been…"

I shook my head into my pillow and somehow found sleep…

A thump. My body shook on the mattress.

A howl.

My eyes flickered open. I smelled her breath before I heard her. Oh God. Not again. She hadn't done this in so long.

"You didn't come and say hiiiiii," she wailed.

I rubbed my eyes to adjust to the light streaming in from the hallway.

"Hi, Mum." My voice so full of sleep I could hardly get the words out. I rolled over to face her. She'd flopped fully backwards onto my bed, her legs straight out in front of her, like she was lying in a coffin. Her pupils were everywhere, her everywhere stank of stale wine. "I was asleep."

"Did you get my message?" she asked, not apologizing.

"I've got college tomorrow."

"The house." Her voice cracked. "Your father's taking away our house."

She began to sob then, just as her words, and what they

meant, hit me in my stomach – each one like a separate sucker punch. Dad had destroyed everything two years ago when he announced he was leaving us for a new family. Just like that. He'd been secretly laying the foundations for months, even getting Jessie nice and pregnant with twins – ready to be delivered only weeks after he slammed the door of our family home behind him and let us combust into ash. I didn't think it could get worse, but now he was taking our house too?

"I gave him everything, Audrey. Everything. It's our house. It's our home..." Her sobbing morphed into ubersobs. She curled herself up into a ball, like a woodlouse – a really traumatized woodlouse. I reached out in the semi-darkness and stroked her hair.

"Why?" she whimpered. "I don't understand why he's doing this to us. Why's he's doing this to me, Audrey?"

I patted her head. "I don't know, Mum," I murmured. Because I didn't. I really didn't.

Mum's sobs faded into whimpers and her whimpers faded into snuffles and her snuffles faded into snores, and I – I stared up at the ceiling for a really long time.

4

THE BEST FRIEND WHO ONLY EXISTS TO BE YOUR BEST FRIEND

Maybe they're gay. Or maybe they're reaaaaally bad with men. Or maybe they're just scatty. It doesn't actually matter, they're only here to assist the main character on their way to happily-ever-after-ville. They don't have their own storyline, their own dimensions, their own...anything really. If they're lucky, they get palmed off onto the love interest's best friend in the last scene.

✭ ✭ ✭ ✭ ✭

Leroy was typically Leroy when I met him the next day.

"Audrey, you look like shit."

I flipped him the finger. "Are you ever nice?" I complained.

"Just being honest. That's nice, isn't it?"

"No."

I yawned as we fell into step on the way to school. It was that really annoying sort of raining where it looks stupid if you put your umbrella up, but your hair frizzes like mad if you don't.

"So, how did it go last night?" he asked, a smidge more concern in his voice. Though, this was Leroy. His levels of empathy were limited. It was why I liked him. No bullshit.

"It was okay, I guess. My boss has control issues. Like, huge control issues. But I don't really care, just as long as it keeps me out of the house."

"Your mum still mental?"

I smiled at Leroy's absolute lack of sugar-coating.

"She is indeed. She got into my bed again last night. Thus me looking like shit. To be fair to her, it's the first time she's done it in a while but we heard from my dad about…" My throat dried and I trailed off, not wanting to go into it.

But any chance of sympathy vanished quickly anyway because Leroy was already distracted, his phone out, checking his messages.

"Sucks to be you." He said it to his phone more than me.

He *did* care. He just also knew I didn't like talking about it. And I also didn't like talking about it. Did I mention I didn't like talking about it?

I nodded towards his phone. "How's the kingdom?"

He nodded, swiped left, tapped and then looked up. "Ahh, buggery fuckdoodles. Someone's claimed they've beaten my time on Rainbow Road."

I faux-gasped. "Surely that's impossible?"

Leroy madly tapped again. "That's what I'm telling them."

Leroy had this weird double life as an anonymous retro gamer. He played games that were out of date before we were even foetuses. But he was good at them, and uploaded videos of him playing onto YouTube. I didn't even understand how it'd happened, but he had over two hundred thousand subscribers.

"I bet that dipshit is using the feather shortcut and still claiming that's his actual time," Leroy muttered. "Cheating bastard." He finished sending abuse and looked up, smiling as he put his phone back into his pocket. "Okay, I'm back, sorry. So, what's Flicker like? The tickets are *so* expensive."

"That's because it's ridiculously posh!" I said. "The customers are dreadful, so up their own arseholes. And there's no normal food..." Leroy pissed himself when I told him about the cinnamon dust. "But the money's okay and there was this one guy there, Harry. He was friendly. Do you know him? He said he knows Dougie."

"What's his surname?"

"I don't know."

"What does he look like? Is he fit?"

I hit Leroy with my bag. "He's not unfit. He has like longish dark hair and he gels it so it's all sticky-uppy. Umm, maybe his eyes were green? Or brown? I'm not sure, it's dark in cinemas. Maybe he's Asian?"

Leroy gave me a Look. "*Maybe* he's Asian?"

"Well, I don't know, do I? He looks a bit like Joseph Gordon-Levitt."

"Audrey, for feck's sake. He's Jewish!"

"Okay! I told you, I don't know."

Everyone in Bridgely-upon-Thames tended to know each other somehow. We only had two secondary schools, and families hardly ever moved away.

Leroy was quiet for a second, running through faces in his head. "Okay, let's figure this out. So an Asian-looking, maybe Jewish guy with either brown or green eyes…"

I laughed and hit him again. "Umm…his friends came and picked him up," I said. "They all seemed to be into rock music. There was this girl with an undercut. He smokes…"

"It might be Harry Lipton. Was he Catholic?"

"Jeez, Leroy. How am I supposed to know? He didn't shove me into a box and confess all his dirty secrets."

Leroy grinned. "You're crap with men."

I hit him for the third time.

"If he's Catholic, then he's Harry Lipton. He's a heathen who left the church. Well, that's what Mum says anyway."

"How would she know?"

He sighed. "She keeps tabs on who goes to church and how often. Actual literal tabs. I found a list once."

"Your mum is so weird." I held out a length of my hair to check how badly it was frizzing in the drizzle.

"I am more than aware of that. But, anyway, if it's the Harry I'm thinking of…I think he slept with Cassie last year and then totally ghosted her afterwards. She was quite hung up on him."

"Cassie from your church, Cassie?"

He nodded.

"Your church has so many secret deviants."

He bowed with the gayest hand flourish the world has ever known. "Audrey, I have no idea what you mean."

Soon talk drifted away from the cinema towards complaining about coursework, complaining about school, complaining about this town – our usual bread and butter. Leroy was the cynic I'd clung onto like an oxygen mask these past few months after Milo. We'd met through Drama Club but became friends when he found me sobbing behind the stage curtains. I knew he was everything I needed in a friend when he said, "No offence, but you're the fugliest crier I've ever seen." Somehow, though my heart was throbbing with pain and humiliation, that had made me laugh.

As we got closer to school, the trickles of other students wearing our navy uniform sloshed together until we were all trudging in the same direction. I said goodbye to Leroy as we split off to go to our separate lessons, but he didn't say it back. He was buried in his phone again, muttering about feathers and Rainbow Roads. I wandered through the cramped corridors towards my Media Studies lesson, trying to rub the tiredness out of my eyes without messing up my mascara. Alice was sitting in our normal spot. She waved, showing off a freshly painted set of long nails, and I went and dumped my stuff next to her.

"New colour?" I nodded towards her hands.

"Yep. It arrived in the post yesterday. It's from America and it has real gold leaf in it – see?" She shoved her fingers practically in my face.

"I see." There was an obvious lack of enthusiasm in my voice but she pretended not to notice it.

"How was your first shift?"

"Okay." Last night felt like a dream. I couldn't believe I had to go back the next night and do it all over again. "You going to come visit me? With the others?" I attempted a smile. I attempted more enthusiasm. Both attempts crash-dived.

Alice pretended again she hadn't noticed. "Oooh, yes, we totally should! Can you get us a discount?" Her attempt at a normal friendship interaction was much more successful – or maybe it was just more genuine. Maybe it was just me who felt the gaping chasm between us that never used to be there.

"I've not asked yet."

"Hang on" – Alice twirled her hair around her finger – "isn't the new Dick Curtisfield out? We can come to that. We love his movies!"

"Sure! Sounds great!" I tried to chirp. "I'm working tomorrow."

"Perfect! I'll ask the others at lunch." Her smile was real but her voice was forced and I felt a jolt of pain. For what I'd done to us, for what I'd done to our friendship.

I was relieved when Mr Simmons bowled into the room

and started the lesson. Relieved to not have to make small talk with the girl who used to be my best friend – the girl who probably still thought we were best friends. I didn't understand how everything that had happened with Milo had changed how I felt about my friends when they'd been nothing but great – but it had.

I'd grown up with it being me and Alice, Becky and Charlie. Two pairs of best friends – the "girlie gang" as our parents called us. We'd made it through primary school, puberty and exams, and all crammed into a caravan together in Newquay after our GCSEs for a crazy holiday. And our friendship had managed to survive the first earthquake that hit me, of Dad leaving and Mum imploding. They held me as I cried, they came over with chocolate – for Mum as well as for me. But then, at the start of the summer after our first year of sixth form, the Milo thing happened and it felt like everything in my life broke. Even my friendships. I was too humiliated to even tell them what had happened. I found spending time with them difficult. *What do you think of this dress? Isn't Russell so good-looking? Don't you think Sarah looked so much better before that haircut? Do you want to go shopping this weekend, I saw this coat, but I'm not sure if it will suit me?* Their cutesy *oh-Audrey-it-will-all-be-okay* positivity turned my stomach and I fled from them, into Leroy's no-nonsense arms. Something inside of me had hardened, while they were the same as ever.

Mr Simmons was pacing the carpet and jolted me back into my Media Studies lesson.

"Right, so it's time for you to start thinking about your Critical Research coursework this year." He turned on his heel and made his way back. "The aim of this module is to teach you how to research an academic topic independently, to help prepare you for university."

Alice made a scared face and I tried to make one back.

"So you need to pick a part of the media to critically analyse. It can be anything. But try and keep it specific."

Another turn. Another trek across the chewing-gum-stained carpet.

A guy, George, put his hand up. "So we get to do whatever we want for the whole school year?"

"Nice try," Mr Simmons said. "I think you'll find this harder than me teaching you what you need for an exam. Most of you will find picking a topic the hardest part."

Alice put her hand up and her nails sparkled.

"Yes, Alice?"

"Can you give us some examples?"

"Of course, of course." He picked up a stack of sheets and passed them out. I took one and looked down at the photocopy of someone else's handwriting. "So, the only real criteria is you examine some part of the media with an academic eye – the news, TV sitcoms, Hollywood movies, it can be anything… Last year a student examined the coverage of women's sports on major news channels compared to male sports. Another looked at product placement in James Bond films. Another measured the amount of screen time given to actors of colour in Oscar-nominated films. Now…"

Mr Simmons sat down and took a sip from his coffee mug. "I know it's a bit overwhelming so let's spend ten minutes jotting down areas that interest you."

Alice and I looked at each other blankly. "Any ideas?" she asked.

"None. You?"

"I dunno." She began doodling spirals in the margin of her notepad. "I guess I could do something about women's magazines?"

"That sounds perfect. And it would look good on your CV when you apply for work experience."

Alice had wanted to write for a glossy magazine since she was seven. She lived in a perpetual state of despair that print journalism would be dead before she got the chance to realize her dream.

"I'll do that then." She sat higher in her seat and wrote down *women's magazines*.

I kept tapping my pen and watched everyone scribble around me. George was the only other person looking perplexed and we grinned at each other. Then I remembered George was one of Milo's best friends and panicked that he knew what had happened. I blushed, feeling vaguely sick, and looked down at my empty page.

What could I spend a whole term researching?

Surely nobody cares about anything that much?

Mr Simmons must've sensed my hesitation because he came over and crouched next to my desk. "Having trouble, Audrey?"

My face screwed up at the strong smell of coffee on his breath. "I can't think of anything."

"Well, what are you interested in?"

I shrugged, feeling exposed with everyone listening. "I don't know."

"How about films or TV? With all the acting you've done in the school plays?"

I flinched as he said it. He may as well have spat in my eye. I shrugged again. "I like films, I guess."

"Brilliant, yes." He acted like I'd just solved an impossible equation, rather than saying the most basic of things. "What sort of films do you like?"

I wasn't sure what I liked any more. I wasn't sure why I was here. Why I was taking Media Studies on to upper sixth instead of Drama. My favourite subject – my *only* subject really – and I'd dropped it. I'd dropped Drama… I'd basically just sleepwalked through my own life this past summer – surviving each day, counting them off, even though I wasn't sure what I was counting down to. Making momentous decisions based on what would require the least effort, bring me the least pain. I had no energy left for anything else after what Milo had done. When it did flare up, it was as a cold-but-simmering anger that pulsed through me, that showed no signs of draining out.

"You like romantic films, don't you, Audrey?" Alice spoke for me and jolted me out of my malaise.

"Oh, is that right, Audrey?"

I felt my face go red.

"She's named after Audrey Hepburn."

"Is that true?" Mr Simmons asked and I half managed to nod.

"Well, she's certainly an icon. Maybe you could do your research about her?"

I gave him my best no-way-in-hell look.

"Oooooor, maybe not. So you like romantic films?"

I shook my head hard. "I did. But I don't any more."

Not taking my hints, he pressed on. "I see, and why not?"

"Because they're full of unhelpful lies." It spat out of my mouth before I'd even noticed myself saying it. I heard George snort and I slumped in my seat, cringing at my own outburst.

At the very least, it shut Mr Simmons up for at least thirty seconds. Alice giggled to try and combat the awkwardness and I felt a rush of hate for her too, even though she was doing nothing wrong.

"It's true," I insisted. "Romance films ruin people's real-life relationships. They offer this idea of love that isn't sustainable in normal life. It's dan…" I was about to say "dangerous" before I looked up to see literally the whole class listening in. My fists clenched. I reached for a lesser word. "It's…pathetic?"

My teacher smiled, in a feeling-sorry-for-you way and I pulled my sleeves down over my hands and leaned forward so my hair covered my face.

"Sounds like you're onto something, Audrey," he said, quietly. "At least write that down. Have a think about where you can take that idea."

"She works in a cinema," Alice chipped in brightly. Still my unofficially appointed speaker for today. "At Flicker."

"Is that right?" Mr Simmons stood up. "Well then, I'll be looking forward to a great proposal, Audrey – with access to all those free film tickets."

"I don't know if I even get to watch the movies yet," I said, but Mr Simmons's back had already turned.

I looked at my notepad.

I'd written:

Why love is never like the movies.

5

I called Dougie at lunchtime, perched outside on the school wall. My bum was already getting damp but the common room was too noisy. That, and I'd seen Milo saunter in holding hands with Her.

It rang off. I tried again. It rang off.

Dougie picked up on my third attempt. "Audrey, what the hell?" His voice was gruff with sleep. "You woke me up."

"Shouldn't you be in lectures?"

"It's first year. Everyone knows first year doesn't count."

I shifted so a different part of my arse sat against the wet brick and bit my lip, knowing he was about to flip. "I'm calling about Dad." There was a long pause. "Dougie?"

"What's he done now?"

I heard shuffling and clicking and then loud music echoed down the line. Dougie's way of drowning out the world.

"He's…he's… He wants Mum to sell the house." I'd bent

over on myself just to get the sentence out – like admitting it out loud finally made it true.

Another painful pause. "You're kidding, right?" he said, finally.

"I don't think so, no. Mum told me last night."

"How was she?" he asked quickly, worry lacing his voice. Dougie was very protective of Mum. Though I always found it a bit half-arsed. He'd spent most of last year – her really bad year – staying out all night with his band. And he hadn't once come home to visit this term, even though it was only an hour's drive. He overcompensated with words and rage and strops at Dad – chucking fire down the phone, hurling insults through his keyboard. It made Mum adore him even more. While I was the one dealing with the actual physical situation. I was the one forced to play bad cop. Forced to say no to her. Forced to go and see Dad and the kids and play peacemaker as Dougie refused. Forced to keep the house clean in her bad weeks. Forced to call in sick for her. And no thanks, no hero badge for me. Just "Why can't you be supportive, like your brother?" – as if words were more what she needed, rather than stopping her dying from scurvy or getting fired for being hungover at work.

"She was…" I pictured her flopping onto my bed like a corpse, the disappointment washing over me like I'd been doused with icy water. "How do you think she was? All the progress she's made has just…imploded."

"He can't do this. Surely he can't do this?"

"I don't know. I'll have to go see him, I guess."

"Tell him if he does this, I never want to see him again."

I looked up at the crisp blue sky, the autumn sun making the bare twigs of trees sparkle. The sky had cleared up since this morning, but everything was still damp. The hum of lunchtime noise echoed through the cold air.

"Tell him yourself."

"Don't be like that, Audrey."

I dug my fingers into the wall. "I'm just saying, it would be useful if you'd help, Dougie. I don't know what to say to Dad either. You know how he's all…weird now."

"Just pretend he doesn't exist, that's what I do."

"Don't you see, I can't ignore him. Not if both you and Mum are. Someone's got to keep us vaguely talking. Plus the twins are our siblings!"

The music in the background inched up a notch. "Half-siblings," he corrected. "And the shit half."

"Dougie…"

"And he can't take the house. It's ours. What does Mum's lawyer say?"

"I'm not sure. She was too…" *drunk* "…ill last night to make much sense."

"Well, get her to ring her lawyer." The screechy plucks of his guitar now. He would hang up this phone call and not have to think about it any more. Whereas I, freezing, exhausted, had to go home to a hungover, confused mother with no option to ignore this.

You're angry at Dad, not Dougie. You're angry at Dad, not Dougie.

"Hey, do you know anyone called Harry?" I asked, changing the subject to save me from my own anger.

More scratchy chords, a riff of a new song echoed down the line. "There's Harry Lipton. How do you know him?"

"I started working at Flicker Cinema last night," I said. "He said he knew you. He's very…umm…friendly."

"Did he try it on with you?" Dougie's voice was harsh again.

"Yes, Dougie." I rolled my eyes. "He pinned me against a wall and declared his undying love the second I put on my new name tag. Why would he try it on with me?"

"He tries it on with everyone, that's all. He's a good guy apart from that though. We hung out a bit in Music Tech. I just don't want him hitting on my little sister. He's into films, isn't he?"

"Well, he works at a cinema, I don't think that means he's definitely into films."

"No no, he is. He makes them. Weird ones. With loads of fake blood and zombies and stuff. Anyway, he's all right. A bit lost…"

Because you aren't, I found myself thinking, then felt guilty the moment I'd thought it.

"But be careful. He's a dick when it comes to girls. Like…"

"Like Dad?" I suggested. The line fell quiet.

"He's not as bad as Dad," Dougie eventually replied.

6

The girls were waiting for me when I got back to the common room – displaying a respectable amount of animosity for the presence of Her. It made me feel guilty for having nasty thoughts about them earlier. I spent a lot of time feeling guilty. I wondered how much the world would change if the people who should *actually* feel guilty in life did feel guilty.

"I hate her new haircut," Charlie said, instead of hello, as I slumped next to them on the squishy sofa. I was trying to keep Milo and Her out of my eyeline but they were with the rest of the Drama people – being loud and obnoxious. It was like they couldn't un-learn how to project their voices. And you can, I would know.

Alice gave me one of her hugs that always last a tiny bit too long. "Her fringe looks deranged," she stage-whispered into my ear.

"She can't pull it off," Becky confirmed, nodding her head seriously.

I gave a thin smile, trying to see this for what it was – good friends comforting another friend. I couldn't understand why they were still being friendly this term when I'd spent the whole summer mostly ignoring their calls and closing the curtains on the sunshine. But I said, "Thanks, guys," in my numb voice. The one I wished wouldn't keep seeping out of me when I was around them. When I was around most people actually.

Charlie moved her chair, blocking my view of the Drama lot and – for that at least – I was grateful. Charlie was pissed off with her new boyfriend, Nick, who went to the big college, because he hadn't replied to her last message and it had been almost twelve hours. I found myself nodding, responding, listening. But more like I was a TV and someone had pointed a remote at me and punched the *NOD! RESPOND! LISTEN!* buttons. They dissected every single possible reason why Nick hadn't got back to her – from the state of his Wi-Fi signal to, eventually, how his family treated him in childhood.

"I think it's because his mum has always been tough, you know? So he finds it hard to show love."

Or Nick is a bit of a cock...

I didn't say that. I just played with my long hair.

"Audrey? Audrey?"

"Huh?" I looked up. The three of them stared at me, wearing the look they always wore these days. The look that said I Wasn't Joining In and therefore they were Worried About Me.

"What do you think, Audrey?"

"Umm, sorry, I wasn't listening properly," I admitted. I saw a twinge of pain cross Charlie's face – at my not caring, at my zoning out, at me not being the Audrey they've known for so long.

"I didn't mean to bore you," she said.

My stomach twisted in on itself, guilt, guilt, guilt – Jesus Mother of Crapcakes, was it my curse to always feel guilt?

Becky coughed, Alice blushed. The awkwardness fell like sleet from the ceiling.

I shook my head. "Sorry, I'm distracted." I tried to smile, and Charlie tried to smile too. Tight ones we didn't mean. "I didn't sleep much. My mum, well, she didn't have a good night. I think she's having a relapse or something, if that's the right word." Charlie's smile grew fatter and she moved over in her chair. Ready to be a friend. A friend I didn't deserve.

"Oh, Audrey, why didn't you tell us?" she asked. "What's happened? You shouldn't just let me drone on about Nick."

"No. You weren't droning on. It's nothing."

Guilty about using Mum as an excuse. Guilty that I was being a dick in the first place. Guilty, guilty, guilty. Charlie's empty space meant I could see Milo and my eyes went straight for him, like they always did. He caught my eye, just for a second. And, in that second, we were in my bedroom, with my music on and my clothes off and my mum not in and his hands were tracing down the sides of my waist and he was whispering that I was beautiful…

Becky came in for a hug too. I could smell the chemical tang of her hairspray. "What happened? Is it something with your dad?" she asked.

"It's…it's…"

I didn't want to be here. In this stuffy common room, in this stuffy school, in this stuffy sixth form stuffed with people too scared to go to the proper college. I didn't want to give the girls a reason for me being difficult, I just wanted to be difficult. I was so fed up of being amenable to everybody. I didn't want to tell them about the house. I didn't want them to ask me questions about what that meant when I didn't know the answers. I didn't want them to feel sorry for me when they should be feeling angry at me for being such a judgemental bunch of crap to hang out with.

Just then, Leroy sauntered through the doors, hand in hand with Ian. I stood up.

"Audrey? Where you going?" Becky asked.

"Audrey, you can tell us," Alice said.

"Sorry, it's just…Leroy. I have to talk to him about something."

I didn't say goodbye, just sort of left and walked over to Leroy. I let the guilt burst the dam and flow through me, feeling like the world's worst person. And Leroy, sensing it, greeted me by kissing me on both cheeks.

"Leroy, seriously, calm the gay down. I've said hi to you already." I gave Ian a quick hug hello.

"I've told him a million times that he does nothing to challenge the stereotypes of Drama Club," Ian said, and I laughed. He and Leroy had been together since *A Midsummer Night's Dream* last Christmas – where Leroy played Puck and Ian the understudy. "But I was the one who got to under…study him," Leroy always joked. I'd played Titania; Milo was Oberon, of course. God, it had been the happiest of winters. High on love, snatching kisses between scenes. Just as I was reminiscing, feeling my heart get heavier with each beat, Milo and Courtney (Her) sauntered past us, his arm over her shoulder.

"All right?" he nodded at us and I was rendered temporarily incapable. My arm moved up in this odd-frozen half wave and I coupled it with a toothy grin that I'm sure made me look like a constipated bear.

"All right?" Leroy replied, because that's how normal people behave. "You auditioning for *Guys and Dolls* next week?"

"Of course, of course," Milo said. His arm hadn't once left Her shoulder. I took a step behind Ian, like his body could protect me from emotional pain. "Who you reading for?" Milo asked Leroy, barely acknowledging me.

"I'm not sure yet. Maybe Nicely Nicely. And you? Let me guess…"

"Sky Masterson," Milo interrupted, not getting the joke. He grinned, in that pretend-humble way I'm sure he'd practised in the mirror. "How about you guys?" He gestured to me and Ian and it felt like a thousand needles flew out from his fingers and embedded themselves into my guts. *You guys?* I'm just one of "you guys"? Ian was talking and I stood there frozen – thinking, *This is my revenge for being rude to the girls. I deserve this.*

"How about you, Audrey?" Courtney asked me. "You're still auditioning, right?"

I forced myself to look at her. Even despite the vaguely-unfortunate new fringe, she looked amazing. Her bright red lipstick, her perfect eyeliner flicks, that mole just above her lip.

"Oh, me?" Bugger, bugger, bugger. I couldn't talk to them. I'd promised myself I'd never talk to them. "I'm not doing the play this year," I managed to garble out.

Both of them looked shocked. Maybe Courtney looked relieved? I mean I guess, until recently, I was Drama Club's golden girl, the shoo-in for every lead going. Our old Drama Head refused to even speak to me when I quit.

"Why not, Audrey?" Milo asked, casually.

I mean, why wouldn't he be all casual? It's not like he'd looked at me this one time, walking home from school, with the light shining behind him and stopped me and said, "Audrey, I can't not say it any more, I love you…"

"I've got a job." I shrugged. All shruggy shrug. "It conflicts with rehearsals and it's not like I'm doing Drama any more. I work at Flicker Cinema now."

"No way," Courtney said. "I love that place. Like, I never knew I needed cinnamon dust in my life before I went there."

I nodded like a nodding dog who had a gun pointed at the back of its head and was told it would get shot unless it kept on nodding. "Don't forget the pulled pork hot dogs." I sounded like I worked in Disneyland. "So, yeah, too busy for the play this year. The cinema's great though. You guys should totally come."

Why was I saying that? What was wrong with me?

Milo looked dubious, but Her eyes lit up. "Amazing, we so should! Could you get us a discount?"

"Yeah, of course!" WHY DID I KEEP TALKING?

"Isn't the new Dick Curtisfield out? Milo, we should SO go this weekend."

No no no no no no no no no.

"Maybe," was all Milo said. Making me breathe a sigh of relief. Though I'd still spend all tomorrow panicking that he'd turn up.

They began to saunter off and I wilted into Leroy, who reached over and squeezed my fingers.

"Hang on," Ian called after them. "Who you auditioning for, Courtney?"

She stopped, turned, smiled. "Adelaide, I think. I would love to do 'Take Back Your Mink'."

My stomach kicked. Of COURSE she'd be Adelaide. The sexy part. Because she was sexy and I was not, which was why Milo was with Her and not me.

Leroy raised an eyebrow. "Whoa, big part. Good thing Audrey isn't auditioning."

We all gasped, myself included. My face went hot.

Courtney's eyes flashed with anger but Milo was already there, pulling her in closer, kissing her head.

"She's going to smash it," he told us and steered her away. He caught my eye one last time, like this was all my fault.

A sudden flash, of him kissing my neck, of me shaking with nerves, but he'd lit candles, and my top was off and I was so shy about him seeing my boobs, but he was so nice about it and it was our six-month anniversary...and then... I'd propped myself on my elbows to try and make it hurt less. "If you'll just relax," he'd said, trying to be soothing, but I could sense the annoyance under his voice. "Hey, hey, hey, it's okay. I love you... Shh...shh. It's okay. Do you want to stop?" I shook my head. He pushed in further. I cried out. He pulled out. I cried. He held me and I was so embarrassed, but he was so, so nice about it being my first time...

Until a week later when he dumped me.

7

I spent Friday night in, like the huge saddo I am.

The rest of the day was nondescript and dull. I used to love school – love coming in, love Drama Club, love my friends, love sauntering the corridors with Milo's arm around me. I was one of those annoying people who *liked* secondary school. But since Milo dumped me and I dramatically decided to drop Drama over the summer – something I'd thought, pathetically, might make Milo realize just how broken I was, turn up at my door, and beg me to reconsider – I didn't even have subjects I cared about. Drama was all I loved, the rest of my options I'd just picked willy-nilly – thinking they wouldn't matter as I was going to get into RADA or something.

So after an afternoon of yawning through English, and head-on-desk sleeping through Geography, I walked home. Alone. The girls had invited me to Pizza Express but I'd told them I was seeing Dad – which I needed to do, but I couldn't face it on so little sleep.

"We'll see you tomorrow though, at work, right?" Alice said, hugging me goodbye. "You can get us in cheap?"

"Yep," I squeaked. Hoping Ma wouldn't go nuts at all the discounted tickets I'd seemingly promised everyone.

I had to walk a slightly different way home so Leroy's mum didn't spot me. I was his cover for tonight, so he could spend time with Ian. Neither of them were out with their families, so they spent a lot of time freezing their arses off on park benches. The other month, when Leroy bounded up to me with a huge "Guess what?" to reveal he'd lost his virginity, my first question was, "*Where?!*"

There had been no messages from Mum all day – which was actually worse than too many. When I let myself in, I saw her work heels by the door.

"Audrey? That you?" Her voice came from the kitchen.

I dropped my rucksack and tentatively made my way in. She stood at the stove, surrounded by vegetable cuttings and ferociously stirring a stir-fry. Her hair was piled on top of her head in an unravelling chignon and she had way too much make-up on to try to hide the hangover. Her foundation wasn't quite the right colour and it sank and flaked into the wrinkles of her eyes.

"Hi." I perched nervously at the breakfast bar. Mum being uber-efficient to cover up her catatonicness was so much worse than just plain catatonic. The other way didn't have a comedown.

"Hi, lovely, do you mind passing me that soy sauce?"

she asked, all breezy, like she hadn't cried herself to sleep on my bed.

"It smells great, can I help?"

"No, it's all under control. I just thought we should eat healthy, you know?"

I sat and watched her twirl and hurl about the kitchen. The work surfaces sparkled, all the empty wine bottles had mysteriously vanished. It wasn't even 5 p.m. yet.

"Why are you home so early?"

She ignored me at first, lifting a wooden spoon to her mouth to taste her concoction. "Mmm, needs a bit more ginger."

"Mum?"

"Audrey, it's fine. I took the afternoon off."

"I thought you weren't doing that any more?"

"Don't stress, Audrey, honestly. I had a meeting. You know how relaxed my office is."

They weren't last year when they had to put you on performance management.

I started laying out the cutlery, not even hungry yet, but knew it was worth stuffing anything down rather than rejecting her efforts. She brought two steaming plates of vegetables and brown rice over, a grin stitched on.

"Mmm, lovely and healthy. All your five-a-day on one plate."

"Thanks, it smells great."

We sat and ate at the breakfast bar. We rarely used the dining room now it was just the two of us. The stir-fry had so much ginger in it that I had to sip my water between every mouthful, yet I made appreciative noises and watched her warily over my glass…waiting…

She pushed her plate away with three bits of broccoli left on it. "So I went to see my lawyer this afternoon. About the house."

"And…"

"And, Audrey, I need you to speak to your father. Get him to change his mind."

I put my fork down. "What?"

Mum was squeezing each of her fingers, one by one. Her wedding band was still on. Even after everything.

"My lawyer says he's got a good shot at making us sell. With you only a year away from uni…your dad's saying we don't need all this space any more. But it's your home, isn't it? You've got to tell him, it's more than space, it's your home. It's our…our…home." That's when the comedown hit. She bent over the table, smashing her head down, getting soy sauce in her hair.

I was up, squatting at her side, moving the plate to one side to get her hair off it. "Mum? Mum, it's okay, it's going to be okay." She wasn't even crying, just kind of wailing, which was worse. "Mum, come on. Tell me what the lawyer said."

She sat up. "He's claiming he needs the money from the sale to help pay for That Bitch and her fucking runts." She pushed her chair back and went over to the drinks cabinet. "Can you believe it? Like she's not taken enough? Like she's not taken EVERYTHING." She clattered down a glass and poured herself a measure of gin. Neat. I winced. "Oh, don't look at me like that, Audrey. It's just one, and I'm an adult, for Christ's sake."

I straightened myself up, my face stinging like she'd slapped me. I plonked my empty plate in the dishwasher and went to walk out the room.

"Audrey? Audrey, I'm sorry!"

I turned back, looking at her. Her hands shook as she poured herself a second gin. A flash. A flash then of how Dad must see her. Revulsion. For a fleeting second I could see why he left. But then she wasn't like this before he walked out. He had done this to her. The flash morphed into pure hot rage at him. Rage I didn't know what to do with, because he was my dad. He was still my dad. I still loved him, and the twins, even after everything he'd done. So I pushed it down and made my guts hurt.

"Audrey, sorry, honey. It's just a little drink. It's been one hell of a day. Please, sit with me."

I reluctantly sat back down – wishing I'd gone to Pizza Express.

"You need to be careful with your drinking. Last night you were…"

"I know, I know." She took my hand, tight. "I've been doing better though, haven't I? It's just the shock, Audrey. If he takes the house…if I lose this place… So, if you can just go see him this weekend. Tomorrow?"

"I'm not sure what good it…"

"Please, Audrey." Her voice was sharper. "Try."

I sighed. Nodded. "I'll try."

Her posture softened even though there was no way Dad would listen to me. But she put the gin away, cleared her plate, perked up again. "So, you in tonight? Why don't we have a movie night? Popcorn? Chocolate?"

Movies. More movies.

"Sure." I nodded.

8

She stayed relatively normal all night though it took me a while to recover from dinner. I'd forgotten how quickly she could flip between fine and drama – it had been months since she was like this. I couldn't believe Dad had set her off again. In a burst of parental obligation, Mum even asked me how school was going and I told her about my Media Studies project.

"Well, we'll have to watch a romance film then. For research, won't we?"

"You sure that's a good idea?"

"Oh, don't be silly, Audrey. I'm a grown woman. I can handle a romantic movie, even in my state."

We shoved a packet of microwave popcorn in, dug out some Cadbury's and settled on the sofa. It was so dark outside already. The heating groaned and clanked up to the high ceilings, the curtains rustled softly from the draught. She picked *Say Anything* – an old eighties film with John Cusack.

"Your dad and I went to watch this at the cinema when it had its ten-year anniversary."

Your dad and I, your dad and I. Why did she still insist on doing this to herself?

But, despite her enthusiasm, Mum fell asleep twenty minutes in. I persevered for the sake of my research but it made my intestines coil themselves around each other. John Cusack was just so…in love with this girl. The way he looked at her, it made me wish someone could look at me like that.

Milo used to look at me like that. But then look at how that had turned out.

Mum snored softly to my left, her feet right up on the sofa, her tights wrinkled and bunched up around her ankles. I tried to tune her out, tried to focus on the film. When we got to the famous scene where John Cusack stands outside her house with a giant boombox to try and win her back, I'd had enough. I hit pause and sank back into the sofa, staring blankly at the freeze-frame.

Nothing like that ever happens in real life…

I pulled out my phone and scrolled through everyone's updates. The girls had uploaded dozens of photos of themselves at Pizza Express – in full make-up, pulling duck faces and taking multiple selfies. Leroy had tagged me in at the local bowling alley and I quickly sent him a message.

Audrey: A bowling alley???! FFS?! If you're going to make me your beard, at least make me a cool beard.

But he didn't reply. He was probably too busy not-bowling with Ian in a not-bowling alley.

I went through all the various sites, catching up on the news from people I didn't like or care about, but still felt shit that they were out and I wasn't. Then I saw Dad had uploaded twenty plus photos and I found myself clicking on them. My brother and sister beamed out of my screen – their pudgy faces filling most of the frame. The album was entitled *Our new vegetable patch* and mostly involved Dad and Jessie smiling and posing with giant spades – their faces dirty and ruddy and healthy from hard work.

It just looks like a pile of dirt now, but wait until the harvest, Jessie had commented. And the white hot rage catapulted back, singing through my veins.

I tried to focus on the photos of the twins – smiling. I couldn't help loving them – after all, it wasn't their fault Dad was an arsehole. But I had to be so careful around Mum about them. I couldn't mention them, or ever have them over. It would be too big a betrayal. I had to tuck away my love for them and save it for the odd few days a month when I could see them. At least I'd see them this weekend, even if talking to Dad was unlikely to work.

God, I couldn't not live in this house. In this room, this beautiful living room. With its mint green paint and warm fire, and memories of how we piled in here every Saturday night for family movie night. We watched every Audrey Hepburn film here – Mum and Dad looking dewy-eyed at each other. *Roman Holiday* always came out at least twice a year.

"This is where he proposed," Mum would say, and Dougie and I would roll our eyes because they'd told the story so many times. But we also secretly enjoyed hearing it again. The story of Them. Mum and Dad. Their epic romance. Their epic proposal. Their Hollywood wedding…

Dad had commented under a photo of Jessie. *Love of my life. My best friend.* Followed by twelve heart emojis.

The comment had fifty-one likes…

Mum's snore interrupted my angsty stalking and I glanced up at her. She moved onto her side, using the armrest as a pillow.

Fifty-one likes.

Poor, poor Mum.

I turned off the TV and got out an old blanket to drape around her. I checked the front door was locked, and climbed the stairs, pulling on Milo's T-shirt and getting into bed.

It wasn't even ten.

I stared at the ceiling for a while. I tried to read a book but couldn't concentrate. So, at half past ten, I sighed and pulled out my phone again – scrolling through the updates of everyone else's better Friday nights.

I found myself tapping in Harry's name.

We had ten mutual friends – one of them Dougie. His profile photo surprised me. It was him holding up a video camera, just one eye staring out behind it. I clicked through some of the photos that had slipped through his privacy settings. They were mostly gigs – blurry photos of his face highlighted by the flashes of club-night neons. But there were a few of everyone dressed up as zombies. Harry stood proudly in the middle, holding up his camera again. That girl from the car was in one of them, their arms around each other. She was splattered in fake blood, obviously playing some sort of zombie. I wondered again if she was his girlfriend, and if so, why Dougie was warning me off him. I was tempted to ask Harry about the zombie stuff on my shift tomorrow, but then realized that would reveal I'd been stalking him.

I was asleep by eleven.

9

THE BAD BOY WHO CHANGES
HIS WAYS JUST FOR YOU

He's tall. He's dark. He's trouble. He just CAN'T COMMIT, you know? He wants to play the field, and the field next to it. Hell, he wants to play in EVERY SINGLE SEX MEADOW THAT HE CAN. Nothing and no one can change his ways. He's a Bad Boy. A sexy Bad Boy. Because, let's face it, you can only get away with being a Bad Boy if you're the sort of good-looking that doesn't actually occur much in real life.

But then Bad Boy meets that girl. This one girl. Who – for inexplicable reasons – makes him want to change his ways. He REFORMS for her. She is special. She is different from the other girls…

✷ ✷ ✷ ✷ ✷

I was woken by my phone ringing.

"Huh?" I said, instead of hello, my head still under the duvet. The house was quiet – Mum not up yet. The heating wasn't on and it was freezing.

"Audrey? I didn't wake you, did I?" It was Ma's voice. All calm and clipped and *of-course-she's-this-awake-at-9-a.m.-on-a-Saturday*. I found myself sitting up in bed, like she could see me.

"Oh no. I've been up for ages. I just got back from a run."

"Riiight," Ma said, unconvinced.

"Is there a problem?"

"Yes, actually. Not a big one though. I was just wondering if you minded doing a double shift today? I know you're new and you're not supposed to start until five. But they need a manager at our sister branch and I need someone to cover the load at Flicker. Could you come in at midday instead?"

Today…

I was supposed to be having a massively awkward and emotionally-damaging conversation with Dad today.

"Yep. I can do it. Was it twelve you said?"

"Oh…" Ma sounded like she didn't know what to do with my compliance. "That's very helpful, thank you, Audrey. Harry and LouLou will be there to look after you, so don't worry. And I'll write you up some instructions before I leave. You'll like LouLou, she's an old-timer."

Oh God, so probably just like you.

"Sounds great."

Ma hung up without saying goodbye.

I grabbed my uniform, which was still crumpled on the floor where I'd left it the other night. I looked at myself in the mirror and scowled. My hair fell long and dank around my face. I just about had time to wash and dry it – which always took for ever because it was so long. I hung my work top on the back of the bathroom door so the steam from the shower would iron out the worst of the creases. Then I shoved some toast and Marmite down myself and dabbed some make-up on. I tried to tell myself that I wasn't putting make-up on in case Milo turned up – but I knew that was a lie.

Just before I set off, I checked in on Mum. She'd migrated from sofa to bed at some point during the night, and she was all huddled up in her duvet, still only sleeping on her side of the bed.

"Mum?"

She rolled over. "Audrey? What is it?" Her eyes fluttered open.

"I'm going to work, they want me to come in early. I won't be home until late, is that okay?"

"What…" She yawned, and her stale breath floated into my face. "What time is it?"

"Almost eleven."

"Oh." And she didn't remark on how late it was at all. She just turned over. "Well, have fun, Audrey." Her head went back under the duvet.

It was raining out – undoing all the hard work I'd put into de-minging my hair. The wind was proper howling, the rain lashing against my hood as I stomped through puddles, soaking my jeans up to the knees, letting the elements blow away all my guilty feelings about leaving Mum for the day. I sent a message to Dougie, not sure what good it would do.

> Audrey: Mum's having a bad day. Again.
> I'm working. Can you call her?

The high street was mostly empty, the bad weather putting everyone off venturing out. I steered my way past the odd determined buggy-pusher, feeling jealous of all the toddlers who get to be pushed around under those snug plastic covers, and dodged down an alleyway to Flicker.

There was a sign on the staff door in scrawled handwriting. *Enter at your own peril.*

"What the hell?" I pulled it off the Blu-Tack holding it up.

All the lights were off inside. The quietness jarred with the howling winds outside.

"Hello?" I called.

Silence.

"Harry? LouLou?" Even though I had no idea who LouLou was.

There was a clattering by the bar. I looked around for signs of life, but all I could hear was the wind hissing at the windows.

"I know you're here. You left a note on the door," I called.

I spotted a foot poking out from behind the bar. A blue

Converse. I walked towards it and found Harry slumped on the ground, lifeless. Face down.

"Harry?" He didn't say anything. I bent down gingerly. Knowing it was a wind-up but still feeling freaked.

I rolled him over and screamed.

His face was covered in blood – what was left of it. Half of it seemed to be chewed off. His T-shirt was ripped and splattered with gore.

A loud crash behind me and this…thing emerged from the kitchen. I screamed louder – pure real terror forcing its way out my vocal chords. It was wearing a ragged wedding dress, the skin behind the veil all grey and gruesome. It staggered towards me and I screamed again, falling backwards over Harry's foot.

That's when the laughing started.

"Got you!" Harry lurched upright like he had rigor mortis. "Shit, are you okay, Audrey?"

I was crouched in a ball, panting for breath. "That. Wasn't. Funny."

The zombie bride pulled up her veil. "Hi, I'm LouLou. Sorry, we're just testing out Harry's new stage make-up."

"Stage make-up?"

Harry clambered to his feet, looking very dead but also very pleased with himself. He held out his hand to help pull me up but I shook my head.

"Sorry, it's my fault," LouLou said. She did look sorry now that she'd lifted her veil. "I'm the assistant manager. I get a bit, well, overexcited when Ma's not here."

And I warmed to her the moment she mentioned Ma in a negative way.

Harry shrugged at my hand reject and ruffled his already-mussed hair. I stood up, not quite looking at him.

"No, it's my fault," he said. "Sorry, Audrey. I make zombie movies and I wanted to try out this new kit."

"Isn't the cinema about to open?"

LouLou shrugged. "Probably. Who cares? What's important is that we scared you shitless!"

"I did not lose my shit," I protested. "I was just confused."

"Oh come on, Audrey," Harry said. "We got you."

"I still can't believe you did that to me when I'm new."

LouLou completely removed her veil, revealing pink hair. "You're right, sorry. As I said, we got…"

"Overexcited, I get it." I was trying to stay grumpy but it was hard. Harry had managed to win my eye contact and was grinning that gravitational-pull smile.

"Let me wash this off." LouLou made her way to the staff bathroom. "Thanks for covering today, Audrey. Harry, can you make the guacamole?"

"Ahh, Ma said she left me instructions?" I called after her and I heard sniggering behind me.

"Ha, yes she has. They're upstairs in the staffroom." LouLou laughed too.

"What? What is it?"

"Just go see for yourself."

She vanished into the loos and I was left with Harry, who was using some of the kitchen paper to mop his face.

"How are your stress levels?" he asked, still grinning.

"I'll recover. So, you make zombie movies, huh?"

"Yep. I'm making one right now. Well, I'm trying to. It's taking for ever because I'm not sure what sort of film it's supposed to be yet and I can't find a good enough zombie bride."

"Why zombies?" I asked.

He was smearing blood further across his face, rather than washing it off. I grabbed a paper towel, wet it under the tap and handed it to him.

"Thank you. And, the real question is, why *not* zombies, Audrey? If you're going to do anything, you need to ask yourself – *would this situation benefit from adding zombies? The answer is almost always 'yes'.*"

His napkin was already smothered in red syrup, so I wet another one and handed it over. "I asked Dougie about you."

He grinned, focusing on getting a big smear off his eyebrow. "And…"

"He warned me off you. Said you were trouble."

Harry's face didn't show even a hint of surprise and I knew Dougie was onto something. "That's not very friendly of him."

Harry was too busy cleaning himself to make the guacamole, so I shoved my rucksack on the floor and got out the avocados.

"So what sort of trouble are you?" I asked, washing my hands before I started. "The *I'm-still-in-love-with-my-ex* kind? The *I-have-mummy-issues* kind? The *I-secretly-have-low-self-*

esteem kind? Or, my personal favourite, the *Just-because-I-can* kind?"

Harry looked totally unoffended. "I just don't know why Dougie would say that about me." He grinned so wide his teeth almost blinded me.

"Ahh, come on, Harry. You even charmed Ma. God, you're not going to get that stuff off with napkins. Go have a wash in the bathroom."

Another huge grin. "Thanks, Mum."

I mashed avocado while the two of them cleaned themselves up. LouLou emerged first, looking totally different. She now had a full face of eyeliner and a lip-piercing I hadn't spotted behind the veil. I guessed she was around twenty-five.

"Sorry about that," she said. "Harry convinced me it would be hilarious. He's very good at convincing people about things." She saw me squeezing limes. "Isn't Harry supposed to be doing that?"

"He had to go wash."

"You see?" LouLou perched on the bar, swinging her legs under it. "He's convinced you to do a job he was supposed to be doing, without you even realizing it. That's Harry all over."

"Sorry. I'll go check Ma's rota, see what I'm supposed to do."

LouLou grimaced and shook her head. "Screw the rota. It's very simple. You do what you did last shift."

"She didn't let me do anything other than make the

food last shift. She said I shouldn't run before I could walk."

LouLou let out a huge sigh then jumped off the counter. "For Christ's sake, that woman! None of it is rocket science. Here, let me show you."

Harry eventually came out, only a hint of red left on his face. It frustrated me that his wet hair made my belly do a thing.

"Only ten minutes till opening and you're going to have to show people to their seats," he said. "Do you think you can handle the pressure?"

I stuck my tongue out. "Tell me again why they need showing to their seats? There's literally one aisle that goes in a straight line. And they either sit on the left or right of it. I mean they've managed to drive themselves here and all – but they need someone to say 'Walk down this only available path'?"

"You know what?" LouLou said, from behind the cloud of popping corn. "I've never thought of it like that before. You should inform Ma. Tell her it would improve efficiency."

Harry shook his head. "She couldn't handle it. Just think what it would mean for The Rota."

"You're right," LouLou said. "Her head would actually explode."

To prove their point, Harry and LouLou dragged me up to the staffroom – Harry unnecessarily taking my hand as he did so. There, on the table, was what looked like a twenty-page dossier.

For Audrey Winters, the top page said. I picked it up, reading it under my breath.

"Here are the five key stages of ticket selling. Number one, greet the customer. Initial friendly contact is integral to customer relations. Number two, ask the customer what they would like. This empowers the customer. Number three, always provide what the customer asks... Oh my God, guys? Is this a piss-take?"

Harry jabbed at the page. "You've missed out number four. *Remember to breathe. Breathing is integral to a human's ability to maintain maximum living potential. I have booked in 0.25 of each second into your rota to allow you to inhale and exhale. If you die during your shift, I will dock your pay."*

I giggled, the paper shaking.

LouLou took the page off me and pretended to read it aloud. *"You must check the rota every hour, in case your duties have changed. If they have, update the rota accordingly to ensure management knows exactly what you're doing and when. Even if there is a huge queue of screaming customers, do not deal with them unless the rota tells you to."*

Harry grabbed it off her, his eyes watering with laughter. *"If you are unable to perform all your daily tasks because you're too busy looking at the fucking rota, do not blame the rota. It is your fault you are not, literally, a human rota."*

We were laughing so hard that we initially didn't hear the door knock. Not until someone tried again. Harder.

"What was that?" LouLou said.

"More zombies?" I suggested.

We descended the stairs to see a long line of harassed parents and kids outside the front door.

"Excuse me," a mum called through the glass. "Aren't you supposed to be open?"

"Ah, bollocks pissing bollocks," LouLou said. "I forgot to open up."

And we scrambled for the doors.

10

I felt more like I worked in a crèche than a cinema in the following hours. There were screams for chocolate ice creams, strops thrown when health-conscious parents tried to order dried fruit instead. One child even wet themselves and LouLou had to get on her hands and knees to scrub the carpet.

"I will take this bullet for you," she told me, when I offered to help. "It will be your time soon enough to clean up someone else's piss."

Harry nodded. "People leave it for us in glasses a lot."

"What?" My mouth dropped in horror.

"I blame the obsession with making all films three hours long. People don't want to miss anything so they just piss in their Coke cup and leave it there for us, all warm and steamy."

"That. Is. Disgusting."

"Oh, Audrey," LouLou said, tipping some bleach into her

bucket. "Hell is other people and what they do in the anonymous dark of the cinema."

Ma rang three times, *"Just to check how things are going"*. But, other than that, it was pretty fun working with Harry and LouLou. So busy my brain had no time to think, which was just about brilliant by me. But after the kids left, I began to clam up.

The girls were coming…

Milo and Her might be coming…

"You okay, newbie?" Harry asked, as we yet again hoovered Screen Two.

I sighed from where I was scrambling under a seat to reach some stray popcorn kernels. I scraped them into the bin bag with my spare hands and righted myself. "Yeah, I guess. My friends might be coming in later. Is it okay to give them a discount?"

"I don't know, Audrey. The MOMENT Ma's back is turned…"

"It's not my fault! They just kind of invited themselves."

He leaned against the wall. "Audrey, I'm joking. It's fine. We all get fifty per cent off for friends and family. The cinema makes most of its money on the food and drink anyway."

I tied up the top of the full bin liner. "Seriously?"

"Why else do you think we charge a fiver for some popped kernels sprinkled with cinnamon?"

"So Ma won't mind as long as my friends order enough black-cherry cordial and pulled pork?"

He shook his head. "Nah, she loves it when my friends

come in. They're always stoned out of their skulls and spend about twenty-five quid on ice cream."

There was still a bleachy-smelling damp patch in the corner and I dodged it with my dustpan and brush. I didn't say anything about the fact he'd mentioned drugs. I'd assumed he and his friends might be stoners. They seemed to be all the clichés I associated with weed – loud metal music, rust bucket cars, zombie films. I was quite sure Dougie smoked drugs. Me and the girls were a bit too, well, girlie for doing bongs, or whatever it is stoners do. Alice, Becky, Charlie and I spent our experimental years drinking cherry Lambrini, or anything else pink and fizzy. The most rock 'n' roll thing I'd ever done was throw up pink vomit into Alice's curtains.

"There's still something bothering you," Harry said, as I went to make my way back up the aisle. "You've been flinching whenever the door opens."

I figured I needed to tell someone, in case I had a nervy fit at the counter.

"My ex may be coming tonight too…" I started. "With his new girlfriend."

Harry put his legs out across the aisle, stopping me from going up. "Now, who would be stupid enough to make you an ex-anything?"

"Harry!"

"What?" His face was the very essence of innocence.

I slowly and deliberately stepped over his leg.

"You know whoever he is, he's an idiot," he called after me as I pushed through the double doors.

11

"I need to warn you about Harry," LouLou said, as we waited for the evening rush to come in. We were almost sold out which made me hopeful that Milo wouldn't be able to get in.

I tossed the pulled pork over with the tongs to stop it drying out. "You're the third person to say bad things about him since I started working here."

"I saw him giving you the eye when you were cleaning up popcorn – thought I'd give you a heads-up. Seems like I've been beaten to it."

I laughed. "Multiple times. Is he really *that* awful?"

"He's a fun guy, don't get me wrong. I'm always happy when we're on the same shifts but he's, well, I'm sure he'll see you as some sort of conquest. You're a pretty girl and all." LouLou scratched her head. "Although he just about tries it on with anyone."

"Why?" I felt strangely unbothered by the whole thing

– or just tired of it. Harry was obviously a flirt and he was obviously flirting with me but he may as well be flirting with an empty margarine tub.

"I don't know, he just always has, and, well, working together can be awkward if you go there. Harry's flights of fancy don't tend to last. We had another girl who quit."

I held out my hand to stop her. "You really don't need to worry. I've made myself immune to boys like Harry." *By still being hung up on one.*

LouLou looked visibly relieved. "Good. Well, I've had the chat now. I have fulfilled my assistant-manager and *woman-of-the-world* duties."

The next batch of filmgoers trickled in and I stood up straighter behind the ticket counter, my fingers twitching nervously. *Would Milo come? Surely he wouldn't come?*

A lady wearing a giant fur coat pulled her husband over. "Two tickets, please," she said, getting out her purse.

"Yes, of course. Umm, for what?"

She looked at me like I was dumb. "For the film."

I nodded very slowly, just as I saw Harry emerge from the cinema with his little torch. He stood behind the lady, laughing.

"Yes, but can I ask what film, please?" I pressed.

"Oh." The lady got it now. "Whoops. Yes. I mean *Walking with Sausage Dogs.*"

"We're a bit busy tonight, but where do you want to sit?" I pulled up the available seats on the computer screen and pulled it around so she could see.

She grumbled a bit. "Aren't there any aisle seats left?"

"Sorry, we're almost fully booked."

"I guess we'll take E3 and E4 then."

She handed over her card and I miraculously managed to put the payment through without breaking anything. The stream of customers poured past me, most with their tickets already on their phones.

Harry pinched either side of my ribs to squeeze past me. "The battery on my torch has gone," he explained, when I glared at him. "She'll complain about the price of the food next," he whispered as the lady walked away. And, with true comic timing, we overheard her say, "Five pounds for some popcorn? That's a bit steep, isn't it?"

"I told you. People always do and say the same stupid things in cinemas." He shoved a new battery into his torch and then crept past me – putting his arms up in the air. "See, no touching." He winked, and my body was suddenly annoyed he wasn't touching me, which was precisely the point. He dashed back to the doors, all gracious with the customers, even bowling over Mrs Complainy. "Seats E3 and 4, you say? Right this way, madam."

I was just shamelessly admiring the back view of him – because you can look at someone like Harry and just enjoy it without ruining your life by adding feelings to it – when Alice's face popped up right in front of mine.

"AUDDDDRREEYYYYYY!" Becky and Charlie were right behind her. They jumped and pulled me in for a hug over the counter.

"Oh my God, look! You're in uniform and everything!" Becky shrilled.

"Hey girls," I said, as un-hollowly as possible. "You made it!"

"We did, we did!" Charlie said. She was the most dressed-up, wearing ruby red lipstick and, by the looks of it, she'd even curled her hair.

I smiled as far as my face would stretch. "I can get you fifty per cent off."

"Ahhhh, that's amazing. Can we all sit together?"

I looked at the screen. "Yes. If you don't mind being in the front row?"

"Nope."

Harry swooped behind them just as I was taking their money. He put an arm around all of them like it was okay to just touch people.

"Ladies," he said. "You must be Audrey's friends?"

I looked pointedly at his hand, which was so over Becky's shoulder it was almost touching her boob – not that she minded in the slightest.

"This is Harry," I deadpanned. "He works here too." I shook my head at him and he smiled. "He's about to say 'Audrey didn't tell me how beautiful you all were', or something similar."

Harry pulled them in closer. "Audrey didn't tell me how beautiful you all were." He kept eye contact with me at all times.

"I told you."

The girls dissolved into unoffended giggles. "How long have you worked here then, Harry?" Becky asked him, in full-on flirt mode.

"Full time since the summer."

"He's in Dougie's year," I added, handing over their tickets.

"Oh." Alice was doing her flirt-smile rather than her actual smile. Alice was always worried she had "too much gum". She even once pitched an article to a women's magazine about how there are no beauty products for too much gum. "So, why aren't you at uni then?"

Harry didn't answer and a tiny wince crossed his face. He coughed. "So, have you girls got your snacks?" he asked and guided them towards LouLou, his hands still around their shoulders.

I was just peering after them, marvelling at how one human being could have that much charm when I heard, "Hi, Audrey."

All my insides turned to shards of ice.

I made myself look up – look right at them. "Guys! You came!" I sounded like I was a wind-up toy that had been wound too tight.

Milo was wearing the American varsity-style jacket that he knew used to make me want to lick him.

"Yeah, I dragged him out," Courtney said. "He's agreed to watch *Walking with Sausage Dogs* if I come watch the new Scorsese next week."

Milo smiled apologetically. "You're going to be sick of us, Audrey."

I closed my eyes for a bit longer than was probably necessary. "Great, well, there aren't many seats left, but hopefully you can sit together." I pushed the screen round, which was stupid because I knew exactly which seats they were going to pick. Harry had warned me about them. The Make-out Seats.

"There's two together right at the back there." Courtney's long nails scraped the screen as she picked the seats I thought she would. "Ahh, how cute! They're on their own little row."

"Righty ho." I clicked *confirm* like someone who said *Righty ho.*

A clatter of heels and giggles and I saw the girls following Harry into the dark of the cinema, each cradling a huge bucket of popcorn and a Diet Coke. Becky, at the back, raised her eyebrows madly at me while pointing to Harry with her spare hand. Then she spotted Milo and Courtney and stopped. She saw my face and mouthed, "*Are you okay?*" and I gave a slight nod, subtle enough so Milo and Courtney wouldn't notice. Milo was digging around in his pocket for money. They hadn't asked for a discount and I sure as hell wasn't going to offer one. Becky put her free hand to her face, with her middle finger up against her cheek – facing Milo – and walked into the cinema, winking at me as she plunged into the darkness. And just that made me like my friends again. It melted the tips of the icicles which were now my guts, sploshing water in and giving me the strength to hand over the tickets to my ex-boyfriend.

The second they were out of my eyeline, I slumped forward on the counter, taking deep breaths.

I heard Harry call out, "You have to go in now, the movie's started."

"We haven't got food yet," Milo said.

"Sorry, it's our policy. We don't want latecomers to disrupt the film for others."

I made a shrugging *hey-not-my-bad* face at Milo as he strode past again, looking Harry up and down, all pissed off.

"We'll just go for dinner afterwards," he said to Her. He kissed her on the lips, right in front of me, and they stepped past Harry into the dark.

The doors swung shut behind them.

I found myself slipping against the wall until my bum hit the carpet. I put my knees up and rested my face into them. I could hear the film's opening music ever-so-softly through the door.

I felt Harry's presence standing over me. "Thanks for being mean to them for me," I said, my eyes still pushed into my kneecaps.

"That was him then, was it?"

I didn't say anything back. I couldn't work out what emotion I was. Angry – that he had the cheek to show up. Sad – that it wasn't me he was taking to the cinema any more. Humiliated – that I was so disgusting and bad at sex that he'd dumped me...

"You want me to say he's obviously an idiot?" Harry said.

"I want you to say something that isn't a total cliché," I said into my knees.

"His girlfriend's boobs are too close together." The shock of it made me laugh and I looked up. "What does that even mean?"

He shrugged and started folding his long body so he was sitting on the carpet across from me. "I'm just saying, there's the nice normal cleavage you can get. That's just... you know." I raised an eyebrow at him. "And then some girls wear these weird crazy bras that push them together so it looks like they're in pain. I felt really sorry for her boobs."

I was still laughing, shaking my head. "You're ridiculous."

LouLou appeared, her quiff all wilty from the heat of the pulled pork machine. "Oooo, carpet party! Why are we all sitting on the floor?" Without waiting for an answer, she sat herself down next to us.

"My ex-boyfriend is here," I explained.

"Ahh." LouLou nodded knowingly. "Is that why you say you're numb to Harry's charms?"

"Hey!" Harry said. "Were you warning her about me, Lou?"

"After Grace quit? Yes."

"She didn't quit because of me."

"Didn't she?"

"How did you meet this butt-plug anyway?" Harry asked, noticeably changing the subject.

I rested my chin on the tops of my knees. "We were in

Drama Club together. We both got the main parts in the school play."

"You act?"

I shrugged, the memories making me achy and uncomfortable. "I did act. But I haven't taken Drama on to upper sixth, I dropped it, and I quit Drama Club." I say it quickly, hoping they won't pry further.

LouLou and Harry shared a look, both of them suddenly smiling.

"What?" I asked. "What is it?"

Harry's eyes were so bright. "Audrey, if you can act, you have to be in my movie!"

LouLou clapped her hands together. "Oh yes, Audrey, you must! We can film tonight, after the cinema closes."

"But the cinema doesn't close until gone midnight."

"Exactly!" Harry stood up, shaking out his legs. "The perfect shooting time for my award-winning film about the walking dead. We need someone to play the zombie bride, Audrey. My friend, Rosie, tried a few scenes but she's only good at screaming and attacking, she's not so good at running lines. Oh my God, this is SUCH good timing. I'll message her now and let her know she's off the hook!"

"I...I..." I leaned further back into the wall. "I'm not very good."

"You just said you were the lead part in your school play!"

"Yes...but..."

I *was* good, at least I used to be good. I used to be able to climb into the skin of whoever I played, lose myself in their life, their emotions, forget who I was, where I was, that there was an audience watching. It was what made me happy. I thought back to last winter, to those heady days of rehearsal, of Milo and I running lines snuggled up on a sofa in a coffee shop, his mouth on my neck, my head heavy with falling in love. My heart so much lighter, something I'd never thought possible after Dad left. "*You're so good,*" he would whisper, his breath hot from his latte. "*I even hate you a little bit, you're so good.*" But that was then and this was now, and now I could hardly even act liking my own friends. I could hardly pull off being a caring daughter. I was already failing the part of efficient employee. I'd been sitting on the carpet for ten minutes.

"Come on," Harry begged, the corners of his eyes scrunched up. "I need you. I'm desperate. It will be the perfect way to get your mind off butt-plug boy."

I laughed at his new nickname for Milo.

"I dunno. Won't your friend, Rosie, mind?" Was Rosie the cool girl from the car?

Harry shook her head while LouLou nodded.

"Nah, she'll get over it. I told you, she doesn't like speaking parts."

"She only wants to do the scenes where she gets to kiss you," LouLou said.

"Oi!" I said. "You didn't tell me about that."

Harry shook his head, his smile well and truly back in place. "Don't worry, Audrey. We're not filming that scene for a while yet, and I'm sure you'll have kissed me all of your own accord by then anyway."

I started to stand up. "I bloody won't have done!"

Just then the front door swung open, letting cold air in and signalling the flurry of activity for the "serious" film we were showing as an alternative to *Sausage Dogs*.

"Hi, are you here for *The Right Side Of Man*?" Harry asked the group of middle-aged women who strode in. They melted under his mega-watt smile. "Come this way," he said, ushering them towards me.

LouLou sprang up to get back over to the bar. "Don't say I didn't warn you about him," she muttered.

12

"Two tickets, please."

"Two popcorns, please."

"Two glasses of Merlot, please."

Cinemas are full of pairs.

Time raced past as we got the fussies into their seats and brought them all their artisan pizzas. Before I knew it, the double doors of Screen One opened and everyone spilled out – most with tears running down their cheeks. I stood with a smile etched across my face, holding out a bin bag that everyone ignored.

"Thank you, thanks for coming, I hope you enjoyed it."

The girls all came out with red and blotchy faces. Alice hugged me again. "Oh my God, Audrey. I think my face is having an allergic reaction to how sad that was. That was the most beautiful film EVER!"

Becky and Charlie hugged me too, causing a blockage. I stepped to one side, still holding the bag.

"Guys, that bit when the sausage dog ran away!" Becky squeaked.

"Oh, and then it had gone to his house!" Alice shrilled shriller.

My grin stayed all grinny. "So glad you enjoyed it."

Alice's face darkened. "We did. But we also saw Milo here with HER. Are you okay?"

"I'm fine." I would have a sore throat tomorrow from all the high-pitched faux-enthusiasm.

"What's he even doing here?" Becky asked. "I mean, he has some nerve."

I bit my lip. "He's Milo," I explained. "Milo is all nerve, that's who he…shh…"

He and Courtney pushed through the doors, the last ones to leave. Her lipstick was smudged and her chin was all red from his stubble. Milo held his hand up without waving it. "Laters, Audrey." They walked out into the night, clutching each other like the world would end if you tried to shove even a sheet of paper between them.

I didn't have any choice about the girls pulling me in for another hug.

"Aww, Auds, he's such an arsehole."

"How can he even treat you like that?"

"You can do SO much better."

I let their words wash over me. I let them hug me. A tiny part of me that wasn't angry and numb – if you can even be those things simultaneously – recognized that I was the problem, not them. But I let go and held up the bin bag as a defensive barrier. "I better go clean up."

"Aww," Alice said. "Can you not come out with us?"

"I don't finish until gone midnight..."*And then I'm maybe acting as a zombie bride...*

Becky stuck her tongue out. "This sucks. You working sucks."

I was about to nod until I realized I'd been here practically all day and hadn't worried about Mum once.

"Who's that Harry guy, anyway?" Charlie asked. "He's cute."

"He's trouble."

"Good rebound trouble?"

I shook my head a LOT then, just as he appeared with the Hoover.

"Audrey!" he called, all coo-ey and feminine. "It's time for our bonding experience picking up people's leftover popcorn."

"Look, I gotta go. I'll see you at school on Monday?"

"Ladies." Harry pushed the Hoover along and then jumped on top of it like it was a horse. "Meet my trusty steed."

"Rebound on him," Alice whispered, as she gave her obligatory goodbye hug.

13

"We're fully booked for the late showing," Harry said as we, yet again, cleaned up the popcorn. "So I guess we'll just need you on the bar, to help out with food and stuff."

"I can't believe this stupid movie is so popular," I grumbled. The complainy lady in E3 had left the most mess – it was like she'd been in a fistfight with her popcorn.

"What's your issue with romance films?" he asked, just as LouLou slid in on an extra Hoover, crying, "*I'm here to hellllllp.*

"Yes, Audrey," she said, plugging it in at the wall. "What's your problem with The Mr Dicky Curtisfield?"

I crossed my arms. "It's simple. Women in most romance movies aren't real."

Harry cut off his Hoover and sat down on a chair, putting his legs on the seat. "Tell me, Audrey. How are they not real?"

I blew my hair up and thought back to all the films I'd

watched with Mum and Dad on our family film nights. "Well, they never have any real insecurities, just like – cute ones! Like, '*Oh, I'm really neat and tidy*', or '*I'm mildly clumsy*'. Where are the woman saying, '*Why the hell haven't you replied to my messages after shagging me?*' or '*Do you mind if we take things slow because I was raped in college?*'"

LouLou pointed at me. "This is true."

"Plus" – I was still warming up – "they're always crazy perfect skinny, even though they're supposedly always munching down burgers and chocolate. That's not real. You can't have thighs that don't rub at the top but also looooove hot dogs and beer. Those two things don't coexist. You have to do squats every single moment of your life and only have one slither of cake, like, once a year, and probably eat it whilst still doing squats."

Harry's smile was so wide. He waved his arm like he was conducting me. "Go on."

"Well" – I sat down next to him – "they always look amazing in the morning. They never have stinky breath or hair all over the place, or boogers in their eyes. And they sleep in, like, tiny pyjama short things instead of an ugly oversized T-shirt with jammy bottoms. I mean, AREN'T THEY COLD? Also" – I began to list them off on my fingers – "they never pick fights with the guy's friends about the fact they're sexist slobs. They never fart, let alone fanny fart, or get their period and accidentally bleed reddy-brown splodges onto their jeans. Their fringes are always impeccable. They're always *one of the guys* somehow, and like sport and drinking beer or watching action movies, because that's so real. They never nag the guy about watching football all the time, or say 'Let's watch Love, Rosie because it's my turn to choose'. They're never stroppy and they're never difficult and they're never needy and they're never bloated and they never wear mismatching underwear and they never have cellulite and they never ask to have sex with the lights off because they hate their stomachs. And even if they ARE stroppy and difficult, it's always something that's MENDED by the end of the film because some guy with perfectly-sculpted arms kisses them in the rain."

"I like you," LouLou said, chewing on her lip stud. "You're allowed to stay."

"Thanks… Umm, can you tell I'm dealing with a lot of anger in my life right now?"

Harry jumped up and grabbed my hand, pulling it upwards. "This is perfect!" he announced. "You HAVE to be my zombie bride. Can you channel all your hate for the human universe into filming? Tonight? Let's do it tonight."

I grinned, annoyed at myself for enjoying the feel of his hand in mine. Deliberately dropping it as a result. "That depends. Can your zombie bride decide that the zombie apocalypse actually SAVED her from a horrid life where she'd be chained to the kitchen sink all day?"

Harry's eyes widened. "A zombie bride who is HAPPY about being a zombie as it saved her from domesticity?"

I nodded. "Yes!"

"Perfect! Yes, this is PERFECT!"

LouLou put her hand up. "Hang on, can zombies have that level of cognitive ability?"

"Shh," Harry said. "Stop ruining it. Let me think... I mean, the thing with zombies is, there's no definite rule on what a zombie *is*—"

"Annnnd half the internet wants to kill you right now," LouLou interrupted.

"But there's not!" Harry said. "Maybe if we tweak how the virus works in the script, so zombies still want to eat brains but also remember their past lives and stuff...?"

I was smiling so wide now. "And my zombie bride wants to use her zombieness to eat the brains of Bad Men?"

Harry grabbed me again. "This is awesome! I wish you'd hurry up and get over the fact that I will end up kissing you, because I totally want to kiss you right now."

"Harry, stop threatening to kiss the new girl," LouLou said.

"She doesn't mind."

"Umm, yes, I do!" I said, though my cheeks ached from smiling. I could feel the zombie bride in me already, her energy twitching up my arms, her thoughts clouding my brain. I closed my eyes and FLASH I was there, on the morning of her wedding, putting the dress on, feeling so much dread and then a crash from the window and fear and blood and gore and then...strength and relief... This was my part. The zombie bride was my part. I could taste her blood on my tongue. God, I'd missed this feeling. I'd forgotten how much I loved this feeling, like the character is crawling under my skin, becoming part of me. "I'll do it," I said. "Filming, I mean. If you let me play the zombie bride like this?"

Harry pulled me into a hug and lifted me off my feet. It should have been shocking, how familiar he was considering this was only our second day knowing each other. But seeing how he was with the customers and my friends, I knew it wasn't me. This was just who he was.

"It's going to be amazing!" he said, eventually putting me down. "Right, I'll message everyone else and let them know. The rain's stopped and everything. It's a sign! We'll film an attack scene tonight so there isn't much script to change. I've already told Rosie you'd do it."

"Harry! I hadn't said yes yet."

He stuck out his tongue. "I know you better than you know yourself, Audrey."

And I was about to open my mouth to protest when the confused head of an elderly man popped around the door and said, "Umm, excuse me? There's a queue at the bar and no one there to run it."

14

We made it through the final showing – hoping nobody would blab to Ma that we'd left the foyer unattended for twenty minutes. It was pitch black by the time we ushered the last of the customers out, dabbing their eyes, snotting into tissues. LouLou led me into the staff toilet and got to work transforming me into a zombie bride.

"I have to say," I commented, as I leaned back so fake blood wouldn't spill into my eyes. "This isn't how I saw today panning out at all."

She laughed with the cap of the fake blood still between her teeth. "I know." She examined my face, deciding where to splodge next. "Harry is a very persuasive person. I knew nothing about filming or zombies until he started here. Now I'm somehow the official make-up artist and also Zombie Number Four."

It was midnight by the time we emerged from the toilets. *What the heck am I doing?* I thought, as I walked towards

Harry wearing a tattered wedding dress, veil and splatterings of blood.

His mouth dropped open. "LouLou, you're a genius. She looks perfect." He had a ton of camera equipment on him – a tripod bag, a big DSLR camera around his neck. He'd changed out of his uniform into a plaid shirt.

I knew he meant *perfect zombie bride* but I still found myself blushing under my veil.

"Where's *your* costume?"

He took off his camera so he could zip up his coat. It was a nice one – a brown leather jacket with fleece inside, like a pilot's. "I'm not in tonight's scene. Alas, Audrey, we don't meet and fall in love until Scene Fourteen."

LouLou, who was playing with the alarm, yelled. "It's set! All out – go go go go GO."

The alarm emitted aggressive beeps and we all hurried out of the staff door, me tripping on my train as we emerged into the stark winter's night.

Harry's friend's car was already parked out front – the music blaring. I went red as the entire car turned to look at me.

"Right, I'm off," LouLou said. "Have a good time, guys."

I turned to her and my make-up must've been good because she jumped a bit. "You're not coming with us?"

"Zombie Number Four got killed off last week," she said. "And by the looks of it, they can do their own make-up."

I followed her gaze back to the scary car full of scary strangers. Their faces were totally zombified – they all had grey skin and odd contact lenses and blood smears. They smiled – except the girl from last time. Rosie.

Harry opened the car door. "Hey, everyone. This is Audrey. She's a proper actress and she's going to play our zombie bride."

The guy at the steering wheel with yellow contact lenses yelled, "WELCOME, ZOMBIE BRIDE," over the music, and everyone else waved.

"I wish you were coming," I whispered to LouLou, who was rifling for her car keys.

"Ahh, you'll be fine. They're a friendly bunch. Just don't do drugs," she added.

"Drugs?"

But she had no time to explain. Harry had shouted for everyone to scooch over and slammed his equipment in the boot. He climbed in first, somehow finding space for his gangly body, while I stood there, arms crossed in the cold – feeling awkward and new and unwelcome. Especially as Rosie stared intently at me through the rear window, chewing gum with proper attitude. She made direct eye contact and blew a neon-blue bubble. It popped without her even blinking.

Harry grinned up at me from the back seat. "You're going to have to sit on my lap, Audrey."

I rolled my eyes. "Really?"

He gestured around him. "Do you see any more room?" He pointed to a guy squashed up next to him, with ultra-blond hair and a scattering of spots on his chin. "I mean, you can sit on Rob's lap here, if you really want to. But considering you don't know him, I think that's going to be weird for both of you."

Rob smiled at me. "Hey, I don't mind it being weird." He patted his knees and everyone in the car groaned.

I chewed my lip. "You planned this," I said, relenting, and climbing in on top of Harry – which was pretty damn hard in a wedding dress.

"Maybe, maybe not."

The car had the strong tang of sweet smoke. Harry introduced me while I sat myself down on his knees. "So, this is Tad, driving. And Rob, whose knees you've so rudely rejected."

"My knees are mortally offended," Rob said, with a friendly smile.

"Up in front is Jay." A boy in a backward cap swivelled in his seat and said "Hi". "And over at the end we have Rosie." Rosie glared at me, still snapping her gum. But she waved, while glaring. Which is quite impressive really. A bit like rubbing your head and patting your belly.

"Are you sure you don't mind I took your part?" I asked her, trying to make peace. Although Harry had reassured me ten gazillion times that she didn't mind.

She chewed her gum and took slightly too long to answer. "It's a bit late now if I do mind, isn't it?"

My stomach flip-flopped with the awkward but Harry just laughed and said, "Rosie, stop being a dick." And she laughed, but with him. Then she glared at me again.

Tad put his car into gear and I twisted around, my face almost right in Harry's face. "Is there a seat belt?"

"Somewhere up my butt crack there is a seat-belt thingy," Rob replied. "I don't think it's going to be easy to remove."

"Relax, Audrey, the woods are only a five-minute drive away." Harry's hot breath tickled the back of my neck.

The car screeched off into the darkness and I grabbed hold of the window winder to steady myself. Harry instinctively – or deliberately – put his arms around my waist. It was an obvious "move" but I was actually quite grateful for not feeling like I was about to fly out the windscreen. I was very aware of his lap, and the things boys have in their laps. He couldn't have planned it better, which I'm sure was the point.

"So, you're an actress then, Audrey?" Jay shouted over the music blasting from the car's speakers.

"Umm, sort of," I yelled back, my bum sliding over Harry's knobbly knees as we rounded a corner.

"She's come up with a brilliant twist on the zombie bride," Harry said, his mouth right in my ear, his hands too tight around my middle.

"She's going to be a feminist freedom fighter," I explained self-consciously.

I felt Harry nodding behind me. "Like a zombie *Kill Bill*. It's inspired. I'm tweaking the script tomorrow."

"Do I still get my brain eaten tonight though?" Rob asked. "Because I've been practising my brain-being-eaten scream all week."

"I can confirm Audrey will still eat your brain."

"Sorry about that." I smiled.

We whipped around another corner and Harry's grip tightened around me again. I saw Rosie notice. She'd stayed silent through the whole exchange, apart from the snapping of her gum. I decided to be the bigger person and make the first move. I mean, Harry insisted she hated acting but I *had* taken her part. It was up to me to make peace.

"So, you all out of college then?" I asked, leading with a group question.

They murmured yes, none of them mentioned uni or anything.

"She's Dougie's little sister," Harry explained.

"Ahh, cool, how's Dougie?" Jay adjusted his hat. "You kind of look like him actually."

"He's good, he's fine. Everyone says we look alike."

Rosie finally spoke. "So, you must be, like, much younger than us, right?" she said, pointedly.

"Just one year. I'm in upper sixth."

"Aww cute. Though you look even younger. Like fourteen."

I ignored her, as that is the only thing you can really do with a deliberate put-down like that. I decided to try again with her later, when she didn't seem so cross. I twisted in Harry's arms. "So, how long have you been making movies?" I asked him.

"Since I was a child."

"Harry's awesome," Rob said. "Don't let his U in Film

Studies put you off this movie."

"You got a U? I didn't even know it was possible to get a U."

His eyes darkened a little but he styled it out with a smile. "They didn't accept my coursework."

Rob laughed. "He was only supposed to make a movie trailer, but he got carried away and made a full-length feature film about a serial killer. I was the serial killer," he said, brightly.

"So they failed you because you over-delivered?" I asked.

Harry's eyes flashed dark again. "Yes."

"That hardly seems fair."

"Life isn't fair, Audrey." It was the first time he'd said anything without a side-helping of charm in his voice.

The car drove through complete blackness and the local woods stretched out creepily either side of us. The car was going way too fast, the music was way too loud. I didn't know any of these people. It felt scary and unreal and odd – but also exciting. I'd been working all day but I didn't feel the slightest bit tired.

"Hey, Harry?" Rosie called over the music. "Remember when we had to film that dirty scene for it, and we almost got arrested?"

I smiled in the darkness. Knowing what she was doing.

Harry laughed. "That was a hard thing to explain to the policeman."

"I was literally in my bra," Rosie told the car. Obviously so the whole car could picture her in her bra.

"They thought we were dogging," Harry explained.

"Me holding a camera didn't help," Jay added.

And I laughed too because I knew Rosie wouldn't expect me to. "Do you always give yourself the leading roles so you get to kiss people?"

"What can I say? I'm the best kisser."

The car erupted into groans and protests. Rob offered me and Rosie a "demonstration" to "let us be the judges" and I couldn't stop laughing. But Rosie said, "You are a very good kisser, Harry," her voice loaded with meaning – and I had to try very hard not to roll my eyes.

The car jolted to an abrupt halt, right in the arse-end middle of nowhere.

"Let the brain-eating commence!" Harry cheered.

15

"I'm not sure I know you well enough to suck your forehead," I said, my eyes hurting from the brightness of Harry's night-vision light.

Rob, spread under me on the muddy ground, smiled. "Do we need to be formally introduced, like in the olden days?"

"Maybe if you bowed?"

"Don't you dare move," Harry barked. "You're both in the perfect shot."

There was not one part of my body that wasn't frozen. It was at least two in the morning and the mushy ground had hardened with a layer of frost. Tad would occasionally start the engine and we'd all cram into his car – fighting over the heaters. But Harry was a surprisingly aggressive director, all his goofiness gone. He'd bark instructions and pull us out of the car, telling us to stop whining. He was a good director though – I could tell that much. I'd been bossed about enough by them in the past. There was this one at the summer school for the London School of Acting who made literally everyone cry once. Before every shot, Harry would sit me down and explain exactly what my motivation was and why, and what he wanted the scene to achieve. Yet he also allowed room for improvisation and was happy if I added stuff here and there. I'd been surprised by how quickly the zombie bride became part of me. Usually before a project I'd spend weeks researching my characters, trying to think like them and clamber into their skin. But it was like the zombie bride had always been here. Harry would shout "ACTION!" and she'd overpower me and the next thing I knew I'd be on top of Rob, his hat hanging out of my mouth, Harry clapping and yelling "CUT!" and then high-fiving me – a look on his face like he couldn't believe his luck that I'd stumbled into his life. I really had forgotten how much I loved acting. I hadn't thought of anything the last couple of hours. I'd just been flinging myself around the woods wearing a blood-covered wedding dress, which, it turns out, is a perfect way to distract from the pain of a broken heart.

Harry clapped his hands. "Okay, so, Audrey, he's going to try and fight you off with the hammer and he's almost going to get you, right? But just as he's about to kill you – Rob, you're going to ruin it. Say something really sexist. Improv – see what comes out. And, Audrey, let the anger give you the strength you need to finish him off. That make sense?"

"Not really," Rob replied. "But my arse is so cold right now I'll do whatever you want to get this over with."

"Rosie, you have the mikes on?"

Rosie stood to one side, holding a big fluffy stick. She nodded, looking bored and pissed off. "Yep."

"Tad, you got the lights?"

Tad had a giant spliff hanging out of his mouth. "I think so. They're, like, really warm." He started stroking the giant spotlight and giggling.

"Stay with me, Tad. Just a little bit longer."

They were all stoned, apart from Harry. In fact, the first thing they'd done when we arrived was roll a spliff and light it up in the car. They'd offered it to me but I'd shaken my head and Rosie had said, "Come on, guys, she's too young," which made me want to smoke some just to make a point. I'd never liked the feeling of getting out of it, not even with drinking, so instead I stood out in the cold as the car filled with fug. Harry had stumbled out the car, coughing, and saying, "I'll stand out here with you, I need a clear head," and Rosie had given him this fierce look that would've made me fear for my life.

"So, are we ready? Audrey? Rob? Five, four, three, two, one, ACTION."

My head cleared. Audrey got pushed to one side and the zombie bride filled me up. I pinned a screaming Rob down, who fought hard, kicking up at me, getting muddy boots on my dress.

"Not the dress," I hissed, anger surging through me. The thirst, the thirst for this man's brain.

Rob kicked me again. He sneered, his face half fear,

half absolute disgust. "I don't know what I'm most pissed off about. Being killed by a zombie bride, or being killed by a zombie bride that's as ugly as you."

I leaned back. "Did you just call me *ugly*?"

"Ugly's an understatement."

I thrashed his head back. "I'm about to eat your brain and you're judging me on my appearance?"

"Yeah, and when you've finished eating my brain, why don't you suck my fat one?"

The rage erupted through my zombie stomach, surging through my bloodless veins. I slapped him across the face – forgetting to do the stage-slap technique I'd learned in Drama Club.

"You're not worth killing," I said, shoving my blood-stained face at him. "You're already a brain-sucking masochistic PARASITE."

"I didn't know zombies could get PMS."

I can't really remember what I did but suddenly there was a pause, then clapping. Loud echoing clapping that bounced off into the night.

"That. Was. Amazing." Harry put his camera down so he could clap harder.

Rob sat up, grinning. "Where did that even come from, Audrey?"

I smiled back, pulling my veil up. "Where did *you* come from? *After you've eaten my brains you can suck my fat one?*"

He shrugged. "I'm good at improv… Hey, can you untie me?"

Harry and I both dived down to help him, our hands brushing as we went for the same knot. "Sorry," we both said. I pulled my hand away and went red. I always feel self-conscious after a scene, after I've lost myself that way. I tried to remember what I'd just done, or said, but it felt like a blur. Harry undid the knots and Rob got up, laughing, and I laughed too – high on knowing I'd done a really good take.

"Audrey, how are you so talented?" Harry looked at me in wonder.

Tad lowered the lamp, his eyes all bloodshot. He giggled softly to himself. "I don't even know what happened there, but it looked cool."

"I love this new angle." Harry kept running his hands through his hair. "I was already excited about this movie, and now I'm *really* excited. Thank you, Audrey."

I felt myself get red again but then...

"I don't think it works," Rosie stated, her voice dry and unimpressed, cutting through the darkness.

Harry spun to face her. "What do you mean, it doesn't work? That entire scene was inspired."

She stepped in front of Tad's light, so it lit her from behind, like a Bond girl in the opening credits.

"Audrey just pissed over the entire rules of being a zombie. I.e. they don't have self-restraint! They can't decide when and where to eat someone's brain. They're not human, they just look human, that's the point, that's why they're scary." She sighed into the night, like she genuinely, proper cared, which I guess she did. "Zombies represent a deep dark fear inside us all," she explained. "A fear of just being a shell, of having everything that's good, everything that makes us *us*, ripped out." I widened my eyes, blown away by her knowledge and understanding of it all. It almost made me like her, until she crossed her arms and said, "So I don't think you can, like, break the laws of zombies just because you're trying to pull a girl with some batshit idea."

Awkward silence descended and Rosie didn't seem bothered by it. In fact, she just reached into her back pocket and withdrew a stick of gum, folding it into her mouth.

Harry coughed and grinned. "I don't need to pretend to like Audrey's ideas to try and pull her," he said lightly, though he'd narrowed his eyes. "I'm capable of pulling Audrey without ruining the zombie film I've spent the past six months writing."

"Umm, well, you're not capable of pulling me." I put my hand up to talk, like I was in class. "I'm sworn off men at the moment."

The others laughed, the atmosphere diluting a bit.

Jay moaned, "Hey, aren't we finished now? Can we just hotbox the car already?"

I had no idea what hotboxing was, but luckily for me, Rosie explained in a primary school teacher voice. I ended up standing outside in the dark again so I didn't get high off the fumes. I leaned against the bonnet as the car filled with flowery fug. Harry didn't hold back now filming was finished. He lit a joint and took several deep drags before finally passing it around. That was all I really saw before the fog of smoke eclipsed my vision. The tiredness hit me then. I was in the middle of nowhere with a bunch of druggies I didn't even know, wearing a wedding dress.

I'd never seen anyone do drugs before. The closest anyone in Drama Club got to living hedonistically was doing improv. I found it mildly disgusting and then worried that made me uncool.

Just as I got bored, the back window rolled down a little, letting a cloud of smoke rise out of the car. Harry's large mouth gaped at the window, his teeth looking even teethier than normal. "You sure you don't want some?" he called over the music, giggling echoing behind him. Like maybe they'd built up to asking me, laughing at my uncoolness as I sat outside by myself.

"I'm fine, thanks," I called back.

Rosie's face emerged through the smoke, her delicate nose pressing against the glass. "She's an innocent girl, aren't you?" she said between giggles.

I shook my head at them. Suddenly tired and pissed off, and really, really not in the mood for a girl I'd hardly met before making me feel like this. Like I was sad, like I was naïve. I'd done a good enough job making myself feel like that since Milo swapped me for Courtney. "I don't do drugs, that's all."

"Oh, so you're too good to do drugs?" she asked, her already-narrow eyes like slits. "Not a bad girl, then?"

I shook my head. "Forget it." Thinking of all the ways you can be bad. Like leaving your loving family to start a new one and not wondering what that meant for the family you left behind. Like sleeping with a girl and then shrugging her off, like she was an ill-fitting coat. Like falling apart when you're supposed to be the grown-up one. Like going away, knowing you're leaving a big mess behind and then getting annoyed by the desperate phone calls of the people you left…

Dougie. Phone.

I dug for it in my bag. I'd asked him to call Mum. How was she? How could I have forgotten?!

I had one message from eight hours ago.

Dougie: Just called Mum. She's bad, Audrey. Really bad. She said you left her all day? You need to look after her better.

I felt instantly sick. With anger. With guilt. With him always guilt-tripping me. Suddenly nothing mattered apart from getting back. Was she okay? What did he mean by *really bad*? His understanding of her good patches and bad patches was not as complex as mine.

I tapped on the window, next to Harry's face.

"I need to go home."

"Someone's wigging OU-UT!" He started laughing. "Only NOW you're scared of the woods?"

I pulled open the door so he almost fell on top of me. A thick cloud of smoke hit the back of my lungs, making me cough.

"Please? Can we go now? I have to get home."

"Relax, Audrey. We'll go in a minute," Rosie said.

"No. I need to go now. It's my mum…"

Even through his red eyes and clouded brain, something in the way I said the word "mum" must've got through to Harry. He stopped grinning and turned to Tad. "Let's go, man."

Tad was using the steering wheel as a pillow. "Man, I'm too stoned to drive right now."

I felt panicked, sick. Why was I here? How had I got myself here? In the woods, miles away from Mum when she needed me? Why had I been so selfish?

"I'll walk," I said, knowing it was useless, that it would take for ever, but it was better than nothing. So I turned and walked into the darkness. My lungs still hurt from the smoke.

She wouldn't hurt herself, would she? There was only that time… That one time. She threatened to. But she hadn't done anything. And Dougie didn't know about that night. She'd made me promise not to tell.

"Audrey, wait!" Harry ran after me. "I'll drive us. It's fine."

I spun on my heel. "You're wasted!" The disgust was all over my voice, bleeding all over my face.

"I'm FINE. I'm a good driver."

"But you're…you're…under the influence." At that, I lost him. He burst into giggles again. "You sound like a grandma." He bent over, propping himself up on his knees.

"Under the influence…" And he was gone again. I reached out and took his hand to stop him, aware of how warm it was compared to mine.

"Please, Harry. I really need to get home."

16

When a dangerously-out-of-it Harry dropped me off, I'd rushed straight upstairs to find Mum happily asleep in bed, snoring quietly. But I was so shaken, so freaked out by what could've happened, that I took for ever to drop off and I was in a whole new realm of tired the next day.

Mum woke me at ten.

"Audrey, wake up. I've made us pancakes," she called through the floorboards.

I stumbled down the stairs, my feet aching from standing up all the previous day. I stopped in the kitchen doorway. It had been too dark to see last night, but it was spotless. Show Home spotless. I turned and looked back at the living room – also spotless. Like a house elf had been overnight.

"Morning, sweetie." Mum was at the Aga, a frying pan in hand, a giant bowl of batter wobbling on the counter. "I've put blueberries in and everything."

"Wow. Thanks."

The surfaces were so clean I could lick them. All the unopened mail and other clutter on the breakfast bar had vanished. There was even a vase of flowers. I perched on a stool and took a sip of my pre-poured glass of proper orange juice.

"How was work? I didn't hear you come in."

"It was long. And then I went out afterwards." I paused, watching her cook, trying to figure her out. Dougie had said she was bad, and, on the surface, she looked more than okay right now. But Mum never made pancakes, and never kept the house this tidy. We'd never, ever, had blueberries. "Milo turned up, with his new girlfriend," I tested, seeing what her reaction would be.

She flipped the pancake over, the raw side sizzling as it hit the pan. "Great, just great. I mean, I didn't even know you could get blueberries in autumn. But they were on offer and everything."

That's when I knew to worry.

"Mum?"

"Yes?"

"I said Milo turned up at work yesterday."

She half-turned around. "He did? Well, I guess that's just like him, isn't it?" She turned back to her pancake while I blinked back tears that had appeared straight out of nowhere. She'd actually been doing okayish the last couple of months or so. I'd thought she might finally be getting over it – after two years in the sanity wilderness – but this house thing had undone everything...

The manicness continued. I ate four blueberry pancakes out of fear of what would happen if I turned one down. She kept up a steady stream of inane conversation, hardly eating. "Sandra told me the blueberries were on offer, so I went to check it out…we don't normally have pancakes, do we? … It's so great you're enjoying your job… What's *Walking with Sausage Dogs* like then? …I finally got that stain off the carpet."

She was bad. Dougie was right. She was wound right up which meant she would unravel fast – flinging mess all around her when the energy ran out, like a Catherine wheel. I shouldn't have left her yesterday. But then yesterday I'd felt free and I'd made jokes and I'd felt like…me again.

"Well, they're amazing pancakes, thanks, Mum."

She beamed at me and sipped at her third cup of coffee since I'd sat down.

"Nice to have a treat at the weekend, isn't it?" Another sip. And then, "Are you still seeing your dad today?"

I nodded slowly. "Yes, I guess. I was going to go yesterday, but then I had to do the double shift."

Mum tipped coffee down her throat rather than sipping it. "And you'll talk to him?"

"I'll try. You know what he's like."

"I thought I did." She smashed her cup down so hard it shattered, pieces of it bouncing off the table. I jumped as she pushed her chair back abruptly, its legs screeching. "OH, FOR GOODNESS' SAKE," she yelled to the ceiling, to me, to nobody, to the world.

I went to get the dustpan out.

"Just leave it."

"Okay." I stood frozen, too nervous to move.

"Just…well…" She seemed to regain control of herself. "Just, well, try to talk to him, Audrey."

"I'll try."

Dad's new wife, Jessie, picked up the phone on the third ring.

"Audrey, hi." There was a distinct amount of screaming down the line. "Hang on… No, Albert, I said, NO. Put it down. PUT IT DOWN. Paul? PAUL? Can you come take Albert?" A clatter and Dad's voice in the background, and more crying, and then quiet. "Sorry about that. Is everything okay? Why are you calling?"

"I was hoping I could pop round today? There's something I need to talk to Dad about."

A long pause. "Today?"

"Yes. Maybe if I can speak to Dad?"

"Today's not great, Audrey." Jessie sighed. "Albert, what is it? WHAT IS IT? Paul? Paul? Can you get him his snuggle?"

"*I don't care, he's my fucking dad,*" I said.

…I didn't say that.

I said, "I won't be long."

"Okay, well, we're having a roast at two, so if you come at one and stay for an hour?"

It shouldn't have surprised me that she didn't invite me to the roast, but it did. It hurt too.

"I'm really full from breakfast so I couldn't eat anyway," I replied. "Mum made pancakes," I added.

But I was only met with crashing down the line and, "Lola? Lola? No. No. Give Albert back his snuggle, give it back NOW." More crying and yelling and clattering. "Yes, Audrey. See you later." She hung up before I even had a chance to say goodbye.

I sighed as the phone beeped. I tried not to hate Jessie, but she made it so easy. I mean, if you'd plucked a husband away from his wife and children, yanked a family apart, chucked industrial bleach on two teenagers' sense of stability…well…you'd think you'd TRY to make up for it. Wouldn't you? An invite for a fucking roast should be the least of it. But not Jessie. It was like she'd declared war. Like Dougie and I were annoying blemishes on her otherwise-perfect life that she wished she could wipe away. Like we ruined the moment just by existing. Like we were a side-plot she wished she could rub out.

Mum crashed into my room, like she'd been listening in. Which, let's face it, she probably had.

"And?"

"I'm going over before lunch."

"Oh, thanks, Audrey. Thank you so much."

"I really don't think it will help."

Screenplay for
ALL THE THINGS I NEVER SAY
TO MY FATHER

Written by
Audrey Winters

FADE IN:

EXT. AUDREY'S DAD'S HOUSE - DAY

‹We're MOVING THROUGH the cottage of
Audrey's father, PAUL, who we find sitting
in the living room, his head in his hands.
AUDREY stands over him, looking fierce
and confident›

AUDREY
How could you do this to us, Dad?
How could you just leave?

PAUL
I don't know. I'm sorry, Audrey.

‹AUDREY throws her arms up into the air›

                    AUDREY
    Sorry isn't good enough. How about not
  doing it in the first place? How about don't
  cheat on your wife? How about don't knock up
  another woman? Do you have any idea how hard
        it's been for me? Having to stop Mum
      practically killing herself? Having two
      siblings I hardly get to see? Having a
        stepmother who makes no effort to
      include me? HOW COULD YOU DO THIS TO
        OUR LIVES, DAD? DON'T YOU CARE?

                     PAUL
      No. I obviously don't. That's why
           I fucking did it.

17

I walked the twenty minutes over to Dad's new house, messaging Leroy to give him updates on my zombie brideness.

Audrey: I'm acting again. In a zombie film.

Leroy: Great!! You going to audition for Guys and Dolls too?

Audrey: No way in hell.

Leroy: You should. HANG ON...ZOMBIE FILM?

Audrey: Yeah, Harry from work is making one.

Leroy: The bad Catholic?

Audrey: He seems to be a good film-maker.

Leroy: Be careful.

Audrey: Leroy, I'm dead inside. When you're dead inside you don't have to worry about being careful.

Leroy: I wish you'd stop referring to yourself as dead inside.

Leroy: ...Tho I guess at least you'll make a good
zombie ;) x

I didn't feel dead inside as I rocked up Dad's gravelly
front path, dodging the pot plants and all the other
manicured garden stuff that surrounded his small stone
cottage. It hurt too much for that. I spotted the freshly-dug
vegetable patch as I pressed the doorbell and scowled.

Dad opened the door, beaming, cradling a topless Albert
on his hip. "Audrey! Hey! Jessie told me you were coming.
Come in, come in."

I couldn't help it. Just the sight of Albert, his pudgy belly
sticking out from above his nappy and the way he beamed
at me... I melted a little, and held my hands out to take him.

"You want a cuddle with Audrey?"

Albert gurgled and made a break for me.

"He's missed his sister!" Dad stepped to one side so I
could get into the tiny hall. "Audrey's here!" he called, then
he kissed me on the head and I closed my eyes, savouring it
for a second.

The cottage smelled of roast lamb, the scent shooting up
my nostrils, smelling of Sundays and Home.

"Where's Lola?" I asked, leaning into Albert's face,
inhaling his lovely toddler scent. He nuzzled into me,
melting off more pieces of my armour.

"AUDEE!" Lola appeared, also topless and covered in
what looked like Nutella. It was smeared all over her,
like warpaint.

"Yikes, what's happened to you?" She toddled at me, colliding with my ankles and decorating my jeans.

"Lola, we need to get you washed up!" Jessie appeared at the door of the kitchen, apron on, her face red from the stove. "Sorry, Audrey, she runs away whenever I try to clean her up. We've got to the point where we have to strip her when she eats, otherwise we'll ruin all her clothes."

"It's okay, these jeans need a wash anyway." I bent down to squidge her cheeks. She squealed and laughed.

"You want a cup of tea?" Jessie asked.

"Please."

I carried Albert through to the living room and Lola tottered after us. The floor was cluttered with primary-coloured toys – cars and blocks and dinosaurs. I sat with them on the carpet and Dad and I didn't really talk – just played with the kids, making car noises, building a tower of blocks that they smashed down and laughed manically at, wiping Lola's belly off with a damp cloth. It was easy when it was like this. If I just slipped into their new life, like a star guest in a sitcom who only stays a few scenes. Jessie brought in my tea and I sat up on the sinking armchair that used to be in my house and sipped at it, watching Dad play with the twins.

He never used to play with us *this much…*

It was a bitter thought, one that arrived already tasting sour. But it was true. Movie Night was the only real time we spent with him. He'd always been so busy with work, leaving Mum to do all the child-raising stuff. I guess now he was older he could get away with taking time out for his family. His brand-new family. His blank slate. His second chance. At what? I still didn't know.

"Audrees, audrees," Albert demanded, and I put my cup down and sat back on the floor.

Jessie left us to it – cooking the lunch I wasn't invited to.

"So, how's it going, Audrey?" Dad picked Lola up and swung her. She screeched and giggled in delight.

"Good…good."

"How's school?"

"It's okay."

"And your new job is working out okay?"

I was surprised he'd remembered. I'd only mentioned getting the job in passing when we took the twins to the park last month. "Yes. I've done two shifts now. I'm getting used to it. Hey, did you know they serve cinnamon dust there? On the popcorn?"

But just then, Lola got upset that Albert had snatched a toy and started crying, and Dad's attention wavered. "Hey hey, play nice, guys. Remember to SHARE." He wrestled the toy out of Albert's grip, and Albert started wailing. I bent down and picked him up, bouncing him on my knee. Meanwhile Dad crouched over Lola, whispering to calm her down, turning his back so Albert wouldn't see the toy that had caused so much drama. And, because toddlers have the memories of fish with dementia, Albert soon forgot why he was crying and started giggling as I waved a Mr Potato Head at him.

Jessie appeared at the door again. "Lunch in twenty minutes," she said brightly. Then she looked at me and realized it was impossible not to invite me. "Oh, Audrey, you're welcome to join us. Isn't she, Paul?"

Dad picked Lola up with an *oomph* and sat back up on the armchair. "Of course, Audrey. You must stay!" He sounded genuine but I couldn't. I'd feel like the universe's biggest traitor. Plus I wasn't sure I could swallow the whole family meal thing. Literally.

I shook my head. "I can't. I've got coursework to do. My new job is eating up a lot of time."

"Oh, that's a shame," Jessie said, though she smiled as she said it, and dashed back into the kitchen. I didn't have much time. I didn't know how I was even supposed to start this conversation, especially with the twins hanging off our necks.

"It's a shame you can't stay, Auds." Dad leaned over and picked a picture book up off the floor, flipping the pages to show Lola. "Jessie makes the best roast lamb. I swear that woman could turn vegetarians." My whole face flinched. He used to say the *exact* same thing about Mum... Did he not remember? "But it's good you're taking coursework seriously. How's Drama going?"

"I quit, remember?"

"Oh yes, oh yes..." He pointed to an apple. "See, Lola? Ap-ple."

No concern that Drama was all I'd ever wanted to do. No comment on why I might've given it up. No, not when

Lola might be on the verge of saying apple. So I just came out with it.

"Dad, why are you telling Mum to sell the house?"

He looked up straight away, and I thought, *Aha, that got your attention.*

"What's she been telling you?"

"Just that your lawyers are saying that you want her to sell the house. Our home," I added. Because if you can't use emotional manipulation against the father who left you and doesn't realize you quit the one thing that made you happy, then when can you?

Dad bit angrily on his lower lip, not answering. The book lay open on *A is for Apple* and Lola clawed at it. Albert shifted on my knee.

"This isn't a great time to talk about it."

"It's just a simple question, Dad."

"Did she send you?"

"No," I lied. "I overheard her talking to the lawyers on the phone and I just wanted to hear it from you."

Is it madness that I still wanted Dad to find Mum attractive? That I protected him from the worst of her just in case it put him off her even more? Even though I was holding his new child? With another woman? I just didn't want him to see Mum as a bitter, angry, terrified, pathetic, spurned mess...even though she was.

He raised an eyebrow, not believing me. Much as I was well-rehearsed in making Mum seem sorted, Mum wasn't so good at keeping up appearances. Dad had to get her phone number blocked. "You shouldn't have heard that," he said.

The twins were losing patience. He picked up the TV remote, switching it onto CBeebies. The twins' heads swung towards the screen like it was a hypnotist and fell instantly quiet – lost totally in the fluffy yellow blob floating around cooing "Ba-boo ba-boo". Albert slid off my lap like he was in a trance and Dad smiled sheepishly. "It's only for ten minutes... Jessie says we're not supposed to show them TV until they're at least three or something but...well... look..." He gestured to his two lobotomized children.

"So, is it true?"

Dad tilted his head back, running his hands through his new beard and the tiny part of me that *wasn't* dead inside gasped its final breath.

"I don't believe it." My voice shook. "Dad, it's our home!" The pain in my voice was so raw that Albert looked away from the TV. "Dad?" My throat closed up, I couldn't say any more.

He didn't even come over to hug me. He just sat in the chair, shaking his head. "It's not for a while, Audrey. Don't you worry yourself. Legally, your mum can keep the house until you've been raised. Until you leave. But we're just looking at the future."

"What does that even mean?"

"Audrey, honey!" He stood up and came and sat next to me on the sofa. I rigidly let him stroke my long hair. "Look, when you go to uni, you won't need that house any more.

Will you? And it's awfully big just for your mum to be rattling around in."

"But it's our home…"

"Audrey, let's not be selfish here. Look at this place. It's too small! The twins are only going to get bigger, and you and Dougie won't be there any more. I'm just being practical."

Practical… The word that covers a multitude of worse words. *Cold. Calculating. Unfeeling.*

"Don't you want Albert and Lola to have their own bedrooms?"

Here's another word: *manipulative.*

"We need an extension, and we can't afford one unless I get money from the sale of the house."

"But…but…" Oh God, there were so many things I wanted to say. Like, *well you should have thought of that.* Or, *what about where I spend the holidays?* Or, *what about the memories?* Or, *what about Mum and how she knows all our neighbours and has lived there for over twenty-five years?* Or how it shouldn't be our problem. How this was HIS mess.

He was babbling now, trying to win me around. "Audrey, this is adult stuff. Don't worry about it. It's a while before you even go away anyway. And, hey, an extension here means there'll be room for you to come and stay… Maybe talk to your mum? See if you can get her to see things like this? I mean, Albert and Lola are innocent in this whole thing, aren't they? We can't punish them for your mum's and my mistakes."

Mum's and his mistakes? MUM'S MISTAKES? Red descended. I had to get up. I had to leave. I had to not be here before I said something un-take-backable. I was the only person holding the bonds of our old family together and I couldn't fold.

I stood up. "I'm off."

"Audrey? Come on. Don't be like this."

I bent down and kissed my brother and sister on the cheek. They hardly noticed. The yellow fluffy blob had found a blue fluffy blob and they were jumping onto each other's stomachs, shouting "Moo-mah, moo-mah". Then I was up, out of the door. I didn't call goodbye to Jessie. I just grabbed my coat and stormed out. Dad called my name behind me, but not proper shouting. Not a shout that would rock his happy little boat. Not a shout that would make Jessie ask questions. Not at a volume that would upset his new batch of offspring. Not a shout that would alter his cosy little Sunday in any way. Whereas, back home, at the home he wanted to rip out from under us, Mum's coffee cup still lay smashed on the table, her feet sticking out from under the blanket on the sofa where she was probably lying, with her eyes half open, staring blankly at the TV until I came home with news that would throw her several rungs further down a ladder. I slammed the front door, feeling better as it shook the house.

I do exist. I am here. I am part of this life, whether you like it or not. I will have reactions. I will be a human. I won't go away quietly. I deserve to be here.

I was standing at the end of the drive, trying to pull myself together, when Dad appeared – holding up his arm, asking me to wait. He tiptoed over the gravel driveway in his socks, wincing with each step.

"Audrey, come on." I tried to read his face but I couldn't. Because I couldn't trust one thing this man, this man who made me, said.

"I'm too upset to talk right now, Dad."

"I didn't mean to upset you, I'm sorry if I did. You took me by surprise, that's all."

"So it's my fault now?"

"No, no, I'm not saying that. It's just a very complicated process, Audrey. I wasn't expecting you to bring it up."

"Well, sorry if I ruined your perfect Sunday." It came out so childishly…

Dad gave a small smile, like he felt sorry for me. "Look, Audrey. This stuff is for the lawyers. If your mum is trying to get you involved at all…"

"She's not. I said! I overheard her in the kitchen."

"I know your mother, Audrey. I was married to her for a long time…"

And you're not any more.

"…and I think we both know that she sent you today. That's not fair of her, Audrey. None of this is fair on you and Dougie, and I'm sorry it happened, I really am." He didn't sound very sorry. He didn't look it. "But I couldn't help falling in love. It's not something you have any control over. One day you'll understand."

I could never understand.

"As I said, this is all still a while away. It's not worth worrying about yet. Just focus on your studies, on work. On your Drama."

"I told you, I quit Drama."

"Oh yes, well, you know what I mean."

The click of the door. We both turned towards it. Jessie stood on the threshold, her arms crossed. "Lunch is ready," she cooed. Knowing she was interrupting something. Not caring. Asserting her dominance. She may as well have run down the driveway, cocked her leg and pissed on him.

"Heel," I said to Dad, raising my eyebrows. He lost his temper. He leaned into me, his voice suddenly gruff. "Don't you DARE talk about Jessie like that. Don't you dare." It was quieter the second time, more violent. His eyes glinted with…something. He jerked his chin up. Then, all he said was, "It was lovely to see you, Audrey," before he turned and waddled back over the gravel, back into the arms of the woman he had chosen over us.

18

THE CHANCE ENCOUNTER

People always say the world is so small. It isn't.
There's over seven BILLION humans on this planet.
Your chance of bumping into someone you know,
somewhere you aren't usually? Minuscule. Your
chances of bumping into someone who is also a
love interest? Not a hope in hell. But in romance
films, everyone is bumping into EVERYONE. Forget
statistical probabilities. Nope. Their love beats
mathematics. Even though they inevitably live in big
cities like LA, or New York or London, the two lovers
are just ALWAYS what-a-coincidence crossing paths
in coffee shops and park benches and cutesy
bookstores.

★ ★ ★ ★ ★

Harry was sitting on my goddamned wall.

I spotted him before he spotted me. His long legs spread out to prop up his gangly body. His whole body jiggled as he tapped his foot. I crunched on a frozen leaf and he looked up, more teeth than anything else as he smiled.

"What the hell are you doing on my wall?"

"Audrey! I need you."

I closed my eyes for a second. Now *really* wasn't a good time for Harry to be on my garden wall. I needed to go inside and tell Mum that Dad was going to evict us the moment I got a UCAS offer. "Why are you on my wall?"

"I didn't have your phone number. Ma wouldn't give it to me. She said it was privacy or something."

"So you turn up at my house?"

His teeth grew bigger as his smile grew wider. "I told you. I need you!"

He jumped down and opened his arms for a hug.

"I'm not hugging you."

"Don't fight your urges, Audrey."

I kept shaking my head in disbelief. "Why do you need me, Harry?"

"It's this script. Your zombie bride has changed everything! I need to rewrite loads and I need your insight into her. I've been up all night trying to get it right."

I tilted my head and peered at him. He did look wrecked. There were circles under his eyes, his face paler than normal.

"Don't you have to be at Flicker?"

"Nah, Sunday Sam works on a Sunday."

"Who's Sunday Sam?"

"He's been there since, like, 1972. Anyway, we're getting off point. Will you help me?"

I moved my body weight from one foot to the other. "I don't know anything about script writing."

"You don't need to. I just need to ask you some questions about how you see the bride. Most of the time you can just lie on your bed and read a magazine or something."

I raised my eyebrows. "Oh, so you're coming inside? Into my bedroom?"

He patted my shoulder and sighed. "Audrey, it would save us time if you just accept the inevitable that I will end up in your bedroom."

"You're actually shameless, aren't you?"

"So, can I come up?"

I hardly had space in my head to think about it, but I was able to make the following conclusions. If I brought Harry in with me, Mum wouldn't be able to react as nutso as I expected her to. Plus, annoying and flirtatious as he was, he was a rather welcome distraction from my planned freefall into emotional oblivion. Finally, I'd LOVED being the bride last night. I had so many ideas for her, for what drove her, for where she came from…

"Okay, you can come up to WORK. Not to flirt."

He beamed at me so hugely I thought I might be blinded. "Perfect! Brilliant. And I promise I'll stop flirting with you as long as you stop flirting with me."

"Hang on, I'm not flirting..." But he was already bounding up the path and rapping on the door.

Mum didn't know what to do with Harry. She flung the door open, still in her dressing gown, obviously expecting me with news. Instead she got, "Hi, you must be Ms Winters, I'm Harry. I work with Audrey at the cinema. How are you?"

"Oh, hello. I didn't know Audrey was having a friend around."

"My fault entirely. I invited myself round. I need her help with a project. Wow, what a kitchen you have here." He stepped past her. "It's gorgeous. Did you decorate this yourself?"

Mum pulled her dressing gown around herself and followed him into our kitchen. "Umm, yes, I did. Some time ago now though."

"You've got great taste. Duck egg blue?"

I raised an eyebrow. How the hell did Harry know what "duck egg blue" was?

Within five minutes, he was sitting at our breakfast bar, sipping tea, making Mum laugh with talk of what Dougie was like in school. Like the rest of the world, she was dazzled by Harry's compliments and seemed to have forgotten I was in charge of saving our home. After tea – "Wow, you really know how to make a good cuppa, Ms Winters" – Harry and I decamped to my bedroom. I mentally ran through the possible mess as we climbed the stairs. Had I left last night's bra on my chair? Or worse? My period-stained knickers from where yesterday's tampon had seeped through on my uber-long shift? I was SURE I'd put them in my laundry basket, but I still pushed through the door first, frantically scanning for gross bits. Luckily, apart from a pile of clothes (*sans* period knickers) on the floor, it was relatively okay. Just as well, as Harry flopped straight onto my bed, belly first, and said, "Come on then. Seeing as you dragged me here. We may as well."

I leaned against my wall and crossed my arms. "May as well what?"

He raised his eyebrows multiple times.

"Harry!"

He just laughed and rolled onto his side, flipping his legs over to sit up straight again. "Okay, Audrey, we'll play your game. Now, help me with this script."

And, just like that, Director Harry took over. He cleared a space on my desk, pulled up a chair and started poring over the script, talking all serious, like this was a UN conference to decide the future of humanity or something. "You see? In this scene? When she meets my character? I need them to fall in love, but she hates men so much, I don't know what can happen to buy him some time, you know? I mean, how do you win over a feminist zombie? Especially as he's not even a zombie yet and she wants to eat his brain."

I smiled, and pulled over my bedside table to perch on. "Well, don't label her as a feminist zombie. That's what she's so mad about. The fact she's spent her whole life being labelled and she doesn't get to decide what the label is."

"You're right! You're so right. You see! I told you I needed you."

We worked for an hour or two, him showing me the script and me adding my input where I could. He never once lost energy, which seemed mad as he looked like he hadn't slept at all. In fact, the more tired I got, the more energetic he was. The flirting stopped and he just started taking everything I said really seriously. "Yes, that's so true!" and, "Argh, of course," before scribbling over his script. I didn't know him very well, but I was seeing a whole different side to him. He even sensed my waning attention, and said, "Hey, don't you need to do coursework or something? Is it okay if I stay here? Just in case I need you? But you can get on with some other stuff."

I did have Geography coursework, which made me feel so bored I could hardly finish saying the word "Geography" without wanting a nap, but I nodded and got tea.

My phone vibrated as I went downstairs.

Leroy: Guys and Dolls auditions tomorrow! Can I run lines with you?

I bit my lip, pausing on my descent. Would it be too painful? To run lines for a play I wasn't going to audition for? For a part I would probably get if I wasn't too humiliated to even try out? Then I found myself shrugging. Actually,

Guys and Dolls wasn't my play. None of those parts were my parts. The zombie bride was.

> Audrey: Sure. Harry is here though.
> Leroy: Harry the non-Catholic Harry?
> Audrey: Yep. He's carving a pentagram into a dead lamb as we speak. He's got blood all over the bed. Rude.
> Leroy: Is he hitting on you??
> Audrey: He was. He's stopped now. He's okay really.
> Leroy: I'll come round to run lines AND protect your honour.

I smiled sadly as I waited for the kettle to boil. Here was the *really* humiliating thing. I wasn't sure if I had any honour left to protect. As in, I wasn't actually sure if I was a virgin or not. Like, what counts as sex? Had I really lost my virginity to Milo? If I was being explicit about it, he had literally…got in… But…like…he hadn't stayed there for very long. Is that sex? A thrust, a yowling of pain, an inability to continue and a withdrawal? Or does the penis have to stay inside for a sct amount of time? Like, enough time for a kettle to boil? Does a guy have to finish? Milo did not finish…he just finished with me.

Mum came in, fully dressed, just as I realized we'd run out of milk.

"So, he's very nice," she remarked. "Harry. Dougie's friend?"

I walked over to the sink to wash out the empty bottle. "Yeah, he's okay. Do we have any more milk?"

"Not unless you bought some. His mum, Jackie, we met at baby massage so many years ago now. She's an odd one. Very strict. I haven't seen him since he was a toddler though."

I fished around in the drawers for some long-life milk capsules that we bought during the power cut last year. I found them and ripped the tops off, pouring them into the mugs. "Not sure how she managed to produce Harry then," I said. "He doesn't seem very...rule-abiding."

"So, what did your father say?"

I spilled some milk, my tummy instantly hurting. Oh God, her face. It was so full of hope. When she saw me falter though, it dropped and sagged. She aged ten years in one moment.

"You couldn't change his mind?"

I hadn't even said anything. "I tried, Mum. It was hard. Jessie and the kids were there. They were all about to have lunch."

She threw her arms up. "Well, GOD FORBID we RUIN THEIR LUNCH with our HOMELESSNESS."

"I know. I know. But, look, he said he can't even put it on the market until I've gone to uni. That's ages away. Maybe, in time, I can talk him round?"

I was lying to her, and myself. I'd heard the way his voice hardened. Ever since Dad left, ever since he fell head over reason for Jessie, he'd made one thing very clear...

We were no longer the priority. It wasn't our turn any more. His heart had changed channels, even though our show was still playing.

"Do you really think so?" Mum was still telling herself fairy tales.

"Maybe. It was just bad timing today, that's all."

"I can't leave this house, Audrey." She gripped the kitchen counter. "It's my home. I've lived here for over twenty-five years."

"We won't leave, we'll sort something out."

For a second, I stupidly imagined a world where Dad got his way and what that would look like. Me and Dougie coming home for uni holidays and having to sleep on the floor of Mum's flat. Christmas spent in some strange new building in a strange new part of town, rather than under the Christmas tree we always put in the bay window. My bedroom – that I'd spent year upon year adapting and evolving with myself – I'd have to peel everything down from the walls. Probably give half my belongings to charity as they wouldn't fit into Mum's downsized life. All of us having to give up and make do because Dad fell in love with someone who wasn't the woman he solemnly promised he'd spend his whole life never wavering from.

What was the point? What is the point in love, and promises of it, when it can just jump from one person to another like that? Tears tickled at my eyes. Mum stood staring at me, like I was The Oracle. I couldn't remember a time when she was the grown-up and me the child. Ever since Dad had packed his suitcase and kissed my forehead two years ago and Dougie had refused to come out of his room, I'd been the adult. I was only seventeen…

Mum wiped under her eyes. "You're right. We'll think of something. Sorry, I didn't want to interrupt your time with your friend." She sniffed. "He's very handsome, isn't he?"

I rolled my eyes. "He's also very trouble."

Mum's eyes darted all over the kitchen, only half-listening. "I better think about what we're going to have for dinner," she muttered to herself.

I knew this wasn't the end of it. That she was only at the beginning of digesting what I'd said, what that meant. For a moment I felt grateful that Harry had unwittingly protected me from her spiralling further.

That was, until, I went up with the tea and found him rummaging through all my stuff…

"What's this?" he asked, waving my college notepad above his head. I stood with the teas frozen to my hands as he opened it and started to read.

"*Romance films are money-spinning cathedrals of love, wobbling on the foundations of unbelievable and damaging stereotypes…*"

"Stop," I interrupted. "You can't just go through my stuff."

He stood up and unclasped my fist to remove a cup. He took a sip, sat down and opened my notepad again. Reading silently this time.

"Stop it!"

"Woooah," he exclaimed. "This is bitter. I can see where the zombie bride comes from now."

I balanced my own tea on my bedside table and snatched the book off him. He grinned as I stuffed it under my duvet.

"Hey" – he gave me the eye over the rim of his cup – "I was hardly going through your stuff. You left it here on the desk, open to that page."

"Still though."

"What can I say, Audrey? I just want to get to know you!"

I laughed in a short, sharp "ha". "Can you please tone down the meaningless charm? I'm really not in the mood for it today."

He must've heard something waver in my voice because, before I knew it, he'd unfolded his spindly body and was by my side. "Shit, Audrey. I'm sorry. Are you okay?"

I shook my head. "Can we just get going on this script? My friend Leroy is coming over soon to run lines for his audition. I don't have much time."

Harry didn't push it. Didn't ask for more info. I liked that. He just said, "All righty," and was back at his desk, firing questions at me, disappearing into his work. I sat there, slurping my tea, analysing him with a kind of stunned wonder as he worked. I didn't know this boy existed this time last week. But now he was in my bedroom, reading my mood, charming my mother, going through my stuff, but still making me feel weirdly comfortable.

After fifteen minutes of solid scrawling, he looked up. "You heard the Ma gossip?"

I shook my head.

"Well you know she went to the sister branch the other day? She keeps doing that. We think she's getting promoted. To area manager."

"Oh, okay, what would that mean?"

He stretched out his legs, putting his feet up on my desk. He had a very small hole in the toe of one of his socks. "Well, the good news is she won't be around as much. Lou is likely to get a promotion."

"So, no more rota explaining how I spend every ten-minute segment of my time?"

"Well, that's the bad news. If she's in charge of several branches, her inner control freak is likely to spiral."

"*Inner* control freak?"

He laughed. "You're right. Well, her extroverted control freak will go berserk. I reckon she'll crack down on us even more than usual... But, like, she can't be there all the time. Anyway..." He reached over and rummaged under the duvet to locate my Media project again. "What's the deal with this? What have you got against romance movies?"

"It's just a project for college," I explained. "We've got to pick a part of the media to critically examine, and I've picked romance films."

"Why?" His eyes had this way of really staring into you. I found myself looking down to dodge his gaze.

"Why not?"

"I feel there's a story there, Rapunzel."

My hand went to my long hair subconsciously. "Not a very interesting one."

Harry came and sat on the bed again without invitation. His bony bum half crippled my toes as he squished on top of them. "Fine then. Don't tell me. But, woah..." He turned a page of my notepad. "You really don't like romance films, do you?"

I bit my lip. "I just think they're dangerous, that's all."

"Dangerous? Like antibiotic resistance? And...umm... SHARKS?"

I kicked him softly. "You know what I mean, I think they're dangerous for, like, society."

"Ahh. They're harmless. I love 'em!"

"*You* like romance films?"

"Yep. I like zombie films better. But I like romance films too. Good ones."

"And what constitutes a good one?"

"You know. Good acting, good dialogue. It has to give you the feels."

I laughed again. "Did you actually just say 'give you the feels'?" I shook my head. "You are SUCH a strange one."

"What? It's a good expression!" He wasn't even blushing. "Anyway, explain please why romance films are a menace to society?"

My eyes filled up as I thought of earlier. I thought of what Dad must've believed when he got down on one knee, in Rome, and proposed to Mum even though they'd only known each other six months. I thought of how happy they had been to tell everyone that story. *Their* story, over the years. So pleased they had their own narrative – one that matched the movies. Love at first sight. Beautiful backdrop. Whirlwinds and grand gestures. I thought of all the films we'd watched together on Saturday nights, the messages always the same. Love conquers all. Love is happiness. Love is fireworks. Love is giving you the feels. Love means never having to say you're sorry. Love is easy. Love is unwavering. Love is for ever.

We watched no films where couples yelled at each other in the kitchen. No films where, ten years after kissing on top of the Eiffel Tower, the couple didn't even sit on the same sofa. No films showing how…bored Dad would look whenever Mum said anything – glazing over, like she was the shipping forecast, rather than the woman he adored so much he pawned half his stuff for a diamond ring…one he tried to get in the divorce. When my parents' love soured, Dad didn't try to resuscitate it. Because there was no one telling him that was possible. Instead he jumped ship and started all over again with someone who gave him *new* feels.

"They're dangerous because they're not real," I said. "Not really." I chewed my lip, trying to gain control of my emotions. "I mean the beginning bit of love is always great, but that's the only thing romance films focus on. It's a cop-out. It's taking the easy way out." Like Dad.

Harry was miraculously quiet, his face uncharacteristically

serious. He looked up at me, and our eyes met properly for the first time. Him staring at me, me staring at him. This boy I didn't know, sitting on my purple duvet. He smiled without his teeth. Small, shyly. I found myself smiling back. Like an impulse.

Then he ruined it by saying...

"You're not like other girls, are you?"

And I activated.

Every single emotion I'd been squashing into my guts exploded like a burst appendix. I jumped off the bed and turned to him with a scowl I was sure he'd need permanent therapy to recover from. *"Are you kidding me, Harry?"*

"Woah, Audrey. Hey, hey, hey. It's okay. It's a compliment."

I felt like screaming. "It's NOT a compliment." I threw my arms up, any motion to get rid of the rage pulsing through me. "It's an insult to every single woman on this PLANET. Don't you DARE try and pull that shit on me."

"What shit?!" Harry was stupid enough to ask. "I was saying something nice..."

I shook my head so hard. "No, you were saying something clichéd and UNTRUE. I AM like other girls, Harry. Don't misinterpret my hatred of romance as some kooky, laid-back, manic pixie NONSENSE. I am DAMAGED. I am not CUTE. I am emotionally-fucking-traumatized right now, okay? I am screaming on the inside. I am too angry and messed-up to contain all the stuff girls spend every day containing. That's why I seem different. That is *not sexy.*"

I started crying then, huge embarrassing hiccups of it. Some of it despair, most of it anger. I pointed at him. Harry was just sitting there, open-mouthed, looking like I'd smacked him over the head with a novelty mallet. "I hate romances because my family is imploding, okay?" I wobbled. "I...I... I'm so fed up of all the LIES everyone tells each other. How none of it lasts. All of it is one big facade..." And I crumbled into ash, sinking into my bed and sobbing into my hands, as Harry nervously patted my heaving shoulders. I gave him credit for not arguing with me. For understanding, even though we were basically strangers, that I needed to cry.

In time, I managed to contain myself. To relock the vault of repressed sadness I'd accidentally blown open, letting everything out. I looked up at Harry through the clumps of my wet eyelashes. "See," I said. "I'm just like other girls. Totally insecure, needy, temperamental and nuts."

He smiled without using his teeth again. "You're just like any human," he corrected. "Stop painting all girls with the same brush. God, Audrey."

And I laughed, almost in surprise. He smiled a bigger grin then. "I'm sorry for multiple things right now, Audrey. Sorry for saying you're not like other girls and mistakenly thinking it's a compliment..."

"It's not. It's sexist bull..."

"Yes, you've made me aware of that. Sorry, I guess, for hitting on you when you're obviously going through a lot. And..." He took a deep breath. "I'm sorry about whatever is happening to your family. That sounds...rubbish."

I nodded. "It really is rubbish."

"I think I can see where the zombie bride's anger is coming from."

"Oh, Harry, you have no idea who you're dealing with."

He grinned. "I'm starting to realize that."

19

We worked in a contented silence until Leroy rocked up. I heard him say hi to Mum in the hall, then he was at my door, leaning against it, raising his eyebrows at Harry and saying, "Audrey has told me ALL about you."

"Harry, Leroy. Leroy, Harry," I said, gesturing to both of them. "And that's not strictly true, is it, Leroy?"

He ignored me and strode in, sitting on my bed, acknowledging Harry with a camp waggle of his fingers. Sometimes I wondered just how in denial Leroy's mum was about his sexuality. "We go to the same church by the way," Leroy said. "Not that you would know, heathen."

Harry was all grin and tooth. "I know. I recognize you."

"It's not hard, babes. Anyway, I'm not interrupting anything, am I?"

I shook my head furiously at him. "We were just working on this script."

Harry was rolling back and forth on my office chair. "Audrey's been amazing."

"That's because she is amazing."

"Can I stay a bit longer?" Harry asked. "I won't disturb you. But I'm totally in the flow and I'm scared if I leave, I'll lose it."

"That's fine," I said. "But we're running lines, that won't put you off?"

Leroy was already digging in his bag for a script. "He'll be put off by just how talented I am."

Harry smiled at Leroy, like he already really liked him. Which is sort of the effect Leroy has on most people. "I'm sure I can cope." He spun round in my chair and walked it backwards to my desk.

"Good, good," Leroy said. "Right, Audrey, we need to run through this a LOT. I didn't have time this morning because SOME OF US still have to go to church. Anyway, can you read Sarah for me? I need to get my suave right."

"Okay." I picked up the spare script and turned the pages to where Leroy had marked them out with a Post-it. I didn't feel the huge sadness I was expecting. Until the other day, thinking of *Guys and Dolls* had hurt me – made me mourn what could've been, if things hadn't gone so wrong with Milo when I was in no way emotionally-equipped for things to go wrong with Milo. But, as I started reading, bouncing off Leroy's lines, I didn't feel sad. I just felt like I was helping a friend.

We read the scene set in Cuba, where Sarah drinks

too much on her date with Sky. Even though it was just a run-through, I felt myself get a little lost in her. Sarah is such a fun part – all the layers of her prude onion slowly unpeeling throughout the musical. And Leroy played Sky just great. Very understated, which was a new way of seeing him. Quietly suave, a little bit messed-up. It was the opposite to how I knew Milo would read him. Ironically enough, the camp gay guy wouldn't make Sky camp, and the straight macho guy would. When we got to "If I Were A Bell", I even sang it, making Leroy laugh as I flopped around the bed, getting drunker and drunker. I'd forgotten we were just in my house, rehearsing. Until…

A slow clap.

I jolted out of where I was, drunk in Cuba, to find Harry applauding. Hard.

"What? What is it?" I asked, feeling dazed.

"Damn, Audrey. How are you so very good?"

Leroy winked in agreement. "I know, right? The gal can act."

I felt myself go red. "Guys, I can't."

"Are you kidding me?" Harry ran his hands through his hair. "I mean, last night you were the most convincing zombie I've ever seen and now what? You're suddenly the most convincing buttoned-up church girl out of her depth in Cuba?"

My blush spread past my neck, down to my chest. "That's just what acting is…" I trailed off.

"I know that. But, honestly, Audrey. You are good."

I was so red at this point, it's likely you could crack an egg on my face and get it perfectly sunny side up.

"And yet she's not even auditioning," Leroy pointed out, clutching his heart like I'd stabbed him. "All because Milo dumped her."

Harry's eyes narrowed. "Is that true? You're not doing *Guys and Dolls* because of that guy at the cinema last night?"

Now my whole body was red. "It's a bit more complicated than that," I said, feeling emotions rising that I didn't want evoked. I took a breath and pushed them down inside myself. "Leroy? Come on, don't lose focus. Let's run the scene again."

But Harry was having none of it. "Audrey, you can't do this. You have to audition. When are they?"

"I'm not auditioning," I said.

Leroy crossed his arms. "I still can't believe you're choosing a zombie film over our school play."

I smacked him again. "I'm choosing MY SANITY over the school play."

"And I, for one," said Harry, "am very grateful to provide the means for Audrey's sanity."

Leroy levelled him with a glare. "Like you did for Cassie from church?"

And Harry didn't laugh it off like I was expecting him to. He just looked down at the carpet.

"Okay, boys, let's get back to work, shall we?"

But Harry stood, picking up his stuff. "Actually, I'm knackered. I didn't sleep last night."

"Oh…" For some reason I really didn't want Harry to leave. "Ignore Leroy, he's horrible to everyone."

Leroy nodded. "True."

"No, no, it's not that. I really have to go." He gathered up the rest of his papers and stuffed them into his grotty backpack. Then, before I had time to think of another comeback, he was out the door, yelling, "See you at work and it was nice meeting you," over his shoulder, before the slam of the front door shook the whole house.

Leroy looked at me. I looked at Leroy.

"Leroy, you scared him!"

He shrugged, unbothered. "I just made a valid point about Cassie. I told you on Friday, he really hurt her! Anyway, what's going on with you two?"

"Umm, nothing?"

"Didn't look like nothing. Looked like something."

I sighed. "I don't even know him."

"Yet you're in his movie? What's that about, Audrey?"

I slid down the bed, into Leroy's weight. "It just sort of happened… And it was fun. And it made me forget about everything for a while. I saw my dad today…" The emotions from earlier flung themselves back like a boomerang. "It wasn't great." And, Leroy, bless him, managed to reach out and scooch me in for a hug. "And this is a good distraction, you know? I like that the cinema has nothing to do with sixth form, or Drama Club, or Milo, or the girls, or the play. Or even home. It's a totally new thing, and I need that right now. Harry just happens to be a part of it."

"A very fit part of it."

"You think everyone is fit. You literally fancy everyone."

Leroy nodded thoughtfully. "That is also true. But, well, I dunno, Audrey. I'd watch him. He was looking at you like you were more than a zombie bride."

"He looks at EVERY girl that way." Though I got a brief flash of the way he'd looked at me when he said *"You're not like other girls"*, and I got a pinch of wanting. "Anyway, you don't have to worry. He tried it on and I told him where to go."

I'd done more than that. I'd essentially yelled so loud I'd probably given him permanent hearing damage.

"That's my girl."

"Anyway, shall we get back to this scene?"

"Yes! I NEED to beat Milo to this part. The world needs MY Sky Masterson, not his."

We went back into our lines, going over and over them until Leroy vanished and Sky appeared. We ran lines until it got dark and Mum called up the stairs saying dinner was ready.

Leroy got his phone out to catch up on all the digital-mingling he'd missed. "I still think you need to be careful," Leroy said, half hypnotized by his screen.

"Careful about what?"

"Harry. You keep claiming you're dead inside but you weren't looking at him like you were dead inside. Don't think he would be different for you, Audrey... Oh bugger. Someone's written a blog post claiming I misuse green shells in battle mode..."

And, as always, before I had time to retaliate, Leroy was swanning out the door, punching madly at his phone, leaving only the strong scent of his woody aftershave behind.

20

I looked right into Harry's eyes and shook my head. "I'm not sure I can do it."

He widened his in return and very quickly squeezed my hand before realizing what he'd done. He withdrew it like I was contagious and stuffed it into his jeans pocket. "You can. I believe in you. We all do."

I hated that I was disappointed at Harry's new, appropriate behaviour. Ever since I'd screamed at him in my bedroom two weeks ago he'd totally stopped flirting. And it was totally bugging me. But I didn't have time to think about that as I somehow had to transform fully from human to zombie in only one take. I was finding it hard enough shooting scenes out of sequence. Add in the pressure of this particular moment, and my brain acting all confused by Harry's professional-only behaviour, and things weren't good.

I swallowed and looked up at the crew around me.

"You've totally got this," Jay said. "Honestly, those fake

blood capsules taste so foul that you'll hardly need to act. Your face will pull all kinds of weird shit all by itself." He looked so smart in his tux, for now. I was about to rip his intestines out of his stomach though, and that would involve a lot of corn syrup.

I glanced down at my perfect wedding dress. Harry had blown a lot of budget buying two decent-looking bridal gowns for this one scene. "An heir and a spare," he'd laughed – but I knew he was really hoping he wouldn't need the spare.

"You're going to be great," Harry insisted. "Don't worry. We still have a back-up dress if necessary, but you won't need it."

Our eyes met again. Damn I was nervous. But the moment was interrupted by Rosie, standing over by the lights saying, "Can we just do this already?"

I didn't know why I was freaking out so much. I'd only ever acted onstage, I wasn't used to the luxury of multiple takes anyway. I'd been trained to get it right first time. But this scene... The turning scene was so key to the film and I could tell Harry was nervous. He'd smoked way too many cigarettes and kept looking at his watch. We only had three hours to film everything before we both had to work. I'd never seen anyone care about anything as much as he cared about this scene, and his nerves were infectious.

"Right, I think I'm ready," I said to my reflection.

I regretted saying it instantly because I could feel I wasn't the bride. I was still Audrey. Audrey worrying that she wasn't going to pull it off. I had to crush a black blood capsule in my teeth, spit it all down my front, die, then turn into a zombie – all with an extreme close-up on just my face. Harry claimed doing any other shot would be a "waste of my talent" but it was a hell of a lot of trust to put in me and my face.

"Is everyone in their places?" Harry called. "Rob? Lights." The lights blasted on, instantly making my face hot.

"Rosie? Sound?"

"It's on," she drawled, sounding bored.

"Audrey? You got your blood capsule?"

I turned round to smile with it between my teeth – acting like I was fine, like I was in the zone. Which was ironic because I wasn't in the acting zone at all. Oh God, if I messed this up we'd have to get me all cleaned up and put the other wedding dress on and then I REALLY would be down to my last shot and what if I messed that shot up even more? And…

"ACTION!" Harry barked.

The room fell quiet. I had my head down, because I was about to look up in the mirror and see my face changing (we were going to CGI that in later). Then I had to burst the capsule and ruin the dress and act my bloody heart out – but she wasn't there. The cameras were rolling but the bride wasn't there. Bollocks, I'd just have to try anyway. I looked up at my reflection and tried to imagine my face changing, imagine how that felt. I still wasn't feeling the bride… But I carried on… And I was about to bite down, I was about to ruin the dress when…

"WAIT!"

Harry's voice.

"Cut cut cut cut cut!" he yelled, stepping out from behind his camera.

"What? What is it?" I asked, almost choking on my capsule.

"Something's up. I can see it in your face. Let's go talk."

I went red. Embarrassed that Harry had noticed my hesitation. He was already marching out of LouLou's flat onto her little patio and all I could do was stand up and shuffle after him. I caught Rosie's eye on the way and she gave me a smug look, like she'd always thought I wouldn't be good enough. I stumbled outside to find Harry lighting another cigarette.

"What is it?" I asked, though I already knew.

He sucked in, paused for a moment then exhaled. "What's going on, Audrey? You weren't there, I could see it."

I bit my lip and wrapped my arms around myself. "I was…" I started to protest then I shook my head. "Okay, you got me. I wasn't there."

"I knew it."

"How are you so intuitive?"

I expected him to make a crack about being good with girls or something but he didn't. Just like he'd not made any flirtatious jokes since I'd yelled at him that time. Instead he took another drag and said, "I'm a good director, that's all. I can see something is up. Now, what is it?"

It was so cold outside my jaw was already shaking.

"I don't know, I just… I don't know where she went. The zombie bride…" I tried to smile. "She's gone AWOL."

"Why?" he asked quietly.

It took me a moment to find the answer. The reason I felt so foggy. For one, I was exhausted. Mum had started talks with her lawyer yet again and kept coming home crying. Two, I'd felt it harder than I thought I would when I didn't audition for *Guys and Dolls*.

"I have a lot going on…" I said eventually. "You know? Some of the stuff I told you the other week." Because I didn't know up from down, left from right, right from wrong. I didn't know what was fair or unfair, what was forgivable or unforgivable. "I just feel all over the place. Usually I can push that to one side when I'm acting, but it's not working today."

"Right." Harry finished his cigarette and stubbed it out against the wall. "Have you thought maybe it's good that you feel like that today? For this particular scene?"

"What do you mean?"

He looked right into my eyes. "I mean use it, Audrey. Whatever's going on, use it. You feel like something has died? Use it. In this scene everything you know is dying, you are dying. Put that in there. Feel it. Release it. Bleed on us."

I thought quietly about what he'd said and I had to look away because of how his eye contact made me feel. "Well, that's the other thing," I admitted. "I'm worried about ruining the dress. I mean, I know it cost a lot and we've only really got this one take and I'm feeling the pressure, I guess."

At that, Harry let out a laugh. "You're worried about letting me down?"

I nodded.

He reached out, like he was about to squeeze my hand again but then stopped in mid-air and bent his elbow to run his hands through his mad hair. "Have I fully explained how screwed this movie would be if you hadn't turned up, Audrey? I mean, Rosie is one of my best friends, and she has an encyclopedic knowledge of zombie theory, but the girl can't act. And, love Rob as I do, I don't think he could've pulled off shoving on a wig and some false eyelashes and being the bride. I still can't believe my luck that you've showed up in my life…" He stumbled and looked away. "Whatever you do will be great. Whatever you do, I'll be grateful for it. Stop worrying about letting us down and just use it all." He looked up again. "Just use it."

It was weird. What he was telling me was basic acting advice, but it was like I was hearing it for the first time. Because I hadn't thought to harness this particular pain. The pain of Dad leaving, the pain of Milo then also leaving. I'd put it in a box and locked it up and then put the box at the back of the cupboard and then locked the cupboard and then set fire to the cupboard. I was too scared of unleashing it. Too scared that it would destroy me, that it would become an insatiable beast that would devour me whole.

"I'm scared that using it will be ugly," I admitted.

His face broke into his wide grin, his teeth almost dazzling. "Which would be a problem in a romance film,

Audrey, but this is a zombie film. I want you ugly. I need you ugly."

I nodded. "Okay."

"Okay?"

I nodded again. "Okay, let's do this."

I felt jittery as he steered me back.

Rosie shot me yet another smug look. "You done?"

And I felt a jolt of anger at her. I mean, I'd apologized about taking her part a million times and tried so hard to be friendly. I'd asked her endless questions about zombies, saying grovelling things like, "*Wow, you're such an expert, it's really cool,*" while she rolled her eyes. But, right then, rather than burying the twinge of anger, I let it grow in me. I felt my fingertips tingle. I needed this pain, I needed this anger. Harry was right.

"Were you guys kissing out there?" Jay asked, but Harry told him to shut up right away.

"Audrey, are you ready?"

I was confused, annoyed that Harry didn't want to entertain the joke of us kissing. And I didn't understand where that confusion came from. So now I was scared and angry and confused and in pain and, actually, when I heard him call, "*AAAAND ACTION!*" I was exactly what I needed to be for the zombie bride to take over.

21

THE KISS

Men in films regularly kiss women who don't want to be kissed. And those are supposed to be the good kisses. Either the woman is taken by surprise, or storming off in a mood, or having a huge go at them, or is engaged to somebody else, or claims she's just plain Not Interested. And, how do men in movies respond to this clear instruction of "no"? They grab the woman's face, and kiss her anyway. Roughly. Using their masculine force. And rather than being slapped or even arrested, these movie men are rewarded for their…well…sexual violence. The women "give into" the kiss after a brief moment of fighting it. You see, according to Hollywood, these women wanted to be kissed all along. It was just the male lead's job to break through the barriers. Barriers like WILFUL CONSENT.

Outside Hollywood movies, there is a term for

being kissed against your will. This term isn't "spontaneous" or "romantic" or "passionate". No, it's called sexual assault. It's a crime punishable in the UK by up to ten years in prison.

✹ ✹ ✹ ✹ ✹

Leroy, predictably, didn't get the part of Sky Masterson. Milo did.

"This is a fucking farce." He slammed his fist against the wall where the listings were stuck. "I could act that arrogant prick under the table."

I pointed to his name, next to the role of *Nicely*. "It's not so bad, you get all the best songs. You even get to sing 'Sit Down You're Rocking The Boat'."

"Bullshit." He went to slam his fist again but Ian grabbed it. "Everyone knows 'Luck Be A Lady' is the best song."

I made cooing noises and tried to comfort him with a pat, but he shrugged Ian and me off and stormed down the corridor, flinging some Year Sevens to one side like they were a door he could open.

Ian and I looked at each other. "He'll get over it," Ian said. "In his next life maybe."

I forced myself to look for Courtney's name. She'd gone for the part of Sarah – Sky's love interest – instead of Adelaide and she'd got it. Couldn't handle the thought of watching Milo kiss another girl every night probably. Maybe she was worried he'd get a flight of fancy and dump her for someone else. I mean, it was a reasonable concern…

To be fair though, over the past few weeks my Milo scars had been fading. Mainly due to being so damn busy. Ma did get promoted and it had messed up all the shifts, so LouLou had asked if I could take more on. I'd said yes without hesitation. Anything to get out of that house – with Mum's constant phone calls to the lawyer, then to her friends to talk about the lawyer, plus her accusing me of not trying hard enough to change Dad's mind, alongside Dougie ringing and saying, "Audrey, you need to look after Mum better," but still not even bothering to visit. So I switched it for Flicker – making guacamole, shredding pork, popping corn and then scraping it off the carpet two hours later. And then there was Harry and the movie…

He'd totally backed off since my *YES I AM LIKE OTHER GIRLS* rant. There was no flirting or innuendo or cheeky winks. He was still friendly but the message had definitely got through. Even LouLou had picked up on it.

"What's with you two?" she asked one evening, as she was frantically trying to make sense of Ma's new super-rota. "I knew it. You've kissed. And it's all gone horribly wrong."

I smiled. "Relax. No kissing. I just told him to stop flirting."

LouLou's eyes widened. "And he stopped?"

He continued being ultra professional during filming too. He stopped getting baked with the others – choosing to stand outside the car with me, asking inane questions.

"*How's Dougie? So why are you doing Geography? Do you think that last shot was okay?*" We seemed to be shooting every single scene that didn't involve Harry and me being on screen together. The main thrust of the film was me falling in love with him, even though he wasn't a zombie – but we hadn't filmed one scene together yet, focusing instead on all my rampage scenes. Rosie, of course, seemed delighted with this turn-out. She went into overly-tactile mode – finding excuses to touch him, leaning her head on him in the car as he drove us back because Tad was too high, smirking at me like I gave one.

I mean, of course I didn't care. I was just relieved that he'd listened to me, that he'd respected my wishes and now we could just be friends…

I mean, of course this bothered me!!

Because even though I wasn't interested or ready or a fool, I missed the attention as soon as he withdrew it. I missed getting the full megawatt smile. I felt a bit strange when Becky and Charlie and Alice kept telling me how hot he was, how lucky I was to work with him. I even found myself caring what I looked like as I got ready for work. Adding the tiniest hint of lip gloss here and there. Even though it was pointless – by the end of most evenings I'd have faux-guts hanging from my mouth.

In other news, my schoolwork wasn't doing too great.

The constant late nights and the fact I couldn't give a flying crap about Geography and English were catching up on me. I was scraping Cs. At best. Essays I managed to produce on time came back littered with red lines and question marks.

Media was the only subject I wasn't flatlining in.

"I've read your initial notes," Mr Simmons said, picking up my draft coursework and slurping from his Star Wars coffee mug. "This is good, Audrey. You'll need to make your writing a bit more academic when you type all this up properly, but it's good stuff."

"Thank you, sir." I almost collapsed in relief that I might not fail all my subjects.

"Working at a cinema seems to be good for this one particular subject." He smiled as he looked up.

"Yeah, I guess."

"I really think you could get an A for this. But you need to collect a bit more cold hard data. Is there a questionnaire you could do? To get people's opinions on a certain aspect of romance films?"

I nodded. "Sure. Sounds good."

"Brilliant, brilliant. Well I guess you can go."

Just as I turned to leave, he called me back. "Audrey?"

"Yep?"

Mr Simmons passed his mug from hand to hand and coughed. "It's just...well...your notes, they were good. But...well...they were a little...er...angry. Is everything okay, Audrey? At home I mean?"

I didn't know what to say. I just stood there, my mouth open. I mean, Mr Simmons wasn't a care-y teacher.

"It's just, you know the school has counselling facilities?

If you ever need to talk to anyone about anything? I can talk to your form tutor. Get them to write a note?"

Counselling...

I shook my head. "I'm fine, sir. Thanks for your concern, but I'm fine."

Am I fine? What even counts as fine?

"Okay, well, the school is always here for you, Audrey. And, good work. I'm looking forward to seeing how this coursework of yours turns out."

"What's this?" Leroy asked, as I shoved a questionnaire into his hand.

"A survey for my Media Studies coursework." I fiddled until I got one for Ian too, passing it over. "I'm on a quest for the best movie kiss."

Ian's blue eyes crinkled up when he smiled. "The best what?"

"Movie kiss," I repeated, handing over a pen. "I'm doing research into romance movies and what's the ultimate goal of a romance movie? The big kiss! I want to see what big kisses everyone else likes, to see if there's a correlation. And if so, why?"

Leroy already had a pen in his hand and was marking up his paper with his illegible handwriting. "Easy peasy. *Brokeback Mountain.* That kiss. The NEED in that kiss!" He started fanning himself.

I raised my eyebrows at the obviousness of the choice.

"The cowboy film?" I asked, just as Ian went, "Oh God, Leroy, really?"

"What's wrong with *Brokeback Mountain*?" Leroy asked. "Don't tell me you're going to pick a straight kiss, Ian?"

"I hated that movie! Have you not read the book it was based on? They totally crucified it."

"Honey, you read?" Leroy put his arm around Ian and Ian lightly punched him.

"What's your choice then, Ian?" I said. Feeling like I was intruding on a moment. A sexual moment.

"Umm. I dunno. Let me think for a while. I may pick a straight kiss, just to piss off Mr Queen over here."

Then, of course, they were kissing. I waited patiently and awkwardly because Ian had my pen.

"Oh, sorry, Audrey." He finally noticed and I held my hand out.

"Thanks."

"Hey" – Leroy pulled himself away – "do you want me to ask my followers what their favourite kiss is? It could get you more numbers?"

"That would be amazing, could you?"

"Sure. I mean, my followers are likely to only choose a kiss between Mario and Princess Peach but it's worth a shot, right?"

I pushed Ian out the way to hug Leroy.

"All right, all right. Just make sure you're pro-*Brokeback Mountain* in your coursework, okay?"

I saluted.

At lunch on Wednesday, knackered from my cinema shift the night before, I made a long overdue effort to bridge the gap with the girls.

"Hey," I said to Alice, Becky and Charlie, as I sat down at their table in the school canteen. It was quiet – sixth-formers always got it to themselves for fifteen minutes at lunch before the rest of the school. A little (shit) perk to keep us from absconding to the local college. They were sharing a plate of chips between the three of them. A dollop of ketchup on one side, mayonnaise on the other.

They all smiled. "Hey."

"Where you been, Auds?" Becky asked. "I swear you're like a ghost these days or something."

"I know, I'm sorry. It's this job." I sat down and picked up a chip, feeling all their eyes on me. I hadn't really sought them out for two weeks – not since the night they'd come to the cinema. Even though they'd been so lovely about Milo and Courtney. I wasn't entirely sure why. I wasn't entirely sure about anything, to be honest. I was hoping the questionnaire would break the all-my-fault ice. "How are things with you girls? How are things with Nick?" I asked Charlie.

They all looked a bit flustered and didn't answer right away. Taking their time to shake off the rust from their talking-to-me skills. I felt a jolt of guilt for being so difficult and inward and essentially dumping them and their well-intentioned sugary-sweet friendship for Leroy's

Death By Honesty approach.

"Good, it's good," Charlie said. "I'm dropping mad hints that he'll take me to Paris for my eighteenth, but we'll see."

"Paris?" My eyes widened. "Oh, wow."

"I know. Wouldn't it be romantic?"

I did a small smile and picked up another chip. "I'm not the right person to talk to about romance these days. Oh, speaking of which..." I reached into my bag and pulled out some of my questionnaires. "I've been meaning to ask you, do you mind filling these out for my coursework? I need to find the best movie kiss of all time."

Alice practically snatched hers. "I've been creating a shortlist ever since you told me in Media," she said. "Can I nominate seven?"

"Only one I'm afraid."

"Meanie." Her cat flick scrunched up in another smile.

"Becks? You got one?"

"I mean, surely it HAS to be the one in *The Notebook*," she stated, picking up another chip. "Why are we even having this conversation?"

"Oh my God, that kiss!" Alice shrieked. "How did I miss that off my list of seven?"

Charlie butted in, sighing. "When it starts to rain...and Ryan Gosling does that speech about how it's NEVER BEEN OVER—"

"And he just grabs her," Becky interrupted. "And she jumps up into his arms and he doesn't buckle under the weight of her."

They all slowly seeped in on themselves, melting into their plate of chips. The doors opened for the lower years and the canteen was flooded by noise and chatting and the clattering of trays and plates.

"What's your seven?" I asked Alice and she actually, literally, pulled out her notepad. "You wrote them down?" I smiled and pulled the pad over. "How did I not know you were doing this?"

"Like Becky said, we've hardly seen you." She smiled as she said it – offering out a million invisible olive branches, even though I probably didn't deserve them.

"Well come on then." I used my hands to create a drum roll on the tabletop. "Let me have them."

"Well, I've gone for Ron and Hermione from *Harry Potter*, because we had to wait sooo long for it."

Becky pulled a face. "Seriously? I do NOT see the chemistry."

"Shh. I do! And it's only number seven. Then, for six, I've put Peeta and Katniss in *Catching Fire*."

"Doesn't she kiss him in that? Rather than him kissing her?" Charlie asked.

"Exactly! See, Audrey, I can be a feminist sometimes." She looked up at me nervously and I smiled back as wide as I could, hating that she was nervous around me. Hating that I'd done this to us.

"Then, top five. At number five I put *Clueless*. The one at the top of the stairs."

"Oooh!" Becky gasped with laughter. "Incest."

"It's not incest. They're STEPbrother and -sister," I pointed out. "And Paul Rudd is GOO in that."

"Then" – Alice rustled her list, ignoring our giggles – "of course you MUST have *Breakfast at Tiffany's*. Audrey Hepburn is EVERYTHING."

She winked at me and I blushed. I HATED being named after her, especially after the divorce.

"Then *The Fault in Our Stars* kiss."

Becky pulled a face at that one. "Really? I never liked the fact they kissed in a murdered girl's house. It always kind of ruined it for me."

Alice's face fell slightly. "Oh...I didn't think of that. I think I was distracted by how much I want Augustus to be real. I will put that one down as a maybe... Then, of COURSE, there's *Romeo + Juliet*." She sighed. "Ever since we had to watch it in English last year I've been OBSESSED."

"The kiss isn't even the most romantic part of that film," Charlie said. "I think the best part is the fish tank scene, where they're both staring at each other through it." She pulled it up on her phone and there was a collective melt as we watched it, with Des'ree's "Kissing You" bleating out of her speakers.

"Maybe not kissing is sexier than kissing?" I put forward as an argument.

"Well, that gets me to number one," Alice said. "I was going to ask you if it counted, Auds. I picked *Pride and Prejudice*. The Keira Knightley one. That scene at the end, where she bumps into him at sunrise. They don't actually kiss in that one…"

I scrunched my face up. "So your favourite kiss is not actually a kiss?"

"They kiss with their eyes!" she protested.

Becky started shaking with laughter. "Imagine if we did actually kiss with our eyes. You just opened them really wide and squelched them together?"

I grinned. "Wouldn't they make a noise as you pulled them apart?"

The whole table *ewwed*.

Alice slammed her book shut. "Thanks for ruining my favourite movie for me," she said, faux-haughtily. "Now all I'm going to see when I watch that movie, is Mr Darcy leaning in with his eyes bulging, and him and Elizabeth Bennet getting their eyelashes tangled."

"I have to tell you how ardently I admire and love your juicy eye juice," I added and Charlie pushed the plate of chips away, complaining, "Can we just…stop?"

The laughter melted bits off me, like I was an iceberg being blasted with a travel-sized hairdryer. Maybe I could find me again? Find my friendship with these girls again? Maybe I could Get Through This, my feelings about Milo, my dad. There must be some old Audrey left, buried deep somewhere.

Eventually I made Alice decide; she picked Romeo and Juliet's elevator kiss. Becky stuck with *The Notebook*. And Charlie picked this film I'd never heard of called *A Room with a View* that she couldn't believe we hadn't seen, and spent the rest of lunch describing it to us. I'd forgotten how good it felt to laugh with my friends. And they must've felt the same because, when the bell went, and we all jolted up, Becky put her hand on mine ever-so-softly, and said, "It's nice to have you back, Auds."

22

Within two weeks, I had over two hundred responses to my questionnaire. A hundred in the last week after Harry had the genius idea of putting a stack in Flicker.

"I despair at people, I really do," I told him, midway through assembling a giant cardboard cut-out of Thor.

Harry turned his head to one side. "I think you've got the arms on the wrong way."

"Stupid Thor." I put him down and walked round to see it from the front. His arms were, indeed, skew-whiff. "Why are these things so hard to assemble? And, also, HOW MANY COMIC BOOK MOVIES will there be?"

Harry laughed. "Here, let me show you." He pulled both of Thor's arms off. "And don't diss comic book movies, Audrey. They keep cinemas like us alive."

I pouted. "Which therefore means I have to work every night this week."

LouLou emerged from the stock room, dragging a half-assembled Iron Man behind her like she was Jesus carrying the cross. "Hey, Audrey. Sorry, we're still behind on staff since the change up."

"Honestly, it's fine. I was just whingeing."

LouLou gave me a tight smile, one of her new special ones. "Well, I'm grateful you can cover." She shuffled into the office, leaving a half-constructed Robert Downey Jr for Harry to deal with. He sighed and got to work putting his head on. Our excitement at Ma's promotion had been short-lived. Though we hardly had to deal with her in person any more, her control-freakery was ruining LouLou's life. She rang the whole time to check and recheck we were following her explicit instructions. Harry was pulling back-to-back shifts most days, and I was on at least four shifts a week rather than my agreed three.

"So, why do you despair of people today, Audrey?" he asked, from behind his cardboard. "What haven't we covered yet?"

I wrinkled my nose at him, though he couldn't see. "I'm not *that* bad. And it's this best movie kiss thing. I've got enough results now and I'm working out all the data." I wiggled to put Thor's arm into the right hole. "And it's definitely depressing."

"I'm intrigued, continue." Harry's smile was revealed like a magic trick from behind Iron Man's head.

"Well, okay, so at least sixty per cent of everyone's favourite movie kisses occurred in the rain."

Harry nodded. "Ahh, yes, the rain kiss. You must kiss

in the rain, Audrey. That is the law of kissing in movies."

"But why? I mean, rain is cold and wet! Plus movie rain is never like normal rain. Nobody ever kisses in drizzle. It's always the really huge rain that comes out of nowhere, with added lightning."

I had a flash of a memory, of my first kiss with Milo. Which was actually in some drizzle. We'd been walking back from rehearsal and he kept trying to hold my hand but I couldn't hold his hand *and* hold my umbrella. When he'd romantically pulled it away, I'd shrieked about my hair going frizzy before I realized he was doing a gesture.

"What else, pray tell, Audrey – you romantic ray of sunshine – did your judgemental survey find?"

I picked up Thor and used it to knock his figure.

"Hey," he said. "You can't make Thor fight Iron Man. They're on the same team." I hit him harder. "Audrey, seriously, stop it. You're breaking everything I believe in."

I rolled my eyes and put Thor down again. "Well, head-clutching is another hugely popular theme. Whenever anyone kisses in the movies, they always seem to, like, grab the other person's head. It's almost always the boy clutching the girl's head to, I dunno, show off the guy's masculinity or something."

Harry smiled again, and, again, I got this notion that he would usually have made a joke or flirtatious comment at this point.

"I've got a rival to the head-clutcher," he said, putting the finishing touches to Iron Man with a "voila". "The perfectly-arranged-thumb-on-cheek kiss. Have you ever noticed that about movies? When the boy reaches out and puts his palm onto the girl's face, with his thumb pointing upward? I only notice, I think, because of my directing, because, to me, it looks awkward. Nobody kisses like that." He leaned against the cut-out, realized it couldn't take his weight and straightened himself again. "I mean, if I want to kiss someone, it's like fighting an addiction not getting to kiss them. When I finally get the chance, I would never waste time gently stroking their face." He laughed. "No, my kisses would probably look horrid on camera, but they feel great." He made straight eye contact with me and I got another flash. But this time a flash of fantasy. Of Harry grabbing my head and kissing me. Our mouths smashing against each other with urgency.

I blushed, hiding it behind Thor's head. God, I was such a ridiculous cliché. A guy likes me, and I don't like it. But then he takes the liking-me away and then, what? I want him to like me again?

Harry, maybe sensing my discomfort, moved on. "So, what else? What else do people want to see in a kiss?"

"Lesbians," LouLou interrupted, carrying in a giant Scarlett Johansson. "Where the feck are all the lesbians?"

I pointed at her. "Yes! That's also what my research unearthed. People only really voted for heteronormative kisses."

"Hetero-what-now?" Harry asked.

"Normative. It means straight couples are considered

the norm. I only had two same-sex kisses nominated, and, yeah, LouLou, you're right. They were both male-on-male kisses."

"I told you." LouLou grinned under her new blue hair. "We need more fecking lesbians."

Now that our cardboard cut-outs were individually constructed, we had to attach them all to the stand. It was a huge faff, the set was a full-on 3D grand-scale display. We paused for a while to swear and bitch at each other, shouting "No no no, Iron Man's foot goes HERE" and "Ouch, you just poked me in the eye with Captain America's finger". When we were finally done, we stepped back and admired our work. Apart from a slightly saggy Iron Man from where Harry had leaned on it, it looked okay.

"Thanks, guys," LouLou said. "If we weren't already sold out, we would be if they saw this. Now, we just have to spend every evening stopping crazed fans from nicking it. Or making the Scarlett figure do nasty things in photographs."

"Seriously?" I asked.

She nodded grimly. "Seriously. Last year Ma found actual ejaculate on the back of a Princess Leia cut-out. She took three days off work to recover. Ma! Taking three days off work. Speaking of which, you two still okay to lock up tonight? I have to go meet Her Highness this evening to 'explain why there is a discrepancy in my use of time rotas'."

Harry and I nodded. "We're fine," he said. "This spunkathon

isn't out for another two days, and most people have seen *The King and Me* now."

"Thanks, thanks." LouLou retreated back into the office, swearing under her breath.

Harry and I looked at each other for a moment – me trying to keep my blushing under control as I kept getting unwelcome flashes of us kissing in the rain.

"I guess we'd better make some guacamole," I said and we both walked to the kitchen.

"So, what other kisses have done well?" Harry picked up the conversation where we'd left off as we became a two-man factory line of avocado mashing. We'd worked together so much over the last few weeks we didn't need to communicate when it came to the making of guacamole. He would half them, I would squish them. Half, squish, half, squash. Our hands touching every time he passed me one, and him not making comments any more like, "*Audrey, I know you can't keep your hands off me, but using avocados as your wingman is a little bit weird.*"

So now, of course, I missed it.

"Grand gesture kisses. Ones where they hire out a baseball field, or stop a party to make a huge speech or something. Essentially kisses where there is applause from random members of the public."

"Eww." Harry pulled a face. "That's actually something I properly despise. How couples these days are all about publicizing their love, rather than enjoying their love? The way I see it" – Harry washed his hands under the tap and moved away to start on the cinnamon dust – "is the more you're trying to prove to people you're happy, the less happy you actually feel."

I watched his arms as he started shaking up the ingredients and my stomach did this annoying flip-flop.

"Agreed!" I said. "Milo was like that a lot actually. He always made us pose for couple selfies."

"Because he's an idiot," Harry mumbled, before apologizing.

"It's okay," I said. "I think I'm starting to get over him." The moment I said it out loud I knew it was true. It had taken half a year, but I didn't hurt so much any more, I just felt…embarrassed. About the whole sex thing. But seeing him and Courtney flaunt themselves down the hall, holding hands, loudly practising their lines in the sixth-form common room so everyone could be reminded daily that they were the main parts…well, I felt cringe-y for them. Embarrassed that I'd behaved like that when I was Milo's golden girl. And, though I was reluctant to admit it to myself, the stirring in my tummy I got when I thought about Harry may have had something to do with that. Is that how hearts work? Is love just a parasite that jumps bodies? It always exists, you always have to yearn for someone, and the only way to get over somebody is to obsess about someone else…?
"And I'm glad I'm not in *Guys and Dolls*. It sounds like a nightmare. Our new Drama Head is a crazy perfectionist and is making everyone rehearse until gone eleven most nights. I actually have more free time working here."

"And time to do my movie." Harry's eyes crinkled as he smiled. "I watched some scenes back last night. The ones where you turn." He put down his shaker and turned to really look at me. Our eyes properly boring into each other. "It's…exceptional, Audrey. The most flawless take I've ever seen. I mean, seriously… You're exceptional." He coughed. "You're an exceptional actress," he corrected himself, and I saw a hint of blush climb up the neck of his black shirt.

His blush made me blush and, to cover myself, I turned around and started clanking glasses about, mumbling about how I needed to mix the special salt for the artisan flatbread.

We worked in silence for a while. LouLou came in to taste-test the guacamole, which inevitably led to us needing to make another batch. The atmosphere felt chilled out. We knew our shift would be quiet. Once all the food was prepped, Harry went to go fiddle with the projector and I cleaned up. I thought about what he'd said, about love and publicizing it. Was he right? *Do* we project to others how we want our love to look to cover up the fact it doesn't *feel* how we want it to feel? Do we cover our relationships with mirrors, so all people get are cutesy projections rather than the truth?

Dad had uploaded yet another album of him and Jessie last night, entitled *We got a babysitter*. The album could've easily been made by two teenagers, apart from the deep wrinkles around Dad's eyes. They'd posed for selfies around London – proving their existence, their love, with St Paul's as a backdrop, Tower Bridge, the OXO Tower. *We are in love here, and here and here and here…* He'd taken Jessie up to the Sky Garden and taken so many photos of her. Some of her looking at the camera, some of her deliberately looking off into the blinking skyline of London. Pretending she didn't know the camera was there, though I'm sure she would've helped negotiate filters and sharpening techniques and the best way to crop it. Instructing him to take it again if she didn't like it, until they found one that reflected "*Them*" to "*Us*" perfectly. Each photo was diligently commented on, with *Such a lucky man* and *How gorgeous?* People robotically clicked *like* because they knew they were supposed to.

But what they didn't realize was there were so many depths to those photos they'd "liked". Depths that you couldn't see. Moments Dad had chosen not to share. Where was the photo of Mum, coming back from the lawyers last week, and sinking to the floor before she'd even closed the front door behind her? Where was the screengrab of the abusive message Dougie sent to Dad's phone, accusing him of being every explicit swear word in the English language? And, most importantly, what about the other photos that existed? We had album after album stacked in the cupboard under our stairs. And Mum still tortured herself by poring over them and littering them around the living room. Dad and Mum in Rome, on the grand romantic holiday that resulted in their proposal. Photos of Mum dressed up for classy surprise dinners. Photos of the four of us, in different incarnations of ageing and growing up, beaming into the camera, the sun on our faces, reflecting the veneer of our perfect lives. Their perfect love.

Until love, the parasite that it was, jumped from Mum onto Jessie.

The door opened and an assortment of customers trickled in for the early showing. I had to come out from behind the till to take at least four photos of people with our new cardboard cut-outs. The films started, the foyer quietened, disrupted only by the noise seeping under the doors. Harry reappeared from the projection room and helped me clean up. LouLou said goodbye in a stressed flurry of putting her coat on and carrying a giant stack of important-looking papers.

"If you get a call from me later tonight, it's because I killed Ma and I need help burying the body."

"Torture her first!" Harry called after her. "Tie her up and show her spreadsheets that don't quite balance."

The double doors swung shut behind LouLou and I seeped onto my chair. Harry groaned, clutching his neck as he lowered himself onto his stool like an old man. "I swear I'm too tall for that projection room."

"I still haven't been allowed into it," I said. "Is everything in it that breakable?"

"Yes."

Silence floated down between us, and for some reason, it was awkward. Neither of us looked at each other. There was nothing left to mop up though, no jobs to do until Screen One finished throwing popcorn into their mouths, missing, and decorating the floor.

"So, any more extra insights into what makes a great movie kiss?" Harry asked after a while. "What's the conclusion you've come to?"

I'd been trying to figure this out myself. "Well, actually, there was this one thing I noticed," I admitted. Staring at the till rather than his eyes. "Some of the winners weren't what I thought they would be. One of the most popular kisses was actually in this film called *10 Things I Hate About You*. Lots of our older customers here voted for it. It wasn't a huge movie, but I looked up the kiss on YouTube and, it's just really simple! All he does is smile at the girl, tuck her hair back and then go in for the kiss. It's the same with the other high-hitters. The common link was just how…normal the kisses were. And just how obvious it was that the characters NEEDED to kiss each other." I made myself look up at him. He was staring right at me, his hair all standing up on end, looking like he was hanging onto every syllable. I felt myself go hot. "The ones where people kiss each other just because they can't not…" I trailed off. Silence descended once more. My stomach twisted in on itself, my heart thud-thudding. I looked down at Harry's hands and he was gripping the counter.

There was something there. I felt it. I could feel it coming off him. Off me. Quickly, like a fucking idiot, my love parasite had jumped. Did I not learn? Was I the most stupid person in the world? But Harry wouldn't do anything. Not now. Not since I'd screamed abuse at him and scared him off. Which was good, I told myself. He would just hurt me; I'd been warned about him enough.

Our heads whipped up as we heard the loud music of closing credits from Screen One. The doors squeaked open, throngs of customers piled out. I sighed, stood, ripped off a bin bag.

"Audrey?" Harry called after me, as I walked towards the screen.

"Yep?" I stopped and turned around.

"Umm…do you want to see the best kiss scene of all time? Later, I mean? I feel you need to see it. For your project."

I smiled and raised my eyebrows, in what I hoped was a jokey enough way to make it clear there *wasn't* anything between us.

"Sounds ominous."

"It's good. Trust me."

I didn't trust anyone any more…

"Sure," I said.

23

It was half eleven by the time the last customers staggered out – leaving the normal trail of devastation in their wake. I was a popcorn-sucking machine by now. Able to clear an entire screen by myself in twenty minutes. But Harry pitched in, and we collected empty glasses and popcorn boxes, leaving the glassware in the kitchen for the cleaners who came in at six every morning to deep clean.

We worked in silence, a weird atmosphere floating between us. I kept wanting to look at him but I fought the urge. Trying to tell myself that I didn't *like* him, I just didn't like the fact his attention had been withdrawn. Because that's how power and lust worked. And Harry knew that. That's why I'd been so warned off him. The one time I did look up, he *wasn't* looking at me. Rather staring down the nozzle of the Hoover, checking it for a clog. I blushed and got on with stacking artisan pizza plates.

By midnight, the place was free from kernels and

discarded Coke bottles. We took out the rubbish bins together, and, once he'd slammed down the top of the skip, Harry broke our silence.

"So, you ready for the best kissing scene of all time?"

"That's quite some statement to make, Harry."

"I told you to trust me."

I followed him back into the cinema, the cold night air making me take short breaths. Harry vaulted over the counter, his long legs only just clearing it, and took two bottles of Coke off the shelf. He added a tub of chocolate buttons and scooted them towards me. "How late can you stay tonight?"

I prodded the chocolate packet, confused. "Mum's usually asleep by now, so as late as I want I guess. Though I've got college tomorrow. How come?"

Harry vaulted back over the counter, landing way too close to me. He grinned, all his teeth showing. Like a wolf...a sexy wolf... *Stop it, Audrey.* "The film's quite long. But it's worth it, and I'll have you home by three."

I ran through the maths in my head – weighing it up. If I didn't get home until three, I'd only get four hours sleep before I had to get up for college. Who was I kidding? There was no way I was saying no. For some unknown reason, I was ignoring every red flag I'd been given about Harry. For some stupid reason I was entertaining stupid thoughts. Thoughts like, *Maybe he would be different with you.* Thoughts like, *Maybe you are just the girl who changes him.* Thoughts that were everything I'd tried to teach myself weren't true in real life. It was like someone had held me upside down and shaken me until all the wisdom had fallen out.

"I'm suitably intrigued. But if you're going to make me stay up that late, it better be good."

His smile revealed even more teeth, if that was possible. "It will be."

He turned and ran up the stairs, taking them two at a time, like the children who came here waaaay too excited for the new Pixar offering. I sighed, smiled and followed him. I saw only the swinging door leading to the projection room. I climbed the steep stairs with apprehension, guided upwards by the glow of a blue light. When I got to the top, I was...underwhelmed.

"I expected it to look more magical than this," I complained to Harry's arse, which was sticking out of a box.

He straightened up, his teeth glowing blue. "It's not what you imagine, is it? Were you expecting rolls of films on reels?"

I looked around what was essentially a cupboard, with two big humming boxes emitting the blue light. "Umm, yeah. I at least expected a flickering noise. Why are we here?"

Harry was rooting around in a giant box in the corner. "I'm looking for a film reel. I know it's here somewhere." He actually climbed into the box, lifting his long spindly legs over the edge. "It must be here," he muttered to himself. "We played it on Classic Sunday just the other week...hang on..." His head vanished into the box, and he re-emerged with a smile, holding a greyish box above his head like it was the FA Cup. "Got it! Right, let me set this up. I'll meet you in Screen Two."

I crossed my arms. "What is it? What are we watching?"

"The best film about cinema ever made."

"Quite a claim."

"Not a claim. The truth, Audrey. Now, I want it to be a surprise. I'll meet you in Screen Two."

I climbed back downstairs, collected up our snacks and pushed through to the cinema. The screen was blank but the curtains had been wound back. I plonked myself in the middle and put my legs up on the seat in front. The lights went down and the screen kicked into life. No trailers, just the film certificate came up.

"*Cinema Paradiso?*" I muttered. "What?"

Harry scuttled down the aisle. He picked the seat right next to me, and grabbed the chocolate buttons out of my hand. I felt like if I hadn't had a huge go at him, he would've made a joke here, like the age-old yawn-and-put-your-arm-around, while I batted him off. But he didn't. He just chucked some chocolates into his mouth.

"You ready?"

"I've never heard of it."

"Prepare for an education, Winters."

I was about to ask more questions when the opening music started. So I settled back in my seat.

The film was subtitled, which I didn't like at first. I kept trying to look at both the movie AND the words at the bottom but found I couldn't. I squirmed in my seat, uncomfortable and slightly ashamed. I'd never watched a subtitled movie before, and Harry certainly didn't comment on it. It was set in Italy, years and years ago and, from what I could make out, it was about this young boy who was obsessed with the local cinema and became friends with the old projectionist who worked there. Then, after ten minutes or so, something just clicked in my head and I found I didn't notice I was reading subtitles.

The movie was amazing. It was beautifully shot, and charming, and so, so funny. The cinema was how I imagined cinemas to be before I started working at Flicker. The projectionist worked with giant reels of old film, where the new releases were biked in, often being carried miles and miles. There was this hilarious scene at the beginning, where the local priest watched all the movies before the town was allowed to, and rang a bell whenever anyone in the film kissed each other. The projectionist had to mark up every single kiss and cut it out – censoring the town from even the most innocent of kisses.

Soon even Harry melted away as the movie bewitched me. I watched in horror as the cinema couldn't cope with modern life, how it stopped becoming the epicentre of the town's community – as video games and technology peeled people away from each other like Cheestrings. I bit my lip as the little boy grew up and left the town and his beloved projectionist friend. And I wept when it cut to many years later, the young boy now a grown man, and he heard the projectionist had died. He returned to his old town and found the cinema in disrepair, about to be demolished. When he was given an untitled film reel, gifted to him in the projectionist's will, I was close to crying. Harry leaned over, his breath tickling my ear, jolting me out of the film slightly.

"Are you ready for it?" he asked. He gripped my hand, really quickly, before withdrawing and tucking it back into his pocket. My hand fizzed from where he'd touched me.

I watched as the man picked up the reel of film and fed it into an old projector. Then he turned off the lights and watched what his old friend had left behind for him.

I started sobbing almost instantly.

Every single kiss that the priest had removed was spliced together to make one short movie of kisses. Shy ones, passionate ones, tender ones, short ones, long ones, nervous ones, giddy ones. Kiss after kiss flickered past as the background music built to a crescendo. It was probably one of the most beautiful scenes I'd ever seen – the bittersweet sadness behind each kiss. The melody of each one, the way they built off each other. I could hardly see through my tears as I sat in the dark and the credits rolled.

Harry jumped up from his seat and vanished up the aisle, while I stayed there and cried. Then the music cut out, the lights came up and the curtains whirred shut.

I blinked and twisted towards the door, where a blurry Harry stood sheepishly at the top of the stepped aisle.

"Umm, did I break you?" he asked.

I tried to laugh, but it came out in an unattractive snort filled with tear-triggered snot. "That was..." I tried to search for a word that came even close to summing it up. "Impeccable."

"I told you." He stepped back down towards me, looking pretty darn pleased with himself. "I feel like I need to prescribe a movie list for you, one to counteract all the bad romance films you're watching for your project."

I sniffed, and ran my finger under each eye to catch the mascara slug trails. "That's a stellar kissing scene. Thank you."

"Any time." Harry scratched his neck, and the quiet between us felt like it had tiny weights attached to every atom in the air. "Are you in a fit state for me to walk you home?"

I nodded, yawned – stretching up, the lateness hitting me. "I can manage on my own."

"Audrey, it's almost three in the morning."

"Exactly, not even the most determined of attackers will stay up this late. Anyway, statistically I'm more likely to get attacked by you..."

Harry's mouth dropped open.

"Whoops," I said, smiling. "I'm too tired to filter."

"Come on, let me be a gentleman."

We locked up, setting the alarm and doing the panicked run to get out before all the red lasers activated. Then we stepped into the icy cold of the empty street.

It could've been the zombie apocalypse, it was so empty.

Harry stopped in the doorway and lit a cigarette then beckoned with his head. "Come on, crybaby, let's take you home."

I scuttled after him, slipping slightly on the crystallized pavement. We crossed the wide crossroads – the traffic lights turning from red to green to red again, commanding no traffic. I felt my thoughts drift to that scene in *The Notebook* – the one where Noah and Allie lie in the middle of the empty road. You could not be that romantic in England. I'd get frostbite of the bumhole if Harry and I lay on the ice tonight. Not that he would want to...

We wandered the deserted streets, leaving icy footprints that would freeze over again before anyone woke up to see them. We didn't talk, either out of awkwardness or tiredness. I wanted to say a million things, but also had no idea what they were. So I just tried not to look at him as we crunched along – the cold biting at the back of my throat, my shoulders hunched up in a failed attempt to keep my neck warm.

Harry seemed tense. He lit one cigarette after another, leaning into the cold, not really looking at me. What was going on? Something was definitely going on. And, as we reached the end of my road, he stopped abruptly, turning to me, but not looking me in the eye. "There's something I need to talk to you about."

"Riiiight."

He took another drag of his cigarette, blew the smoke out over my head. "Umm, well, it's two things, I guess.

Firstly, I wanted to apologize. For…well…for being flirty when you first started. It wasn't on. Sorry. You should be able to start a new job and not have some random dude hitting on you."

My tummy twisted. "It's okay," I said.

"Well, I'm sorry. I'll leave you alone, like that, I mean."

I bit my lip to stop myself yelling out, *No! I've changed my mind. Flirt with me shamelessly, please.*

"And, well, with that out of the way…" He hadn't made eye contact with me once. "I, umm, well, we kind of need to film the kissing scene this week. I've been holding off, because I know you're mad at me, and I made you uncomfortable. But it's got to the point where I really need to film the scenes I'm in… Sorry…I mean, I guess you're a good enough actress to kiss someone who pisses you off, right?"

My tummy plunged. *This* was what tonight was leading up to – not anything romantic. It had just been a gentleman-like buttering me up, so he could tackle this awkwardness. I wasn't replying, only digesting. So Harry gabbled on.

"I mean, we can try and do it in one take. And I promise I won't be all, like, well, like me. LouLou had a go at me… told me off too… I mean, I was going to apologize anyway, but I thought you'd like to know she kicked my butt."

"Harry, it's okay," I managed to stammer out. "I've done kissing scenes before." Although only with Milo, who I was also seeing, so I'd never actually kissed someone I didn't like. Not that I didn't like Harry. Actually, some sliver of me plummeted with the knowledge that acting was the only way I would get to kiss Harry now.

"Yeah, I assumed so. Even so, I wanted to talk it through with you, check it was okay."

"It's fine," I insisted. "But I appreciate you...umm... apologizing. And taking the time to talk it through."

"So, it won't be awkward?" He still wouldn't meet my eye, so he couldn't see my forced smile.

"It will if you keep asking if it's awkward."

He laughed, a hacking one that bounced around the empty street. "True, true. Anyway, that's all sorted. Come on, I'll walk you to your door. Like the gentleman I really am not."

It was my turn to laugh. Though I still felt disappointed. In a way I didn't have a grasp of yet. We walked the twenty metres or so to my door, past the sleeping Victorian terraces. When we got to my doorstep, I stopped, hovering. Exhausted from how late it was, but also, part of me not wanting to say goodbye. All the kisses from *Cinema Paradiso* flickered past my eyelids, making the bottom of my stomach ache.

"Thanks again," I said, reaching in my bag for my keys. "For the movie, and the apology, and walking me home and all."

I looked up once I'd found my keys and this time Harry was staring right at me. Our eyes met. Breathing got tricky. He reached up and ran his hands through his mad hair. "I'm sorry for the comment I made too. About you not being like other girls. You...well...I guess you're not like other girls in that you didn't melt into a puddle when I said it."

I raised my eyebrows. "So you *have* used that line before?"

"Maybe." He grinned, but didn't look proud of himself.

"I knew it."

"If it means anything, for what it's worth, I actually meant it when I said it about you. But you were right. I shouldn't be, er…turned on by your emotional trauma." He leaned forward, so our breath mingled. "I'm sorry for suggesting you are anything other than perfectly ordinary."

I instinctively leaned closer. "I'm practically dull."

Then, before I could compute what I was doing, I leaned forward to kiss him. An urgent need spreading through my stomach, up my arms, bypassing my brain. I was going to, I was going to…

"Ouch. What?"

Harry had dodged back at the last moment. I clashed my head into his jaw, the pain radiating through my skull. It was like someone had injected a syringe full of humiliation directly into my heart.

"Shit, I'm sorry. I'm so sorry," I yelped.

Harry was rubbing his jaw. "What was that?"

My keys were in my fingers, my back was to him. I fumbled with the lock. I had to get out of here. Oh my God, I'd tried to kiss him and ended up headbutting him. Like a freaking…WWE wrestler.

"I don't know what happened. I'm sorry. I have to go. Thanks for…everything…sorry."

The door opened. I couldn't get through it quickly enough. What was wrong with me? Seriously, what was I doing? I HEADBUTTED HIM. I needed to not be here. I needed to escape what I'd just done, how embarrassed I felt.

I heard laughter as I bowled through the door. "Audrey? Wait. Come on! Audrey, come back."

But I was safely over the threshold and I swung the door shut in Harry's face, running up to my bedroom. Peeling off my coat and scarf, like they were layers of humiliation I could remove. I heard him call through the glass one last time, more urgently. I ignored it. I got into my bedroom, dived under the covers and curled up in a ball.

24

It's safe to assume I didn't sleep much.

Whenever I closed my eyes, it all came back. Me lurching in like an unattractive freight train. Lunging with my mouth open. Smashing into Harry's face.

One thing was very clear. I needed to stop doing sexual things with boys. I was obviously incapable. Of being alluring. Of putting my head in the right position. Of knowing someone was interested. Or even where their mouth was, as opposed to their jaw.

The shame was so huge that I even cried, smothering my face into my pillow so Mum wouldn't hear me.

He'd laughed.

I'd tried to kiss him, and he'd laughed.

Why had I tried to kiss him?

The night dragged on. I grabbed snatches of sleep where I could. But it was like a film entitled *Audrey's Sexual Humiliation* had been pushed into my mind and some evil twat had pressed the *play* button repeatedly.

Flashes of Milo's hands on me, and then how they flopped off my body when he couldn't get in. Flashes of him saying *It's okay, it's okay* over and over, but not looking me in the eye. Harry's laugh bouncing off my shoulder. My head hitting his jaw… I'd tried so hard to repress this. So hard to run away from the zinging shame of what happened with Milo and now, kissing Harry and embarrassing myself AGAIN, sent it catapulting back. All the more vividly as the humiliation had had months to stew inside the locked vaults of my mind.

I was jarred awake by my alarm clock. I lurched up in bed to bash it onto snooze. I closed my eyes slowly, feeling sleep finding me, then…

It all came rushing back and I was too humiliated to even doze for ten minutes. I got up and showered, to try and wash off my shame. I gathered my hair up, squeezing it into Mum's flowery shower cap so I could stand totally under the water. Then I dried off. I shoved on some clothes for school and lumbered downstairs.

Mum was whistling in the kitchen, stirring a pan of porridge. "Morning. Didn't hear you come in last night."

The only way through this morning would be coffee. I went to put the kettle on. "I stayed at work late, there was this…umm…thing I had to watch after closing."

A beautiful film made of kisses where people didn't lurch in madly and smack heads…

"I worry you're not getting enough sleep."

"It's fine, I'm good. I like my job."

Mum's whistling turned to humming as she poured her porridge into a bowl. "I've made enough for you."

"Amazing, thank you."

We ate in what I guess she would assume was contented silence. I was too tired to analyse why she was so cheerful. Mum finished before me and clattered around the kitchen, asking if I wanted to maybe watch a film later tonight as I wasn't working. "Although you're probably sick of movies, aren't you?"

I grunted non-committally, dripping porridge into my mouth like a baby bird, thinking.

I had some initial thoughts:

- I needed to quit my job, sharpish – even though it was the only thing I liked right now
- And the zombie movie
- And then go hide somewhere where Harry would never be
- ...and possibly get some advice on how to go about doing this.

I needed brutal, honest advice.

I needed Leroy.

He couldn't stop laughing.

"Leroy, stop it! It's not funny!"

He threw his head back as we skidded along the icy pavements to school together. I was already doubting if tough love was actually what I needed this time.

"Oh, but, Audrey, it is. You HEADBUTTED him."

I shook my head and tried to storm off in a mood, but it was too slippy to really storm off anywhere properly.

"Audrey? Come on, Audrey!"

I sighed, stopped.

"Sorry," he said eventually. "I'm just in shock. I thought you were sworn off boys?"

"I am."

"So headbutting him was an attack?"

My face glowed again at the memory; it was going to take a long time to get immune to it. "No, I was trying to kiss him."

"But…" It was no good. Leroy collapsed into laughter again and I couldn't laugh back. Not yet. It was still too raw and ripe and, oh God…I could never see Harry again! I was too ashamed.

Also, as I thumped Leroy on the arm and told him I didn't want to talk about it any more, I realized I was something else.

I was confused.

Nothing about what I'd done last night made any sense.

I had Media first thing. Mr Simmons paced the room, talking about the different types of film shots we would need to know for our exams, but I couldn't concentrate. I descended into a confused-about-Harry abyss, trying to make sense of my emotions. Alice scribbled notes eagerly and I watched her pen move over the page. She was the only person I knew who still put circles as the dots of her i's. She must've sensed something was wrong because she pulled out a page of her notebook.

Everything okay??

I picked it up, wondering what to do. When Milo broke up with me, shattering any emotional progress I'd made since Dad left, I'd thought I only wanted harsh honesty. People who didn't sugar-coat. Or bullshit. Or simper. Or say things would be okay when they wouldn't be. That's why I'd gravitated towards Leroy – he was the embodiment of that. But now my heart had begun to open again. Working with Harry on the movie, embracing my pain rather than staying numb, I'd started to actually work through some of it. And the crushing embarrassment of yesterday was my big wake-up call. I couldn't shut out what had happened any more – it was resurfacing like potent acid reflux and I didn't know what to do or where to go or how I felt. It made me realize I needed…girls.

Not just girls, The Girls.

I shook my head and scribbled back.

Not really. Can we do coffee later?

Alice was still. She stared at the page, probably as shocked as I was. After essentially freezing her out for six months, she was entitled to write *Piss off, Audrey.*

Instead, she just wrote *Sure*, followed by two smiley faces with hearts for eyes, and I almost welled up at the kindness.

The lesson dwindled on and I took no notes. So when Mr Simmons asked me to stay behind, I prepared myself for a telling-off.

"Audrey, sit." He gestured to a chair he'd pulled over to his desk. "You got a class right now?"

"I'm free until after lunch."

"Good. Well then, I've been meaning to chat to you."

The apology was on my lips when he charged right on. "It's about this coursework of yours. I read through the kissing research you did and, well, Audrey. It's impressive."

"It…it…is?" I'd never excelled at any subject other than Drama before.

"It is. It was very interesting, but more than that, I like how you've interpreted the statistics. I was marking last night, and I hope you don't mind, but I showed my wife. She was riveted. She also told me to tell you that it's a travesty that *A Room with a View* only got one nomination."

"Hey, don't shoot the messenger."

He laughed. "Anyway, I didn't call you back just to share my wife's opinions. It's about two things actually. The first is about the project itself. I thought you'd benefit from maybe adding a professional opinion."

"Sir?"

"Like interviewing an expert? See what they have to say about *10 Things I Don't Like About You*."

"I *hate* about you."

"You know what I mean." He batted my correction away with his hand. "But maybe ring a relationship therapist, someone like that? See if they'll talk to you."

I chewed my lip. A relationship therapist? Was there such a thing? "Will I get extra marks?"

He rolled his eyes. "Yes. And, God forbid, Audrey, you may also find it interesting."

"Okay…" It couldn't hurt. My other grades were tanking. I fiddled with my bag strap. "What's the other thing?"

"I was just going to ask about your uni application. Where are you thinking of going? What subject do you want to do? Do you know?"

I shook my head. It was always going to be Drama, Drama, Drama. That's all it had ever been. What I'd spent my whole life working towards. And then Milo had happened and I'd just dropped it.

Hang on…

For a second, the hugeness of that thought hit me. WHAT THE HELL? I DITCHED Drama because of Milo? Because I was embarrassed?

It was like a ton of concrete dropped on my head. Not only had I allowed my shame to mess up my relationships with people, but I'd allowed it to screw up school as well. Not just school – my whole future. I twisted my hands around on themselves, hardly listening to Mr Simmons blah on about UCAS as the enormity of that decision grabbed me in a chokehold, making me gasp for air. How had I allowed this to happen to my life? How had Mum and Dad let me do this? They were too busy imploding to save *me* from imploding. I mean, Leroy had tried, once, to talk me out of it but all I could remember was crying so hard in humiliation that I could barely hear what he said. My Drama teacher had tried before he left but I was so, so determined to quit.

"Audrey?"

I mean, what was I thinking? I'd just given Milo that power over me? To ruin my chances, to take away the thing I loved the most?

"Audrey?"

Mr Simmons's voice cut through my fog of revelation.

"Yes?"

"I was just saying, I could help you write your personal statement. If you *did* want to apply for a Media Studies degree that is."

"Huh? You think I should do Media? At university?"

"Yes." He had his hands together in a praying motion. "It's something to think about. The deadline isn't for another month or so, but you should really get a move on."

I smiled through closed lips – his words unleashing all sorts of emotions. I guessed I should feel good. That he thought I could get into uni, that I'd found a subject, besides Drama, that I was okay at.

"I guess I could apply…" I trailed off. I hadn't even thought about university. Dad obviously wanted me to go so he could turf Mum out of the house. But since he left, and especially since Milo, I'd just focused on getting through each hour, each day, each week. The Future was something intangible. Something I would worry about later, once I'd got through the complicated act of continuing to breathe when it felt like my world had caved in.

"That's great, just great." He beamed at me, like I'd jumped up and air-punched with joy. "Well, shall we check in next week? You can have some time to think about it. Plus" – he screeched back his chair, lifting his arms up to reveal small sweat patches seeping through his shirt – "a friend of my wife's is a couples counsellor, shall I ask her if she'd be willing to talk to you?"

I nodded slowly. "Yeah, umm, sure. That would be… ace."

"I look forward to reading the interview then!"

"Yep."

He smiled and held his coffee mug upside down. "Whoops, out of caffeine. I better go top up my levels."

I pretended to laugh. He swooshed out of his classroom, leaving me sitting at an empty desk, surrounded by empty chairs, blinking a lot as if the act would dislodge all the thoughts cramming into my skull – punching each other in the face. The school was quiet – everyone had finished migrating from one lesson to another, the corridors eerily empty. I picked up my bag and strode through them, looking at my phone.

Alice: Can chat now? At Nero. Hope you're okay x

Reading it melted away some of my bad feelings.

Audrey: On my way x x x

The conversation with Mr Simmons had taken my mind off things for a whole ten minutes, but the shame bloomed in me as soon as I stepped off school property.

I really did need a girl to talk to.

25

Alice had managed to bagsy the squashy sofas at the back –
the prime Nero seats. She had a hot chocolate with cream
and marshmallows in front of her and was reading her
Media notes. I ordered a cup of tea and then brought it over,
feeling nervous for some reason.

"Hey," I said, and she looked up. "Thanks for agreeing to
meet me."

She frowned. "Why wouldn't I?"

*Because I've been a judgemental bitch and essentially cut
you and the other girls out since summer...*

I put my drink down and fell into the sofa. It immediately
swallowed me whole, sinking me towards Alice so our
thighs were touching. "Well, I know I've been a bit off these
past few months."

The wings of her eyeliner twitched. "You've been through
a lot, Audrey. We understand."

She said *we*. Implying that she and the girls had discussed it, discussed me, made a joint decision on how to handle my sudden iciness.

"It's not an excuse though," I said. And it wasn't. I was realizing so many things that day. Headbutting Harry had been like dousing myself with ice-cold water. The embarrassment of it had awoken all the senses (and sense) I'd buried – made me look back at my numbness, and bad decision-making and think: *What the actual hell?*

Alice smiled and took a sip of her drink – the cream sticking to her nose. I tapped my nose to let her know.

"Whoops, thank you." She rubbed it off. "So, what did you want to talk about? Is everything okay?"

I nodded my head, then shook it again. "No, not really."

"What is it?"

I leaned forward, trying to figure out where to start. "You know that guy, Harry? The one I work with?"

"Yes," Alice replied seriously.

"Well…umm, last night, he kind of did this really nice thing for me. After work. And, well, he walked me home after and…" I squeezed my eyes shut – the memory smacking me round the head like it was made of steel. "I… I tried to kiss him."

"You *tried*? What does that mean? Did he push you off?"

I squeezed my eyes shut tighter, digging my thumbs into them, like I could claw the memory out. "No. Well, he didn't have the chance to. Cos I…well… I, just, like, lunged at him…but I missed." I opened my eyes, to find Alice staring at me intently. "I headbutted him, Alice."

"Right..."

"Like, my jaw went for his, but he moved his head, so I just careered into him." I covered my hands with my eyes, but rather than crying, I let out a laugh.

"Did you hurt him?"

I giggled again. "Maybe."

I heard a snort and removed my hands to see Alice struggling to contain herself. "It's not funny!"

"I know. I know it isn't..." But she snorted, covering her mouth to catch it. "It's just...well..." She really lost it then, and I did too. We crumpled into hysterics, sinking into each other, each of our giggles setting the other one off. I'm not sure why I could laugh with her but not with Leroy. Maybe it was still too raw this morning and now I'd had time for it all to sink in. Or maybe there's a type of laughter that only feels good with old friends. But we laughed and laughed until the final ice particle in my heart thawed out completely.

My tea was lukewarm by the time we managed to stop.

"I am sorry." Alice wiped under her eyes to catch any stray eyeliner. "It just wasn't what I was expecting. So, what happened after you headbutted him?"

"Nothing. I ran inside and slammed the door in his face. I'm going to quit my job so I never have to see him again."

"Audrey," she sing-songed, rolling her eyes. "You can't quit your job. You love it there. I know it's embarrassing..."

"It's more than embarrassing. I want to die."

"Come on. We've all had a false-start kiss somewhere

along the line. Remember that Jake boy, the one I pulled on the French trip? And he bit me?"

"That was someone biting you, not you biting someone else."

"Well I'm sure I've been a bad kisser in the past."

I couldn't imagine it. Everything Alice did was neat. Her perfect cat flicks were the tip of her orderly iceberg. She'd never once messed up the hard-to-do hand when applying nail polish.

"Oh God." I flopped my head back, sacrificing it to the gods.

"Oh, Audrey, stop torturing yourself," she said, a laugh still in her voice. "What were you doing kissing him anyway? I thought you said he was a fuckboy?"

"He is."

"So, what happened?"

So I sipped my lukewarm tea and filled her in. On the warnings I'd had about him, of his flirtation, of the zombie filming. I told her about our not-like-other-girls fight, and she smiled, and said, "Honestly, Audrey," but let me continue. Then I filled her in on the previous evening – the late-night private show, the way he'd backed off, apologized, respected my wishes and then…then…then I'd headbutted him. And I found myself crying, wiping frantically below my eyes to try and catch my tears.

Alice sprang into action immediately, sitting closer, saying, "Hey, hey, hey," blocking my tears with her body, so the rest of the coffee shop didn't stare. "Why are you crying?"

"I just…just always make stupid decisions about boys." I sniffed. "I always end up making a massive twat of myself. After Milo, I told myself I'd do better. And I just caved and have humiliated myself all over again."

"Hey, Audrey. Hang on, I've got a tissue." She dug in her bag and handed it over. I took it gratefully. "You didn't humiliate yourself with Milo. I mean, it's shit that he went off with Courtney, but you didn't do anything wrong…"

"I did. I put him off me."

"What? How?"

I brushed more tears away. Could I tell her? I hadn't told anyone. I'd just tried to vanish into the walls. It was my most shameful moment. Even saying it out loud could rip me into shreds.

"We…had sex," I admitted, not looking her in the eye. "Well, we tried to. It didn't quite work. Then he broke up with me."

I heard her intake of breath. "You lost it to Milo?" I nodded, then shook my head again. "We tried to. I'm not sure if what happened counts… It…it…hurt, Alice. Is it supposed to hurt? He, like, literally couldn't get in…" My face was so red, tears shooting out of my eyes. I could hear my voice shake.

Alice picked up my hand and squeezed it and the kindness of it flooded my body. Why had I shut out my best friend? Why did I think that was the answer to anything?

"No, Audrey," she said. "It's not supposed to hurt. Tell me if I'm being too explicit, but, like, did he do anything…

beforehand? To, you know? Make you ready?"

I flinched at the memory, because he hadn't. Not really. Not ever. We went from kissing straight into sex, that weekend when Mum going away miraculously coincided with our six-month anniversary. We'd been kissing and it had felt amazing, and he'd been kissing my neck and it had felt amazing, and he'd asked if it was okay to take off my bra, and I'd said yes, and he'd kissed me there, and it felt amazing. Then he'd asked me if he could take off my knickers, and I'd mumbled yes, and I'd even been impatient for it, because if everything else had felt so amazing, surely this would? And then...then... I flinched again. His fingers had just jerked inside me. Prodding, angry. Ripping through me. I'd had to bite my lip to not scream out from it hurting. And Milo's finger had just pummelled at me, poking in and out aggressively, each time scratching even more. But I hadn't said anything, because, well, maybe this was just what being fingered was like? And maybe something was wrong with me for not enjoying it? Milo had slept with other girls, so he *had to* know what he was doing. I had to be the one who was wrong. So I pretended to moan, and that made him harder and more aggressive, and I'd had to turn my head so he wouldn't see me cry, as I really didn't want to ruin the moment. When he'd stopped, I'd been so relieved. But then he was taking off his boxers and I knew whatever he had planned next would hurt even more...

I snapped back into the present. "No," I said. "Well, he tried. But...umm...what he tried wasn't very nice."

Oh God, the shame of it. She was going to think I was a prude, a buttoned-up, dysfunctional prude.

But then Alice said... "Let me guess? He prodded at you like he was a farmer shoving his arm up the backside of a cow to pull out a baby calf, and you're wondering why you didn't come?"

I turned to her, my mouth open. "You could say that." I wasn't sure if I could handle saying any more. But this was Alice. Alice. And she seemed to understand. And I'd been carrying it with me for so long. Maybe I should let it out. "He couldn't really get high up. It hurt too much." I chewed my lip. "I'm not sure what happened but it was like my vagina sort of...sort of...rejected him..."

Alice smiled, ever so slightly. "So, when he tried with his...you know."

I nodded, astonished at how she got it. "You know that bit in the first *Lord of the Rings* film? Where Gandalf stands up to that fire demon on the bridge and yells, 'YOU SHALL NOT PASS'? Well..." I paused, feeling so ashamed. "Essentially my vagina had a Gandalf standing at the entrance, and he thought Milo's dick was a fire demon."

Alice snorted so hard, the hot chocolate she'd been drinking shot out her nose, dribbling over her perfectly made-up face. "Oh God! Audrey!"

I couldn't laugh with her, it still felt so wrong. "You see why I'm upset now? It was bad enough as it was, and then Milo dumps me because of it. And then, for some reason I don't even understand, I try to kiss Harry and can't even do that. I'm sexually defunct. I should just have sex with myself, like potatoes do."

Alice was still cleaning up her face with a napkin. "Why are you blaming yourself for this? Milo is so obviously the arse here."

"You can't blame him."

"For what?" she said, her hand on her hip. "For prodding you like you're all the buttons in Willy Wonka's Great Glass Elevator, and then dumping you for not creaming all over the elevator?"

"I think both of us need to stop with the metaphors right now."

We both giggled. I couldn't believe she'd made me giggle. With everything I'd just told her. "How do you know all this anyway?" I asked her.

She blew her fringe up. "Oh God, because I've been there, Audrey! You remember when we went to Newquay?"

I nodded. The four of us had gone on this ridiculously clichéd drunken week away to Cornwall after our GCSEs. I still slept in my souvenir T-shirt sometimes, when Milo's was in the wash. It had a faint stain on it from the night I vommed up a lifetime's supply of jelly shots.

"Well, you know that guy, Jared? The sexy surfer I met?"

I nodded again. We'd all been so jealous when she'd pulled him. He had long, blond dreads and could actually surf.

"Well, there was this one night, I think it was the night you were really sick from those jelly shots? Well, he invited me back to his caravan, and, you know I was a virgin…

and I thought, *I may as well lose it to someone as good-looking as him.* Because that's the sort of stupid thing you think about virginity sometimes."

I stayed quiet, stirring my tea with a spoon. She hadn't mentioned this, or Jared, again since that holiday. It was well over a year ago.

"Well, we did it. And…it wasn't great, Audrey. For some stupid reason, I thought because he was so good-looking, he must have had lots of experience and know what he was doing. But, well, he didn't. It hurt, I bled everywhere, he complained he'd have to pay a fine for me getting blood on the sheets."

My mouth fell open. "What? I had no idea! You never said anything!"

She looked down at her hot chocolate. The marshmallows had all melted, leaving a gooey crust on the top. "Well, I was embarrassed. And ashamed. I thought there must've been something wrong with me."

"Do the other girls know?"

She surprised me by nodding. "Yeah, they do. It sounds ridiculous but I was so upset that I eventually ended up ringing a helpline to talk about it. To check nothing was wrong with me. They were amazing and so reassuring. And that gave me the courage to tell the girls in the summer. I got drunk when we went to V Festival and eventually told them…" She trailed off. Politely not mentioning the fact they'd invited me but I hadn't gone. Glossing over the fact their friendship had grown and evolved and they'd shared things without me – which was totally my fault. But she never said as much. Still though, she'd kept that to herself for a year.

"So, what I'm trying to say, Audrey, is Milo is the dick. Milo is the person who is crap in bed, for not caring about whether something feels good for you or not. You shouldn't feel humiliated. I think what you had happen is quite… normal."

I was quiet, digesting, before I said, "That's a depressing thought. On behalf of all women everywhere."

She shook her head. "I can't believe he dumped you right afterwards. No wonder you've been…" She trailed off and went red, burying her face in her hot chocolate.

"An antisocial bitch?"

She rolled her eyes again over the cup. "That's quite a strong statement, Auds. But, well, we've missed you."

I felt like I was waking up from a coma. But a coma I'd been complicit in creating over the last six months. Why had I shut the girls out? Why had I judged them so harshly? Why had I let Milo, and his behaviour, hit me so hard? Potentially even ruining the rest of my life? I'd dropped Drama because of him. No…that wasn't fair on him. I'd dropped it because of me. I'd chosen to blame myself; I'd chosen to be too ashamed to confront him, or what happened. I'd chosen to hang out with Leroy, feeling like I didn't deserve the subtle, supportive hand-squeezing of my oldest friends. In trying to outrun my shame, I'd left so many important things behind.

"I'm really sorry." A cry caught in my throat. "I know I've not been very friendly. There's just been so much going on. The Milo thing, and it hurt so much when he got together with Courtney. And my dad. He's making us leave our house, and Mum's a state and...now this fucking Harry thing has happened. But it's not an excuse."

I was blown backwards by the force of her hug. I'd forgotten Alice was a hugger. My tea almost went flying as she launched into me, flinging her arms behind me, squeezing me like I was a teddy bear.

"Don't be stupid, Audrey." The smell of her vanilla perfume was so strong. "You've been through a lot. And it's not like you've been horrid to us. You've just been a bit distant, that's all."

I relaxed into her hug. Enjoying it even though I felt I didn't deserve it. "Thanks," I mumbled back. "I'll try not to be so...solitary from now on."

She broke free, smiling sweetly, her lip gloss smudged from our embrace. Her hand flew to her face and she dived into her handbag and got out her hand mirror and Clinique Chubby Stick to sort it out. "We're friends, we're here for you. And maybe this space did you some good. Allowed you to figure things out? And, well, through it you met Harry?"

"Oh God," I groaned, slapping my hands over my eyes. Reliving it for the ninety-millionth painful time.

"Honestly though, Audrey," Alice said. "Headbutt aside. What's going on with you and him? Do you like him?"

I shook my head slowly. "I don't know. I think so. I mean,

it's really hard not to. He's so freaking charming, but it's more than that. He's so…passionate about films, and he makes me laugh when I least expect it. Agh, I don't know." I picked up my drink, sipped some and plopped it down. "*Everyone* has told me he's trouble. I'm not sure what came over me last night. He's not the sort of guy to get involved with after getting dumped by someone like Milo. I will definitely end up with my heart stamped on."

"You don't know that for sure. I mean, the guy sat up with you until 3 a.m. to show you a romantic film. Maybe he likes you…"

Those words. Just hearing those words was like someone had tipped sherbet into my intestines. Oh God, that wasn't good. That's what happens when you like someone.

"I think he's just intrigued by me. Because I didn't fall for him straight away. You know?"

Alice raised her eyebrows. "God forbid he actually likes you for you. No, according to Audrey, it's only because you're a challenge."

"But I *am* a challenge. Well, I was… And now I've fallen for him, like everybody bloody else, and now I've also headbutted him…" I covered my eyes again. "It's probably a good thing. Maybe the headbutt was my subconscious deliberately sabotaging things, so I wouldn't get hurt? It's just a shame I have to quit my job now."

"Don't be ridiculous. Don't quit your job! You like it there. No offence, Audrey, but you've got to stop running away from stuff. Drama, us. And you have to face Harry if you want to carry on with this zombie movie, right? I mean, you're enjoying that?"

I nodded. I was. I really was.

"Just be a grown-up and pretend it never happened." Alice beamed. "Like I did with Jared. I managed to keep that up for a whole year!"

I tilted my head at her. "I'm sorry about what happened with him. It sounds awful."

She shrugged. "It's fine now. I wasn't, like, permanently damaged. I've just learned to wait for a guy who makes sex feel unpressured and, dare I say it, pleasurable. Wait until I find a guy I really like, and maybe, I dunno, build up to sex with him rather than jumping into it. Maybe that's what you should think about with Harry. Are you just repeating a Milo situation? I mean, you fell for him even when me, Becky and Charlie were warning you he was a bit of a dick. But you were so upset about your family, you just seemed to get lost in him."

I'd forgotten that. Forgotten that the girls had never liked Milo. Her words hit several nails on several heads. "I guess that's what my concern is," I admitted. "I mean, I worry Harry won't be any different for me to how he is with other girls."

"Well then. Don't go there if you don't trust it, or him. Or do go there, but keep your eyes open. I mean, if I were you, I would go there and keep my eyes WIDE open, because, well, look at him."

"Alice!" I thumped her.

"I'm just saying."

And, just like that, we were back. We laughed and slurped our drinks and caught up on news and the walls I'd carefully constructed around myself fell away. I didn't even flinch when she insisted on taking ten million selfies. Because that was just Alice. Mentor and beauty junkie – capable of both incredible personal insight and brilliant knowledge of the best filters. I'd opened up to her and she hadn't judged me. I could only do the same for her. She asked about Dad and I told her everything and she hugged me again. She even invited me to a girls' night in they'd planned that weekend. And I found I genuinely wanted to go, even though I couldn't as I was pulling a double shift.

For the first time in a long time, I felt good. I felt warm. I felt less alone. It was like my hardened defences had been hacked through with the back of a spoon, like the top of a crème brûlée. We hugged goodbye before I went into lessons, and I said I'd have lunch with them. I did, and it was nice. And my afternoon lessons weren't so boring. And I'd almost forgotten everything, until…

…until I came home and found Harry sitting on my front wall.

26

THE BIG DATE

<u>Common dates in romance movies:</u>
Seats in a box at the opera or ballet
Walking around a beautiful foreign city
Night-time picnics in empty parks
Finding some gorgeous abandoned house that the
boy fills with candles

<u>Common dates in real life:</u>
Nando's…

✱ ✱ ✱ ✱ ✱

Harry held his hands up when he saw me, and pretended to duck. "Please don't hurt me again."

I stopped in my tracks, heat starting in my little toes and shooting up through my body like when you shove a Refresher into a bottle of Coke. "What are you doing here?"

He rubbed his jaw. "I'm not sure. You see, I had a bit of a thump last night and I have short-term memory loss. Where am I? What year is it? What's my name?"

"Your name is Arsehole."

He stood up, slightly blocking my path to the house and smiling apologetically. "Audrey, we are British! We MUST make a joke about something awkward happening. Otherwise we'll combust."

I blinked, and made myself look at him. "How's your jaw?"

God, I wanted to DIE.

"It's okay, a little bruised. How's your pride?"

I raised my eyebrows. "It's okay, a little bruised. It's my sense of judgement I'm most worried about, to be honest."

At that, his smile drooped. He took a step closer, and just his closeness made my heart thud against my ribs. "Okay, can we be serious?"

I let my silence be my yes.

"Audrey, I like you," he said, just like that. "I didn't think you liked me back. In fact, I was quite sure you hated me, so I've been killing myself trying to be polite so I didn't get yelled at again. But your headbutt, Audrey…" I was blushing and suffocating at the same time. "Your headbutt taught me to hope in a way I've never hoped before." I shook my head in disbelief and he held up his hands. "I told you, I'm being serious. So, umm. Can I ask you on a date or something? For like, now?"

I didn't know what to say. I felt paralysed by his words,

how they made me feel. "Why aren't you at work?" I managed to ask.

"I asked Sunday Sam to pull an extra shift. It's his first time working a not-Sunday since the dawn of time."

"Is he going to be okay?" I asked. Sunday Sam was old and easily confused. He kept complaining that he didn't believe in this "barcode on phone thing".

"I don't care," Harry answered. "I only care whether you're going to let me take you out or not."

I looked up at my house. I wasn't sure how I felt about Harry standing outside it. I wasn't sure if Mum was home yet, what state she'd be in.

"You do realize waiting outside my house like this could constitute stalking?"

He shrugged. "I didn't think you'd answer your phone. And, if you tell me to piss off, I promise I will never sit outside your house ever again."

I sighed and pushed my hair back over my shoulders. "Where does someone like you even take a girl out, anyway?"

Harry released his teeth. "Why do you keep answering my questions with other questions?"

"Because I don't know what my answer is, to be honest."

He stepped forward. "Your answer is yes, Audrey."

Was it? He was being very forward which I liked, even though I knew I shouldn't. Different parts of my body had different answers – like someone had scribbled all over me with crayon, dividing me up like a butcher's chart. I let out a huge breath, blowing my hair up off my face, not quite able to look at him. "Oh God, okay then. I think."

His smile was so huge that I almost fell over from the strength of it. "That's a yes!"

"It's an okay then."

"Okay means yes."

"Kind of, but less definitely."

"Audrey, I think it's important to be honest. Not only with me, but with yourself. You like me."

I crossed my arms, still smiling. "Oh do I?"

"Of course you do. Why wouldn't you?" He gestured down at himself. "And I've already told you, I like you." He held up his hands, as if expecting another attack. "And not because I think you're special, or different, or magic, or not-like-the-others, or that you're going to save me from my coma of a life. Nope. You're just a girl, with a collection of hormones and body parts and life experiences and characteristics – like everybody else. I just happen to *like* the particular combination of those that you have, and would like to take you and your ordinariness to the seaside." He sucked in the breath he'd used up from all his long sentences.

I blinked at him. "The seaside?"

"Yes, the seaside. Why not the seaside?" He stepped closer and closer, invading my personal space. Our ribs almost touching. His nearness made my body take control of the steering wheel, karate-kicking my logic out the passenger door, where it rolled onto the dusty roadside with a groan.

"Umm. Because it's midwinter? It will be freezing."

He looked me up and down, in a way that made me go even redder. "Audrey, you are wearing a coat. And I'll let you go inside and get a hat and scarf too. That is the sort of gentleman I am."

I felt the twitch of the curtains from the front room. I reluctantly turned away to see Mum's face disappear behind the netting. Harry followed my gaze. And, sensing my hardening, he stopped taking the piss, his eyes all serious when I turned back.

"Audrey? Let me take you to the seaside. It will be fun, I promise."

I watched this amazing documentary once, called *Man on Wire*, about a tightrope walker who pulled off a huge feat to tightrope walk from one tower of the World Trade Center to the other. There was this bit where he talked about the moment he had to step off the ledge, onto the tightrope. He had one foot on the ledge, and one foot on the wobbling rope. All he had to do was shift his balance and he'd go from safety, to the potential of plummeting head first.

I looked into Harry's eyes, searching for answers I knew I didn't have. *Can I trust you? Will you break my heart? Am I really stupid enough to think you will treat me differently? Are we going to do this? Is it going to be worth it?*

Then I sighed again, shifted my centre of gravity and stepped out onto the rope. "Let me get my stuff."

27

Mum was in the kitchen, pretending she hadn't been spying on me.

"Oh, hi, Audrey," she said, chopping up a butternut squash. "You here for dinner?"

I smiled at her, as my entire body seemed to be smiling for some reason.

"Umm, actually Harry's outside, I'm going out with him tonight." I rummaged amongst the coat hooks in the hallway, looking for my hat and gloves, pondering whether to be honest with her. "It's just for this movie thing," I said, deciding against it. "We're doing some filming."

She smiled at me as I returned fully bundled up. "Just for filming then?" She raised an eyebrow. "Of course."

We laughed at each other and I felt a warm pang in my body. For this small moment. Where she was acting like a normal mother and me a normal daughter. Both of us pretending the heap of emotional debris scattered over the house didn't exist.

"Well, have fun. I've got Sandra coming over tonight anyway."

"You have fun too."

Harry was smoking when I re-emerged, but when he saw me, he chucked the cigarette over his shoulder where it landed, still lit, in the middle of the road. "And she is a vision of layers."

I stopped and twirled on my garden path, like I was on a catwalk. "And you can't even see my incredibly sexy thermal underwear."

He laughed until it turned into a heavy smoker's cough and he had to bend over on himself. "Please don't talk about your underwear on a first date." He coughed again before straightening up and leaping off the wall. "We are in the beginning stages, Audrey. Even your thermal underwear will do it for me."

I blushed so much I was glad practically all my face was obscured by winter clothing, and followed him as he started walking down my road. He wore only his aviator jacket over his jeans and shirt, and a grey beanie hat, and I wondered how he wasn't dying of cold.

"The beginning of what?" I asked, just as we stopped outside Tad's car. Harry must've borrowed it for the evening. He ignored me for a moment – clambering in to unlock the passenger door from the inside. He opened it with a hard yank, his face appearing in the gap.

"I'll let you be the decider of that," he replied, and I climbed in.

The car stank of stale weed and leftover McDonald's, like it always did. I noticed it wasn't quite as filled up with crap as it usually was. Harry must've cleared out the piles of polystyrene boxes that normally hid under the seats. I was just putting on my seat belt, when I found his face right in front of mine.

"Woah, hi, Harry," I said, the tip of his nose almost touching mine.

"Audrey, it's important we get something out of the way."

"What is it?"

Harry just gently grabbed my face and kissed me.

28

My thigh was wedged into the gearstick. And when Harry's hands moved down to my neck, I almost jolted because they were so cold. But, generally, I just melted. Of course he was good at kissing. Of course he didn't slobber or dishwasher or tongue-dart or do any of the things that sound horrid but, actually, would be remarkably useful when it came to nipping this potentially dangerous liaison in the bud. Alas, when he leaned away, my mouth almost followed his, wanting more.

He started the car and pulled off, like nothing had ever happened.

"You grabbed my head," I said dumbly.

"I did indeed. I didn't stroke your cheek though. As I said – much too awkward to pull that one off in real life." He indicated and revved out onto the local A road.

I wanted to touch my lips, to check they were still warm from his. To check it was real.

"The thing is, Audrey…" He put the car into fourth. "Is that yesterday, you headbutted me."

I was about to blush but he leaped on.

"And I thought maybe you'd be embarrassed about that. Even though you shouldn't be. Because that headbutt showed me I may actually have a chance with you. So I thought I'd exorcize the memory of the headbutt, so we can move on with our day. Our date."

Harry was speeding and I tugged at my seat belt to make sure it was still tight. "So it was a tactical kiss?"

"Oh, yeah. No meaning to it whatsoever."

I rolled my eyes when he wasn't looking.

It was about a thirty-minute drive to Brighton, probably quicker because Harry drove too fast. My hands clenched onto my kneecaps as he soared down the A23, gabbling about how the filming was going.

"So, well, we're almost there. I just need to film the scenes between you and me, which I was putting off due to you totally having a go at me."

"With good reason."

"Yeah yeah, manic pixie. Anyway, now you've made it abundantly clear you have no qualms about kissing me. Which, can I just say, I totally called when we first met… Woah…don't try and hit me when I'm driving. I almost crashed the car!"

But, when he wasn't shamelessly winding me up, he was so into his film that it was intoxicating. "I mean, I want to change the way we see zombie films, and I'm hoping this will do that. *The Walking Dead* and *World War Z* have helped a lot but they're too glossy. They've lost all the hilarious bits of B-movies. Zombies can represent so much, you know? So, like, I'm hoping I can take this to the London Film Fest. Hopefully get it shown? You never know, it may even win something. And, like, your acting. I mean, I know I'm obviously trying to impress you today, let's not even pretend otherwise, but also, like, it's quite clear I don't need to impress you, judging by how much you're hoping I'll kiss you again and…woah, seriously, Audrey! Do you want us to crash and die? Ouch! That hurt."

We were soon creeping along the traffic-clogged road of Brighton seafront. We pulled into an underground car park and Harry reversed into a tiny space, almost smashing a wing mirror. Then the engine was off, the handbrake yanked up, Harry was smiling and, pretty quickly, Harry was kissing me again.

This kiss was more aggressive. His hands dug quickly into the back pockets of my jeans, squeezing my arse. The sort of kiss where you can only kiss back. It was heady and tongue-filled and overwhelming and also really, really great, and just like that, all my logic and defensive barriers were obliterated, crumbling with each mouthful of him.

Again, it was Harry who broke off. "For Christ's sake, Audrey, stop kissing me!"

"I…"

He was out the car door before I could even object,

running around to open my passenger door. "Do I get points?" He bowed as I stepped past him.

I shook my head, feeling a little dazed. Being around Harry was like being plugged into a tornado. "Umm…" I didn't even have time to process the joke. He was off ahead, jaunting his way through the dank car park towards the steps.

"Audrey, hurry up. The rides close at seven."

Rides?

I caught up with him and he slung an arm around me, casually, like he'd been allowed to put his arm around me for years. We pushed through to the stairwell, which stank of urine and I put my sleeve over my mouth as we climbed two flights of steps and emerged into the black, wintery night of Brighton.

Every part of me was instantly freezing – the harsh wind blowing us sideways. Brighton seemed dead. Only office workers clogged The Lanes as we stumbled through them.

Harry pulled me closer, tucking me into his jacket. "So, whatcha fancy, Audrey? The rickety rollercoaster that makes you think you're going to fall into the sea? The loop the loop? The ghost train? Don't say I don't offer you the world."

I could hardly hear him above the wind. When we left the cosy alleyways of The Lanes, it hit us even harder. I actually thought it was going to blow us over.

"There is a reason people don't come to Brighton in winter."

"Piffle," he declared, though his eyes were watering. "Where is your sense of adventure?"

"Did you just say 'piffle'?"

"Shh, Audrey, I'm concentrating on not letting you fly off into the sea." He grabbed me around the waist and began nuzzling my neck. I squealed and laughed. But this was too fast. I felt it was too fast. There'd been no build-up. No romantic prolonged eye contact. But…but…my arms flung themselves around him and I surrendered into it.

Eventually, among distractions, all of them involving Harry and either his hands or tongue, we made it to the pier. It was all lit up, the neon lettering blurring in the drizzle, but most of the kiosks were shuttered down.

"I don't think it's open," I said, looking around dubiously.

"Of course it's open."

We ducked into one of the arcade halls and found other human beings. The aggressive honking of the machines greeted us, especially as two younger teens appeared to be involved in some sort of elaborate dance-off on the dance game. We stood and watched, warming up from outside, as the two of them ignored us, ignored each other, and leaped around the dance pads, their arms up, spinning and twirling while the machine occasionally shouted out *"WOWSERS"* and *"YOU DID IT"*. I stared longingly at the stuffed toy crane machines, even though I'd learned, over coming here most summers since childhood, that it is scientifically impossible to grab a toy.

"Come on," Harry called, pulling me ahead.

It didn't really feel like a date.

That was the niggle that kept pushing into my mind. It felt like we'd skipped all the courting, the nervousness, the uncertainty, and jumped right into, well, by the way Harry kept pawing at me through my several layers, intense physical contact. He'd run off ahead, darting through the over-eighteens fruit machines where a few crusty-looking oldies stood mesmerized, pumping in coins, jabbing buttons, waiting for it all to be worthwhile. I stopped for a second, an invisible force holding me in my tracks. What did I really know about Harry? Somehow, with a late-night cinema showing, a headbutt, and a kiss in the car, I'd made myself vulnerable. Just like that. Like the last six months hadn't happened. I wanted to feel his vulnerability too. Otherwise…otherwise… LouLou's voice came back to me. *"Harry's flights of fancy don't tend to last. We had another girl who quit."*

Harry turned back and fixed me with his very best grin. "I've made a decision," he said. "We are going to go on the log flume."

I walked over and when he tried to put his arm around me, I ducked. Giving myself the space I needed to work through what was going on and why.

"Harry, it's November."

"It is November, Audrey. Right you are."

"Harry, it's cold and dark."

"That is why we should do it. Think of the log flume man! Think of how sad he must feel at this time of year –

everyone spurning his ride because 'It's not the right time'. Think of him, Audrey, coming into work every morning, thinking, *Today, maybe today will be the day I'm not discriminated against. Today I will get to bring joy to the hearts of people who want to go down a log flume.*"

There was no way it would be open so I just said, "Okay, whatever."

It was even colder and darker and windier at the end of the pier. The wind hit me so hard I literally squealed. The place looked like the apocalypse had hit it. There was no one around, just a few disgruntled employees, hugging steaming flasks, staring at us gloomily as we walked towards them, all like, *What the hell are you doing here?*

Harry beamed at them, seducing them with his smile. "Hello," he said to the man behind the central counter. "We want to go on the log flume. How do we make this happen?"

The man raised his eyebrows. Well, I think he did. He had so many hats on it was hard to tell. "Ha ha, very funny."

"Seriously," Harry said. "It's only 6 p.m. The rides are still open for an hour, right?"

"Mate, it's minus two degrees. And you want us to start up the log flume?"

I pulled on Harry's sleeve. "Harry, come on."

He shrugged me off. "Is it closed?"

"Not technically."

"So, we can go on it?"

"Well, yes, technically."

"Well then, two rides, please."

Harry turned back to me, beaming. "You ready?"

My delayed onset of emotional whiplash was catching up on me fast. What was happening? This time yesterday, Harry was just a work colleague. Now he was kissing me, groping at me, whisking me off to Brighton and demanding I get on a log flume in the middle of winter. He took my silence as a yes. And before I knew it, he had grabbed my hand and tugged me over to the ride. While the guy followed us, muttering and, yes, actually swearing under his breath. "Fookin' youth of today. Have to get the whole ride going… almost home time."

I felt so embarrassed as we waited for the ride to start up. It looked dormant in the dark – sleepy and lurching and just plain creepy really – all the logs stood clogged up along it, like a constipated intestine. There was a crank and the ring of a bell and then, slowly, the sound of water gushing. The logs began to move.

"It's happening, Audrey." Harry pulled me into him, trying to get me to snuggle in but I stiffened.

More logs clogged round, some starting to swoop and splash as they hit the bottom of the drop. It was so dark you could hear them more than see them.

The grumpy guy appeared at the gate. "It's all ready, you nutcases," he said, and stepped aside.

Harry pulled me after him. I wanted to have it out with him, but now wasn't exactly the best time. So I just sighed and let him hold my hand as I lowered myself down into a log, coldness seeping through the bum of my jeans. Harry clambered down behind me, opening his legs so his were around mine. With a jerk, we were flung forward, our log floating out into the blackness. Harry put his arms around my waist, pulling me further into him, his crotch completely touching my bum. "Here we go, Audrey," he whispered into my ear, then he kissed my neck as we jolted along.

This time I didn't simper or swoon, I just felt a warm rush of anger. I held it in though, thinking, *This is something I have to tackle face-to-face not groin-to-butt*. So I looked out at the gorgeous lights of Brighton – how they reflected off the dark water and stretched out for ever in the cold, clear night. Until I was suddenly tipped upwards, my body squishing into Harry as the log made its ascent.

"Woah, Audrey, please, come on, it's only our first date." He grabbed me tighter, and that's when I lost it.

Just as the log teetered on the edge of oblivion, I twisted my head and shouted, "Oh for fuck's sake, Harry, how stupid do you think I am?"

We plummeted down, down, down into the darkness and freezing water erupted either side of us, drenching every inch of me. I screamed as my skin erupted into goosebumps. I heard Harry coughing violently behind me – he must've had his mouth open in shock when we landed. We juddered to a shivering halt, crashing into the log in front of us and Mr Grumpy stood, hand out, ready to help us up.

"I hope it was worth it," he murmured.

I took his hand, said thank you, and then I stormed off,

leaving puddles of water behind me before Harry was even out the log.

"Audrey? Audrey?" he called. But I kept walking, my fists clenched, my lip wobbling with shivers. I ran to the warmth of the arcade dome – pushing through the doors, letting them swing madly. I heard an *oomph* as they crashed into Harry. He was catching up with me. I picked up my pace. The arcade lights blurred past me, the carpet squelching underneath my soaked Converse.

"Audrey? What's going on? AUDREY?"

Then Harry was in front of me. Blocking my path. Holding my arms to stop me. I batted him off. "Audrey, what's going on?"

The cold made me more angry. "Sorry, was I supposed to find that CUTE?" I yelled. "My apologies for not melting into your quirky, let's-go-crazy, romantic, whimsical, *carpe-diem*, ooh-let's-go-on-a-log-flume BULLSHIT!"

He tilted his head. "It was colder than I thought it would be. Sorry." Then he raised an eyebrow. "I know what we can do to warm up."

I pushed him with all my might, and stalked past him – thumping a machine as I passed, just to let out my anger. Then I stopped and turned back.

"You've done this before, haven't you?" I asked. "You've taken girls on the log flume before?"

His face, the shock on it, confirmed my suspicion. Of course he had done it before. How else did he know it would be open? In midwinter? That the flume even closed at seven.

242

"Does everyone else fall for it?" I laughed. "Do they think this is a special, unique thing you've shared? When it's just engineered NONSENSE? I really thought…" My voice broke then, I passed it off as a shiver. I really thought what? That maybe I was different? That maybe, because we'd had time to get to know each other, he would treat me differently? Fall for me? Change for me? When I'd been so very warned otherwise.

"Audrey, please. Look, let me explain."

I'd already turned my back on him, looking frantically for a toilet. I needed space, and to dry off and warm up and to not have him say or do anything that made me lose myself. A female icon appeared overhead with an arrow and I turned abruptly left, following it until I found a matching icon on the door.

"Audrey?"

I swung through the door and it slammed shut in front of him.

29

Thank God for hand-dryers, that's all I'm saying. I turned it upside down and blasted my hair first, vaguely remembering some fact that you lose most of your body heat through your head. Once I was only damp, instead of drenched, I put it the right way again and squatted underneath it, taking it in turns to shove random body parts underneath so my insides didn't feel like ice any more.

I pushed down the loo seat and sat there for a while, my face in my hands, trying to catch up on the past twenty-four hours. Too much had happened, that was all I was certain of. And somehow, from just a moment of wanting to kiss Harry and accidentally headbutting him, he'd grabbed the steering wheel and driven me over several canyons. My power – that I'd finally started to grow back after Milo – had been ripped off me like a sticky plaster. And what made it worse is I didn't think Harry even knew, or cared, that he'd done it. Or what giving it up meant to me.

Well, I didn't think he cared, until I opened the bathroom door. And there. There he was. Shivering so hard he was practically a blur.

I paused in the doorway.

"Audrey." He looked up, his jaw shuddering.

"Harry, you're freezing."

"Are you okay?"

"No, but I can't yell at you until I know you're not going to die of hypothermia."

He grinned, but as he did, his teeth chattered. "I didn't think this through, did I? Getting us to go on a water flume in midwinter?"

I raised both eyebrows. "The problem is, Harry, I think you DID think it through. That's the whole thing."

He scratched his head, blinked slowly, then he sighed and said, "Look, let me just dry off, then I'll drive you home. I've obviously messed up here. I'm not quite sure h-h-how."

"Oh, come on, Harry. You're not stupid." It was my turn to sigh. "Look. Go dry off. If you haven't figured it out by then, I'll at least explain to you why you're a massive arse before you drive me home. If you really want me to?"

"I mean why else would I take Audrey Winters on a romantic date to the seaside? I've been waiting for this bit all night."

I crossed my arms, reluctantly smiling. Impressed at his ability to constantly regain snippets of power, even in the most undesirable of circumstances. He asked me to wait for him and I moseyed around the mostly-empty arcade, shoving a few ten-pence pieces into the 10p machine.

"Screw you to hell, 10p machine," I said, a pound down later. "Will I never learn?"

"It appears not." Harry appeared at my side, looking slightly warmer and drier.

"Some things I learn." I looked at him pointedly and his face literally fell, like his nose was a dimmer switch and I'd grabbed it and turned it off. He stuffed his hands deep into his pockets.

"Okay, so I can drive you home now."

I didn't want him to drive me home. I wanted his arm back around me, his mouth on my neck, his whispers in my ear. But I wanted him to MEAN it, I wanted it all to mean something. I wanted the Harry behind the grin. The one I'd seen so many glimpses of until this date. The Harry who could sense I needed more time before a take, the Harry who backed off when I told him to, the Harry who told me I needed to start embracing my pain rather than hiding from it. I could sense us becoming an us, but a real us. An important us. A good us. But he was suddenly treating me like I was just another conquest he'd get bored of. Maybe I was…

"Do you want to drive me home?" I asked, trying to coax something back out of him.

"Well, not particularly. Especially as we have to work together tomorrow, followed by our first ever kissing scene. And, charming as I may be, I don't like awkwardness, it hurts my vibe."

"Did you just say 'vibe'?"

"Yes, because I probably have the first stages of hypothermia. Can we please, at the very least, go somewhere warm for you to tell me I'm an arsehole?" He took off his beanie and ran his fingers through his hair and, for one moment, his face was the picture of genuine upset. The actress in me could sense absolutely no acting in him. He was hurt. Maybe that was too big a word. But I'd spooked him at the very least. Could I explain? Could I say anything to get him to understand? To want to understand? Could this still be something?

"Okay," I relented. "Let's go for a drink."

30

"So, hit me with it." Harry's arms were thrown wide, his chest puffed out. A pint in a warm pub with a crackly fire had truly revived him.

I sipped my wine. "Hit you with what?"

"Tell me what I did wrong."

I eyed him over the rim of my glass. "Do you actually care?"

Harry lowered his arms, picked up his pint and took a sip. "Yes, I do, actually," he admitted. Once again, his mask had fallen. I pointed at him. "You see, there, that."

"What?" He touched his face self-consciously.

"You weren't bullshitting me. Just then, for that one whole sentence, I didn't feel like I was getting rained on with bullshit." I tilted my head to one side. "To be fair, it's very well branded, tied up in a pink ribbon bullshit, but it's still all bullshit, Harry."

He shook his head. "I don't understand."

I took another sip of my red wine while I pondered over my words. "Look, you know I was warned off you. Multiple times, in fact," I added, as I saw him about to protest. "By people who I respect and trust. And more than anything tonight, I think I'm mad at myself. For thinking I was different…"

"But you *are* different."

I held up my finger to show I wasn't finished. "For thinking, maybe, you liked me for me. Not because you couldn't win me." He went to interrupt. "Please, let me finish… Last night, with the film. And, well, how it's been with the filming, and working on the script. I thought maybe there was something… But now, you've taken me here to Brighton, and this is so obviously a thing you do, Harry. You've so obviously taken girls here before. And you're not being the Harry who walked me home last night, or who respected my wishes to be left alone. It's like the old one is back. The one I've been warned off. And, well, I'm not interested in him." I bit my lip. "I feel like I'm just someone you're trying to win over, rather than someone you're trying to get to know."

He reached over and took both my hands. His touch made my tummy squiffy but I still yanked them away.

He sighed and smacked his forehead down on the table. "I am trying to get to know you, Audrey." He spoke face-down into the wood.

"Tell me, honestly, that you've never taken another girl on the log flume before?"

He swung up. "It's a good place for first dates!"

"But it was a routine. I was just part of it!"

"No. Argh!" He finished his drink in three gulps, glowering, then clashed the glass back down on the coaster, empty.

I pointed to him again. "See, real Harry. Angry Harry."

"I AM angry!"

"Why?"

"Because you're making it so hard for me!"

"Oh, I'm sorry, is this usually easy?"

He looked me right in the eyes. "Yes," he admitted.

"And how did things work out for the last girl it was easy with?"

He laughed, shook his head, but the anger had broken. "Okay, so not great for her. She doesn't work at Flicker any more…"

I raised a triumphant eyebrow. "You see!"

"Oh stop gloating!"

We both stared at each other. I felt realness bubbling to his surface. This was what I'd felt last night. I took a breath. "Look," I said. "I'm not asking you to declare your undying love. I just…can't…when you're being all…on. I need to know that a tiny bit of this is real. Even if it comes to nothing."

He took my hand again and this time I didn't have the strength to pull away. In fact, I squeezed his fingers, hating myself for how it made my heart go berserk.

"The annoying thing, Audrey, is that how I feel is real,"

he said. "I just don't know how I can prove that to you."

"It's actually quite easy. You just need to be vulnerable."

"*Vulnerable?*" He said the word like it was dirty.

I nodded. "Yes. You know? Drop your own barriers, rather than spending all your time dismantling mine. Let me get to know you. Be interested in getting to know me, and not just the inside of my pants."

"Can I not be interested in getting to know *both*?"

And, even though it was a Harry line, it was coming from a better place.

"Tell me three things about you that make you vulnerable." I extracted my fingers, picked up my wine glass and took another sip.

"What?"

"Go on."

"I can only have one pint, I'm driving."

"I'm waiting."

I thought maybe he'd tell me to piss off. Or just drive me home. Or come out with something like, "I'm vulnerable because of how much I fancy you." Instead he muttered about needing another drink, went up to the bar, ordered a lime and soda, sat down in a huff and said, with no introduction, "All right then, Miss Shot-Caller. One, I had ADHD as a child. Two, my parents hate me…" He counted them off on his fingers. "And three, I want to make movies so much and the thought that I won't get my big break fills me with dread." He downed half his drink, wouldn't meet my eye and sat back heavily into the leather chair.

I didn't know where to start. The ADHD revelation made about ten million things click into place, but I wasn't sure if he'd want to discuss it. "I'm sure your parents don't hate you," I ventured.

He gave me this look then, a warning one. "They're Catholic, Audrey. And I'm…well…where do I even start? I don't believe in God for one. And I smoke, drink, get stoned, failed my exams, hang around with the people I do, work where I work, and, well, date enough girls that other girls get warned about me."

"Is that why you don't live with them?" I asked. I'd always wondered why he lived with Tad and Jay.

"Yeah. They hate me. I only ever see my parents at Christmas and Easter. I don't know if you're religious, but those two days are kind of a big deal."

I smiled at his attempt at a joke, and opened my mouth in faux-shock. "No way, really?"

"Oh yeah. This guy called Jesus did some stuff. Those were the days he did the biggest stuff."

"Harry, if it doesn't work out for you with the film-making then I really think you should consider becoming a priest. No one's ever explained Christianity to me like that before."

"Anyway, what about you? Now it's your turn."

"You already know all my drama with Milo," I pointed out. "I made myself vulnerable to you, like, on the first day we met!" It hadn't gone unnoticed that he'd not elaborated on his other two points. But it was something.

"You got dumped? That's your big bad secret?" He tutted. "Nope, not good enough, Audrey. Try harder. Some dude being too stupid to realize what he had is not a trauma, sorry."

"It still counts as one." I narrowed my eyes playfully. "I only have to reveal two."

He narrowed his eyes in return. "Are you *sure* you want to be an actress? Because you'd make a great lawyer."

I tipped my head back and finished my wine. "Okay, okay, vulnerabilities." I took another deep breath. "My dad left my mum," I said, staring determinedly at the beer mat, picking it apart with my fingers. "You know when I told you stuff was going on with my family? Well, that's what it is. They were, like, the most romantic couple ever. I'm even named after Audrey Hepburn because he proposed in Rome. And then…then, well, he fell madly in love with someone else. Jessie. He just left. Not just Mum, us." I gulped. "He left us. Started a new family with Jessie. He's just…not that into us any more. My own dad."

Harry leaned back and put his fingers together. "Woah, that explains most of Dougie's fits of rage in college last year then, I guess."

I looked up. "Dougie had fits of rage?"

Harry nodded, his face solemn. "Yeah, he punched a locker. He wrote all these weird songs in music…"

I shook my head, to dislodge the bad thoughts. "Anyway, that's why I'm so down on love, I guess. Because I've seen what happens when you fall for charm, or the promise of a happily-ever-after. I think there's this huge void between what people think love is, what they want it to be, and what it actually is. I can't…" I stuttered and Harry reached out and enlaced his fingers through mine. His raggedy eyebrows raised upwards in serious concern.

This moment was real. This Harry was real. And he was holding my hand. I felt like I'd started to remove all the bandages wrapped up around my wounds from the past two years. I'd begun to let in the oxygen needed for them to heal. But opening them up made me vulnerable. I looked right into him and said the most honest thing I would probably ever say to anyone on any first date ever, breaking every single rule of how you're supposed to behave. "I can't get hurt again, Harry," I said. "I need honesty. That's all I can handle right now… I'm worried you're going to hurt me."

He blinked slowly, then tilted his head. "That's strange," he replied. "Because I'm worried you're going to hurt me too. In fact, right now, Audrey, I'm fucking petrified I won't get a second date."

31

We drove home in happier air where it didn't feel like I was about to trip a landmine. We'd walked back to the rust bucket car, stumbling over the cobbles, getting lost in the pitch black of The Lanes, squealing whenever the wind hit us, holding hands. Then we'd skidded down the dark motorway, planning our scene for the next day – chatting through how he planned to shoot it. The radio was playing, Queen came on and we sang along at the tops of our voices. The radiator blasted my face, making me feel so warm. Harry kept stealing glances at me.

Once, we both looked at each other at the same time, and burst out laughing.

It was in that moment that I really started falling for him.

Not that I realized it at the time. I maintained a delusion that things like that take longer, that I had some kind of self-control over my heart.

But, the way he smiled…his teeth too big, his eyes scrunched up, shaking his head, muttering, "Oh God, I'm in trouble." That was the moment a piece of my heart broke off and got thrown into his, where it would lodge for ever. Because you always leave a little piece of your heart in whoever you fall in love with.

We drew up outside my home far too quickly. I could see light leaking out from a gap in the curtains. Sandra was probably still around, getting Mum drunk in the kitchen.

I unclicked my seat belt, not sure where to look all of a sudden. "So," I said. "I guess I'll see you at work tomorrow."

Harry was biting a hangnail. "Yep. Are you ready for the hell that is a Marvel movie release weekend?"

"I'll bring caffeine." I twisted my hands in my lap. "Thank you. I think I had a good time."

"You think?"

I laughed. "Okay, I don't think. I know. It was good." I smiled over at him. "After I broke through your layer of nonsense."

"Just the one layer? You've demolished multiple layers. I feel actually naked right now."

A sudden vision of Harry naked popped up behind my eyelids, and I blushed, twisting away again so he couldn't tell.

I knew I needed to open the car door, but I didn't want to open the car door.

"So," I said.

"So," he repeated.

"I better go. I need to sleep. Last night is catching up on me."

I went for the door handle as slowly as humanly possible. Begging him to stop me, to kiss me, though the thought also made me feel impossibly nervous. I pulled down the handle and the door clicked open. No grab. No kiss. The cold air leaked through the gap. No grab. No kiss. I had no choice but to scramble out.

"So, bye."

"Bye."

God it was cold. Every muscle in my body cramped up as the air hit me, and I pulled my coat around myself. Feeling stupid and unfinished, worrying that, again, I'd read it wrong. Read him wrong. I slammed the door shut and shuffled down the garden path, listening for his engine to rev off.

It didn't though.

"Audrey, wait."

The crunch of gravel as Harry caught up with me, shivering in his flimsy aviator jacket. He stepped closer until our stomachs touched. My body danced at the contact, even with the winter layers between us.

"What?"

He took off his beanie hat, looking everywhere but at me.

"What!?" I pressed.

"It's just…well…I can't believe I'm going to say this but…I'm nervous. About kissing you."

My stomach felt like I'd just necked a whole tube of Berocca, fizzing and exploding like fireworks.

"You? Nervous?"

He pushed a hand through his hair, standing it all on end. "I'm just as confused as you are. I don't get nervous about things like this."

"You don't have to kiss me." It was true, but I'd probably explode if he didn't.

"No…" He reached out and put his thumb on my cheek, in exactly the way he claimed was so hard to do in real life. His hands shook. "I guess I don't *have* to."

I looked up at him, taking in his face. The lines around his eyes, the shadowy curves of his cheekbones, the dimples that seemed to be permanently stapled into his face.

"Well, don't then. We can just shake hands and…"

Harry leaned in and kissed me. Gently. His mouth closed, his other hand pulling around my neck, gently tugging me into it. It was different from the earlier kisses. Better. The sort of kiss where time slows, the rest of the universe fading around the edges. I didn't feel nervous. I didn't worry or stress about him or his other kisses, or LouLou's and Dougie's and Leroy's warnings. This kiss erased it all. His kiss told me everything I needed to know. His kiss told me it was time to open up my heart again. I kissed him back. My hands running up into his hair. I got lost in the feeling. And we only stopped when we both heard the actual loud chattering of my teeth.

Harry pulled away reluctantly and laughed quietly. "I better let you go."

"No…I'm-m-m-m." I laughed. "I'm f-f-f-freezing, actually. Yeah, I sh-should go."

His eyes scanned my face, still scrunched up from smiling so hard. "You have to kiss me all over again tomorrow, you know that, right? For filming?"

"I don't think it means much romantically if I'm going to spit a crushed blood capsule into your mouth and then feed on your f-f-forehead."

"I wrote that into the screenplay, especially. It's always been a fantasy of mine."

I hit his chest, and he caught my hand and pulled me in for one last kiss. "Night, Audrey."

"Night."

I dragged my feet towards the front door, every part of me wanting to stay on the path with him. I heard him crunch back down the gravel, heard the slam of his car door. I fiddled with the lock, my hands shaking so much that I struggled to get the key in.

"Hey, Audrey," he called, just as I'd pushed the door open. Harry leaned out the car window, his hat back on, the edges of his huge smile vanishing into its lining. "I won't hurt you," he said. "I just wanted to say that. I have no plans of doing anything to hurt you."

And he drove off, music blaring, tyres screeching round the tight corner. I stood on the threshold, sinking into the door frame.

Every part of me felt full. Every part of me felt good.

And, you know what? I'm sure he meant it when he said it.

32

THE MONTAGE

So, the couple have got together. To be honest, usually they leave it right there. Roll the credits. The end. They smooched. You feel fulfilled. You know everything's going to be okay because the camera has panned slowly out, and the leading female has just cocked her leg backwards. But, if they don't end a romance film here, this is where The Montage comes in. You know? When a lovely pop song plays in the background as you watch scene after scene of the couple doing cute things together to show how they're falling in love and time is passing.

Cute things that tend to happen in The Montage:

- Repainting something, like a room, or a shed, and then the guy daubs paint on the girl, and she squeals and soon they're both having a super-sweet paint fight
- A long walk along the beach, and then they

both run into the sea and splash water on each other. She will jump onto his back and he'll carry her through the waves

- A shot of them sitting drinking coffee, right in the middle of the front window of somewhere. They're talking with wild gesticulations to prove they're having deep and meaningful conversations

- Lying with their heads together in a field or a meadow, looking up at either the clouds or the stars

- A shot of them both in bed, but not having sex. Just talking. Their heads close on the pillow. The girl falls asleep first and the boy just looks at her all meaningfully.

Audrey and Harry's montage of the following eight weeks

(The Beach Boys: "Wouldn't It Be Nice?")

I walk into school the next day and tell the girls what happened. They all squeal and start jumping and flapping their hands and I smile shyly to myself.

Harry and I keep sneaking glances at each other at work. He throws a piece of popcorn at me when the counter is empty. I throw one back. Soon we're chucking handfuls of it at one another until Ma arrives out of nowhere, sees the carnage, hits multiple roofs, and shouts at us while we struggle not to laugh.

Harry kisses me too passionately while we're filming his scenes for the movie. Jay, the temporary director, keeps having to yell "CUT!" and make us retake. His friends cheer and clap Harry on the back, while I pretend I don't love it and push him off. A slow pan to Rosie, standing off to the side, covered in zombie make-up. She has her arms folded and is glaring at us.

Another late night at the cinema. Harry digs out THE WAY WE WERE to watch until the early hours. We kiss passionately as the film flickers over our faces. Harry tries to put his hands down my jeans and, when I stop him, he apologizes. I go deep red, and say, "It's not that I don't want to, it's just...well...I'm on my period." He leaps away like I just told him I have highly contagious leprosy and we watch the rest of the movie in awkward silence.

Going to watch Leroy in the school play to show our support, and Harry covering his mouth with his hands to shout "BOO!" in Milo's first scene. The whole audience turns to glare at us and I hit him and refuse to talk to him on the way home, while he trails after me, still laughing, saying, "Come on, it was a bit funny!"

LouLou watching us intently as we piss about hoovering up popcorn. Harry leaves to fiddle with the projector and she comes up to me and says, "I hope you know what you're doing," shaking her head, like I should know better.

Harry meeting and charming my dad and Jessie, and taking the twins out to the park for the morning. He has Albert on his shoulders and is running with him around the playground, until he slips on black ice and they both fall to the floor in a heap of shrieking pain. Albert is screaming his head off and we have to go back to the cottage to patch up his head. Harry apologizes ten million times but still gets glowering looks from Jessie.

Dougie coming home for Christmas and pretending to square up to Harry. Then,

within minutes, hugging and bonding, and
leaving me bored and left out on the edge of
the sofa while they chat about EVIL DEAD II.

Watching a rough cut of one of the scenes
we'd filmed together, the blue light glowing
off our faces. Me pointing at it excitedly,
him smiling...and then, him snapping the lid
of his laptop down and pulling me on top of
him on my bed...

33

Christmas zipped past in a haze of work, family arguments, more work, and me continuously dodging Harry's invitations to come back to his flat. Sex, and the somewhat inevitability of it, loomed over me and I was tortured with flashbacks of what happened with Milo. Kissing Harry was good. Kissing Harry was amazing, even. But I dodged many opportunities to be alone with him in scenarios where more-than-kissing could happen. And he wasn't pushing it. In fact, he didn't bring it up. Just shrugged whenever I said, "Oh I can't come round tonight, I need to be with Mum." Once, he opened his mouth to say something but I just sort of flung myself onto his mouth and kissed him until he forgot whatever he was going to say.

Dougie returned for the holidays, dragging two guitars behind him, and quickly told me everything I was doing wrong with Mum.

"You can't keep leaving her," he said, after finding all

the empty wine bottles in our recycling.

"I'm working, Dougie, and she's not alone, she's with Sandra a lot of the time."

He pulled a face. "That pathetic alky? Audrey, you've got to look after her better."

Dougie's idea of *looking after her better* involved spending many evenings listening to her whinge on about the legal process and nodding whenever she laid into Dad. He even refused to go visit Dad and the twins on Christmas Day – acting like I was the universe's biggest traitor for popping round in the afternoon to give the twins their presents. They clawed and pawed at me, while Dad kept asking why Dougie hadn't come, his mouth a thin straight line, and when I babbled about the house, Jessie's mouth got even thinner than his. She sniffed in deeply, gave Dad a "look" and said, "Audrey, I don't understand. She always knew she would have to sell the house. This was part of the divorce settlement. You're almost eighteen... God, that woman!" And I'd stood up and said, "What do you mean by that?" And Dad had to come between us, shouting, "Hey, hey, hey!" and I'd picked up the kids, kissed them each on the forehead, decanted my presents and stormed back home. Where Dougie and Mum were curled up in a duvet, sipping brandy and watching *Love Actually*. They ignored me, even though I'd fought her corner. I sat mutely on the carpet, messaging Harry and trying not to roll my eyes as the little kid chased that girl through the airport.

"Just imagine how that would've turned out if the kid

wasn't white," Leroy always says about the airport scene in *Love Actually.* "It would be renamed *Shoot-Dead-First-Ask-Questions-About-Romantic-Intent-Afterwards Actually.*"

Harry came over in the evening. "Aww, Audrey, Christmas is always bollocks," he'd said, kissing my shoulder, moving his way up to my neck. While I half relaxed into it, half freaked out that he would try and slide a hand into my knickers. "I've had to go to church TWICE in the past twenty-four hours. Midnight Mass and then morning mass. And then Mum and Dad spent lunch asking me disapproving questions about my promotion to shift manager. I mean, only *they* could think a promotion is a bad thing. They still want me to be an accountant or something boring and sensible, rather than a director. Anyway, do you want a present? I heard somewhere that the birth of Baby Jesus means I have to get my girlfriend a gift, one that will be judged on adequacy by everyone who asks her what her boyfriend got her."

The fact he'd just referred to me as his girlfriend was present enough. And a total shock. But I didn't say anything about it.

"Well, if Baby Jesus says so."

In true Harry style, he'd got me a giant square marshmallow, with his face printed onto it. "So you can literally eat my brains, my zombie bride."

I'd also given him a zombie-themed gift. Tickets to do this local zombie fun run – "I've asked LouLou if we can get the same day off." Harry had been so happy he'd put his hand up my skirt, and I'd been so happy with his present – both the intentional and unintentional ones – that I hadn't freaked out about it. In fact, I'd actually even enjoyed it until Dougie smacked on the door, asking if we wanted to watch *The Muppet Christmas Carol*. Then he'd grilled Harry all the way through about his "intentions" while Mum laughed and I felt frustrated that Harry's hand was no longer up my skirt.

I really didn't understand sex sometimes.

Christmas faded into New Year (where Harry got so stoned he vomited all over Tad's car), and New Year melted into Oscar season. Work was nuts – I was pulling back-to-back shifts like they were normal, hardly able to keep up with college work. LouLou had a crazy expression wherever she went. Ma kept dropping back in to "see how things are going", pulling a grim face when she saw how long the queue was for snacks, even though she hadn't approved the budget for us to hire an extra person.

"I've actually had to order in tissues to give to customers," LouLou said one evening, her eyes darting all over the place, like Ma could jump out at any second. She hadn't had time to re-dye her hair, and it was now an offish sludgy colour. "I swear the production company for *The End of Childhood* should provide them."

Just as she said it, another customer emerged from the darkness, her eyes red, nose dripping. "Do you have any tissues?" she asked.

I handed a packet over.

She took one gratefully, blew her nose and said, "I'm not sure I can go back in there."

LouLou and I shared a look. We'd started betting each session how many customers would need to come out to have a breather. I had bet a pound on more than five. Here this lady was, and we hadn't even got midway.

The lady blew her nose again. "Okay, well, I better go back in. Thank you." She handed me back her snot-filled tissue and I pulled a face as she pushed through the double doors.

"LouLou, someone literally just handed me a snotty rag."

She laughed for the first time that day. "At least people don't make out in sad movies. I don't even want to identify the wet stain I found in the duo seat last week."

When I'd suitably shuddered, we got back into the kitchen, preparing for the next huge influx of people. We were showing *The End of Childhood*, an Oscar-contender weepy, on both screens and had tweaked our timings to squeeze in an extra showing. But we still didn't have enough tickets, enough showings, enough staff. I delved into the fridge, retrieving a giant collection of avocados, while LouLou mixed up yet more posh dust.

"So, you coming to filming tonight? After closing?" LouLou asked. She turned her face away to sneeze.

"I can't. I've got to fill out my UCAS form when I get home. It's due in two days." And I hadn't even started it. "And my mum...well...she needs some time. I guess I'll end up watching yet another crappy romance film."

Mum had got even more obsessed with them since Christmas. We'd gone through all the decent ones, and were now dredging the inner-sanctums of Netflix for anything with a whiff of a happy ending. After Dougie's telling-off, I'd dutifully sat through *Ski Trip Girl*, *Complicated Love* and *It's Only Love When You Kiss on the Lips*.

"Why is your mum so obsessed with romance when her own love life is a freakin' mess?"

"God knows," I sighed. "You'd think she would want to watch slasher flicks, or zombie movies, but no. What scene you guys filming tonight anyway?"

LouLou grinned. "Like you don't know! Rosie's death scene. That's why I thought you'd wanna be there. You know, to watch it? Imagine it's real?"

I bumped my butt with hers. "I don't want Rosie to die. I just want her to be nice to me, like, once. And to stop looking at Harry like she wants to eat him."

"Well, he gets to eat her tonight."

I bit my lip. "I know…"

I was pretending I didn't care about the scene because I didn't want to come across as pathetic. Tonight they were heading back into the woods to film Harry's turning scene, and Rosie was his first victim. Even though we'd been dating for almost two months, Rosie still made me feel uneasy. She kept undermining our relationship, making "Aww, how cute" comments whenever Harry and I held hands or something, but in a way that made me feel embarrassed.

I was trying REALLY hard not to hate her, but it was tough. Especially since Harry had revealed that, yes, they had once had "A Thing" as he called it. Which I knew meant they'd slept together. Which didn't make me feel any better, especially with my very apparent lack of sleeping with Harry.

LouLou finished making the dust, and started fiddling with the ancient computer, making sure all the seats were sorted. We heard the gasp of the audience. Another lady came out, red-eyed. LouLou silently handed her a tissue and the woman nodded, took it and ran into the toilets.

"So, you decided on Media Studies then?" she asked, in reference to my UCAS form.

I nodded with non-existent excitement. "Yep. It's the only subject I'm not totally failing."

"Sorry, that's my fault. I'm working you like a Trojan."

"It's fine. My subjects are so boring I'd be failing anyway." I missed Drama so much by now it was an almost constant ache. It highlighted how much I hated my other subjects, but I couldn't go back in time and shake myself out of making such a stupid decision.

I'd hardly looked at which universities did Media or which were good for it. Uni unearthed so many conflicting emotions in me. One, I wasn't doing Drama. Two, leaving meant Mum would be turfed out the house. Three, it would mean being away from Harry, which was, yes, I know, a totally terrible reason not to want to go to uni.

Like he knew I was thinking about him, Harry barrelled

through the front door – arms flung open, smiling before he'd even got to me.

"Who's winning the blub-a-thon bet?" He wrapped me into his arms. The cold air lingered on his jacket and I encased myself in it. Smelled his smoky smell. Felt my knees jellify. He kissed the top of my head before releasing me. LouLou had made her opinions on inter-office groping very clear.

LouLou nodded towards me. "Audrey," she admitted, reluctantly.

"That's my girl." Harry jumped over the bar, saw the state of my guacamole, sighed, "Audrey, oh Audrey, why do you never add enough lime juice?" and got to work. The second crying lady, suitably recovered, emerged from the toilets. She thanked us and went back inside. Harry, avocado all over his hands, wrinkled his nose when she shut the door. "Such hypocrites," he said. "I hate Oscar season."

"Here we go." LouLou rolled her eyes.

"What's wrong with Oscar season?" I asked. "Apart from pulling so many double shifts."

"Don't encourage him, he'll—" LouLou began, but Harry interrupted.

"Do you not see it?" he asked. "Look at all the films coming out right now, that all these middle-class people pay to see so they can rah on about how brilliant the acting was at their next dinner party. There's the *Wasn't Slavery Awful?* one. And the *Isn't Rape Terrible?* And the *Let's Be Trans Aware* one. And, next week, there's the Winston Churchill one."

"So?" I shrugged as I cut a lime in half.

"So…" Harry threw his hands at the screen doors. "So, most of the women in there are clutching handbags made in factories where the staff are treated hardly better than slaves. They'll no doubt think, *Oooh, well, she had a short skirt on* when they next read about a rape in a newspaper. They're probably secretly signing online petitions to ban trans people from public toilets. And, well, what can I say about Winston Churchill?" He coughed while muffling the word "Bigot". He dumped his finished batch of guacamole to one side, and began washing his hands under the tap. "People think watching some stupid film with decent acting in it is a way of showing how much they care about a certain issue. When all they've actually done is pay a tenner to sit on their arses, chucking popcorn down their faces, leaving us to clean it up, have a cathartic cry, and then come out feeling like they're Mother freakin' Teresa. Just for watching a movie." He pulled down a napkin to dry his hands.

"Are you finished?" I asked.

He grinned widely and tilted his head to one side. "Maybe."

"I didn't know ranting was contagious. You need to stop hanging out with me so much."

We stood smiling at each other, laughing with our eyes, feeling…feelings, until LouLou barged between us.

"Aren't you off now, Audrey?" she asked. "Got your UCAS statement to do? Crap on the telly to watch?"

I groaned. "Don't remind me."

I faffed about, getting my coat, making sure they were both okay. The busy period had brought out a huge sense of camaraderie in us, none of us wanting the others to work too hard. I also didn't want to leave Harry. I had visions of his face so close to Rosie's – getting lost in the scene. Having the acting turn into not-acting – the performance triggering feelings. I shook my head. He'd said he wouldn't hurt me. He'd promised.

"I'm off," I announced, my coat on, scarf wrapped a gajillion times around my head to keep the cold out. "Let me know if I win my bet," I said to LouLou. "And…" God it killed me to say it. "…have fun filming tonight."

I turned and smiled at Harry, but couldn't kiss him properly, not with LouLou watching and disapproving. I shrugged and waddled outside in my many layers. I'd just walked to the traffic lights, when I heard footsteps behind me.

"Wait up," Harry called.

I stopped, my insides turning to goo as I waited for him. He was already shivering in his thin work shirt but the smile on his face stretched from earlobe to earlobe.

"Umm, Auds? Where's my goodbye kiss?"

"You know LouLou will…" I didn't have time to finish, his face was already on mine. His hands digging into my jeans pockets to keep his fingers warm.

He broke off, a giant grin everywhere. "That's better."

I nuzzled my head into his chest. "I hope tonight goes okay," I said, with the least sincerity ever.

Harry pushed my chin up. "Audrey Winters, are you jealous?"

I wouldn't look him in the eye. "No. It's just...well you know Rosie doesn't like me...that's all."

"Ahh, Rosie's just like that with everyone," he said. "You don't have anything to worry about."

I wanted to say, *Don't I?* But I just kissed him again – because that is cute, and not-needy, and all the other things girls are supposed to be.

"Well, have fun."

34

GOOD SEX

In Hollywood sex, they always have an incredible first time. Even though the two characters don't know each other's bodies and what each other likes yet. The women can always orgasm through penetration, and don't need foreplay before they're ready to be...mounted. Their underwear is always matching, their bras always easy to remove. They don't seem insecure about their bodies – never covering themselves with as much of the duvet as possible so the dude can't see their cellulite or floppy belly. Or just because it's freezing cold.

Whereas the guys never lose their erections and never have a problem getting it up in the first place. The couple always orgasm at exactly the same time...because...yeah, that soooo happens. And... actually...I really don't want Mr Simmons to read this, maybe I'll leave this bit out.

Mum was in an unexpectedly good mood. She'd cooked a stir-fry again. She'd bought in hardcore amounts of ice cream, and she'd managed to ask me about my day, my UCAS form, and not mentioned Dad or the house once. We snuggled up on the sofa with the duvet that she'd dragged down from upstairs. She even picked a less naff romance movie for us to watch – *Before Sunrise*. It was set over one night in Vienna, where a young American guy gets talking to a French girl on the train and they spend the whole night wandering the streets together just talking and getting to know each other. I was actually pretty captivated. It was all going fine until…

"Your dad and I stayed up all night in Rome after he proposed," Mum said, emptily.

"I remember you saying."

"We were so young, Audrey. It was so…" She trailed off, leaving a silence that I had no idea how to fill.

But she didn't cry and she didn't get out the gin. She just curled into a ball and continued to watch the rest of the movie, and I think maybe that was worse. The not-drama-ing. The hollow way she stared at the movie like it could've been anything. In the last scene, where the American guy has to get on a train and they promise to meet again in the next six months, she snorted. A small one, that was all. But it said so much that I almost cried. Mum didn't snort at romantic endings to films. That was my job. She simpered.

"You okay?" I reached out to rub her back but she jolted away, sitting abruptly upright and getting to her feet.

"I'm fine. Tired though. I might go to bed."

I looked at my phone; it wasn't even eleven yet. Harry and LouLou still had an hour of work before filming started.

"Okay, sleep well."

"Night." She dragged her duvet behind her, like she was a toddler with a comfort blanket. I didn't hear her go to the bathroom to brush her teeth or anything. Just the click of her bedroom door.

I sat staring at the menu screen of the DVD, the music playing on a loop over and over. Then I got out my phone.

Audrey: I'm worried about Mum.

He wrote right back, even though it was a Saturday night.

Dougie: What's she doing?
Audrey: Nothing. She's just...I don't know...
She's not drunk tho. That's good I guess.
Dougie: I guess. Pls keep an eye on her tho.
Audrey: I will x

I faffed about in the silent house for a long time before bed. My body clock was all messed up from working so many late nights. I read back through my personal statement. Even with all Mr Simmons's help, my enthusiasm for Media Studies didn't quite ring true. But it was something, I guessed. I then read back through my notes for my project, trying to keep myself busy so I didn't think about Harry and Rosie. It was midnight now. Somewhere, in a wood not too far away, they'd be rolling around in the leaves, him biting her face, which is almost like kissing if you think about it. The girls had a group message going, competing over who could take the ugliest selfies. It distracted me for a while but at half midnight I made myself go to bed, just for something to do.

I was woken by pebbles at my window.

"Huh?"

I sat up in bed, still in my clothes, my head fuzzy from sleep. Another flecking of noise at my windowpane. I reached over and turned on my bedside light, the brightness scorching as my eyes struggled to adjust. I pulled out my phone. It was gone 2 a.m. And I had three messages.

Harry: AUDREY – I'M SO COLD. I'M COMING OVER TO LET YOU WARM ME UP.
Harry: YES I MEAN THAT IN A SEXUAL WAY.
Harry: I'M OUTSIDE.

I shook my head, still feeling dreamlike and out-of-it from being woken. I twisted to open my curtains. Peering out, there he was. Harry, standing under the orange street light, wobbling slightly from being drunk or stoned or whatever he was. He must've seen me in the window, because he got to one knee, and shouted, "OH, AUDREY, AUDREY – WHEREFORE ART THOU, AUDREY? DENY MY SOMETHING AND REFUSE MY WHATEVER IT IS, BUT PLEASE LET ME IN BECAUSE I'M DYING FOR A PISS."

I opened my window, letting the freezing air stream in. "Shut up! You're going to wake up the whole road."

His teeth shone orange. I could see the crinkle of his eyes from the second floor. "AUDREY!" Even though he was clearly wasted, his pure childlike enthusiasm at seeing me made me feel all sorts of brilliant.

"If I let you in, do you promise to be quiet?"

He put his hands around his mouth to make a megaphone. "I PROMISE."

I shook my head and went to close the window.

"NO! Whoops, I mean, no." He lowered his voice to a dramatic whisper. "I'll be quiet, I promise. I just wanted to see you."

I checked on Mum and was surprised to hear her still softly snoring, somehow sleeping through Harry's yells. I smiled as I pulled on my old spotty dressing gown and went downstairs to open the front door. He was leaning against the wall like James Dean. A really wasted James Dean.

When he saw me he started singing the lyrics to "Breakfast at Tiffany's" really, really loudly.

"Harry, shh! You'll wake Mum."

He swayed in, his eyes red, and engulfed me in a hug. He stank – of the sweetness of alcohol and smoke. Then he started kissing my neck, his hands pawing at my body.

"Harry, I swear. Can we at least get through the door? Why are you so wasted?"

He kicked off his shoes, shrugging his coat onto the floor.

"I'll get you a glass of water."

"Yes! Water, water would be amazing!"

I left him where he was and went to the kitchen, figuring out how I felt about his sudden arrival. Touched, that he'd thought to come here, I guessed. Especially if he'd spent the evening with Rosie. Pissed off – that he'd woken me, worried he'd wake Mum. When I returned with a pint glass he wasn't anywhere to be found downstairs. But he'd left a trail of Rizla papers leading up the stairs. I sighed, smiled and followed them, picking them up after him.

Harry was in my bed. No top on. Both hands behind his head. Grinning. I stopped in the doorway and tried not to drop the glass.

"Hello, Audrey," he said, in a suave film-star voice.

My stomach did ten million things at once – squirmed, clenched, melted. "You'd better have your trousers on in there."

His smile grew wider. "Why don't you come over and find out?"

I dallied on the threshold, looking at Mum's closed door, wondering if she was stirring from the noise. Freaking out about getting into bed. Not knowing what I felt, why he was doing this. Though I assumed alcohol and weed had something to do with it. I closed the door, put the glass on my bedside table and climbed into my cramped single bed with him, still encased in my fluffy, unsexy dressing gown.

Harry didn't have any pants on.

He moved to kiss me straight away, his mouth tasting of cigarettes, digging under my dressing gown. I kissed him back but...but...I didn't know how I felt. I pulled away.

"Why are you so wasted?"

He answered between kisses on my neck. "Rosie. Made. Me. Do. A. Bong. Said. I. Was. Getting. Soft."

I rolled my eyes and pushed him off. "So you're high?"

He looked down mischievously. "I'm both high and unsoft." And he went to kiss my neck again. But I twisted away. Annoyed at him, at Rosie. "Harry, I'm not going to have sex with you tonight."

It was the first time I'd even said the word "sex" out loud to him. He stopped kissing my neck, but kept his mouth there. "I know."

"So why are you...?" I didn't know what else to say.

He sighed into me, his hot breath tickling my hair, then propped himself up on his elbows. His eyes were so red there was no white left in them. "Why aren't we having sex, Audrey?"

There it was, falling out of his mouth. The issue I'd been skirting around for two months. That I'd naively hoped he wouldn't mention. That we wouldn't need to tackle. That would get magically resolved somehow. Also, that I really hoped he wouldn't try and solve like...this.

"Why are you bringing this up *now*?"

Deflection. Which, I reckoned I had a right to. Considering he'd put himself naked, in my bed, at 2 a.m., off his face, as a way of fixing this.

He shook his head. "Argh. You're pissed off now, aren't you?"

"Yes."

"Ergh." He rolled over onto his stomach, his whole face in the pillow. "I knew you'd be pissed off."

"What's going on?" I asked Harry's back, feeling my tummy tighten, not wanting to hear his answer.

But he was mumbling an apology. "Sorry, I'm an idiot. I shouldn't have just turned up here. Sorry, it seemed like a good idea. It was something Rosie said..."

The knot in my tummy doubled, the adrenaline of anger surging through me, waking me up. "You spoke to *Rosie*?! About *this*? What did she say?" My voice was so sharp it could've carved diamonds. Into daggers. To stab Rosie with. And Harry. I mean, how could he?

He turned over and looked me in the eye. "She just asked if we'd slept together yet. And then, well, she was surprised that we hadn't."

I wanted to kill her. I wanted to actually be a zombie bride so I could rip out her brain with my teeth and then spit it back into her eyes.

Harry sensed me stiffen. "Hey, don't get mad at her. She was just asking...as a friend, you know?"

I didn't reply. I just turned and grabbed the water, shoved it at him. "You said you were thirsty?"

He pushed the glass away. "Audrey, come on. Don't be like this. It wasn't like that...it..."

I interrupted him, my voice a whisper but with a lot of venom in it. "You spoke to another girl about our sex life? One you know doesn't like me? One you had a thing with? And now you want to talk about sex? Now? While you're off your face? Naked? Here uninvited? In the middle of the night?"

"I thought it would be romantic."

"Harry, I can feel your fucking erection sticking into my thigh."

And, at that, he burst out laughing. Proper laughing. A high-pitched hee-haw, like someone had stamped on a donkey. His face was bright red. "You're right!" he managed to get out. "This isn't very romantic, is it?"

I shook my head, dazed from his laughter. "No, it's not. It's also totally unfair of you."

He was giggling too hard to listen though. I was brimming with anger and insecurity and just confusion but I let him laugh himself out, the bed rocking – not in the way he'd planned – as he eventually calmed himself down.

"Will you put your boxers on?" I asked. Feeling like I was on the verge of A Big Talk, and really not wanting to do that with...*that* lurking underneath my duvet.

Harry saluted and wiggled back into his pants, still letting out the odd small grunt of laughter, while I hit him with my pillow and said "Shh".

I looked at Harry. Harry looked at me. "This isn't going

at all how I planned," he said.

I raised both eyebrows. "I don't think you had a plan really, did you?"

"No," he admitted. "Just urges."

"Are you in any fit state to talk about this sensibly?"

He sniggered again. "No, not really."

I hit him with my pillow again. "Harry!"

He put his hands up in defence. "Okay, okay, I'm sorry. Honestly, I'm sorry...I am...wasted. Just a bit, it will pass. I wanna talk though, but can I wee? And also, I found a new film about love that isn't totally awful! Can I show you?"

Is it possible to have emotional whiplash? I had no idea what was going on, but Harry was digging out his phone. Then he was up saying, "Man, I really need a wee," and running out of my bedroom in just his boxers. I winced as he set off at least three creaky floorboards but heard no stirring from Mum's room. So I flopped back down on the bed, feeling rising panic and rage and other emotions.

Fuck fucking Rosie.

Fuck fucking Harry for listening to Rosie and then thinking that turning up twatted was the best way to deal with this.

Fuck fucking me for being so messed up about what happened with Milo that I wasn't able to talk about, well... everything with Harry.

He came back, looking a little less of a mess. And a lot more sorry. "I feel like I should make some sort of grand apology before I'm allowed back into bed, but it's freezing and I'm only wearing my pants," he said.

"And whose fault is that?"

"I'm sorry."

I sighed and lifted up the duvet to let him back in. "Oww, Harry! Your feet are like ice!"

He deliberately ignored me and pushed them on my legs to warm them up further and I let out a small shriek, before covering my mouth with my hand. With us just messing around, the pressure lifted, my body unravelled from being able to touch so much of his skin – to feel his bareness in bed next to me. All my senses jumped to attention, my skin suddenly longing to be touched – though the thought had terrified me only minutes before. Harry meanwhile seemed to have forgotten entirely about the sex thing and was pulling up a YouTube clip on his phone.

"This one is going to break you, Winters."

He'd started his own counter-project recently in retaliation to my Media coursework. Harry said I'd get too cynical if I only focused on the bad bits of love stories, so he kept trying to find examples to show me "true" love as he called it. It had started with *Cinema Paradiso*, morphed into *The Way We Were* and now…

"Who's Marina Abramović?" I asked, peering over his shoulder.

"Just wait for it, wait for it."

He hit *full-screen* and *play* on his phone and pulled me down so I was lying with my head on his cold chest. It was a documentary called *The Artist Is Present*. I'd started to learn that, with Harry, you just had to go with it. And so, at 2.30 a.m., I kept my head where it was and watched the film. It was about this artist called Marina who created incredible conceptual feminist performance art. She travelled around Europe together with her artist boyfriend, Ulay, in a clapped-out van. But they started to fall apart. For their final project together, they each travelled to opposite ends of the Great Wall of China and spent months walking towards the middle, where they embraced for one last time. That's how they broke up. With that one hug they'd marched hundreds of miles for.

"Wait for it," Harry kept saying, my head bobbing on his chest as he did.

I moved into the warmth of his body and kept watching, captivated. Years later, Marina started a performance at the Museum of Modern Art in New York where members of the public could share a minute of silence with her. She would sit with a table between them, and both would look at each other in total quietness.

"It's coming," Harry said. "Get your tissues out, Auds."

Because on opening night, Ulay, her ex, turned up to sit in front of her.

Oh God…Marina's face, when she looks up and sees him there. The shock, the sadness. Ulay blows out his breath, all like, *Look where we are,* and tears spring instantly to her eyes. You can see her visibly fighting her emotions as they sit in front of each other, not sharing a word, but sharing a lifetime of what-ifs. Tears were already leaking down my own face when Marina bent forward and stretched both hands out onto the table. Ulay took them and they held eye contact, both of them silently weeping. Then, she lets go, he stands up and he walks off. Just like that. You see Marina struggle to get a hold of herself before she lowers her head, recovers, and then looks up and waits patiently for the next person.

I was a wreck when the music faded out. I buried my face into Harry's collarbone, wetting it with snot and tears, my shoulder blades jolting with sobs I hadn't expected. He laughed quietly, seeming so much more sober now, stroking my hair. Weaving his hand all the way through it, untangling it gently with his fingers.

"Did you like it?" he asked.

"I am broken."

He laughed again. "I told you! I will not let you become a cynic, Audrey. You are too young. I will keep finding examples of love to keep you going."

I raised my head and looked into his face. "Like turning up on my doorstep in the middle of the night and then removing all your clothes?"

"I mean, Audrey, I can't believe you turned me down."

We both laughed, the noise dislodging any discomfort. Almost. Because then Harry looked hugely serious and said, "Why haven't we had sex, Audrey? I mean, I don't mind... Well...'mind' isn't the right word. I guess...argh... I mean, I'm happy to wait, even though, I mean, look at you, it's hard to wait."

I turned purple.

"But, it would be nice to know why I'm waiting. I mean, you won't come to my flat, and I know why. And sometimes when we…do stuff…you're fine, and other times you stiffen up and I feel like the world's worst guy and…argh…I'm going to stop talking now."

My heart was beating so hard I was surprised it wasn't causing *Jurassic Park*-style vibrations in the glass of water on the bedside table. He had asked. Should I answer?

He saw me hesitate, open my mouth. "There's something. Tell me, Audrey."

"I…" I closed my eyes slowly. He was still staring at me when I opened them again.

"Please."

Oh God, did I? Did I? I mean, he was my boyfriend. I guess you're supposed to be able to talk to them but I was so mortified. "Something happened with Milo," I garbled out, like it was a plaster to rip off. "He didn't just break up with me and go out with that other girl. He…well…we had sex…well I think we had sex…but it didn't really…er… work…and then he dumped me and went out with that girl."

Harry didn't look away. That was the first good sign. "You *think* you had sex?"

I squirmed, literally. My body was wiggling around under the duvet like a tortured worm. "I'm not sure if it counted. It…it hurt. He didn't, like, get to…" I coughed. "Finish or anything."

Harry shoved his hands through his hair, digesting it.

He didn't reply for a long time. I could almost see the cogs in his brain whirring. Would he think I was damaged goods? Would this make me unsexy?

Eventually he just said, "It shouldn't hurt, you know that, right? Even if you're a virgin, it doesn't have to hurt."

I dared myself to look up at him. "And you know that, how?"

He stared straight back. "Do you want to know?"

"Actually I don't."

He smiled then. "Wise girl." He sighed. "So, you're scared I'm going to hurt you?"

I nodded, blushing. "Yeah, I guess. Emotionally and… well, physically."

He shook his head a little. "You know Milo is an arseweasel, right? You shouldn't think I'm like him. I told you I wouldn't hurt you."

"You say that…"

"I'm glad you told me. Everything makes sense now." He started laughing.

"It's not funny!"

He shook his head. "No, it's not that. I just wish I'd known all this, before…earlier. You must've been scared witless. I really am sorry, Audrey. I thought, in my drunken state, that it would move things along, you know?"

"Well, I guess it has," I said, allowing myself to relax. I'd told him and the universe hadn't imploded. He hadn't looked at me with disgust or sorrow. He'd just absorbed it. That was the moment I fell totally in love with him. The moment the feeling bubbled to the surface, shouting so loud that I was surprised he couldn't hear it.

We started kissing. Just like that. Announcing the end of the conversation with no real solution. But things were out there now, flying out of Pandora's box – though I'm sure the Greek gods didn't give a shit about Audrey Winters's virginity – and they'd dissolved in the air like throat pastilles. Harry's kisses were tender and sleepy and not-pushing-me-into-anything. I kissed him back lazily, the lateness of the night catching up on me, lulling me to sleep. Soon we broke apart, my head back on his chest, half-chatting to each other through a tide of tiredness.

"I really did like that documentary," I said.

He kissed the top of my head. "Good, wasn't it?"

"Yeah. I mean, that's what love is, isn't it? Moments like that. Not chasing someone through the airport."

I felt his smile. "Or holding a boombox outside their house."

"Or sending them a message in a bottle."

"Or standing on their doorstep with some handwritten signs."

We shared them back and forth, our voices getting sleepier and sleepier. And, just as I reached unconsciousness, I had a thought. This, right now, was one of those moments. Me sharing the Milo thing and us talking about it. Him not judging it. Not judging me. Accepting it. Taking it on. Working our way through the misunderstanding and the ill-timing and the bad behaviour and the pressure to do what you think you should do rather than what you feel ready for.

And, as sleep flowed through my limbs, making them heavy one by one, Harry must've thought the same thing. Because as I rolled over, my back spooned up against his front, he murmured, "I think I'm falling in love with you, Audrey Winters."

35

I woke slowly at first. Then, as I felt the intense heat of another body next to me, I jerked up.

Morning. Sunshine.

And Harry was in my bed.

The shock of him and everything that had happened bolted through me. It was way too much to catch up on in only a few seconds of consciousness, but it crammed itself in anyway.

The most pressing concern was Mum. Had she heard? Did she know he was here? I wasn't allowed boys to stay the night. I climbed out of bed slowly so I didn't wake Harry. He looked so much younger while he slept – his hair all over the place like a mad scientist, still smiling. I shoved on my furry slippers and tiptoed out the door and downstairs, but there was no one there to greet me. No Mum. The house felt undisturbed. I padded into the kitchen and found a note on the counter in her handwriting. She was out?

I picked it up.

Gone to church with Mrs Williams. Be back this afternoon x

Church? Since when had Mum gone to church? Especially with Leroy's mum?

Still, there was nothing in the note about being woken up, or night-time visitors, or boys in beds that they shouldn't be in. We must've got away with it. And that's when it hit me. Harry was upstairs. In my bed. With essentially no clothes on. And we were alone. Sunday Sam was covering the morning shift. We had the house to ourselves. And suddenly, because of last night, because of how great he was, because there was no pressure, the thought of all that and what it meant excited me. I had a glass of water and then padded back upstairs, feeling…things stir all over my body.

Harry was still dozing as I pushed through my door, the mess of his dark hair invading most of the pillow. He grunted and turned over, revealing his face, chin covered in stubble. The duvet rode down revealing the top of his chest that was covered with a thin, dark layer of fuzz. His eyes were creased shut, his hands large. He was a man. An almost-naked man. In my bed. Who I thought I loved. And, even when unconscious, was making me want to do things. I took a deep breath, weighing it all up… Wondering…worrying… did I want this? Was I ready? But my body answered for me.

I was already undoing my dressing gown, already stepping out of my knickers, shrugging off my T-shirt. My legs shook as I climbed back under the covers, completely and utterly naked.

Harry stirred at my movements. An eye cracked open, he smiled into the pillow. "Morning." His voice was gruff from sleep, deep, even more manly.

I smiled, waiting for him to notice my nakedness. "Morning."

He reached out and pulled me into him, and that's when the penny dropped. His hands ran up and down my body and he sleepily raised an eyebrow as he explored each inch of my skin…checking. Then, it's like he knew I didn't want to talk about it. He just turned me so I was facing him and kissed me deeply.

I'm sure my breath stank, as I'm sure his did too. We'd both only just woken up, we hadn't brushed our teeth or anything. But I didn't notice. All I cared about was Harry's mouth on mine, his tongue playing with my tongue, the way his grip tightened on me. The feel of so much of his skin against so much of mine set off tiny grenades of lust, like I wanted every single part of us that could touch, to touch. Soon Harry's hand slid down my chest, in between my legs, pushing to open them and then I gasped, at the feeling, at how good it felt. We stayed kissing, him touching me, bringing me to a hazy pool of gasping and melting and forgetting where I was. Suddenly, it wasn't enough, I needed more. The closeness wasn't enough. I needed him, wanted him. I broke off the kiss, bit on his ear and found myself whispering, "Do you have a condom?"

Harry stilled, his hand between my legs stilled. He coughed. Swallowed. "Audrey, are you sure?"

I nodded, expecting him to smile or say something cheesy, taking the piss. But he was still being all Man Harry, not Boyish Harry. He leaned out to rummage in the pocket of his jeans. He had his back to me for a second while he put the condom on. The strong rubbery scent of it hit me and it brought back a jolt of memory. Of Milo. Of that awful night. And my body tightened up again. I suddenly thought, *Oh God, what if it happens again? Will it hurt? Will it hurt?*

Harry started kissing me again – his tongue going deeper. He clambered on top of me, between my legs, and I adjusted to his weight. I could feel his erection digging into my stomach. It was a shock how hard it actually was. And weird – just sticking out of his body like someone had glued it on at the wrong angle. Then he was wiggling down, positioning himself, his mouth moving to my neck and just feeling him that close made me want it. Just the tip of him slid into my body. And, there, like it was a muscle memory, I tightened up and Harry hit a brick wall. Well, not a brick wall. But you know. It suddenly hurt, a piercing tearing hurt that made me take a sharp intake of breath. I closed my eyes with shame, waiting for Harry to leap off me, or just determinedly push in further like Milo had – making it hurt more, tighten more. I waited for him to say something, knowing whatever he said would make me feel so humiliated and cringe and oh God, why was this happening to me again? I WANTED to have sex, why was my body not complying?

But Harry didn't do any of those things.

He just tilted my chin up, looked me right in the eye, like it wasn't fazing him at all that my body was literally rejecting his, and started kissing me again. My eyelids, my cheeks, my neck, back to my lips. At first I knew what he was trying to do, and that made me tighten up further. But then, his kisses and how good they felt made things go hazy again. My stomach relaxed and unfurled. I even threw my head back when his mouth moved down to my chest. And then he slowly moved in an inch further. And stopped. Kissing me again. Melting me again. Then another inch. And another. Until Harry was completely inside me and it didn't hurt at all. I felt stretched and weirded out. Part of my brain was screaming, OH MY GOD, AUDREY, HARRY IS INSIDE YOU. YOU ARE ACTUALLY HAVING SEX WITH HARRY NOW. THE SEX. THE SEX PEOPLE HAVE. YOU ARE HAVING THE SEX. HOW WEIRD IS THIS? WHY DOES NOBODY TALK ABOUT HOW FREAKING WEIRD IT IS THAT PEOPLE DO THIS TO EACH OTHER? But then he started moving slowly, carefully, checking with his eyes that it was okay. And it felt…nice…good, even. I closed my eyes and everything slipped away and there was just the sensation of him moving with me, me moving with him, our bodies finding a rhythm, my fingers digging into his back and I could sort of see what the fuss was about.

It wasn't all romantic. Near the end, Harry kind of zoned

out on me. He stopped being slow and caring and tender and something seemed to take him over entirely. He thrust fast and strong, kind of like a zombie when it gets a scent of brains. I looked around, for a clue as to what was going on, not sure how to handle this. Finding that, yes, this bit did hurt a little. But then he quickly let out this strange guttural groan, buried his head in my neck and well… He stilled and collapsed onto me, not using his elbows to support his body weight so I was sort of pinned to the bed by him. He didn't talk to me or even acknowledge me for a good few minutes. So I just lay there, half-heartedly stroking his back, biting my lip, wondering if this was normal. Then he recovered, withdrew, turned his back while he dealt with the condom. Then his smile was all teeth and his eyes were so squinted they were practically closed. Our eyes met. His smile set off my smile.

And we both started giggling.

36

<u>Blooper reel from ALL THE TIMES
I TRIED WITH ROSIE</u>

<u>Annnnd ACTION:</u>

AUDREY

Oh, Rosie, I love your top. Where did you
get it from?

ROSIE
‹Stares at Audrey blankly›
A shop.

AUDREY

Right.

<u>Annnnnd ACTION:</u>

AUDREY
Hey, Rosie? I was wondering if you could
help me with this scene. You see, you're
so good at zombie law and...

‹Rosie walks off›

<u>Annnnnd ACTION:</u>

ROSIE
‹To Harry›
Oh my GOD, do you remember Leeds Festival
last year? Harry, I still can't believe
you made us all zip our sleeping bags
together.

HARRY
That was one of my most brilliant of
ideas, I have to say.

ROSIE
Yeah, apart from I woke up with your
erection poking into my leg.

‹Audrey coughs and Harry starts stammering›

                    ROSIE
Oh sorry. Audrey, we were all asleep in
the same giant bag. It didn't mean
anything. Don't stress out.

                    AUDREY
          I'm not stressing out.

                    HARRY
              Audrey...

                    AUDREY
     I SAID I'M NOT STRESSING OUT.

             Annnnnnnd ACTION:

‹Rosie and Audrey are holding two mikes
while Harry eats Jay's brain but they're
     laughing too hard because they're
           all stoned - bar Audrey›

                    ROSIE
            ‹Watches them fondly›
Those are my boys.

                    AUDREY
            ‹Sighs quietly›

Do you have any, like, friends who are
girls?

                    ROSIE
What's that supposed to mean?

                    AUDREY
I was just asking.

                    ROSIE
Well...no. For some reason girls don't
like me. I've always got along with
boys better. There's just less drama,
you know?

                    AUDREY
...

37

Once Harry and I started having sex, we didn't really do any activity that wasn't having sex if we could possibly help it. Whenever we managed to squeeze in alone time together, the whole thing was just an elaborate game of pretending we weren't going to have sex. It started raining one day and didn't stop for three weeks, postponing the filming. So we had a lot of sex. I even got over my aversion to going to his flat. Which showed just how much I wanted to have sex, because the place was disgusting. The toilet bowl was more skid mark than porcelain, the kitchen sink unreachable through the tower of dirty dishes, and don't get me started on the pubes in the shower. But Harry washed his sheets and the bed was the only part of his flat I was interested in.

The sex was sometimes good, sometimes bad. Not yet great. I made Harry get an STI test. "This must be serious, if I'm getting a giant cotton bud shoved up my willy hole for you," he'd grumbled. And then we had to wait until my period started before I could begin taking the pill. In the meantime, Harry bitched about condoms and, once, when he'd picked me up from a late shift, stoned off his brain because he'd been with Rosie, he'd lost his erection trying to put one on. I was mortified and started crying, "You don't fancy me," while he just laughed hysterically, patted me on the back and said, "Of course I fancy you...it's just I'm high and I hate condoms... Can we go out and get some pizza?"

I found I couldn't orgasm through sex, which Harry seemed miraculously unfussed by.

"You should let me go down on you." He shrugged. "You will then."

I turned purple at the thought. "No, I'm too shy."

"About what?"

I buried my face deeper into his blue sheets and mumbled.

"What was that, Audrey?"

I pulled the sheet down so only my eyes were showing.

"I said...I'm not sure I want you so close to...there. I'm worried it's...it's...ugly."

He grinned before he laughed. "Don't be ridiculous. It's not ugly. It's fine. It's sexy! You'll like it. I'm good at it. Hey, where are you going?" ...As I buried deeper under the covers to hide my mortification. But then, one night, after a particularly gruelling shift, LouLou had said, "Screw this, we're drinking," and let us go mad on the cinema's bar. Back at Harry's, I was just drunk enough to not feel too shy about letting him try. He was right. He was good at it. And I did.

He was also such a smug prick about it afterwards I had to thump him.

"Stop puffing your chest out."

"I'm not. This is just what Sex Gods do with their chests."

Another thump.

Leroy sauntered over while I was having lunch with the girls and smacked a ripped poster onto my table. "Tell me you love me."

"What's this?" I picked it up. "Royal Welsh College of Music and Drama..." And put it down again. "Why are you giving me this?"

He pulled up a chair and made the girls move down. "Read it! I stole it off the Drama noticeboard. We don't want Milo seeing it. Not that he'd have a chance after missing that high note in 'Luck Be A Lady'."

Milo missing that note was the happiest day of Leroy's life.

I pushed the poster further away, my heart aching. "Leroy, I quit Drama. They're not going to let me into an acting school with a D in Geography."

"OH WILL YOU JUST READ IT ALREADY," he shouted, before turning to the girls, and apologizing.

Alice, Becky and Charlie just grinned at him. The more we'd all been hanging out, the more they'd got used to his theatrics.

Leroy turned back to me and punched the page with

his finger, almost ripping it. "Look. They're doing VIDEO auditions this year, Auds! To show how with-the-times they are. All you have to do is send in a clip. You have a clip! You can send your zombie bride stuff!"

I looked down, the words blurring with excitement. "Don't you have to apply through UCAS to go there?" I asked. It was a question I'd already learned the answer to, when I'd stayed up late, clicking through the *apply* pages of uni websites, cursing myself for dropping Drama.

"Yes," Leroy said. "But this is for two special places, SEE." He jabbed at the page again. "They want a diamond in the rough! Not someone doing the Macbeth soliloquy for the eighth time in a row. Surely you should at least TRY and send something in? Harry will give you some footage, won't he? Make you a showreel?"

I shook my head, my mouth open. "I…I guess. But I'm not exactly a diamond in the rough."

"They don't have to know that!"

I looked over at Alice and the others. "What do you think?"

Becky rolled her eyes. "Erm. Are you stupid?"

"But what about uni?"

Alice reached out and took a chip from our shared bowl. "You can still send off your UCAS form for Media, but enter this too."

"I'm WAITING for you to say thank you." Leroy crossed his arms. "You're lucky I'm choosing to focus on IT-related world domination rather than Drama-related world domination, otherwise we'd have to fight each other for this."

I leaned over and hugged him. "Thank you. I'm sure I won't get in…" Everyone started protesting. "…but thank you. It's worth a shot, I guess." It felt like someone had shoved a valve into my belly button and started pumping hope right into me. I shook my head to dislodge the thoughts. I wouldn't get in anyway. I mean, there's "edgy" and then there's playing a feminist zombie bride in an overtly B movie in some shit local woods.

"You are very welcome, now givuss a chip." Leroy leaned over me and grabbed a handful from the bowl, ignoring Alice's attempt to slap his hand.

We all started chatting but I kept looking down at the scrap of paper. Thinking…wondering…hoping… Until Leroy said, "Your mum keeps going to church with my mum. It's weird."

I sighed. "I know. It's her new thing." I still couldn't figure out if this new thing was a good thing or a bad thing. It was certainly different, but it appeared to be stemming the drinking at least.

"Does that mean she's hanging out with Harry's parents too?"

I shook my head. "I don't think so. She grumbled about trying to talk to his mum, apparently she was rude."

Leroy nodded. "Sounds like Harry's mum. She's a big cheese there. Not a fan of hanging out with the Babybels."

I didn't like the thought of them meeting. From what

Harry had told me, I wouldn't like his parents. They were strict, cold, too religious to see straight, judgemental. It worried me too that Mum had randomly found God. We'd never been a religious family, not even at Christmas. But it seemed to keep her calm. And Leroy's mum was there to look out for her. I was willing to hope on anything when it came to Mum at the moment.

"Argh, I don't know what to do, Leroy," I said. "I'm worried about ever going away to uni and leaving her. She's so…lost."

Leroy squirmed in his seat, never that comfortable with me talking about the deep and meaningful. "It ain't your job to find her, babe."

38

The Relate counselling office was probably the most depressing building ever.

It had a tiny door with a broken intercom, sandwiched between two bins and at the back of a badly-lit car park. I half expected to be mugged as I knocked and knocked at the door.

If your marriage was failing, this really wouldn't help inject the spice back into it, I thought, shivering in the cold.

The door eventually opened and a youngish funkily-dressed lady appeared in the frame. "Hey, Audrey? Sorry, this door has been broken for ever. Come inside." I tried to shake her hand but she was already disappearing down a narrow corridor of scratchy grey carpet. I pulled the door shut and followed her, past children's drawings tacked to the wall that said things like, *Daddy was home late again last night. I really miss him.*

Jane – Mr Simmons had told me her name was Jane –

pushed through a tiny door to the right and sat herself down.

"Er. Thanks for seeing me," I said as she gestured to one of the two chairs facing her.

"Please. Sit. I'm happy to help."

I dumped my bag down and rummaged through it to get out my notepad, while Jane crossed her legs. She wore a pinafore dress with yellow tights and these really cute maroon Mary Jane heels. She couldn't have been older than forty and all her blonde hair was piled up in a giant bun. She smiled. "I'd offer you a cup of tea but the machine's turned off for the night. I can get you a glass of water?"

I shook my head. "I'm fine, thanks." I took out my phone and held it up to her. "Is it okay if I record this?"

"Yes, of course." She smoothed down her dress. "So, how can I help? Jack told me you were doing a project for school?"

Jack? I realized she must mean Mr Simmons.

"Umm, yes. It's about romance films," I explained, hitting record on my phone and setting it on the small table between us.

She smiled and recrossed her legs. "Ahh, yes. Those old chestnuts."

I explained my project to her, flicking my pen around my fingers with nerves. "So, yeah, it would be really good to get your take on them. How useful they are, how problematic. And, yeah, anything you could add about relationships and what you see here would be great?"

There was a silence. "Sorry," she said. "I don't quite know what the question was."

"Oh, yeah, right. Umm, I've never done this before. So, well, what do you do, I guess? We can start there."

God I wanted her yellow tights. I wanted them so much I didn't quite hear her begin. "Well, we offer counselling to couples *and* individuals who want to explore their relationships."

I made a note in my book. "And what sort of people come in. And for what?"

She blew out some breath. "All sorts, I guess. I mean, we mainly get married couples, in their middle age I guess, but it's not definitive. We have a lot of couples come in because one of them has had an affair. Or because they want to get divorced but they don't want to upset their children. We get younger couples in too though. And lots of individuals who just want to break patterns in their relationship behaviours that aren't making them happy."

I had a sudden thought. Would Mum and Dad still be together if they'd come and seen Jane? Would it have made a difference? Would he still be at home, waiting for me to get back tonight?

"You must see the very worst of love then, right?" I asked.

She smiled again, a small one, through tight lips. "You see good stuff too. You see couples fall in love again. You also see some couples who, after counselling, learn that actually the best thing is to walk away."

"So, what's your take on romance films?"

Her smile grew tighter. "Lots of people find them enjoyable. I guess the word I would use for them is…" She looked to the ceiling tiles for inspiration. "Unhelpful?" she offered. Then she broke into a wider smile. "How about you give me some famous romances, and I'll try and offer my professional opinion on them?"

I sucked on the end of my pen lid. "Er, okay," I said. "Umm, *Romeo and Juliet*?"

She laughed and clapped her hands. "A good start! Oh, where do I begin?" She leaned forward in her chair. "Well, let's see. One of the issues I have with romantic movies is they always tend to end way too early. The movie either ends when the couple gets together, or someone dies before you can see the relationship develop. So you only see this perfect *idea* of this couple. You don't see the niggles that can become cracks and how those can become giant crevices over time." She leaned back again. "I mean, in *Romeo and Juliet* they *both* die. But, if they hadn't, my professional guess is that the warring families would really have caused issues between them over time. It may seem romantic to fight against your family for True Love at first, but, well, your family plays a huge part in how you understand your relationships. Plus you shouldn't ideally ask your partner to reject their entire family just for your love. Where would they spend Christmas? Who would come to the christening of their first child? How would Juliet cope with Romeo making underhand digs about her parents all the time?

It would definitely cause conflict."

I decided then that I liked her. Very much.

"*Dirty Dancing*," I put forward, and her face lit up. "Oh, I love that film! I had a couple in here once who did the dance at their wedding. Umm, another thing to point out about relationships is that often what attracts you to someone in the beginning is what starts to bother you over time. There's this theory that we look for a mate that colours in a blank part of ourselves. That's why opposites attract. But what drives that initial attraction is often what causes the issues eventually. So, let's see, Baby and Johnny in *Dirty Dancing*. He's attracted to the way she sticks up for what she believes in, because he wants to be more like that. And she's attracted to his subversive way of living." Jane's foot tapped in her gorgeous shoes. "But, give them ten years, and I can bet Johnny's maybe rolling his eyes whenever she starts ranting about the Gulf War again. And she's getting pissed off that he can't hold down a regular job. She feels insecure about how sexually experienced he is, when, initially, that was part of the sex appeal—"

"So they'd break up?" I interrupted. "They wouldn't last?"

"Ahh…" Jane put her hand up, stopping me. "I'm not saying that. All I'm saying is, love changes over time. No person is ever perfect for another person. No couple goes through life without an argument or a bad patch, or even just a dull patch where they look at the other and think, *Is this it?* But romance films never really show those parts."

She sighed, staring past me to the tissue box as her thoughts organized themselves. Then, she looked up. "Can I ask *you* a question?"

I nodded, finding myself hanging on her every word.

"Do you think love is a feeling or do you think love is a choice?"

"I don't know."

"There's no wrong answer. But if you had to choose one?"

I thought about Harry and Milo and how I didn't seem in control of how I felt about them. My stomach curdling, my dry mouth, my heart being plugged into an electric chair that shot me with yearning and emotion. "It's a feeling," I said.

She raised an eyebrow. "You're sure?"

"Well, yeah. Love…it's something you feel. You can't help who you fall in love with."

She pointed her finger. "Ahh, well you say that, but ask any couple who've been married a few decades the same question? They *all* say it's a choice. Every last one of them."

I wrinkled my nose. "A choice? Like what to have for breakfast? Or where to go on holiday?"

Jane nodded. "Yep. They get up every single morning and make a conscious decision to stay with the person they're with. On the good days, that choice is easier. On the bad days, they really have to fight the *feeling* in them to make the opposite choice. To leave. To find someone else. To walk away."

I shook my head and I was surprised to find I wanted to cry all of a sudden. Being a therapist, she sensed it.

"Oh, I'm sorry. You're upset," she said.

"No, I'm fine." But my voice squeaked. "I just...I just hadn't thought of it like that before."

Because it was easier to see what Dad did as something beyond his control. It was easier to tell myself he couldn't help his feelings. I mean, I guess you can't help your feelings. But you can choose what to do about them. He chose. He chose to let them overwhelm him. He chose to leave Mum. He chose to leave us.

"I didn't mean to make you sad," she said, her face somewhat panicked now. "I thought you may even find it reassuring? That every couple has these moments of wanting more sometimes – it's normal. It's just we don't see these moments in romance movies."

I nodded and gulped and insisted I was okay.

But I wasn't sure if I actually was...

Harry thought everything Jane had said was brilliant.

"I love it," he said, Hoover in hand. "She sounds awesome!"

"She was." I moved over on my belly to drag out an espresso cup someone had left in a tucked away crevice. "But, don't you think it's a bit depressing? Like, surely there must be SOME couples who don't get sick of each other."

I emerged to find him standing right in front of me,

his smile stamped across each cheek.

"I don't think I could ever get sick of you." He yanked me over and I squealed as we fell onto the popcorn-laden floor. He leaned down on top of me, grinning as he went in for a kiss.

"Get off," I said, reluctantly pushing him away. "We don't want LouLou to find us and have another go."

She'd already walked in on us in a compromising position in the stockroom. After yelling, "AGH, MY EYES, MY BEAUTIFUL EYES," she'd actually given us a Proper Talking To in her office. "Don't make me be that boss. Now, please behave."

I clambered to my feet. "Anyway, that's very sweet of you, Harry," I said. "But we've only been together a few months. I'm sure, in time, you'll find all sorts of things that piss you off."

We'd already had our first fight, coincidentally. About Rosie. Unsurprisingly. He'd turned up outside my house. Wasted. Again. And I'd not found it endearing. Again. And I'd blamed it on Rosie. Again. And he'd defended her. Again. And then I'd started crying and saying "She fancies you" and he'd called me paranoid and I'd told him I wasn't and he just didn't see her how I did, and he said they'd been friends for years, and I said I didn't know getting stoned in a car with someone counted as friendship, and we'd woken up Mum shouting and Harry had stormed off into the night and not answered his phone all day... But then we'd made up at work and...well...that was the day LouLou found us.

"NONSENSE," Harry said, pulling me in for a quick hug. "Now that we've sent off your incredible zombie showreel, you're going to bugger off to Wales and become all famous. And I'm going to have to trail after you saying, 'Audrey, it's me, YOUR BOYFRIEND', and you'll *have* to stay with me otherwise the tabloids will say you've lost touch with your roots."

I stiffened, as I always did whenever he brought up Wales.

"Harry, I've not even got an audition yet. And the zombie bride is not their sort of thing."

"It will be, when they see you... HANG ON..." He jumped up on one of the folding chairs and almost fell off it again.

"Harry, get down! What is it?"

He pointed down at me. "You've got it, you've totally got it. The ending! I know how the film will end now." He tumbled down again, picked me up and lifted me off my feet. "You, Audrey. Why are you such a good muse? Such a sexy, brilliant, wonderful, lovely..." He kissed me between each adjective. "...insightful, sexy, perfect, sexy muse."

I started laughing. "What are you on about?"

Harry gave me one last kiss and put me down. "The zombie bride! She needs to get married. The film should end with a wedding!"

I opened my mouth. "Where has this come from?"

"Think about it, think about it." He started racing around the screen with the Hoover. "She didn't *choose* to be a zombie. And, initially, she didn't choose to be a bride. But she got turned BEFORE the ceremony, right?"

"Riiiiight."

"But what if she and him" – I assumed by "him" he meant his character – "find a way to be together? And they get married. Have a zombie wedding! Oh man, we can throw guts as confetti and the wedding favours can be little jars of brains and…and…"

I held up my hands. "I don't get it. And, why would a feminist zombie end up getting married?"

He danced back to me, his face ablaze. He was in that sort of Tasmanian Devil tornado where I could never quite get through. "Yes, but what you were just saying about choice. It's given me an idea. We should end on her CHOOSING the one thing she didn't want at the start of the film. And and…"

The doors swung open and LouLou's new purple Mohawk appeared between them. "Are you two *still* not finished? Do I need to start putting you on separate rotas?"

Harry ran up the stairs of the aisle and hugged her. "LouLouLouLouLOU, I've got the ending for the film!"

"The only thing I care about is you having the end of the Hoover in your hand. This place needs to be ready for the next showing."

He batted her comment away and picked her up too. She squawked like a bird.

"Ahh, it's dead at the moment, Lou. All the Oscar films have finished, and DID YOU NOT HEAR ME? I HAVE

AN ENDING FOR MY MOVIE."

She looked over at me and I shrugged, still holding the empty cup. "He wants to marry off the zombie bride," I explained. "He is having a light-bulb moment."

"Not just a light-bulb moment, an apple-on-the-head moment! A bullet-time moment, a...a—"

"Harry, you're not the Wachowski sisters," LouLou interrupted. "You're just late. Can we get this place clear? I need you both in the staffroom."

"Okay okay," he grumbled.

We cleared up the rest of the place quickly, acting like kids who'd just been told off. Soon enough, it was sparkling clean again. The seats and floors devoid of any popcorn bits for a whole half an hour.

"You know what this is about?" I took Harry's hand as we walked to the tiny staffroom.

"Nope. But Ma was here again yesterday."

"Oh God, they're not going to change our uniforms, are they? Make us wear some ridiculous neon get-up with a matching beret or something?"

Harry leaned over and kissed my neck. "You'd look hot in a beret. All your hair spilling out of it? I'd like that. You could put on a French accent and...oww...stop hitting me."

LouLou held her head in her hands in the staffroom.

"Whatever it is, it's going to be okay." Harry perched on the edge of her desk. "Now, what is it?"

She didn't smile, but stared up at us both. "It's about the gents loo."

Harry threw his hands up. "No way. Not again, LouLou. I'm not unblocking it again after that dude's bum exploded. I still have nightmares. I wake up scratching underneath my nails to make sure the shit is still gone!"

"Calm down, nobody's defecated all over the loo," LouLou said. If her face hadn't been so worried I would've laughed at LouLou saying the word "loo". "But…" She paused. "You know how the one on the end has been playing up?"

We both nodded. It had been flushing itself non-stop for about four days now.

"Well, Ma came yesterday and, instead of fixing just that one, she wants all the toilets refurbed now, as it's quiet season. So we're closing for a week. Next week." She gulped. "Sorry, guys."

Harry jumped off the desk. "What about our shifts? My rent?"

LouLou shook her head. "I'm asking to get you transferred to our sister branch in Richmond."

"It will cost as much to get there as I'll earn!"

"I'm sorry, Harry. It's out of my hands. Audrey, I'm sorry too."

I coughed. "It's okay. I mean, I'm here to get a break from Mum more than for the money."

Harry kept running his hands through his hair. I reached over to squeeze his arm but he pulled away, leaving me feeling stupid and confused.

"Oh God," he was saying under his breath. "I'm going to have to ask them for help. They're going to be UNBEARABLE."

"Ask who?" I wondered, but LouLou gave me a warning look.

"Fuck this!" Harry shouted. And before I knew what was happening, he'd stormed out the door, slamming it behind him.

I went to follow him but LouLou called, "Audrey? Don't."

"But he's upset."

"And I've worked with him long enough to know when to leave him alone. Trust me. He doesn't want you to follow him."

"But…" But I was his girlfriend. Surely I could help? Talk it through? But LouLou looked so sure of herself that I perched where Harry had been.

"I'll try and sort him some shifts. I feel terrible, but you know what Ma's like."

"It's not your fault. Are you sure I shouldn't check he's okay?"

"Honestly. If he has to ask his parents for money, it won't be good. He just needs to calm down."

I pulled a face. "His parents can't be that bad."

LouLou's mouth dropped open. "You mean he hasn't told you about them?"

"I know they're super religious and they don't get on. But, I mean, he still sees them. Why? What do you know?"

She stared at me, like I was a maths problem she couldn't do, and I felt a creep of dread. What did she know that I didn't? Why did LouLou know this and not me?

"It's not my shit to tell," she said. "But there's drama

there… It's weird he hasn't…" She held her hands up. "I'm not getting involved. You two can figure things out for yourselves." She blew out a long breath. "Bloody Harry. He's not the only one having to commute all the way to Richmond."

I smiled at her tightly, my stomach feeling like someone had punched a hole in it and then released a can of maggots. I knew we were new. I knew we weren't, like, the most talky couple, but still… It hurt there were bits of him, important bits, that he'd chosen to keep to himself.

Still to this day, I don't know what went on between Harry and his parents.

Because the week the cinema closed?

Well.

That was the week we broke up.

Ahh, come on. You knew this was coming.

39

THE FORMAL EVENT

FACT: A girl in a romance film cannot be fallen in love with unless she's wearing a very pretty and important dress. But such a key moment in filmic courtship would look out of place in regular settings. Therefore, the couple MUST attend some kind of formal event so she can showcase her perfect body and demure-but-ravishing beauty in some sort of couture gown. And, of course, there must be the moment the boy SEES HER IN THE GOWN and you get a reaction shot of his face, while she twirls self-consciously and pretends she doesn't know she looks like an A-lister (even though she _is_ one, she's in a romance film, godammit).

✱ ✱ ✱ ✱ ✱

"Well, this is weird." Alice stared at my face, sucking on the end of a make-up brush.

LouLou loomed over me too. "You're telling me. How am I supposed to add blood to that perfect eyeliner flick of yours? I don't want to ruin it."

Alice smiled at her. "Aww, thank you! You've made the bite marks in her skull look so real."

LouLou beamed back. "Thank you. It's this new putty I've been trying out. It really looks like brain, right?"

I looked up at both of them. "Okay, so this is *super* weird."

Alice tutted. "Shh, zombie bride, or I'm going to mess up your eyeshadow."

Charlie and Becky barged through the door, cradling five mugs. "We've got tea! ...Oh my God, Audrey! What the HELL do you look like?" Becky stopped in actual shock in the doorway. We'd achieved a lot in the make-up department since they'd vanished off to buy milk.

I tried to grin but Alice yelped, "Don't smile! You're going to mess up your lips!"

We were about to film the last ever scene for Harry's film. He'd been sulky and weird about the cinema's current closure for the two days before it actually closed. Getting way too stoned – after work, before work. I'd found him standing once at the back entrance with Rosie, sharing a spliff and giggling together uncontrollably. When she'd seen me, she'd not even said hi, just saluted. And, for some reason, Harry found this hilarious. He'd apologized later but...still...

Anyway, LouLou had managed to secure him three days

of back-to-back shifts up in London and he'd stayed on the uni floor of one of his friends, Joel. It made him just enough money to dodge asking his parents for help. "Let's use the free days to film the wedding scene in the DAYLIGHT," he'd said, trying to kiss me in the storeroom to apologize. Because I'd yelled at him. About Rosie.

"*Why are you pretending she doesn't fancy you?*"

"*Because she doesn't.*"

"*She does. And she so obviously hates me.*"

"*She doesn't hate you. Rosie's just like that.*"

"*Or…she fancies my boyfriend.*"

"*Don't you trust me, is that it?*"

"*You KNOW that's not what it's about. How would you feel if I kept getting drunk with Milo?*"

"*I'd be fine with it.*"

"*Yeah, right. I'll just ring him now then, shall I?*"

"*I don't think this is about Rosie, I think this is about you hating me smoking weed.*"

"*Well, I'm not over the freaking moon that you do it, no.*"

"*You knew this about me before we got together.*"

"*That doesn't mean I have to like it though.*"

"*I can stop any time I want.*"

"*Oh, because that's not a clichéd thing addicts say.*"

"*I'M NOT AN ADDICT.*"

And I'd weighed up whether I could be bothered to continue the argument, or just lean into his mouth and let it go.

"Come on," he whispered into my ear, pulling my hair

back to get better access to me. "It's the last scene. We can have a huge wrap party to celebrate." And he'd lifted me onto a crate of organic crisps and cupped my face in his hands and we'd made up…

"Audrey, you look so awesome," Charlie said, handing out the mugs of tea. "I love that dress."

"Don't get too attached."

I went to sip my drink but Alice slapped my hand and said, "Not until your top coat of lip gloss is set."

I pouted at her. "It's going to get covered in red syrup and intestines soon."

Alice shuddered. "I don't know how you're going to handle that."

I shrugged. "Acting, isn't it?"

LouLou made me tilt my head to one side while she dribbled a trail of fake blood down me. "Almost done… Okay, zombie bride. You are as pretty as a picture."

Alice removed the towel around my shoulders and I stood up, examining myself from all angles. I looked the oddest mix of beautiful blushing bride, but also, well, a zombie – my long hair ringletted up with daisies, my cheeks flushed, make-up dewy…and a bit of brain dribbling down my head, blood spilling from my rosebud smile. Because I'd managed to do my turning scene in just one take, I had the gorgeous blood-free spare wedding dress on.

"You guys are miracle workers," I announced to my reflection. "It's perfect. Harry's going to go ape-shit."

I saw them all beam in the mirror.

"Well, I couldn't have done any of that fancy-pants proper make-up," LouLou said, taking a sip of her tea.

Alice looked at her in thanks. "Well, I couldn't have done any of your stage make-up. We make a good team."

The air fizzed with different people getting on and I grinned.

"Now…" LouLou said. "I have to make myself look like a zombie wedding guest." She plonked a chair down in front of the mirror, budging me to one side. "If I do all the gore, will you help me look more like a lady?" she asked Alice.

"Sure."

They both got to work and I reached out to finally enjoy my tea. I picked up the many layers of my wedding dress in my spare hand and shuffled onto Alice's bed, next to Charlie and Becky.

"Will you take my photo?" I asked. "I want to show Harry."

Harry was at the church, setting everything up. LouLou planned to zombify his face at the last moment, "In case the vicar sees and doesn't let us film there any more." Needless to say, he wasn't filming in his parents' church.

"You sure you guys don't want to be extras?" I asked the girls, taking my phone back to pick the best one to send.

"We were all for it until you mentioned the guts," Becky said. "But, funnily enough, we'd rather go see a movie than get intestines thrown on our heads as confetti."

LouLou twisted away in the mirror. "Oi, where you seeing a movie? Flicker is closed this week."

"Uh oh. You're in for it now," I murmured, smiling as Becky stuttered out an apology.

"It's only because you're closed. And I don't think you would show it anyway. It's just that new film, *The Last Days of a Broken Heart*. You know, the weepy one?"

LouLou winked. "I'm only winding you up."

My phone buzzed.

Harry: How do you look that beautiful with half your brain hanging out?

The blood cracked on my cheek as I smiled. Charlie leaned over and read it before I had a chance to snatch it away.

"Oh my God, you two are SO IN LOVE, Audrey. What happened to the cold angry cynic who hates romance films?"

I was cowering too much to stop her swiping my phone and showing it to everyone else. They all cooed, apart from LouLou, who stuck her tongue out.

"Hey, I still think romance films are unhelpful." I stood up to retrieve my phone. "I interviewed an expert and everything. But yes…" I felt myself get red. "I may not be as…umm…anti love itself as I used to be."

Their squeals were *very* high-pitched. I flopped back onto the bed, my skirts exploding beneath me as air rushed up them.

"Has he said he loves you yet?" Alice asked.

I twisted my hands around each other. "Not quite. But he has said he thinks he's falling in love with me."

More squealing.

LouLou put her hand up to stop it. "Please," she begged. "This is too weird for me. I know them both too well. And, well, this is not the sort of thing I want to know."

They ignored her though.

"Oh my God, I bet he says it soon."

"Do you love him? You're blushing, you do!"

"Seriously, today is, like, your practice wedding."

"Maybe he's waiting for tonight? When the filming is over?"

"You HAVE to message us when he does."

Soon the make-up got finished, the tea got drunk, LouLou and the girls even swapped numbers.

LouLou and I sat on a wall, waiting for our taxi. She didn't say anything while I just kind of smiled and felt warm from my friends, and the message from Harry, and also a tiny bit sad that this was the last scene I'd ever shoot as the zombie bride, but also, stupidly, thinking it was kind of magical that Harry and I were sort of getting married today. And, with Rosie killed off, she had to film it for us. That should get the message across without me even looking like I was trying to get a message across.

Then LouLou said, "So he said he *thought* he was falling in love with you?"

I grinned, feeling more dried blood crack across my cheek. "Yeah."

More silence.

"I thought you didn't want to hear about it anyway?"

She tilted her head. She looked so cool as a zombie. I mean, she looked uber-cool all the time anyway, but having blood splattered all over her really polished it off.

"I don't…I didn't…I just…"

"What is it?"

"I shouldn't get involved. I said I wouldn't."

"LouLou…?"

"It's just, well. He only *thinks* he's falling in love with you? Audrey? Are you sure that's romance, and maybe not just a cop-out?"

40

LouLou's words haunted me for the entire cab journey. She apologized, but she'd still said it. And it had still seeped in – turning what had been a happy memory into a confused one. I mean, saying you think you're falling in love is the natural precursor to the actual drop, right? Not a cop-out. And it's not like I'd said it to him, even though I felt it. I was waiting for him to say it first... I knew he did. I mean, he must, right? He was caring and affectionate and honest and loyal and...and...right now looking SO GOOD in a tux that every single thought that wasn't *I LOVE HARRY, I LOVE HIM SO MUCH* evaporated the moment I stepped out of the taxi and saw him.

Jay, Tad and Rob all cheered when they saw me. Jay and Rob put their hands up to form an arch and whooped out the tune "Here Comes the Bride". LouLou and I gave each other a look and she took my arm, like she was my proud father, and walked me underneath. Towards Harry. Who was waiting there, beaming… In front of Rosie. Who was standing there, glaring. When I reached Harry, he leaned over and kissed me, smearing my bloody lipstick and everyone cheered. It was a bright winter day, the sun throwing gorgeous wintery light onto everything. The air buzzed with the high of it being the final scene. Oh, and the fact Jay opened up his suit jacket to reveal a half-empty bottle of Jack Daniel's.

"What?" he asked, when LouLou made a disapproving face. "It's our last day. The wrap party starts here!"

Harry took my hand. "Here, let me show you the set-up," he said, leading me into the church. I lifted my skirts to scuttle after him, keeping a hand over my face as the bright sunlight made my eyes water. Behind me, I heard LouLou say, "Now, who wants to be attacked by my make-up brush first?"

Harry led me through the giant double doors, that were so huge and old it was like being in the Hogwarts great hall. Stone pillars held up the high arched roof and the sun flooded through all the stained-glass windows, casting rainbows that bounced off the walls. At the front stood an ornate altar with a stone-carved angel.

"Harry, it's perfect," I whispered.

There was film equipment everywhere. Two cameras stood on tripods, three big professional lights were erected around the front – there were even two silvery umbrellas.

He grinned and squeezed my hand. "Isn't it? I blew all my savings on hiring the extra camera and lights. But I had to make the most of the set."

"It's so nice of the vicar to let us use it."

"Yeah, well. He won't be happy if he ever asks to see the finished footage. I told him we were filming a *Save Yourself For Marriage* education video."

"Harry!"

He laughed and dragged me down the aisle to show off the rest of his handiwork. "It's fine, he won't ask. He's a vicar, he's trusting! God, this church is something, isn't it? Anyway, you'll stand here... Let me check the lights are okay."

I stood on the small bit of Sellotape he'd put on the floor as a marker, and listened to his clattering noises echo around the high walls. In a blast, I was plunged into bright lights that made me blink and feel instantly hot. Harry pushed another button and another light glared at me. I blinked several times more, knowing Alice would murder me if I let my eyes water and wreck her make-up.

When I'd finished blinking, Harry stood right in front of me, a smile so wide I could hardly see his eyes.

"You're so beautiful."

"Even with half my skull missing?"

"Yes."

He stepped forward and we were on the verge of kissing, there, bathed in light and stained-glass rainbows, when...

A cough, just as he leaned in.

We looked up and Rosie was standing at the end of the aisle, scowling. "LouLou wants you for make-up," she told Harry.

"Ahh, cool." The moment evaporated and Harry took off, calling to us to turn the lights off.

The doors swung shut, leaving us alone. I smiled with my mouth closed and walked into the harsh rays of the nearest light to try and turn it off. I couldn't find the switch though. "Ouch!" I accidentally touched the bulb and burned my wrist.

"Hang on, I'll help." Rosie walked down the aisle. She turned the light off easily then jumped over and did the other one.

"Thanks," I said, still cradling my wrist.

"No problem."

Big awkward silence.

"Is your wrist okay?"

"Oh, yeah, I think it's fine." I was surprised she even cared.

Big awkward silence. Rosie stood right where the sunlight hit the floor through the stained glass and her face was a paintbox of colours. I tried to think of one thing to say to her, but couldn't. Eventually I managed, "I like your jumper," just as she said, "That dress is cool."

We both smiled at the jinx before remembering who we were smiling at.

"Thanks," I said. "Er…it's great that you can film today. What with everyone else in the scene."

She didn't reply straight away, just looked up at the window. "Well, Harry killed me off."

"Hey, Rosie," I found myself saying. "Can I ask why you

have a problem with me? It would be nice if we could get on. I mean, I know you had a thing with Harry once…"

Both her eyebrows went up. "Is that what he told you?"

"Yeah, well… He said you guys…you know…" I was already regretting starting this.

Her eyebrows drew higher and she smirked. "I always wonder what he tells you."

"So you didn't?"

"Oh yeah. We did."

"Right. Okay then." The twist of jealousy in my gut was instant – like someone had just shoved my intestines into a spiralizer. In my head the sex was incredible between them – panty and sweaty and she did all the right things. Her smirk confirmed my suspicion that she wasn't finding this awkward at all – in fact, she was enjoying herself. The rush of dislike overwhelmed me, made me incapable of speech.

She laughed. "Harry and I go way back, that's all. We lost our virginity to each other."

I almost choked on her revelation.

"Didn't he tell you that?"

"No."

"You just have a connection when you share something like that." She picked off her nail polish. "We've always been very on again, off again, you know? It's like, no matter what happens, we always come back to each other." She was talking to me like I was a friend and we were reapplying make-up in the loo. Not like I was Harry's girlfriend. What did she mean by *on again, off again* – they wouldn't be on again, surely?

She examined her nails, looking bored. "So, yeah, sorry if it makes you uncomfortable, but we're in each other's lives, Audrey. I've known him since he was seven. You've known him, what? Four months?"

"I'm his girlfriend." It was supposed to come out as a statement, but it came out more like a plea.

She smiled. "For now. Yeah, I guess you are."

"What's that supposed to mean?" I couldn't keep the disdain out of my voice. How *dare* she? Come here and tell me *that* about Harry and her? Knowing it would upset me. Implying their relationship was closer than ours. I was only trying to clear the air. But before I could have it out with her properly, everyone burst through the doors.

"We're ready!" Harry yelled. His face was the epitome of childish excitement and all zombified. He stopped when he saw Rosie and I glaring. I may've imagined it, but he looked momentarily concerned. Then he clapped, grinned and said, "Amazing, they're actually getting on!"

Rosie gave me the fakest smile the universe has ever seen. And all I could do was grin inanely back whilst I was dying inside.

41

It took a while to get the shot set up. I had to stand on the Sellotape for ages while they fiddled with the lights. With nothing to distract me from Rosie's words...

They'd lost their virginity to each other.

That was huge. Or was it? It wasn't like Harry had lied. Just, er, withheld the whole truth. Oh God, the visuals. The visuals of them sleeping together – his hands on her body, mouth on her neck...

Rosie smirked, well aware of the internal hell she'd unleashed. Harry was totally oblivious – all fired up and barking demands and smiling like it was running out. I tried to get into character. I imagined how happy the zombie bride would feel, to finally get what she wanted, the man she loved, on her own terms... Oh God, was Rosie better in bed than me? I mean, the first time with Harry had been... fumbly...but we were good at sex now. Sort of. Whatever that means... Whoops. No. Zombie bride, zombie bride...

How does she feel? What's her motive? Did Harry really love me, or was it a cop-out? Like LouLou said?

"Audrey? Audrey?"

"Yep?" I shook my head to try and dislodge the insecurity spiral.

"We're ready for you to walk down the aisle." Harry tilted his head. "Now, I know you probably want to wait until we're older or something, but I'm afraid zombie love waits for no man."

I smiled thinly and got into position at the back of the church.

Harry kept grabbing the camera lens off Rosie, leaning over her to explain the shot. "So, you need to hold it tight on Audrey's face for this take, got it? Are you okay walking backwards? Here...like this." At least eighty per cent of their bodies were touching. She raised an eyebrow at me and the surge of hatred I felt almost bubbled over. I narrowed my eyes, so noticeably that Harry said, "Woah, Auds, it's your wedding day. You're happy, remember?"

With a final whoosh of instruction, everything was set up. Rosie stood with the lens right in my face. The aisle was empty, ready for me to walk it. I ran through my lines under my breath.

"*I, zombie bride, take thee, undead. To have and to maim, for richer times of brains, and poorer times of brains, in sickness and in general zombieness, to love and to cherish the brains, till undeath do us part...*"

LouLou gave a thumbs up.

Harry yelled, "AAAAND ACTION." The red camera light bleeped on. "Walk, Audrey, walk."

I found one foot stepping in front of the other but I didn't feel like the zombie bride. I felt squidged and confused and conflicted. When I got to the top of the aisle, I turned, paused, and found Harry at the end of it, his smile erupting at the sight of me. And, because I wasn't acting, because I wasn't lost in my part, I felt this surreal mist descend down on me. I was in a wedding dress and walking down the aisle to my boyfriend. My boyfriend who said he thought he was falling in love with me. Who was grinning like I could mend his life. My boyfriend who had picked up the jagged pieces of my humiliated and shattered heart and glued them back together with jokes and care and tenderness, but had also withheld the truth from me. I was supposed to be smiling. This was supposed to be the happiest day of my zombified life.

I loved him…

Each step towards him made me surer of that. The ache in my guts, the jealousy pumping around my body. I was in love with Harry. I'd tumbled back down the rabbit hole and swallowed ten tiny bottles of love potion. More steps, the congregation of zombies grew closer. Harry grew closer, his smile unwavering. I'd made myself so vulnerable to him. This boy. This one boy. And, in that moment, I wasn't sure if I was delighted about that or horrified. I walked and walked, clutching my bouquet of wilting flowers we'd nicked out of a florist's bin. He got closer and closer. Within seconds I'd get to him and we'd film the service. The zombie bride's special day. Her happy ending. The happy ending she'd chosen. A lifetime of being undead shared…

And I was supposed to smile and simper beneath my veil…

…

But I found myself screaming and knocking Harry to the ground, attacking his face.

42

The whiskey bottle was almost empty.

"I'd feel bad drinking in a graveyard," LouLou protested.

"NONSENSE." Rob was already wasted. He was wasted before Harry had even called "Action". "People drink wine in church every Sunday, remember?"

Harry's face was already very red. "Dude, it's not really wine though, is it? It's the blood of Christ."

"Oh, shut up, Catholic boy, you've had the most."

The last shot had been filmed, the equipment packed away, the blood and fake intestines washed off the stone floor outside. Everyone was so wired that I hated to point out that I was still covered in fake blood. It was matted into my hair, it had sunk into my wedding dress and dried hard against my body. We stood in the winter sunshine, huddled around the car, and poured the rest of the whiskey out into plastic beakers.

"A toast." Harry's smile was so huge I'm surprised it didn't have its own gravitational orbit. "To Audrey! The zombie bride who COULDN'T EVEN STAND HER ZOMBIE WEDDING."

Everyone cheered (apart from Rosie) and clunked their cups together.

"I'm sorry, I know I didn't stick to the script," I said to everyone.

"No, you didn't," Harry replied, still beyond grin. "But you did give the film the most epic twist OF ALL TIME so I can't be mad at you."

Everyone cheered again, making me even redder. Not that you could tell through all the dried fake blood. I hadn't planned to change Harry's ending. The *she chooses to love* ending. But I just flew at him and improvised the hell out of it and launched into this speech about how I shouldn't conform to societal pressures put on me just because I'm a zombie bride. I'd thought Harry would go mental, but all he did was grin from the floor I'd knocked him to and say, "I LOVE IT." We'd reshot it over and over – ending with the wedding guests celebrating my single zombie status by chucking intestine confetti over just me. Then Harry screamed, "IT'S A WRAP!" and picked me up, getting blood all down his tux and whispering in my ear, "*God, you're great. How are you so fucking great?*" while everyone piled on top of us.

"Right, guys!" he said. "WRAP PARTY AT MINE. LET'S GET WASTED."

We all cheered so loud I'm surprised we didn't resurrect

the people buried in the graveyard. The whiskey scorched my throat and made me wince. I noticed Rosie drank hers without even a grimace and another pang of hatred flushed over me. I wasn't done being mad at her yet – even with my triumphant ending. With the whiskey gone, it seemed urgent to Harry to get back to his quickly. LouLou sighed, said she'd drive as she hadn't had any whiskey, and we all somehow managed to squeeze into the tiny car. I sat on Harry's lap, feeling a rush of nostalgia, remembering that first time I'd sat on him. So much had changed since then.

"The blood is seeping off your arse onto my lap." His breath was hot in my ear.

"Yeah, I think you're going to have to let me go home and change."

We rumbled back to mine, music blasting from the speakers, everyone but me knowing all the words. I almost flew off Harry's lap as we rounded a corner but he grabbed me round the waist, pulled me to him, and said, "Nope, you're not allowed to die, please. I like you way too much."

LouLou screeched us to a halt. "You did good, Audrey." She looked so proud behind the steering wheel, like a mum. A cool mum. "I'll see you next week when we re-open."

"You not coming to the party?"

"Nah. Too old." She scrunched her face up. "But you kids have fun. And don't get too wasted. Haven't you and Harry got your zombie fun run tomorrow?"

"Oh God, don't remind me," I groaned. "A 3k run with a

hangover is a stupid idea. I'm tempted to go in this costume so nobody chases me."

"That would be cheating!" Harry yelled over the music. "We'll be fine, Audrey. I am the epitome of health…" He started coughing.

I rolled my eyes at LouLou. "Anyway, I better go shower. I have red food dye in places that no one should ever have red food dye."

Her face scrunched up. "That's disgusting. Anyway, see ya! Have fun tonight. Enjoy it."

I stood and waved, calling, "See you in an hour," as the car took off again.

I ran through everything I needed to do as I walked up the garden path. I certainly needed to wash my hair, wash my everything. What would take off red food dye? And what should I wear? Should I sort my running gear so it was ready for tomorrow morning? I fumbled for my key in my bag, but as I went to put it in the lock, the door swung inwards.

It was open.

43

My stomach dropped into my toes as I paused in the hall. Then a crash. One that rocked the walls, reverberated through the air. My mouth went instantly dry as fear surged through me.

A wail.

Mum's wail.

Then a scream and a bigger crash from the living room and I ran as fast as I could to the source of the noise.

I stopped in shock as I took in the obliterated room. Mum stood swaying in the middle. She looked a state – her face red from crying, in jogging bottoms, her hair all bunched on the top of her head. But the living room looked worse. Glass littered everywhere from smashed photos. Thousands of fragments decorated the sofa, carpet, table...

"Mum?"

She ignored me, let out another guttural scream and

chucked a family photo she was holding against the wall. It exploded like shrapnel.

I ducked. "Mum!"

"WHAT'S THE POINT? WHAT'S THE FUCKING POINT?"

She didn't even note my entrance, let alone the fact I was drenched in fake blood. She just walked over to our display shelf.

"Mum, you're barefoot! The glass!"

She picked up another framed photograph – this one showing all of us on holiday in Italy.

"Mum, no!"

It careered through the air and hit the wall. More shrapnel rained down, I ducked again.

"I GAVE MY WHOLE LIFE. EVERYTHING. FOR WHAT? WHAT THE FUCKING HELL DID I GIVE IT FOR?"

"Mum." I trod gingerly across the glass, feeling it crack under my heels. Until I was right in front of her. "Mum! What's going on?"

She looked up, finally noticing me. I could smell alcohol on her breath.

"Oh, hi, Audrey. We're losing the house, ISN'T THAT JUST FUCKING FANTASTIC?" She picked up a letter from the table and shoved it into my hand. "See! SEE! We're losing the house. His lawyers, his EXPENSIVE LAWYERS. Taking everything. Because I can't afford someone as good because HE LEFT ME ON MY OWN."

My eyes blurred at the writing.

Dear Ms Winters,
I regret to inform you that... As we discussed yesterday
on the phone... As you initially did agree to a Mesher
order it's very difficult now for us to retract it...
Regretfully...expecting the house to be put on the market
within the next six months...

"SEE?" she yelled. "SEE?!"

I scrunched the page shut, not even able to process my
own emotions. "Mum, you need to calm down," I said softly,
like she was a child I was trying to get to sleep. "Come on,
let me make some tea."

"I WILL NOT CALM DOWN, I HATE HIM, HATE HIM,
HATE HIIIIIIIIIIIM!"

Three more photos exploded. She was demolishing them
without even looking at them now. Dougie's leaving ball
combusted into nothingness. My baby photo cracked
against the ceiling, raining glass snowflakes down onto us.

I covered my head with my hands, my heart shaking with
fear. "Mum? MUM?"

But it was like I wasn't there. I walked out of the living
room, my hands trembling, hearing another smash behind
me. I grabbed my phone out my bag and rang Harry.

"Pick up, pick up, pick up." But it rang on until the
answerphone kicked in. I winced as I heard more smashing.
I pulled up Dougie's number, hardly able to hit the right

button. It was Saturday. He *had* to answer, he must…it rang…SMASH…oh God, Dougie…pick up.

"Hello?" There was music on in the background.

"Dougie?! You have to come home. Now! It's Mum. She's gone mental."

"Woah, Audrey. What's up? What's going on?"

"Get a cab! Just get here. Dougie, it's bad. It's really bad."

"What what what? Hang on, I can't just come, I have to go out tonight. It can't be that bad…" He was interrupted by a louder crash and a long scream. "What was that?!" "It's Mum! She's got a letter from the lawyer. Dougie, she's trashing the place. She's probably got glass all in her feet. Please. Get home. Please." I started crying.

"I'm leaving now. I'll be an hour or so. Can you ring someone? Leroy?"

"She won't want anyone to see her like this!"

"Is Harry with you?"

"He won't pick up."

"Okay, okay." Dougie's voice shook but I could sense him trying to keep it together. "Just hang on, Audrey. I'm on my way."

I hunched over my phone, almost hyperventilating as I stared at the dimming screen. Another crash. This one so huge it shook all the walls.

"Mum?" I called. "Dougie's coming round."

No answer. I made myself breathe in, breathe out, in and out. Then returned to the mess of the living room.

It was trashed. The coffee table had been flung against

the cabinets – smashing everything inside. Two of the shelves had collapsed. The broken table lay at the bottom, covered in shattered ornaments, photos, fallen books. The armchair had been tipped upside down and the bottom fabricky bit had been kicked in. By the looks of it, she'd attempted to pick up and throw the sofa too. The cushions lay strewn on the floor, the rug all pulled up around the legs.

Mum wasn't there any more.

"Mum?" I called brightly, like I was calling her down for dinner or something.

I jumped as she appeared in the doorway.

"Hi, Audrey." She left a trail of blood on the white-painted floorboards. She was bleeding quite badly from her feet, smears of it everywhere. My stomach curdled. She was acting calmer now. She wasn't crying. She'd retied her hair. She was holding an old tin of blue paint from when we painted Dougie's room.

"What's the paint for, Mum?"

"Well, if he wants the house, I figure, give him the house, yeah? But WHOOPS." She pinged the top off the paint tin like she was a magician. "BUTTERFINGERS." And, before I could yell "Stop!" she'd chucked it all over the place. It sailed through the air, as if in slow motion, and then splattered against the floor, the walls, the sofa, the dilapidated cabinet. She laughed manically. "Whoops, Paul! I hope that doesn't lower the value! God forbid that ugly slag can't afford a new Dyson."

"Mum! Mum! Stop!"

She smiled, ignored my cry and dug a pen out of her jogging bottoms pocket. "What do you say, Audrey? Want to do some decorating?" She hobbled over to the wall, leaving bloody footprints in the pool of paint.

I could hardly breathe. I definitely couldn't speak. It was like I was hovering above it all. Like my brain had identified "a trauma" and had pressed the emergency parachute button. She ripped the pen top off.

The pen hit our gorgeous wallpaper. The wallpaper I'd grown up with. The wallpaper that had been there when I took my first steps, ate my baked beans and sausages in front of children's TV.

TAKE IT ALL, YOU BASTARD, she scribbled in huge letters.

I stood with my mouth open, tears frozen on my face as her graffiti took up the whole main wall. She looked slightly lost when she was finished, and that was my moment to grab her. Stop her. Bring her to her senses. But I was too frozen, too slow. So she just laughed and hobbled back into the kitchen, slipping slightly in the paint. More smashing jolted me into action. I slid over the ruined living room to the kitchen and almost got hit in the face with a flying plate.

"Our wedding china," she explained, tossing it like a frisbee. The shattering pierced the air as it collided with the tiled wall. "Got it in the divorce, but it's not like I'm going to have any space for it now, am I? In whatever shitty flat I can afford."

Spin crash, spin crash. I ducked, dived, weaved my way

to her, trying to grab her arms to get her to stop. The alcohol on her breath was stronger this close. I grabbed at her hands but she fought me off.

"LEAVE ME ALONE, AUDREY!"

A giant bottle of gin lay empty on the kitchen table. When she ran out of plates, Mum dropped it on the floor.

"Mum?" I pleaded again. Trying to get eye contact. But, before I knew it, the kitchen drawer was open and she had a pair of scissors clutched in her hands. Dread pulsed through me at the sight of the blades. "Mum!" I ran towards her but she pushed past me, knocking me to one side, running to the hall. She held out the scissors and scoured a deep line across the wall as she stumbled past the stairs. She staggered out of my eyeline, leaving only a trail of bloody footprints.

I breathed in and out, noticing how it was catching in my throat, not making it to and from my lungs. I couldn't lose it. Not till Dougie was here.

Then I heard her scream.

The sort of scream that replays on your brain in dark moments for the rest of your life. I skidded and ran to the noise where I found her with her arm out, the scissors held up against her wrist.

Every part of me ran cold.

"Mum." I coughed it out. Not good enough, not caring enough. Oh God, the fear. Where was my phone?

"Would he even care?" Mum asked, pushing the blade harder against her skin. "Or would he just be relieved?

Oh well, how sad, but at least I don't have to deal with my whingey ex-wife any more." She laughed hollowly and pushed the scissors in.

"No! Mum, please!" My phone was in the living room. The scissors weren't sharp but I didn't know what damage they could still do. "Mum, I love you. I need you," I begged. "Please. Stop."

She looked at me for the first time. "Audrey," she whimpered, shaking her head. "It hurts, Audrey. I'm so… so…h-h-humiliated and alone. It hurts me but it doesn't hurt him. It's not fair."

I took a step forward. "I know it's not fair. It's really not fair. It's not your fault, none of this is your fault."

She flinched at my step, pressed the scissors harder still. A very small dot of blood shone on her wrist. Oh God, oh God. "Mum, don't! I need you. Dougie and I. We need you. We love you. You have us."

Her eyes met mine again but they were veiled with a sheet of tears. Her lip wobbling, her hands shaking on the scissors. I didn't breathe and then…then…she screamed so loud, so high, so full of agony that I felt part of my soul shrivel up. The scissors flew against the wall and she collapsed in on herself, her knees buckling under her, falling to the ground like a dropped egg, smashing into pieces as she hit the floor.

I ran to my mother.

"It's-s-s-s no-o-t f-f-f-air." Her back heaving and lurching with pain. "I g-g-gave him everything, Audrey. My h-h-heart.

My life. My youth. I g-gave him his children. He t-t-told me it was going to be for ever. He p-p-promised. He made a v-v-vow."

Tears spilled from my eyes, snot from my nose, pain from my heart. I hugged her so tight. "I know. I'm sorry."

"What does it all mean? What did any of it mean? Why? Why did he do this to us? What didn't I do? Au-Au-Audrey, what didn't I do?"

"You did nothing wrong."

"I must've d-done. Men don't just leave their w-w-wives. You have to give them r-reason to leave."

"Don't say that. Please don't think that."

"Where am I going to live, Audrey?" Her voice was so faint, so high-pitched, so empty of hope.

"We'll find somewhere."

"This is my h-home. Our h-home. Audrey, he said he loved me. He…it…everything was so romantic. How can th-th-this come out of that? It doesn't make sense. None of it makes sense."

"I know, I know." I was crying so hard – tears for me, tears for her, tears for Dougie. Tears of anger, grief, shock, relief and pain merged with each other, carving rivers out of my make-up, joining ranks as they fell off my chin, dripping onto the blood-stained floor.

I hugged her, pulling her into me. She started shivering so I wrapped my big wedding skirt around her. We sobbed together, spilt like milk on the floor, the pinching scent of paint making our eyes water even more. I rubbed her back,

I stroked her face, I murmured reassuring nothings. I felt her calm down. I felt her come back. I felt the adrenaline lift, only to be replaced by the dead weight of grief.

She lifted her head only once to look at me. "He's not coming back, is he?"

44

We'd both stopped crying by the time the key scratched in the lock. Dougie pushed through the front door, banging into our huddle on the floor. I can't imagine what we looked like, what the house must've looked like.

"My blood's not real," I whispered. "I've been filming."

He hid his shock well and just crouched down and put his hand on Mum's shoulder. "Hey, I'm back."

"Dougie?"

His appearance made Mum sob again. She reached out, her arms wobbling, and he fell into her embrace and started crying too.

"I love you, please, we both love you so much."

Instinctively I stood to give them some time alone and walked back to the trashed kitchen. It looked like a crime scene. Blood everywhere, china everywhere. I pushed debris off the breakfast bar – the same breakfast bar I'd sat at every Saturday morning while Dad whistled and made pancakes – and put my head on the cool surface. I closed my eyes and stayed like that until I heard Dougie cough.

I looked up.

"I've booked a taxi. I'm going to take her to hospital."

I nodded. So glad it wasn't me who had to call the taxi, to make the decisions. So grateful there was someone else here. Someone else but me finally here.

"You can come? Or, I guess, maybe you want to clean up? It might be hard for her to come back to this."

"You're right. I'll stay here."

"Are you okay?"

"Are you?"

"No."

"Me neither."

We smiled at each other. Then, "*Dougie?*" floated round the door.

"You'd better go."

I heard them shuffle out to wait for the car. Mum wincing, "Ouch, ouch, ouch," with each step she took. Then the door clicked closed and I was left, just me. To digest whatever the hell had just happened. That could never be taken away.

Harry.

I picked my way through to the living room where my phone lay dormant on the upturned sofa. I was expecting multiple missed calls. I'd been ages. He must be worried.

Just one message though.

Harry: Hey baby, where u at?

I'm not sure what part of my brain was capable of thinking, *Why hasn't he called?* considering everything that had happened. But, part of my brain did think that. And I found myself constructing a melodramatic reply.

Audrey: Can't come. Things really bad here with
Mum. Proper drama x

I left it dangling like a carrot, for him to ask me what was up. So I could go into detail and he could come running over and let me cry on him and him tell me it was all going to be okay.

He didn't message back though.

The house was quiet. The only noise was the sound of paint dripping onto the floor. I surveyed the scene around me, trying to work out where to start. I dug in the cupboard for a paintbrush and got to work just spreading the puddles of paint out a bit. Before they dried into pools that would be impossible to chip off. The paint had splashed mainly across one wall, with only small splatters on the other three. So, when I'd finished, it looked more like a badly done "feature wall" than a post-divorce mental health crisis. I hoovered up as much glass as I could with the nozzle attachment and then spread the paint around on the floorboards – covering up a lot of the blood. It was pitch black outside though I had no idea what time it was.

My phone buzzed and my heart jumped ten feet.

> Dougie: Waiting in A&E. She's not cut a tendon, so it
> should be okay. We're going to be here a while
> though. Are you okay? X

Relief flowed through me and my hands shook as I tapped out my reply.

> Audrey: I'm fine. Tell her I love her. See you when
> you get home x

I put my phone down and looked around again, figuring out what to do next. I got a bin bag out, crouched down and picked big shards of glass off the destroyed cabinet.

"Ouch." Blood appeared on my finger. I shoved it into my mouth to stop the bleeding. I picked up the offending piece of glass with my spare hand and saw something behind it, nestled in a pile of crushed ornaments.

Mum and Dad's wedding photo.

She'd never taken it down. We'd argued so many times about why. But, after tonight, I understood. She'd always believed he'd come back. This photo was like leaving the windows open for Peter Pan. I traced their faces with an unbleeding finger, smiling sadly. Mum looked so hip. The same blunt fringe as Audrey Hepburn in *Roman Holiday*. Dad so suave in his suit. They looked so…happy. Raw, unpacked happiness. This particular shot especially.

An unposed one, their heads together, laughing outside the church. Tears tickled at my eyes as I stroked Mum's face through the glass. How could a couple so besotted with each other end up like this? Paint and blood and graffiti and heartbreak and jealousy and screaming? It made no sense. I put it down and looked up at the wall. At Mum's angry message adorning most of it. Something clicked inside of me, like someone had pressed a button labelled *Activate*. I stood up, my fists clenched, and I turned.

Then I ran out of the front door, smashing it closed behind me.

45

It was freezing cold as I ran through the quiet suburban streets, but I hardly noticed. I passed two women and they both screamed as I dashed by. It took me a moment to realize I was still in full zombie bride get-up – streaked with fake blood and now real blood, my make-up halfway down my face from crying. The rage spurred me on through the night, my feet finding a rhythm as they thudded the pavement. I didn't even pause as I got to the gravel driveway – just skidded down it and thumped hard against the door.

Jessie tentatively opened the door a crack, her mouth falling open when she saw me.

I pushed the door open wider. "Are you happy now, you HOMEWRECKING WHORE?" I screamed, pushing into their hallway. "Mum's in hospital. IS THIS WHAT YOU WANTED?"

Her eyes were wide with shock, disbelief. I used it to launch a further attack. "Do you think you're different?

That you're not like other women? That you're special compared to my mum? *'Ooooh',"* my voice was screaming and high-pitched, *"isn't she pathetic? Hasn't she let herself go? I'll never let myself get like that. No wonder he left her."*

Dad arrived in the hallway in his pyjama bottoms. "Audrey, what's going on?"

"I'M NOT TALKING TO YOU, I'M TALKING TO YOUR SLUT OF A WIFE."

Jessie's face jerked back, too stunned to reply.

Dad wasn't. "Don't you DARE talk to Jessie like that. And keep your voice down, the twins are asleep."

I spun to him. "I DON'T CARE!" I screamed, so loud it hurt my lungs. "Mum's in hospital, HOSPITAL, because of you! Because you couldn't *just* rip out her heart, could you? That wasn't enough. To bunk up with this homewrecking bitch and pretend to be father of the fucking YEAR when you were already a dad, you were already a husband. No, you want to take HER HOME on top of that. She gave you EVERYTHING, Dad. And THIS is how you repay her?"

He stood taller, his fists clenched like mine. The same blood as mine pumping through him. But I'd never be like him, I'd never hurt anyone the way he'd hurt us.

"Audrey, you cannot come into my house and do this. Apologize to Jessie, now!"

I crossed my arms and mock laughed. "I'd rather die than say sorry to you."

She was standing there, vacant, placid, passive. Just how Dad liked his women, it seemed.

"AUDREY!"

I spun back to him. "How can you love her, Dad? A woman who doesn't mind breaking up a marriage? Who then tries to strip that family for everything she can get?"

"AUDREY, I'M WARNING YOU."

Jessie was inching further and further towards Dad, like he was a defensive spell.

She was smiling...the bitch was smiling.

"And how can you love him?" I screamed. "A man who cheats on his wife? Who fucks up the family he is supposed to raise? Who is so quick to break his FUCKING VOWS. How can you love that? WHAT THE FUCK IS WRONG WITH YOU BOTH?"

A loud wail belted out from down the hall. I'd woken one of the twins.

Jessie narrowed her eyes and ignored everything I'd said. "Look what you've done now." She actually rolled her eyes before retreating to the twins' bedroom. I heard her say "Hush" and crank up the musical mobile while Dad and I squared off at each other like we were in a Western shootout.

I hated him then.

I hated Jessie, but I hated him more. For what he'd done, for how little he seemed to care.

"Audrey." His voice was calmer. "I want you to apologize, and then I want you to leave. We can talk about this another time when you've calmed down."

"Don't you even care about Mum? She's in hospital!"

One shake of his head. "Your mother and her…drama is not my concern any more."

"YOU CAUSED HER FUCKING DRAMA."

The crying got louder from the other room.

"KEEP YOUR VOICE DOWN."

I shook my head. "Dad. You can't. You just…can't… expect me to accept everything. Jessie. What you've done. How you've treated Mum. You've got to put us first sometimes. We're still your family!" My voice broke and I shouted to stop the tears flowing. "I'M STILL YOUR DAUGHTER, DAD, DON'T TAKE THE HOUSE. DON'T DO THIS. DON'T CHOOSE THAT BITCH OVER US."

"Careful, Audrey." Dad's voice crackled with tension. He crossed his arms, looking bored now, rather than angry. Bored was worse. The crying softened behind him, Jessie's voice cooing a lullaby. "Don't ask me to choose between you and Jessie," he whispered sharply. He paused for impact. "Because I'll choose her."

Jessie came out cradling Albert, patting him on her shoulder, smiling with a wince. Dad stepped forward, like a protective bear, blocking me from getting to her.

I wilted.

The words, their meaning, hitting me like bullets. *I choose her. I choose her over you, my child.*

And I realized that had been the case from the beginning. He hadn't even tried to juggle the two families. He'd just jumped into another one, leaving us behind, like we were an old pair of trainers. He wasn't just a slave to his feelings of love, he'd made a conscious choice to throw us away. To practically delight in throwing us away. I shook my head, tilted my chin back to not let my tears spill. Not yet. I would not give him the satisfaction.

"You two deserve each other," I said quietly, honestly. Then I turned. I needed to get home for Mum, to be there when she got back. Because we still existed. His love for Mum had created me and Dougie and we still fucking existed – even if maybe now he wished we didn't.

"I'll see you out."

He walked me down the hallway of their perfectly adequately sized home. Jessie followed him, cradling Albert still. I could only interpret it as a gloat. God knows why she felt the need – when she'd already won everything that meant anything from me.

"Goodbye, Audrey," she said, still with a smile on her face. And it was goodbye. Because I would not come back to this house again. I would not give my love to this man any more. That was my choice.

Just as I got to the threshold, I stopped and turned back. Matching her smile. "Be careful, Jessie," I said. "All I can say is, if he did it to Mum, he can do it to you. The years are long. See how much he loves you in ten years' time, see if he gives you everything he's promised."

Dad's face soured. "Audrey, that's quite enough…"

And the door shut in my face.

I couldn't figure out if it was him who had pushed it shut, or her.

It didn't matter.

I stood there, gulping for breath, the cold night hurting my lungs. Blinking back the tears. There was no love for me here.

So I gathered up the skirts of my battered wedding dress and made my way home.

46

Still no message from Harry when I got in. But an update from Dougie.

> Dougie: Just waiting for them to take the glass out.
> God I hate A&E. They want Mum to talk to a
> psychiatrist too. Joy. Will be home late x

The mess of the house still shocked me, bringing everything back. I collapsed onto a kitchen chair and allowed myself to cry. For Mum. For Dougie. About Dad. For the mess they'd left for me to clear up. I tried Harry again but it went straight to voicemail. When the tears had dried as much as I could manage, I stood up and got back to cleaning. The work soothed me. Kept me busy as the outside air got colder and the heating clicked on. Two hours later, the house looked as normal as it could – considering the blue feature wall, the abusive graffiti and the blade marks across the hallway. I took a shower, making the water as hot as I could stand. Steam filled the room as I shrugged out of my wedding dress. It fluttered to the floor gracefully, pooling at my feet in a sodden ruined mess. Then I stepped under the water and washed the long, wretched day from my skin.

When I was clean, warm and dry, I curled myself up in bed and tried to read my book. The adrenaline was flooding out of me fast though, making each muscle heavy. My eyes kept flickering closed but, whenever they did, the image of Mum holding the scissors to her wrist jerked out at me and I'd sit up with a start.

At around one, I heard the click of the key in the lock, the murmuring of hushed voices. I pulled on my dressing gown and padded out, peering round my door. Mum's feet were both heavily bandaged and she hobbled into the hall on two crutches. She looked exhausted and stale and like all the life had been slurped out of her, but she looked like Mum again. There wasn't a disconnect. I could see it in her face. She was back.

Dougie helped her out of her coat. "Let's get you to bed, Miss Painkillers."

I retreated to my room as he helped her upstairs, not wanting to gawp. I heard her shuffle past my door, Dougie murmuring things that made her laugh, their whispers coming from her room. I waited and waited...

Finally, "Audrey?"

I got up and tiptoed over to her bedroom as casually as I could. Mum looked like a child, all curled up under a million covers. But she smiled when she saw me and Dougie did too.

"I'm going to put the kettle on," he said. "Night, Mum."

"Night, Dougie. I love you. Thank you."

He squeezed my shoulders before leaving. Switching off the light as he left, so just Mum's orange bedside light was on.

Mum opened up her arms. "Come here, love."

I tentatively perched on her bed, not wanting to hurt her feet, but she pulled me down into a proper hug and rested my head in her lap.

"I'm so sorry about tonight, Audrey." Her voice was quiet, soothing, adult again.

"It's okay." Even though it wasn't okay. And I didn't think anything would be okay for quite a while.

"It's not… I didn't mean to lose it like that. I…I… It's just…I really thought…" She started stroking my hair. "But I'm going to get help, to deal with the divorce. I thought I had a hold on it but this house thing… Anyway, the people at the hospital gave me the number of someone to talk to. It's a start, I guess. But, sorry."

I turned to look up at her. Her face looked weird from my angle, looking right up at her nostrils. She looked so… old. The skin around her chin loosening at the jaw, her eyelids wrinkled up like she'd spent too long in water.

"None of this is your fault, Mum."

She smiled. "Maybe. Maybe not. It takes two people for a relationship to fail, honey."

"No, don't defend him. Don't blame yourself."

She closed her eyes, a wave of exhaustion visibly hitting her body like a tsunami. "Well, let's get some sleep. I just wanted to say sorry. And thank you. For handling tonight, calling Dougie, stopping me. I'm so proud of you, Audrey. I know it's not been easy. But I think things may change now. I mean, they have to."

"Are your feet okay?"

She laughed softly, eyes flickering shut. "They'll be fine. I just won't be disco dancing any time soon."

With another small laugh, her face relaxed further. I watched her quickly find medicated sleep. The trouble leaving her face the moment she lost consciousness. She looked so small and fragile. And I thought of that young woman in Rome, being proposed to in front of the fountain. Every fairy tale she'd been told to wish for coming true. I carefully scrambled off the bed without waking her and went downstairs. Where Dougie was sitting in the kitchen, nursing a cup of tea, his body slumped over the breakfast bar.

"Tea?" he asked when he saw me.

I smiled. "Well, it's gone one in the morning," I replied. "But we've had a bit of a drama and we are English after all. So tea it is."

I perched on a stool opposite him and watched him fill the kettle, get out the milk. He made it just how I like it — strong, with loads of milk. He looked wrecked though. He pushed the steaming cup in front of me and sat back on his stool across the breakfast bar. We didn't speak for a few minutes, both of us just staring into the steam and sipping at our mugs.

"Thanks for clearing up," he said after a while. "It looks… Well, better."

"Thanks for taking her to the hospital. Do you really think she's going to see somebody?"

Dougie's fingers clenched the handle of his mug. "I hope so."

"Me too."

More quiet. More sipping. More digesting the night and all that it had contained.

"Audrey?"

I looked up.

"You shouldn't have had to deal with all of this on your own," Dougie said, not making eye contact. "That's what I've been thinking all night. I should have visited more. I should try harder."

"You're at uni."

"Yeah, but look at how quick it was to get here. I wish I'd visited more. Rather than just relying on you doing everything, making you feel bad, when it shouldn't all be your responsibility."

I bit my lip, felt tears well up in my eyes. "But I've not been doing a good job or anything," I protested. "I've been working at Flicker so hard, trying to stay out of the house." The tears resurfaced, straying down my face. "Spending all my time with Harry."

"It shouldn't be all on you though," Dougie said. "No wonder you tried to escape. I shouldn't have put that pressure on you." I heard his voice wobble and when I looked up he was crying. Openly, unashamedly. I reached out and he grabbed my hand, squeezing it tight. He sniffed and shook his head. "God, I'm so angry at Dad. I know you defend him but—"

"I don't defend him," I interrupted. "Not any more. I saw him tonight. I went over, still in my zombie outfit."

Dougie's face perked up in surprise.

"I basically told him he was a selfish bastard, then called Jessie a homewrecking whore and told them they deserve each other."

He raised one eyebrow. "Go, Audrey."

I shook my head. "It didn't make any difference." I snorted. "Dad called Mum's hospital visit 'drama'." Dougie's hands tightened on the mug. I sighed. "I'm done with him. For now, at least. I wanna see Albert and Lola still, but... I just can't..."

I sipped at my tea, marvelling at how it really did make problems seem smaller. We didn't talk about Mum any more. Or Dad. I asked him about uni. We compared notes on the last Marvel film.

"So, how's it going with you and Harry?"

I gave him a look. Dougie and I didn't really do talking about relationships. "Okay, thanks."

"Just okay?"

"You met him, you know him. You like him."

"I like him as Harry, I'm still not sure how I feel about him dating my little sister. Where is he tonight anyway?"

I paused before answering. "He's not picking up his phone. But, it's the wrap party tonight. I think he's just wasted."

"He's not wondering why you're not there?"

Dougie was saying everything I'd been thinking. "I sent him a message saying I couldn't make it."

"Hmm."

"Come on, Dougie, he's making me happy!"

"Is he?"

"Yes!"

It took him a while to smile. "Well, as long as it stays that way…"

"It will," I insisted. "Actually, we're supposed to be doing this zombie run thing tomorrow. I guess we'll have to cancel. He might be too hungover anyway."

Dougie shook his head. "Don't cancel. Hey, if he's making you happy. Go."

"But…"

"I'll stay here with Mum. I don't have lectures until Tuesday."

I opened my mouth.

"Honestly, Audrey. Go. I told you. I'm not going to let you deal with this by yourself any more. Go out, have fun." He wrinkled his face. "Not too much fun."

I giggled, and it set Dougie off. And soon, as the night grew later, we stopped being two messed-up siblings dealing with the horrors of our parents' divorce, and seeped back into being a brother and sister, staying up too late and taking the piss out of each other.

And, in that moment, I didn't feel alone. I felt so full of love that, at 3 a.m., I fell asleep the moment my head met my pillow.

47

THE BIG MISTAKE

The course of finding true love cannot run smoothly. Hero and heroine can never simply meet, get along, kiss and The End.

Nope.

We need an OBSTACLE for them to overcome before they're allowed to disappear into the sunset. This usually involves one of them messing up in some way, about seventy per cent into the movie. To make the audience think they're not going to make it.

However, these big mistakes can't be too big. The audience still has to root for the couple. So they make "cute" mistakes, like lying, but only for a really plausible reason. Or freaking out about the strength of their feelings and going cold, but not in a too harsh, unforgivable way. Then, of course, this minor misunderstanding can be sorted out at the ninety-five per cent mark, allowing for the big finish.

PS: Most of these big mistakes in romance films could be resolved if the couple only had a freakin' conversation. But for reasons unknown, lovers in films seem incapable of sitting down and having it out over a cup of tea.

✸ ✸ ✸ ✸ ✸

The winter sun shone directly into my eyes, rousing me from my uneasy sleep.

I'd not closed my curtains before collapsing into bed. So, at around eight, I blinked awake, moaned and shoved my head under my pillow.

It took about ten seconds to remember everything that had happened.

It crashed through my skull like a burst water pipe, spilling everywhere. The smashing sound of china, the scissors on Mum's wrist, Dad's quiet voice saying, "*I choose her.*" And, you know what? Maybe it was a good idea to spend the day running away from zombies. I felt like I needed to pummel the shock and grief out of my system. I still didn't have a message from Harry though and it pissed me off. I could guess why – he'd just got too wasted too quickly. I'd been dating him long enough now to know how quickly he could fling himself into oblivion. But he wasn't to know what had happened last night and I couldn't handle being pissed off at him on top of everything else. I tiptoed to the bathroom, not hearing any stirrings from Mum or Dougie, peed, washed, then returned to my room to dig out some running stuff. *Still* no message from Harry. But I'd see him soon enough and he could smile with his teeth and pull my head into his armpit and tell me he'd missed me and complain about being hungover and everything could be golden and normal for a day.

Audrey: You still on for today? Or you dying? X

It took a while to find my proper trainers. They'd lain abandoned at the bottom of my cupboard since the end of Year Eleven and compulsory PE lessons. I was also lacking in the jogging bottom department. But I shoved on some leggings, a T-shirt and hoodie and spent some time scraping all my long hair into a ponytail. Even though the run was advertised as "only" 3k and "fun", I was still slightly concerned about Harry's and my physical abilities. I hadn't worked up a sweat doing anything other than, well, unspeakable things with Harry for about two years. And Harry smoked, drank, took drugs, and I'd only seen him eat one piece of fruit during our entire courtship. In short, we were going to get caught by zombies very early.

If we even got there on time… It was almost nine and the race started at ten. I was about to call Harry, wondering how much he'd hate me if I woke him, when my phone went off. It was him.

"Audrey?" He sounded like a bear. A bear with a cold

that had been up all night screaming karaoke.

I broke into a smile. It was so nice to hear his voice after everything. "Speaking."

He coughed violently for a few seconds, his voice even hoarser when he was back on the line. "You okay? You didn't come last night?"

"It's a long story. I'll tell you later. You are still on for today, right?"

"What? Yeah. Of course." More coughing. "Umm, when is it?"

"In an hour."

"Shit. Okay. I'll be round in fifteen minutes, I guess."

He hung up before I had a chance to ask how last night had gone. Puzzled, I shrugged and put my phone in my hoodie pocket, and crept downstairs to have a small breakfast. The state of downstairs still shook me up a bit. It would be harder for Mum when she saw it for the first time and I felt a stab of guilt for running off today. But mostly I just felt relieved that Dougie was there, that it wasn't just down to me. I put the mugs from last night into the dishwasher and plucked a banana off the bunch – finding some glass shards I'd missed the night before. I swept them into a paper towel and shoved them in the bin. Then I took the banana and went to wait for Harry on the wall.

It was another gorgeous day with a hint of spring lacing the air. I didn't even feel that cold. I ate my fruit and checked my phone. Nine twenty-five. We were really pushing it. Just as I considered firing off a *trying-not-to-nag* message,

I heard the revving engine of Tad's car. Harry pulled up in front, and my first sense that something was wrong was that he didn't turn to smile hello. He just stared right ahead out of the windscreen. Not even pulling the handbrake up. I shoved my banana peel into the wheelie bin and climbed into the car. There was no music playing. More weirdness.

"Hey, you made it," I said brightly, leaning over to kiss him on the cheek. "You ready to be chased by zombies?"

"Hey. Yeah, it should be good." He didn't turn, didn't smile. Just pulled into first gear and started three-point turning.

He looked like utter shit. Not even his handsomeness could carve through what looked like one hunky-dory of a hangover. He'd stuffed his hair into his beanie, stubble littered his chin, his eyes were more slit than eye, his skin all grey and sallow. And he…well…smelled a little. And not in his regular gorgeous way. More a stale sweetness that made my nose wrinkle.

"Harry, are you okay?"

"Me? What? Oh yeah, I'm fine. Drank too much. You all right?"

I squirmed in my seat, annoyed he had only asked now. "Well, no, not really. About last night…"

He did turn to me then. "What about it?"

"Well, it's nothing." I squirmed in my seat. Had he not seen my message? "Well it isn't. It's just, Mum went a bit crazy. It was quite intense. She ended up in hospital."

A curious collection of emotions crossed Harry's grey

face, none of which I could figure out. He gulped, he flinched, his hands tightened on the wheel. He focused on the road.

"Shit, Audrey. Is she okay? Are you okay?"

"Umm, she's all right. Dougie's with her. I'm all right. I tried ringing you..." I let it trail there, not sure how naggy it would come across if I finished the sentence. Harry had sped us through town now and we were out in country lanes. I saw my first *Zombie Run! This way* sign – all red stop signs and garish font. I would've felt excited if I didn't feel conflicted by Harry's response.

"Yeah, sorry about that. I...er...well, Rob made me do absinthe the moment we arrived. It was...I was..."

I tried to smile. "Probably not in a fit state to be doing a 3k run this morning then."

A short burst of laughter. "Ha! No. But it will be fun." He smiled, but his eyes winced as he did. He reached out and patted my knee, which made me feel much worse rather than better.

I was trying not to feel pissy about his reaction. Trying not to judge his response to my mum news. But I wasn't impressed. He'd not asked any more questions, wanted any more detail. I mean, it wasn't like I was expecting him to be a professional therapist or something but still...he didn't seem fussed. My mum had gone to hospital! We slowed into a line of traffic and men in yellow reflective jackets appeared to direct us all into some muddy field. Everyone in the surrounding cars looked ten million times healthier than us

– suited up in Lycra and all glowy of face. Harry muttered and grumbled and didn't really look at me as we were guided into a parking space. Then he pulled up the handbrake and was up and out, leaving me to scramble after him.

"Harry? Something is up."

He kept walking, not looking at me. "What? No! It's just, doesn't it start soon?"

I took his hand and he turned and gave me his wince-smile again, making me want to let go. We funnelled into a crowd of other latecomers. Everyone else seemed to be in big groups, mostly men, all taking the piss out of each other and joking about how long they'd last. There were fake body parts strewn around the field and dangling from trees, dramatic signs everywhere.

CONTAGION ZONE – DO NOT ENTER.

Loud eerie music blasted from speakers set up in the trees. It was everything I'd hoped it would be, everything I'd thought Harry would love. But his face was still grim and unresponsive. So I let go of his hand and walked to the side of the people river, crossing my arms, waiting for him to realize and follow me. Which he did.

"What's up?" No eye contact.

"I'm not going any further until you tell me what the hell is going on," I said. "We just passed an actual burned-out car and you're not even excited. Tell me."

He looked over my shoulder and I thought, *Oh God, something bad has happened,* but then he took a deep breath and finally, finally made eye contact.

"Audrey, I'm sorry." He smiled. And this time most of his face was involved. "I'm just really, really hanging. Please, don't be angry. I'm not being off, I'm just trying really hard not to vomit."

His smile always made me smile back. "Is that all?"

He nodded. "Yes, that's all. Honestly. It's just whenever I open my mouth, I get scared I'm going to legit puke."

"Harry we're about to run 3k. We're about to get CHASED for 3k."

"I'm trying to pretend that isn't happening."

Just then a huge siren went off, startling everyone. "EVACUATION HAS BEGUN, EVACUATION HAS BEGUN. WE ARE NOT SAFE, I REPEAT, WE ARE NOT SAFE. GET TO THE MEETING AREA STAT."

Everyone cheered, whooped, some people screamed. Harry and I met eyes again and both giggled.

"I don't think this is something you're going to be able to ignore," I told him.

"Argh, come here." He pulled me in for a hug and it was everything I needed. I smushed my face right into him, even if he did smell a bit, feeling better, whole. Then he turned and whispered in my ear, all dramatically, "If I fall, you have to go on without me, Audrey. Leave me behind, okay? If you love me, you'll live. For me. Live for me."

I laughed, clicking into the joke. "I can't live without you," I said in a hysterical female voice. "I'd rather zombies eat my brains than live even one day without you."

Harry's body shook with laughter. "We'll make it through,

Audrey. The zombies may have being undead on their side, and super-speed, and, well, the function organizers have probably hired professional runners but...our love...our love can help us beat them."

And, just like that, things were okay again. The siren blared louder and Harry flung his arm around me casually and we walked to the starting point where hundreds of runners were gathered, looking expectantly at a giant TV screen.

"We need to register," I said, and Harry steered us to this little tent, splattered in fake blood. There was no queue, just a harassed-looking woman dressed in one of those plastic forensic suits, playing on her phone. "Oh," she said, when she saw us. She coughed. "I mean, you're late. The evacuation is about to begin." Her voice was deliberately over-the-top, and I couldn't help but judge her obvious lack of acting talent.

"Sorry," I said. "But we're here."

"Give me your names. You may just make it to the boat in time."

She ran through a list, before finding our names and crossing them off in pencil. She handed us numbered stickers to attach to our fronts as well as five coloured scarves which she told us to tuck into our trousers. Then, in her normal voice she said, "Toilets are around the back. Be quick if you need to go, it really is about to start."

We emerged from the tent into the bright sunlight. "Do you need the..." I began to ask Harry, but deafening music started and the face of an actor dressed as a politician appeared on the giant screen. The whole field went nuts. People cheering or booing. Harry grabbed my hand in excitement and pulled me forward to get a better view.

"Hello? Hello? Are you receiving me?" The actor on the screen said and everyone cheered, while I winced. "Okay, let's hope so. There's no easy way to put this, folks. Parliament has fallen. The zombies have breached the walls. The Prime Minister is dead." Everyone cheered at that. Some macho guy next to me, made entirely of protein powder, laughed and said, "I wish."

The actor coughed. "We've arranged evacuation for survivors. Boats to the Isle of Wight leave in an hour. For safety reasons, they will leave with or without us. You've got to make your way through the woods to get there. It's okay, it's clear. We checked, we're going to be fine, everyone. Bravery comes when you most need it..." Just then a zombie appeared to the side of the screen and launched himself at the man. More screams and cheering.

Harry turned to me and said, "This. This is the best thing ever!"

The actor clambered at the screen and yelled, "THEY'VE BREACHED THE WOODS. THE ZOMBIES ARE COMING. RUN! RUN FOR YOUR LIVES..." And then he was pulled out of shot again and the camera was splattered with blood. The screen turned to fuzz and everyone around us went ballistic.

"My hangover just vanished." Harry pulled me in to

nuzzle my neck. "Why do I have such an amazing girlfriend who takes me to such perfect things?"

I smiled. "Shh, we're missing the instructions."

A bossy lady in an official-looking costume walked under the screen and started explaining the rules through a loudspeaker.

"There will be many paths through the woods to the finish line. Some longer than others. There is no right or wrong way. Though there are some ways that are more…infected than others." Everyone cheered again. "Choose carefully."

"Oh God, I am worried about legitimately having to run," I said to Harry, pulling my body further into him. Craving close contact after his weird mood. "I can only run lines."

He kissed my forehead and hugged me back. "We'll stick together. It will be fine. It will be fun!"

The lady barked out further instructions. "You have five tags attached to you. The zombies will try and snatch these off you. The aim is to get to the finish line without losing all your tags. If you do lose them, the woods are full of supervisors wearing yellow jackets. Find them, and they'll escort you to the losers' area."

Everyone booed.

They'd started to shuffle us towards an inflatable starting arch. People were half listening, half going over their game plans with friends, some stretching their legs and arms. My phone buzzed, the vibrate pulsing through my hoodie.

"Bollocks. I forgot to leave my phone in the car. Do you think I can run with it okay in my pocket?" I asked Harry, who kept a protective arm around me as they squidged us in closer.

"Are you ready?" the lady yelled. Everyone whooped, the energy floating off the crowd like vapour clouds.

"Maybe it's Mum." I pulled my phone out and unlocked the screen. An unknown number.

Then my heart fell out.

Harry and I got together last night. I thought you should know. Rosie.

The screen blurred as nausea raced through my shaking hands, plummeting through my stomach. My face drained of blood.

No.

No no no no no no no no no.

Harry's voice.

"Hey? Audrey? What's wrong?"

No.

No no no no no no.

The nausea felt sour, like my insides were pickled. My face flushed with heat. I couldn't…couldn't…

"READY? TEN, NINE, EIGHT…"

I made myself look at Harry, whose face was arranged into puzzlement. Concern even. I could hardly bear to look at him. Everything hurt, and yet everything was numb at the same time. I held up my phone. Watched his face as he read the message. Watched as his mouth fell open, eyes bulged.

"Audrey, it's not what it looks like. Audrey! Audrey."

I was turning away. Looking for an exit but we were crammed right in with the runners, excitedly counting along, waiting for the gun. I'd already been shot. I was bleeding out on the muddy grass.

"What the hell does it look like then?" I snapped back, part of me floating above myself, thinking what a clichéd line that was. That I was acting in a bad movie. "While I watched my mum go to hospital, you were fucking someone else. What else does it look like?"

"Please, Audrey. I can explain." Oh God, this really was a bad movie.

"GO!" A gun fired and the crowd rushed forward, pushing us along, euphoria and excitement blending with the shock and horror falling off me in chunks. I let myself get jostled along to the side, trying to lose Harry.

We got together last night…

Last night, while my mum bled onto our floorboards, smashed all our belongings, trashed our house, held a blade to her wrist. While I desperately tried to clean up a spill that just kept spilling…he was…he was…

I was at the side, runners streaming past me like a herd of gazelles. I saw Harry's hat bob and weave through them, his face desperate, eyes searching for me. I'm not sure why I waited for him but he got through, people swearing at him as he bumped into them. I crossed my arms. The tears not here yet. The shock still too raw.

"Audrey!"

I shook my head, shrugged him off as he tried to grip my shoulders. "Don't fucking touch me!"

"Please. Let's go somewhere."

"That's why you didn't pick up your phone last night, isn't it?" Things fell into place. Puzzle pieces of a painful jigsaw assembled themselves in the air.

"I was wasted, Audrey. I was so drunk. The absinthe... Ouch."

Another runner knocked into him and called, "Watch it, mate," before sprinting off into the woods. Most people were past the start line now. I heard screams and laughter echo from the trees as zombies attacked.

"But you were sober enough to remember it happened?" I could hardly talk my voice wobbled so much.

Because he must remember. He was so weird this morning. Not weird. Guilty. Not able to look me in the eye.

"No!" he protested. "Not at first. I woke up, your message woke me up. I...I..." He shook his head, looked away, looked back. "I...woke up with Rosie. I...I didn't know what had happened. I had to ask her."

I closed my eyes as if it would shield me from the pain his words caused. It didn't work. I blinked again and again. But the pain, and the images of them. Curled up naked in Harry's bed, light streaming through his red curtains, their bodies entwined, unclean from the things they'd done the night before.

I didn't believe him.

I didn't believe a word of what he was saying.

My ribcage caved in then, falling in on itself, crumbling into dust, taking my heart with it, falling, falling into a blackness inside of me.

A steward came up to us, looking baffled. "Hey, you guys running or not?"

And I realized I couldn't stand to be in this moment any longer. Couldn't stand to be having this conversation. Couldn't stand to be confronting this new reality. I had to leave, go, get away.

I had to run.

"Audrey! Where are you going? Come back."

His voice ricocheted off me as I sped past the start line and ran into the woods, my arms pumping, adrenaline kicking in, pain pushing me forward. It was much darker in the canopy of trees, and the shrieks of runners ahead were much louder. I paused for a second as the path split into five, my brain incapable of decision-making. It allowed Harry to catch up with me. He grabbed me, trying to force me to look at him again.

"Please, don't run away," he begged. "Please, Audrey. I'm sorry. I'm so sorry. Please."

I pelted down the far right, along the edge of the woods. He was hot on my tail.

"I'm not going to let you go," he called through huffing and puffing. "You have to hear me out, please, I'm sorry."

We didn't come across any zombies. Only runners who'd already lost all their tags, walking with their heads down, trying to find the supervisors.

"Keep going," they yelled at us in encouragement, unaware of the massive domestic I was running from. "It's clear ahead, they're further into the middle of the woods."

It was impossible to know if they were being honest, or luring us into a trap. I didn't really care. It became obvious which one when, suddenly, a zombie jumped out from behind a bush.

"BRAINS!" the actor yelled, his head dripping with fake blood, clothes ripped.

I didn't even flinch. "Fuck off!" I dodged out of his grasp and pounded further into the woods. I heard Harry thundering behind me, followed by, "Fuck off, mate, leave me alone!" When I allowed myself to look back, I saw he only had four tags on him. It got quieter and I emerged into dappled sunlight, in a small clearing. I leaned over, taking huge gulps of air to replenish my overworked lungs. And that. That's when the tears came. A flood of them, bursting the banks of my eyes, falling down my face, onto my cheeks, splattering my legs.

Harry.

Harry had cheated on me.

Oh God, it hurt. It's so simple, happens so often, but how it hurt. Like a sting. Like an ache. Like a burn. Like being punched. No one ever tells you how much heartbreak physically hurts. How it literally feels like you've been kicked down the stairs. How you can't swallow. How every muscle aches. How your heart lurches inside you like it's been poisoned. Nobody tells you that.

People should tell you that.

I heard panting and Harry staggered out into the clearing. His face was practically yellow, snot all down his face. From his crying.

Because Harry was crying.

And that, that inexplicably bought him five minutes.

"Audrey, I'm so, so, so sorry. It's not as bad as..."

"I get to decide how bad it is." My voice choked.

He took a step closer and I bolted back. He sensed it and put his hands up, signalling that he wasn't going to get any closer. We had the clearing between us.

"You knew..." My voice was so strained, so high-pitched as I fought to get the words out. "You knew...after Milo... after my dad... You promised not to hurt me... You knew how..." I didn't finish the sentence. He did know. He knew how vulnerable I was. I hadn't lied about it, or hidden it. I'd owned it, exposed it. Spelled it out to him that I was holding out my battered heart on my palm and offering it to him. And he'd taken hold of it, sworn to help me nurse it back to health.

He'd lied.

"It really didn't mean anything... I don't even really remember it..."

"So you do remember it?" Liar. He was a liar.

"Hardly! Audrey, I was so drunk. If you'd been there! It wouldn't—"

"MY MUM WAS IN HOSPITAL!"

"I know, I know this is all my fault. And I'm so sorry

about your mum. I didn't know… Fuck, Audrey…I was so drunk… But it's not as bad as you think. We didn't… We didn't have sex."

A scream echoed around the woods, scattering birds. We both watched them fly off. It wasn't from far away. The zombies must be near.

They didn't have sex.

Didn't have sex.

Didn't.

Have.

Sex.

Didn't.

Was this salvageable? Was it? Was this not what it looked like? Could I handle a kiss?

"What happened?" I asked, my tears temporarily disabled. "Tell me exactly what happened. And don't lie to me about being too drunk to remember."

"We didn't have sex."

"But?"

He paused, sniffed, wiped his snotty nose with the back of his arm. Shook his head. That's when I knew it was bad. The fact he paused. Wanting to prolong the moment where he still had a chance, knowing he wouldn't have one after this. I started crying again. It wasn't just a kiss. Not that I was sure I could even get over a kiss.

"But…oh, Audrey… I didn't do anything to her but she…she…"

"Tell me." My voice was a squeak.

"She gave me a blow job, okay?"

I found myself touching my chest, checking my heart was still there. Harry was spluttering on. "It was nothing! I mean, I can't tell you how wasted I was. I told her this morning, that it meant nothing. That I loved you." He hiccupped a sob, then looked into my eyes across the clearing. "I didn't do anything to her. I love you, Audrey."

I shook my head. "No." The word came out instinctively. "No," I repeated. "You don't tell me you love me. Not now. Not after…" I sighed and threw my head up to the golden sun, like the sky might have the answers. It hurt so much.

A blow job.

I mean…

What even?

"I do love you. I was going to tell you last night. After filming finished. I'm not just saying this, Audrey. I was going to."

I blinked away more tides of tears and looked back down.

It was then I saw them.

The zombie actors. Creeping up behind him. Four of them. Faux-staggering. Totally oblivious to our drama. Harry totally oblivious to them. They noticed me notice and smiled, made the *shh* sign, their blueish fingers held over their mouths. I had a good ten metres on them.

Harry… He was going to get taken out.

"So, you were going to tell me you loved me but you let someone suck your penis instead?" I said dully. "Bit of a contradiction, isn't it?"

"Please, Audrey. I'm sorry. I love you. I love you so much."

"BRAAAAAAAAINS!" The zombies charged. Harry's eyes widened. I shrugged at him.

"Hang on, guys, we're trying to have a conversation. We're not in the race any more. Guys, come on. Please. GUYYYYYYYYYYSSSS!"

And my feet were thundering under me, my aching body carrying me away from them, away from Harry, back into the woods, as his surprised yelp scattered more birds, which flew with me deeper into the trees.

48

Harry: Audrey, I'm so sorry. Where are you?! I can't find you anywhere. X x x x x x x x

Audrey: I got a lift home with a zombie who is less dead to me than you. Now will you please kindly fuck off.

Harry: Please hear me out. Please let me come round. I love you. I wasn't lying. I'm in love with you.

Audrey: Harry cheated on me…

Alice: What!?

Becky: OMFG THE BASTARD. Are you okay?

Audrey: No.

Charlie: We're coming over. We'll be there in half an hour.

Harry: Why won't you see me? Your mum said you're not in but I know you are. Please. I'm not giving up on you, on us. I love you. X x x x x x

Leroy: The fucker! You can do SO much better, sweetheart.

Harry: I can't stop thinking about you. Please give me another chance x

LouLou: Okay, so Harry told me what happened and you also didn't turn up to work today. Audrey, I'm so sorry. Are you coming back into work? I can fire Harry if you want? He deserves it. I hate that I was right about him.
Audrey: Hey. Don't fire him. He needs the job. LouLou, I hope we can still be friends but I'm not coming back to Flicker. Sorry x

George Dyson Estate Agents
10 Bridgely High Street
Bridgely-upon-Thames
BT5 6TY

Dear Ms Winters,
Thank you for choosing us as your estate agent. We endeavour to get you the best price for your property. You mentioned you don't want to move until September, but we can put the house on the market now. Due to the location of the property and the current selling climate, we think we'll be able to get you a high offer.

Yours sincerely,
George Dyson

Harry: The movie is finished. It's amazing. You're amazing. I wish I could show it to you. I still love you, Audrey. I will never stop being sorry.

Harry: PLEASE I L(VE YOU SU FKCING MUCH WHY WONTY YOU TALK TO ME IM SO MESSSED UP IMSORRY I LOVEYOU AUDREY IM SORRY SO SORRY PLEASE PICKUP THE PHONE PLEASE I L9VE T x

Dougie: You need to leave my sister alone otherwise I'm going to gut you.

Royal Welsh College of Music and Drama

Dear Audrey Winters,
We are delighted to invite you to audition at the Royal Welsh College of Music and Drama. We were blown away by your video audition. It was unlike anything we've ever seen before. Below is the audition date, alongside information about how to get here, where to stay and what to expect. We look forward to meeting you, Audrey.

Yours sincerely,
Joe Headley
Course Leader

Audrey: I GOT AN AUDITION AT ROYAL WELSH.
Leroy: OMFG SERIOUSLY? I am so jealous I could
DIE. When is it?!
Audrey: Next week.
Leroy: Wanna run lines?
Audrey: I love you!

Audrey: I can't stop thinking about him, Leroy.
Leroy: Don't go there babes, trust me x x
Audrey: I know… It's just…I love him.
Leroy: No you don't.
Audrey: It doesn't work like that. It's not as easy
as that.
Leroy: Isn't it?

LouLou: Hey Audrey, how have you been? We all
miss you! When can we grab a catch-up coffee?
Sorry to bother you, but Ma is getting on at me
about your uniform. Do you mind dropping by to
return it? Otherwise she's threatening to charge you.
Audrey: Hey, I'm good… I think. How are you? I can
drop it round tomorrow morning, before I have to
go to Wales. That work for you?

LouLou: Wales? What's in Wales? Yeah, 10 works
for me.
Audrey: 10 it is x
Audrey: Lou, he won't be there, will he? <deletes>

49

THE GRAND GESTURE

Sorry isn't good enough in romance films. Sorry does not cut the romantic mustard. No. At precisely the ninety-five per cent mark of a romance film, one of the characters has to make a Grand Gesture to make up for the aforementioned Big Mistake. These gestures usually include killer lines, dramatic weather, flash mobs, mad dashes through busy places and heartfelt speeches.

And they always, always pay off.

A lesser known cliché, known as "The Dream Denial", often goes hand in hand with The Grand Gesture. Usually the spurned lover has used their heartbreak to do something amazing with their lives. Maybe bag a dream job, or accept an offer to move abroad. Whatever it is, this dream conflicts with the couple's ability to be together. But, as long as the Grand Gesture is big enough, the lover is willing to let go of their dreams and fall into their lover's arms. Who needs dreams when you've met the love of your life? Isn't that the ultimate dream anyway?

I stood outside Flicker for a long time, waves of nostalgia crashing over me. It had only been a month and yet my time here still felt like it was the past. I cradled my silk shirt over my arm and looked up at the posters displaying this week's current films.

I hadn't heard of any of them. Oddly enough, I hadn't watched a film for a while. And, now my A-starred Media coursework was done, I didn't think I'd be watching romance films for a long time. I took a deep breath, summoning the courage and energy I'd spent the last month building up, then I walked up to the big entrance doors and pushed through them.

The lobby was empty.

"LouLou? I'm here," I called out. "Bearing highly flammable uniform with a stain I couldn't seem to wash out."

Only silence replied. Odd. The bar was empty, the staffroom empty. I glanced up at the rota to see who'd taken over my shifts. Some girl called Lauren. I wrinkled my nose, not liking the feeling of being replaced.

"LouLou?" I called up the stairs, but still nothing. So I pushed through the heavy doors of Screen One.

I wasn't expecting candles.

"What the hell?" I said, stopping in shock.

And there he was. Him. Harry. Flickering in a hundred tea lights…that smile…that face. I was crying instantly and he stepped through the flames and touched my face. I'd been so strong. I'd managed a whole month. But his touch melted me and I felt powerless.

"Can you just stay?" he begged.

I couldn't look at him. If I did, my heart would win. So I looked everywhere else but at him. I stared at the candles adorning every available surface, at the giant cinema screen behind him. Rose petals scattered the aisle. Of course he'd used bloody rose petals. Harry's thumb rubbed my cheek again. He whispered sorry again. My face, the traitor, leaned into his touch. Finally, I looked up at him.

Those eyebrows. He raised one, like he knew. There was still so much longing and love there.

"Please?"

I didn't know what to do. I didn't know what the "right" answer was. If there even was one. Oh God, I'd missed him. Just his smell, now, filled me up whole, made everything feel right. His touch, him, he felt so right. He was so right. But what he had done…

"Audrey? It's less than ten minutes, I promise. Then you can go."

I looked up into his eyes, knowing that, by doing so, I was surrendering. Somehow I was smiling. "What will take less than ten minutes?"

His grin grew wider, his ego filling in the gaps inside of me. "Take a seat."

I slowly cottoned on as he led me to one of the best seats in the cinema. Middle. Aisle. Best view. He sat me down. Then ran down through the ocean of candles and came back cradling a giant cardboard box of popcorn. "With extra cinnamon dust!" he exclaimed.

I took it, our fingers brushing, the feeling short-circuiting the section of my brain marked *Sense*.

"Please, just, stay here," he said. Then he was off through the candles again, leaping over them with his spindly legs, racing up the stairs. I heard the doors close behind me. I was alone, surrounded by flickering light, clutching overpriced popcorn, wondering what the hell was going on and why I was putting up with it when the screen flickered into life and then...then I got it.

A fake film certification popped up, glowing green. It was rated 12A. The title: *The Apology*. A warning underneath. *May contain some cheesy scenes that cynical viewers will find distressing.*

Because Harry had made me a movie. And there he was. On the screen. Filling it with his teeth and charm. Beaming across the cinema in a pool of yellow light. He held up a stack of giant white cards in front of him and Jeff Buckley's "Hallelujah" started from the speakers. Harry on the screen lifted up a stack of handwritten signs – just like that scene with Keira Knightley in *Love Actually*.

Audrey, the first sign read as the song floated around

the candle-filled cinema.

Harry pulled another page to the front. *I am so sorry I hurt you.*

And another. *I will never stop being sorry.*

And it will never happen again.

Tears poured down my face, the popcorn lay forgotten on my lap.

I know you've had to watch a lot of romance films recently.

He winked as he pulled another sheet of card forward. *And I know you're not a fan.*

But I thought maybe…

…hopefully…

I could use them to prove to you how much I love you.

Because I really do love you.

He looked right down the camera lens, smiling with so much pride. *And here's the proof.*

The music faded out and then faded into "Kissing You" by Des'ree. I knew that song because…because…

Because Harry's face was now much bigger on screen and he was staring at me through a fish tank. Just like in Baz Luhrmann's *Romeo + Juliet*. I say "fish tank", but he had to be in the London Aquarium or something because an actual shark floated in front of him and he jumped and I found myself laughing through my tears. Then it cut out again, to a shot set up in a dance studio, the walls lined with mirrors. Harry now stood, head down, in the middle of the wooden floor. And then "(I've Had) The Time Of My Life" came on and Harry launched into the beginning of the *Dirty Dancing* finale dance. He was terrible. My mouth dropped as he spun and leaped around the studio, hardly keeping in time, but the steps were roughly the same as the film's. And, when it couldn't get any more surreal, LouLou's Mohawk appeared. She floated up in the corner of the screen, cradling a giant watermelon over her head with the words *He's sorry* written across it, winked into the camera, then floated back down again… We cut away. This time Harry was in his flat with LouLou and all the guys. Everyone wearing party hats. I felt instantly ill as I looked for Rosie but she wasn't there and my stomach relaxed.

"TEN, NINE, EIGHT, SEVEN, SIX, FIVE…" they all yelled behind Harry as he walked towards the front of the shot, smiling shyly.

"Now, Audrey." He spoke into the camera, his cone party hat off to one side. "I would say something here vaguely along the lines of when you realize you want to spend the rest of your life with somebody you want…hang on… If I finish that sentence I'm going to have to pay a lot of money to the creators of *When Harry Met Sally* but—"

"HAPPY NEW YEAR!" Tad, LouLou, Jay and Rob erupted behind him and all started singing "Auld Lang's Syne".

"But I don't have that kind of money," Harry continued. "So I'll have to use my own script. Audrey, I love you. I've never loved anyone before, and I can't imagine ever loving anyone else…"

It cut again. This time to a shot filmed in sepia tone – all old-fashioned and yellowed. Harry was standing in exactly the same spot but he wasn't wearing a party hat any more. He wore a period costume, with a ruffled blouse. He'd even pasted on sideburns.

He stared right out at me. "Audrey, you must allow me to tell you how ardently I admire and love you," he said, just like Mr Darcy says it.

Then, the film cut again. He was still in period costume but he was in our local swimming pool. LouLou and the others were bobbing around in the water on foam floats from the Sunday fun swim, yelling, "Help! Help! Iceberg! Fuck you, iceberg!" Harry looked down at his ye-olde clothing, then cheekily looked back at the camera, and said, "Now, apparently it really does it for girls if I do this…" And, with that, he dived into the swimming pool just like Colin Firth in the BBC version of *Pride and Prejudice*. His head emerged and he switched roles, suddenly re-enacting Jack from *Titanic*. A novelty float bobbed past and he grabbed it and tried to climb onto it but kept falling off.

"I'M NOT GOING TO TRY VERY HARD TO GET ONTO THIS LIFESAVING DEVICE," he yelled, in the world's worst American accent. "AND NOW I'M GOING TO FREEZE TO DEATH TO PROVE MY LOVE TO YOU."

I was beyond laughing and crying at this point. All I could do was watch, mesmerized, as the most creative, beautiful, funny, poignant romance film of all time continued to play on the cinema screen. Celine Dion's "My Heart Will Go On" came on and I rolled my eyes. That song! But then the scene cut again, to Harry, wearing a long beige coat and standing outside my house. MY house. Holding a giant boombox just like John Cusack in *Say Anything*. Apart from the fact he was blasting Celine Dion out of it. It was broad daylight and our neighbour, Mildred, shuffled over and complained, "Turn that down, please!" Another cut and Harry was in Gatwick airport, the camera struggling to keep up with him as he ran through the terminal, leaping over suitcases and dodging customers, running, running. He wheezed into the camera, "I had to buy a plane ticket to freakin' Manchester to get airside for this shot." And I laughed before I heard security in the background saying, "YOU ARE NOT ALLOWED TO FILM IN AIRPORTS, PUT THE CAMERA DOWN NOW."

And, finally, there was Harry standing in the rain. Drenched. And it wasn't dramatic rain like in films. Just grey drizzle but rather a lot of it. And a determined pigeon trying to get off with another pigeon in the background. Harry smiled, shrugged and said, "You always have to include some rain, don't you, Audrey?" The camera zoomed in, so it was just his face. His smile. Rain running off it. Him blinking it away as he spoke. "Audrey, I love you. Please forgive me. Being with you makes me feel like I'm in the movies. I honestly, truly, want you to be my happily ever after. Please..."

The screen went dead. The movie was over. I put my head into my lap, tears well and truly back now. And, when I lifted it, Harry was there. Real Harry. Serious Harry.

Crouching in the aisle, clutching my hand, saying, "Do you forgive me?"

I gently tugged the collar of his shirt and I kissed him, pulling him towards me. Every bit of me needing him. He sort of fell on top of me but he kissed me back. It was full of meaning and feelings and our tears ran off our faces and merged before dripping off our chins. It was the best kiss of my life. The most real kiss of my life. Between two people just being there – raw and honest – just kissing like the universe would end if they stopped.

Tiny fragments of myself fractured all over when I broke off the kiss.

And I said the truth.

"I can't forgive you, Harry," I whispered in his ear, my voice cracking. "I'm sorry, but I can't."

Because I couldn't forgive it. I couldn't forget it. That's just me. I'd seen too much pain from love. I couldn't be with someone who had stung me so sharply so early on. I wasn't strong enough. I wasn't…romantic enough to work through it. Because what I'd learned was, love isn't just a feeling. Love is a choice too. And you may not be able to help your feelings, but you are responsible for the choices you make about what to do with them. Dad had loved Mum. He had fallen for her hard. Then they'd grown old, grown dull, and he'd developed feelings for Jessie. He chose to act on those feelings. He chose to rip our family apart. He could've chosen not to. So many people choose not to. And Harry… Harry…he chose to drink too much that night. He chose to betray me. Even if he was drunk, even if he regretted it, even if he was sorry. I loved Harry. I felt it so hard, so deeply, that I was sure it would never go away. A part of me would always love him. The boy with the teeth, who made me a Hollywood ending. My love was something I couldn't help, that I felt so deeply it was a scar.

But I was choosing to walk away from that. Because my heart…my heart was too fragile for someone who had chosen to break it.

He looked up at me, his face filled with horror. "What! I don't understand. I thought…"

I nodded, crying so hard none of my face was dry. "I know… I do love you. I do…" I choked on my words. "But I can't be with you. I can't be with someone who cheated on me. It's not going to work. Us…we're not going to work. I'm not going to change my mind about this."

"No, Audrey!"

I nodded more determinedly. "Yes. I thought maybe our relationship was different. Maybe it was, for a little while. But I'm not giving you the opportunity to break my heart again, Harry. Maybe this time you've broken your own too and maybe you won't do anything like this again. I'm not willing to take that chance though."

He didn't fight it.

Instead his face collapsed onto the armrest and then he jolted up and grabbed me into a hug. We squeezed each other so hard we almost couldn't breathe, salting each other's shoulders, saying goodbye.

"Thank you," I whispered. "For the film. It was amazing. I hope you get all your dreams. You are so talented, Harry. I've always thought so."

"You are too."

I closed my eyes and inhaled his smell one last time, using up all the moment when I could touch him, be this close to him, have this access to him. This was going to be the last moment in my life where I'd be able to, where it would be appropriate. I drank him in, trying to savour it, knowing my memory would never recall it properly, never do it justice. It was a fleeting moment of beauty, of romance, of love, and like that…it was gone. I stood up, my feet shaking. I accidentally knocked over the popcorn.

"Whoops," I said, tilting my head. "Sorry. You're going to have to clean that up."

He stood with me, wiping his eyes, putting a brave face on it. Like we all do. When the moments to be honest about our feelings have passed, when it's appropriate to play manners again. "Nothing I'm not used to."

"Do you have any credits you can roll to give me some music to walk out to?"

His eyes were so sad but he still smiled. "Nope. I was relying on us making out heavily at this moment. Anyway," he shook his head, "this may sound cheesy but, I didn't think you and me were ready for credits yet. I didn't think… I hoped…we still had a few more scenes."

I reached out and wiped a tear from his cheek. "We do," I said. "We have so many scenes left. Just not with each other."

"Cheesy line, Winters."

"Oh, you can talk Mr *Ikea Now Has A National Shortage of Tea Lights.*"

And, like everything with us, despite everything with us, it ended on laughter.

I stepped over the candles, I left my uniform on the counter and pushed through the doors. The bright spring sunshine disoriented me and hurt my eyes, like it always does when you step out of a cinema. Emerging into the real world. Where the lines aren't scripted, where the characters' motives don't always make sense, where the lighting isn't flattering, where boring days are things you have to endure rather than skip past in a montage, where the couples don't always work it out, where the rain makes your hair frizz, where love is sometimes complicated and hard and dull and painful and grey and ever-changing and compromised and flimsy, rather than only perfect and soulmates and kisses in the rain and knowing they're going to live happily ever after.

It is both.

Every love affair is always a mixture of both.

You just don't see both in romance movies.

The only love affair I needed to invest in right now was one with myself. Spend some time with me. Figuring out myself and why I picked the relationships I did. I was holding out my heart to me. Because I'd realized I was the only person who could give me a happily-ever-after.

My phone buzzed, and I dug it out of my pocket.

Mum: Car all packed. Wales here we come.
Road trip!

And, the final shot is of me smiling as I reply. Then I put my phone back into my pocket, and I walk down the street. The camera pans out slowly as I merge into the crowd. Becoming, slowly (*and with a killer end song of your choice*) just another face. Another normal human. Whose love story is over…for now.

⟨Roll credits⟩

The ten movies that made me
by Holly Bourne

Despite writing an entire novel that rips apart romance films, I'm actually a wildly romantic person. Falling in love is pretty much the best thing about being a human – but it can also be the worst. I spent years working as a relationship advisor, and therefore gravitate towards films that show the real sides of love. Here are the films that made me the cautiously optimistic romantic that I am today. (You'll recognize some of them from the book.)

Before Sunrise/Sunset/Midnight

Ideally, you need to wait a good nine or so years between these films for the full effect. They start with Jesse and Céline falling in love when they're both idealistic students. They share one perfect romantic night strolling around Vienna – the sort of thing you just WISH would happen to you. But the second film catches you up with them in their late twenties, and the last film another nine years later. You see how the characters' love, and their ideas of what love is, evolves as they get older. They're painfully realistic, but there's so much beauty in them.

The Way We Were

Barbra Streisand as Katie is EVERYTHING in this film. This is a love story about a "difficult" woman who refuses to adhere to society's expectations of her, and how this makes love with (a useless) Robert Redford difficult in return. This is a film for anyone who's ever had one of those near-miss relationships, a film for any girl who's ever been told she's "too much". You're not too much, you're brilliant. Watch this film and find your inner Barbra.

Eternal Sunshine of the Spotless Mind

After the pain of a break-up, it's common to think, *What was the actual point of all that?* *Eternal Sunshine* is about precisely this feeling. Clementine and Joel have a turbulent two-year relationship that ends with them both going to a specialist service where they can wipe their memories of the whole love affair. It follows their story backwards, as Joel realizes halfway through the process, that, actually, it was all worth it and he would do it all over again. Can he stop the procedure and save the memories before it's too late? A gorgeous, quirky, brilliant film.

Lost In Translation

I adore Sofia Coppola and I adore this film so much and the last five minutes are actually perfect. On the surface, it sounds a bit gross. A jaded and aged film star, Bob, meets a young bored wife, Charlotte, in a Tokyo hotel. But the film manages to bypass any uncomfortable, sleazy vibes and instead tells a story about how unexpected people can help each other when they're both lost.

How to Make an American Quilt

I mean, this film has Maya Angelou in. What more do I need to say? Reluctantly-engaged Finn spends the summer at her grandma's house to get her head around marrying Sam. While there, her grandmother's quilting circle make her a wedding quilt – each elderly lady telling Finn the story of their own love and heartache. The film's a great examination of the perils of modern monogamy, but I mostly adore it for its tribute to female friendship and the power of stories.

When Harry Met Sally

Can a boy and a girl ever be friends without sex coming into it? That's what you initially think this film is about, but it's not. It's more about how the best love comes out of knowing someone really well – their quirks, their neuroses, their annoying habits. True love is about taking that all in, and saying, "Yeah, I'm still here." It also just has one of the best endings of all times.

(500) Days of Summer

Sometimes boys…not all boys…but a lot of damn boys, fall in love with the idea of a girl, rather than the girl herself. This film is all about a boy called Tom doing just that with a girl called Summer, despite her repeatedly telling him she is not able to give him what he wants. Not only is this movie a brilliant takedown of the Manic Pixie Dream Girl trope, it's also just a stunning piece of film-making, with all sorts of random techniques, including surprise musical numbers.

Roman Holiday

Oh, it's just so stunning and Audrey Hepburn is brilliant in it, and Gregory Peck is SEX and you literally cannot watch this film and not fall in love with it. It's a scientific fact.

High Fidelity

I like any film that highlights the fact blokes totally have feelings too, and can get as upset about broken hearts as any girl. Record-shop owner Rob is hurting from yet another break-up. This leads him to revisit the five girls in his past who broke his heart the hardest. The soundtrack is stellar, Jack Black is funny in it, and the book it's based on is pretty brilliant too.

Four Weddings and a Funeral

Look, so I know I write for teenagers, so a lot of you won't understand the significance of this movie. But come back to me when you're in your late-twenties/early-thirties, yeah? And watch this. Because never has a film so hilariously shone a light on what it's like when you hit that age and everyone and their cat are getting married. It also has the best un-proposal ever. In some top-notch rain.

Acknowledgements

As this book is movie-themed, please imagine me saying all this in a couture gown like I'm at an awards ceremony (even though I'm currently typing this in my pyjamas).

A huge thank you to all the talented wonderwomen at Usborne – Rebecca, Sarah S, Becky, Sarah C, Amy, Anna, Stevie and Alesha. Thanks to Will Steele for my amazing front cover and Lenka Hrehova for the gorgeous font. To my incredible agent, Maddy, and her accomplices Alice and Hayley – I feel so strong with you guys on my side. To all my incredible author friends who keep me sane – Lexi, Christi, Mel, Sara, Lucy, Holly, Jess, Harriet, Eleanor, Lisa, Non… the list goes on. Getting to be friends with folks like you is the best part of this job. Cheers to everyone who took part in the #BestMovieKiss on Twitter – apart from those of you who picked *Love, Rosie*. Thanks, as always, to my family. And the biggest thank you of all to my readers. God, you're a brilliant bunch. I'd choose you lot over Ryan Gosling in the rain any day.

For more fabulous Usborne YA reads, news and competitions, head to
usborneyashelfies.tumblr.com
www.usborne.com/yanewsletter
www.usborne.com/youngadult

 @Usborne @UsborneYA